OTHER TOPAZ ROMANCES

BY MARY KINGSLEY

In a Pirate's Arms
Masquerade

BEYOND THE SEA

Mary Kingsley

A TOPAZ BOOK

TOPAZ
Published by New American Library, a division of
Penguin Putnam Inc., 375 Hudson Street,
New York, New York 10014, U.S.A.
Penguin Books Ltd, 27 Wrights Lane,
London W8 5TZ, England
Penguin Books Australia Ltd, Ringwood,
Victoria, Australia
Penguin Books Canada Ltd, 10 Alcorn Avenue,
Toronto, Ontario, Canada M4V 3B2
Penguin Books (N.Z.) Ltd, 182–190 Wairau Road,
Auckland 10, New Zealand

Penguin Books Ltd, Registered Offices:
Harmondsworth, Middlesex, England

First published by Topaz, an imprint of New American Library,
a division of Penguin Putnam Inc.

First Printing, June 1999
10 9 8 7 6 5 4 3 2 1

Copyright © Mary Kruger, 1999
All rights reserved

 REGISTERED TRADEMARK—MARCA REGISTRADA

Printed in the United States of America

For Samantha, the sunshine of my life

Chapter 1

"And, I fear, everything will have to be sold," Mr. Rodman said, looking up at last from the papers he held.

Abigail Palmer snapped to attention, aware that she'd missed something important. She was still in a daze, since her father's unexpected death and the discovery of his debts. It wouldn't do. She sat straighter in the burgundy velvet chair. "Everything?"

"Everything." Seated across from Abby, Mr. Rodman, her father's lawyer, cleared his throat almost apologetically. "The house and its contents. I'm sorry, Abigail. It will leave you with a modest amount to live on."

"But where will I live? This is my home." The wave of her hand encompassed not just the grand house at the top of the hill but her heritage as well. Losing her parents, first her mother to childbirth and now her father, had been devastating. Losing all else she held dear would destroy her. "I know it's a big house, but surely there's some way?"

"I'm sorry, Abigail. I wish I had better news for you. And I wish I knew what had possessed your father. Whaling may not be what it was, but his ships have been turning a profit, and he had planned to invest in the Potomska mill. Speculating money as he did." He shook his head. "It's a dangerous game, gambling on stocks. Likely he thought he'd recover his losses."

"But then he had the stroke," Abby finished for him, rising and pacing to one of the tall windows overlooking the gardens. Outside, past the verandah, the roses that her mother had so carefully tended were just coming into bloom, while the green-latticed pergola drew her, an oasis of calm on this sultry, oppressive day. The thought that all this was no longer hers was very strange. "Will I be able to keep anything?"

Mr. Rodman cleared his throat again. "Your personal possessions, of course, though they'll have to be evaluated."

"I have my mother's jewelry. Not very much. Mama didn't care for jewels." A strand of pearls, worn on her wedding day. A locket that opened into three compartments, holding miniature portraits of her parents and a carefully conserved lock of Abby's baby hair. And now, her father's gold watch.

"We may be able to save those. There is one more thing," he added reluctantly.

Abby turned. "What?"

"The Palmer ships will be sold when they return to port, and the countinghouse as well. But there is one item that is in your name, rather than your father's."

"The *Aquinnah*," she said.

"Yes." He nodded. "The *Aquinnah*. The whaleship you own. We can try to sell her, though I doubt we'll succeed."

Abby nodded, turning back to contemplate the view outside. Past the green board fence that lined the property, people traveled on the elm-shaded streets, on foot or in fine carriages. Life went on. New Bedford in this summer of 1870 was flourishing, with no signs of distress at the loss of one of the city's wealthiest merchants. Abby's eyes suddenly stung with the tears that had so far eluded her. Her entire life was about to change, and she had no say in the matter.

Briefly she closed her eyes, and then turned back to the attorney. Nothing was gained by turning away from troubles. "Is the *Aquinnah* seaworthy?"

Mr. Rodman pursed his lips. "I doubt it. Not after sitting idle at the wharf for three years, and without refitting from her last voyage."

"Mm." Instincts that Abby hadn't known she possessed clicked to life within her. She was her father's daughter, and he had taught her about the business side of whaling. The *Aquinnah* had been a present for her sixteenth birthday. She smiled as she remembered the excitement of seeing her very own ship, flag-bedecked and festive, being launched. Unfortunately, reality had soon intervened.

Time had not been good to the *Aquinnah*. Any whaler faced enormous strains and demands; it had to be sturdy enough to withstand the freezing waters of the Arctic whaling grounds and yet nimble enough that a small crew could work her. The ship had left port with fresh paint and varnish glistening and brightwork sparkling. Returning four years later, she had looked very different; dirty, oily, and sooty from the whale oil boiled on her deck and badly in need of repairs. The real problems, though, were not so tangible. Just two months out of New Bedford, the *Aquinnah* lowered her boats in pursuit of a whale. Unfortunately the line on one of the boats fouled, carrying one of its crew overboard. One man lost. Another two went shortly after, when an enraged whale attacked their whaleboat, smashing it to splinters. Men often died on whaling voyages, but to lose three in so short a period of time was rare. The rumors started, then, of strange sounds in the forecastle, the crew's quarters. Soon the *Aquinnah* had the reputation of being haunted, and unlucky. Though she had made a small profit, no one wished to sail on her again. Times had changed, and whaling was indeed not what it had been. Whales were growing scarcer, making longer voyages necessary, while the recent Civil War and the discovery of petroleum in Pennsylvania had struck serious blows to the industry. Papa had told her that, giving it as his reason for investing in the new Potomska mill just being built. Whaling's heyday was past. Textiles were the future of the city.

Now that investment was gone. "Do you think it's worth it to refit her and find a crew?"

Mr. Rodman frowned. "It's unlikely. We'll have a hard enough time unloading the other ships. The best thing to do with the *Aquinnah* is to sell her for scrap."

Abby flinched. "Oh. Well, yes. Probably that would be best, though I would like to think about it."

"Of course."

"As to everything else—will you make the arrangements?"

He nodded. "Certainly. There'll be an inventory, and then likely an auction."

Abby flinched again. "I see," she said, with a calm detachment that astonished her.

"I'll see to it." He rose. "I'm sorry to be the one to bring you such news."

Abby held her hand out to him, managing somehow to

smile. "It's not your fault, and I do have relatives to help me."

He nodded. "We'll do all that we can, Abigail," he said, and making his farewells, he departed.

Left alone, Abby crossed to the parlor door and surveyed the house. She would miss this. She dimly remembered living in a much smaller house when she was young. Once Benjamin Palmer had become successful, though, he'd moved his family away from the increasingly rowdy waterfront to this mansion atop the hill, with its fine gardens and splendid views. She'd taken it all for granted: the ormulu clock on the marble mantel, the oriental carpet, the fine Waterford crystal chandelier. More precious than those, though, were the memories. Mama and Papa arguing, and then Papa saying something that made Mama laugh, ending that quarrel. The three of them toasting the *Aquinnah*'s launch with the Venetian wineglasses bought on her parents' honeymoon. Papa, heady with the success of a recent investment, waltzing Mama, laughing and protesting and looking very young, down the length of the hallway that bisected the house. Abby was smiling as she moved into the hall and looked far, far above, at a chandelier that hung over the stairwell, at the paintings by Audubon or Bierstadt or William Wall, at the pianoforte, just visible past the door of the music room. Then her smile faded, and she turned to the stairs. Not all her memories were happy.

In her room Abby searched for the volume of poetry she had been glancing at earlier and then started toward the back stairs. She would go out and sit in the pergola, she decided, in search of a sanctuary. She had just reached the top of the stairs when Martha, the housekeeper, called to her from below. "Someone to see you, Miss Abigail."

Abby frowned, though she had heard the door knocker a few moments earlier. "I don't want to see anyone, Martha. Could you handle it for me?"

"I think you should see this one, miss."

"Oh? Who is it?"

"Captain Howland."

Abby paused, one hand on the railing. "Nathaniel Howland?"

"Yes, miss. Not that he's calling himself captain, I'll say

that for him, but he did work for your father all those years."

"Yes." Abby gnawed her lower lip. Of all people, Nathaniel Howland was the last she had expected to visit. "But if he's just paying his condolences—"

"He says it's business, miss."

"Business? But why would he come to me, and not Mr. Rodman? Oh, well." She ran a hand over the top of her hair. "All right. I'll be down in a moment."

In her room again, Abby splashed water on her face and regarded her reflection dispassionately. Her mourning gown of black foulard, with its straight front skirt, short train, and trimmings of puffed rosettes, was both cool and stylish, the best that her dressmaker could provide, but the color was singularly unflattering. She looked washed-out, she thought, pinching her cheeks in an attempt to bring some color to her face. Though wisps of her hair had escaped to frame her face and were curling in the humidity, the rest of it was caught neatly back in a black net snood. She knew what Captain Howland would see when he looked at her: a short, overly plump woman past her youth. Not that it mattered. He was here only for business. She'd see him, send him on his way, and then try at last to make some sense of what had happened to her life.

The day had darkened in the few moments since Abby had gone into her room, making her pause at the top of the stairs. In the gloom below, the man who waited in the hall loomed tall and broad and shadowy. She took a deep breath, glancing for a moment out the front windows and seeing only that thunderclouds were moving in. She was in for some kind of storm. Might as well face it. Taking a deep breath, she at last began to descend. She was about halfway down when two things happened: the sun broke through the clouds, and Captain Howland looked up at her.

Abby's feet stopped; her fingers stilled on the mahogany balustrade. With the sun streaming in through the open door behind him, turning his hair to molten gold, Captain Howland looked mythic, a Viking god come to life. She forced herself to continue down the stairs, aware all the time of his keen blue gaze. Mercy, but it had been years since he had been in this house, and then only to be fired from the Palmer employ. Once he had been a superlative skipper. Why, he had even managed to outsail the Confederate raider *Shenandoah,* which had destroyed so much of New Bedford's fleet. That feat, along with his successful voyages, had made him a legend. When he was home he had visited frequently, and the combination of his dazzling good looks and his fame, worn so nonchalantly, had produced an acute case of hero worship within Abby. Perhaps that was why she had been so devastated by his downfall, when his heavy drinking, along with carelessness, had caused him to wreck his ship in the Arctic ice. It was the ultimate crime for a shipmaster. No one had hired him since, not even as a common seaman.

"Captain," she said as she reached the hall. Closer to him she could see changes—lines in his face that hadn't been there before, fraying cuffs on his black frock coat. His blond hair, though, was carefully cut and looked healthy, while his shirt was blindingly white. He may have come down in the world, but he was fighting his way back. He would fight for her. Odd thought. "Is there anything I can do for you?"

"Miss Palmer." He folded her hand within his large one, and she was swamped by a peculiar sensation. No harm could ever come to her with him. It was so strange and frightening a thought that she nearly pulled away. He was taller than she remembered, and his shoulders were broad, a bulwark against the world. "I was sorry to hear about your father," he went on, jolting her out of her reverie. Mercy, what was she doing, clinging to his hand, and to fantasies that she'd given up long ago? "I was at the service for him."

"You were?" she said, startled into looking at him, though that blue gaze was almost more than she could withstand. "I didn't see you there."

"You had other people with you." *Surrounding her,* he thought. Abigail Palmer did not lack for friends or family. Yet now she stood alone in this house. "I wonder if I could have a word with you."

"I—yes." She looked down at their hands, as if just then realizing that they were still clasped, and let go. "In my father's office, I think."

He nodded, stepping back to let her precede him. *Little Abby Palmer,* he mused, gazing down at the top of her head. She'd grown up. Last he'd seen her she'd been a shy, bright-eyed young girl, eager to face the world. He'd always liked her, but then, he liked women. He'd never denied that, he thought, glancing appreciatively down at the curve of her bustled skirt. There were many things about himself he'd tried to change in the past years, but that wasn't one of them. Life's troubles had taken their toll on Abby; her face was grave and pale, and her eyes shadowed. Still, there were copper gleams in her chestnut hair, and her posture was erect. In her quiet way she was a brave woman.

The house, built years earlier by another of New Bedford's merchants, had been designed for business as well as for living. Someone come to see Palmer about any of his many interests would enter the front door, be confronted with the large mahogany door to the house itself, and be shown into the office to the left. It was into this room that Abby led Howland now. Here he had received word that he was, at last, being given a ship to command. Here, too, he had seen it all come to an end, three years ago. "The last time I was here your father had some things to say to me," he commented.

Abby, sitting at her father's straight, cubbyholed desk on a plain, worn wooden chair painted ocher, looked up, startled. "I'm surprised you'd mention that."

He shrugged and dropped into a chair like hers, similar to those from his cramped childhood home near the waterfront. The Howland family had never had such a view, he thought, looking out the wide front window. "I deserved it."

"He had a temper," she said. He looked back to see that her lips were curved in a smile. Full, lush, red lips. Kissable lips. Damnation, but she was pretty. Why hadn't he ever realized it before? "When he was angry everyone knew it."

"I can't imagine he got angry with you."

She gave a short laugh. "Oh, but he did. Something would upset him and he'd roar about it. When I was young and he fought with my mother I'd think it was the end of the world." She looked away, blinking. "He loved my mother. He loved me. But we never knew what would set him off. It was . . . difficult."

Nat, too, glanced away. He hated it when women cried. "I'm sorry. I didn't mean to upset you."

She smiled, though her eyes were bright with unshed tears. "I miss him. It's just—I miss him."

"I understand." He let the silence lengthen. "But what he did to you is criminal."

"Excuse me?"

"Leaving you with all his debts."

Abby's eyes closed. "Oh, mercy. How do you know about that?"

"Everyone knows. I'm sorry," he said again, more gently this time, as her eyes flew open. "I thought you knew."

"No. No." She rubbed her temple. "I found out only today. Everything will have to be sold."

He cursed softly. "Everything? The house, too?"

"Yes." She managed a smile. "It's probably just as well. This is a large house for just one person."

"But where will you go?"

"Oh, that's not a problem. All my aunts have offered me a place, so I could go to Boston or Maine or even New York." She smiled, as if the prospect intrigued her. "But I think I'll stay here, with my cousin Elizabeth."

"Does she still take snuff?"

She smiled. "No. I think she did that only to shock people. I know it shocked me. But I was young." She straightened. "But you didn't come here for that. Is there something you wanted to discuss?"

"As it happens, yes." For a disconcerting moment she resembled her father, leaning forward from the desk, impatient and no-nonsense. He'd do well not to underestimate her. "I've a business proposition for you."

"Mr. Rodman is handling everything like that."

Rodman had turned him away. Nat wasn't about to tell her that, though. Not yet. "This doesn't have anything to do with your father's property. I'd like to buy the *Aquinnah*."

Abby's heart constricted. "No," she said, reflexively.

"No?" He was watching her, with those sharp, disconcerting eyes. What was it he saw, when he looked at her? "Why not?"

She set her lips. Had Mr. Rodman come to her with such an offer she would have leapt at it. Why not, indeed? "Why do you want to buy her?"

"I want to go to sea."

"But you—"

"I was stripped of my command, yes, but not my master's papers." He leaned forward, his eyes more intensely blue than before. "I don't deny that. I don't deny why it happened, either. I was a drunkard, Miss Palmer, and I lost my ship. But I am not a drunkard anymore."

Abby let out her breath, feeling somehow freed as he leaned back. "You're not a sailor anymore, either."

"No." Some humor returned to his face. "Actually, for the past two years I've been a spinner at the Wamsutta Mill."

"A spinner!"

He shrugged. "I had to eat. No one would give me a berth. Not that I blame them." He leaned forward again, and she was caught by his gaze, unable to look away. "I deserved what happened to me. There's no excuse for what I did. But I've paid for it, and I want to go to sea again."

"I'm sorry." Abby rose. "The *Aquinnah* is not for sale."

"I've the money." Nat stayed seated, a breach of manners that annoyed her. "If that's what concerns you."

"No."

"Maybe not what you'd like, but likely more than she's worth. We both know no one else will take her off your hands."

Abby braced her hands on the back of the chair. "The answer is no, Captain. Now, if you'll excuse me—"

"What will you do with her, then? Sell her for scrap?"

"No." Abby paused in the doorway. An idea had come to her that was so outrageous she couldn't believe she was considering it. "No, while I'm her owner I won't see that. She's a fine ship, Captain. Well built and strong."

"But in need of work."

"Oh, without a doubt. But she has good lines, and she's sturdy. No. I won't sell her." She would soon lose her house and would be obliged to depend on the charity of relatives. All she had left was an old, unwanted, yet very precious, ship. "What I will do," she said, walking back into the office and sitting down again, "is send her to sea myself."

Nat's eyebrow raised. "And who will sail her for you?"

"Why not you?" She went on before he could protest. "I need a partner, Captain. I've the ship, but no money to overhaul her. You've the money, but you need a ship."

"A partnership." He frowned. "It's not what I had in mind."

"No, nor I, but it's what I'm offering."

He rose, crossing to the window, and then turned. "Would we have an agreement for me to buy you out once she's made her money back?"

Now Abby frowned, her instincts screaming to hold on to what was hers. "Perhaps, but I'll need to think about it."

"Do so. I won't take you up on your offer, elsewise."

Abby's heart began to pound. "You'll agree to be my partner?"

"If it's the only way you'll allow me to skipper the ship, yes. And with a clause to buy you out at some future date."

She paused, and then nodded. She could agree to that. By the time the *Aquinnah* made one or two voyages she'd be back on her feet. Perhaps then it would not hurt quite so much to give up the ship. "Very well. Then we have an agreement."

He smiled, and it was as if the sun had broken through the clouds. "Splendid. I'll have the papers drawn up."

"There is one condition."

Nearly at the door, he stilled, his eyes wary. "What?"

Abby took a deep breath, stunned at what she was about to suggest. It was ridiculous. Outrageous. She was mad even to think of it. The alternatives were worse, though. She would forever have to live on someone else's charity, forever give up her one remaining link to her father. The *Aquinnah* was hers. "I will be sailing with you."

Chapter 2

Nat reared back. "No."

"No?" Abby said. "Why not? It's my ship."

"That's why not," he ground out.

"Excuse me?"

He paced the room, and she realized for the first time that he was angry. "Your ship, not mine."

Her brief alarm at his anger faded. "We both realize that, Captain, but—"

"I came here to make an offer to you, in good faith, to buy the *Aquinnah,* to have my own ship. To be my own man."

Her brow wrinkled further. "Are you saying you think I'll tell you what to do?"

"As the owner, yes."

"I wouldn't."

"Oh, you would. You would."

"But I don't even know anything about running a ship."

"Well, I do. It's what I've worked for all these years. Working at the mill— Damnation, I know how to handle a ship."

"And how to take a drink."

Silence fell heavily. "You've a nasty tongue, Miss Palmer."

"I'm sorry." She stared at him, appalled at herself. "I don't know why I said such a thing."

"I haven't had a drink in over a year."

Abby nodded. Not that she believed him, but what she had said was nasty and uncalled for. It was almost as though she were trying to provoke him, and that was strange. She'd spent most of her life avoiding confrontations. But then, his refusal of her idea had filled her with sharp, bitter disappointment. Until that moment, she hadn't known how very much she wanted to leave this house, this city. "I'm sorry," she said again, assuming the mask of poise she used to cover her emotions. "But you understand that I've reason to be concerned."

His face was grim. "Aye. Along with every other worthy shipowner in this city." He couldn't escape it; the stain of his past would follow him forever. Nathaniel Howland, who had lost his ship due to carelessness and drink. No matter that he hadn't touched a drop in over a year. She had a right to be concerned. He could fall back into his old ways next week. Or tomorrow. Or today. Damnation, but he wanted a drink.

"Let me be certain I understand you," he said quietly, as he did when he was truly angry. "You'll name me master of the *Aquinnah,* if I allow you to sail on her?"

"The other way around, Captain." Her gaze was steady, in spite of his anger. She had courage, he'd say that for her. "As owner I allow you to take command."

"And what happens, Miss Palmer, when everyone in this pious city finds out what you've agreed to?"

"Women have been going to sea on whalers for years."

"Wives," he bit out. "Or do I have to marry you, too?" She recoiled. "Mercy, no!"

"Why not? Aren't I good enough for you?"

"You're—it's not that! That has nothing to do with it." She paced across the room. "What happens to my reputation is my business. As for what people will say, I really don't care." That wasn't strictly true, but she rushed on. "I am the owner of the *Aquinnah.* If I decide to sail on her, I have the right."

The silence was broken only by the ticking of the old grandfather clock in the hall. "Then it seems I've wasted your time, and mine."

Abby bit her lip as disappointment surged through her again. Why in the world did she feel this way? Her suggestion was utterly ridiculous. Wasn't it? "Then this meeting is over. If you'll excuse me, Captain, I've had a trying day."

He nodded briefly as she turned and walked out of the office, her shoulders very straight. Her posture remained erect as she entered the foyer, as she passed through the inner door into the hall. Only when she reached the parlor and was, mercifully, alone, did she slump. Of all that she had faced lately, somehow this was the hardest.

"Abby?" a voice said. Male, familiar, but not Captain Howland's. A shiver crawled up Abby's spine and then dissipated. She turned, smiling in welcome. "There you are."

"Jared." Her smile broadened, though her shoulders remained stiff. She didn't know why. Jared Swift had been her friend since childhood. "Mr. Rodman told me you'd made port, but I didn't expect to see you so soon."

Jared stood in the opening between the pocket doors that separated the parlor from the music room. No slouching for him; no lounging in a chair or sitting while a lady stood. "I came as soon as we cleared quarantine. My poor Abby." He held his arms out, as if to embrace her. "I would have been here earlier if I could have."

Abby shifted, so that his hands fell on her shoulders and his kiss on her cheek. "Thank you. Oh, it is good to see you! Did you have a good voyage?"

"Yes, but that doesn't matter," he said, dismissing the four-year-long voyage with a jerk of his head. "Abby." He pulled her closer. "What a difficult time you've been through."

Strange, but his sympathy left her unmoved. "I'm fine, Jared. Papa's death was quick. It's hard, but I'm managing."

"He left you with nothing! How could he do that to you?"

"You once told me he was like a second father to you, Jared," she said softly. "Or were those just words?"

His hands fell away, and she was finally able to breathe. "No. No, I meant it. I suppose it hasn't sunk in." He wheeled away from her, pacing to the center of the room. "Your parents were both very good to me, Abby. I haven't forgotten that. With my father gone and my mother sick so much—it meant a lot to me. I can't believe he's gone."

Pity welled up within Abby at the lost look in his eyes. She remembered all too well the lonely boy he had been, his father at sea and his mother unable to care for him. Though he was only a neighbor's child, Abby's parents had come to treat him almost as their own son. Now he, too, was orphaned. "I keep expecting to hear him yell my name," she said.

"Did he still do that? Shout as if you were miles away?"

"Oh, yes, and expect me to drop whatever I was doing to see what he wanted." She smiled. "Funny, but that doesn't bother me anymore."

He turned. "You're alone."

"No, not quite, Jared." Again she braced her shoulders, not sure why. If she'd faced any threat today, surely it had been from Captain Howland, with his temper and his poor reputation. Not from Jared. "You know what New Bedford is like. Everyone's related. I wonder . . ."

"What?" he prompted when she didn't go on.

"Nothing." Why hadn't Captain Howland's ship-owning relatives given him a command? Oh, she knew the answer to that question. "Everyone's been kind."

"Everyone's left you alone."

"I wanted it that way. I'm tired, Jared." She spread her hands in a gesture of apparent frankness. "I need time to sort through what happened."

His face darkened. "You took time to see Nat Howland."

"How do you know that?" she exclaimed.

"Your housekeeper told me. What did he want?"

"To pay his condolences." Mercy, why was she lying? And who was she trying to protect, Captain Howland or herself?

"Stay away from him." He watched her from across the room, motionless, only his pale, restless eyes belying his alertness. "He's bad, Abby."

"Oh, now really—"

"I'm serious. He's worse than you could know. I don't want you seeing him again."

She frowned, holding back her protest. He had no right to order her about, and yet her impulse to fight, so strong against Nat, had faded. "Jared, I appreciate your concern, but I really am tired. Please, let's leave this till tomorrow—"

"But what will you do, Abby?" he asked, nearing her and jolting her into awareness. He was tall, with dark, straight hair and finely molded bones—a very handsome man. Somehow she tended to forget that. "You can't stay here."

"No." She evaded his grasp, standing still in the center

of the room, with nothing to block her way. "I'll probably stay with cousin Elizabeth."

"What?" He frowned. "Abby, you're acting strangely."

"No, I'm not."

"You're very distant. I suppose it must be grief. Abby, surely you realize you can't stay with her?"

This time she held her ground as he neared. "Why not?"

"Bad enough that you'll be a poor relation, but—"

"You needn't remind me of that."

"It's true. But, Abby, the woman is insane."

"You haven't seen her in four years."

"I've known her all my life. She doesn't like me either." He wheeled away, and she let her breath out. "What the dickens has she done to her house? It looks ridiculous."

Abby smiled. Last year, deciding that the new style of fancy turreted homes was to her liking, Elizabeth had had her perfectly fine, but staid, Federal house rebuilt with dormers and cupola and mansard roof. It now looked something like an overburdened wedding cake and had caused much talk. "I like it."

"I don't. I won't allow you to stay with her."

"You won't, Jared?" From somewhere, she found courage. "I don't think you have any say in the matter."

"But I do. I spoke to your father before I left."

"And you had my answer then!"

"I haven't changed my mind, Abby." He was close again—too close, but pride kept her from stepping back. This was still her house. "I want you."

Panic flared within her. "Jared—"

"Marry me, Abby." His hands shackled her upper arms. "It's what I want. It's what your father wanted."

"That's not quite true, Jared."

"You won't have to leave this house, you won't have to give anything up. Abby, Abby." His gaze was intense. "This was meant to be. Don't you feel it?"

"Jared, let me go."

"Don't reject me again, Abby." The pressure of his fingers tightened. "Marry me."

"She can't," a voice drawled, and abruptly Jared released her. Abby looked past him to see Nat, leaning against the doorjamb from the hall.

"Captain." She smoothed down her skirts, her hair, as if caught in something illicit. "I thought you'd left."

His eyes shifted briefly to her. There was no warmth in them. "Have you forgotten our agreement, Miss Palmer?"

"Our—agreement?"

"What agreement?" Jared said at the same time.

"So she hasn't told you yet." Nat's lips stretched into a fierce smile. "We have an agreement, haven't we, Miss Palmer?"

"I—" Abby's head was spinning, as though a chasm had opened beneath her and he had thrown her a rope. "Yes, I believe we have."

"You have no business here, Howland," Jared snapped.

"Yes. Yes, he does, Jared."

"Abby, the man's a drunkard. I forbid you to have anything to do with him."

"Do you, Jared?" A strange calm settled over her. Her old life awaited, its bonds like tentacles to hold her fast; a new, more frightening, life beckoned. "But he's one of the best men ever to sail for my father. Yes, Captain." She held her hand out to Nat. "We do have an agreement."

"Good." His hand closed over hers, though he kept his gaze on Jared. "If you will let me skipper the *Aquinnah,* I'd like you to come aboard her as owner."

Chapter 3

Jared's gaze darted back and forth between them. "You can't be serious," he said flatly.

"Oh, but I am." Abby smiled, surprising herself. "Don't you think it's about time I make my own decisions?"

"This was your idea." Jared, his face dark as the thunderclouds, rounded on Nat. "She wouldn't do this if not for you."

Nat was still propped against the doorjamb, hands tucked into his pockets. "True." he said.

"You admit it? Hellfire." Jared swung back to Abby. "You don't know what this man is like."

"I've heard the rumors," Abby said calmly.

"Not all of them. Abby, Abby." His expression changed, became concerned. "I understand why you're doing this."

She frowned. "You do?"

"Oh, yes." Jared's gaze flicked contemptuously over Nat and then settled on her again—benign, warm, suffocating. "You feel alone in the world. You think the *Aquinnah*'s all you have and you want to cling to it."

"That's not true!" she cried, angry because he was right. She did feel alone, and she did want to hold on to her ship. There was more, though. She glanced at Nat, who still stood in the doorway watching them, for all the world like a spectator at a play. More, and though she didn't know quite what it was, she had to grab it, or she'd never have the chance again. "All right." She let out her breath. "Maybe that is true, to some extent. But," she hurried on, "it's not all. It hasn't fogged my thinking, Jared. I know what I'm doing."

"Abby, I love you." His voice was low, throbbing. "Doesn't that mean anything to you?"

She took a deep breath. "Of course it does. You've always been like a brother to me. No." She held up her hand to silence him. "Now we're friends. If you care about me you should want my happiness—"

"I do, blast it!"

"—and I won't be happy staying here."

"Do you really think sailing off with this drunkard will make you happy?" he demanded.

"I don't know, Jared." She held his gaze. "I only know that I have to try."

Jared stared at her for a moment, and then, snorting, he jammed his hat on his head. "You'll regret this. And don't think to come to me for help when you realize your mistake." He wheeled away, pulling up short at the door, where Nat still watched. For a moment the two men eyed each other—one dark, one fair, and yet alike in their intensity. Then Nat straightened, shrugging lazily. Jared's color, already high, deepened. "You'll regret it," he said again and stalked out, slamming the front door behind him.

"I've hurt him," Abby said into the sudden silence. "He's been a good friend to me."

"Didn't sound like it to me."

She glanced at him, annoyed. "You don't know him."

"Oh, but I do," he said softly. "Or have you forgotten? He was first mate aboard the *Nantucket*."

Abby's breath caught. Nat's ship, the one he had lost in the Arctic ice. She had forgotten. "He was the one who got the crew off safely."

"So he says." Nat's posture was rigid, in contrast to his earlier slouch. "Well? Are you changing your mind?"

"I don't know." Hand at her forehead, Abby gazed out at the garden. "He is right about one thing. Everything has happened too quickly."

"I can skipper that ship, Miss Palmer, and turn you a decent profit as well."

"I'm not arguing that," she said, frowning. Jared's words had found their mark. "This isn't just business. It's my future."

"Then you have to decide what future you want. You can stay here, doing the same things you've always done, meeting the same people, talking about the same things. Or you can make your own life, with no one to order you about."

It stopped her. No one to tell her what to do, after years of enduring her father's benign tyranny. Frightening thought. Exhilarating. "Don't expect me to believe that, Captain. You'll likely tell me what to do."

"As skipper? Aye. I'll have to." He ambled toward her. "But I won't tell you how to run your life, and when I do give you an order you'll know it's for the good of the ship. For your own good."

"And yours."

"Aye," he said, after a moment. "You'd expect no less, would you?"

"Papa always liked to hire men who cared about their own futures. Why would you be concerned about the ship if you didn't have anything at stake?"

"I do care about that ship, Miss Palmer."

"I know you do." She paused and held out her hand. "We still have our agreement, then."

Nat looked at her outstretched hand a moment too long. She pulled back, to spare herself the humiliation of rejection, when of a sudden his fingers touched hers in a quick, light grasp. "Aye, God help us." He grinned. "We've an agreement."

He had a ship. The joy and the wonder of it buoyed Nat's steps as he strode along Union Street, down the hill to where the waterfront beckoned. A ship at last, and by Neptune he was going to prove himself this time. This time he knew how easily opportunity could be snatched away and what living with failure was like. He didn't expect his reputation to be completely rehabilitated, but things were looking up. He wanted to shout the news to the anxious store clerks who busily cranked in striped awnings at Haskell's Dry Goods or Thompson's Confectionery in readiness for the coming storm; he wanted to stop in at Taber, Read, and Company, men's clothiers, and order suits befitting his position. He had a ship again, and all it had cost him was his pride.

He grimaced. That wasn't quite true, but it was not what he'd expected when he'd gone to see Abigail Palmer. For the past three years he had worked hard, changing spindles in a constantly moving loom at the Wamsutta Mill and taking on any odd job he could find. He'd saved his money for the one thing that meant anything to him anymore: a ship of his own. A whaler, to take to the Arctic, the scene of his downfall, to prove to everyone that he was good at his work, that the drinking hadn't destroyed him. To prove it to himself. His own ship, his own master. Instead, he'd entered into a devil's agreement. What in damnation was he going to do with Abigail Palmer?

The door to a tavern opened abruptly before him. Nat sidestepped on the slate walk to avoid colliding with the two men who came tumbling out, speaking a language he didn't understand but immediately recognized. Portuguese. It could as easily have been Norwegian or German or Creole, the tongue of the Cape Verdean mariners who were so prized as boatsteerers. For years men had come from all parts of the world to New Bedford, lured by tales of adventure and the tantalizing prospect of wealth. Few ever made it past the taverns and brothels lining the waterfront. His father had been one such, and so, all too recently, had he. The mingled odors of sawdust, tobacco, and beer wafting from the tavern made him pause. He hadn't had a drink in a year. Surely he could handle one now. Just one, to celebrate his good fortune. A whiskey, with a beer chaser, because everyone knew that beer wasn't really a drink. Just one.

And another, and another. Nat wheeled away and continued down the hill, some of the lightness gone from his step. He'd been down that road before, when the need and the craving grew too strong to ignore. Just one drink, aye, but it always led to more, until before he knew it he would be out on the street, just another drunken sailor marooned on the beach. It wouldn't happen this time. He hadn't worked as hard as he had, or sweated out those first difficult days without alcohol, for no reason. All that work, all that discipline had been aimed toward one goal—commanding a ship again. That the circumstances weren't ideal was something he would have to accept. He did, indeed, have a ship.

A breeze from the water brought the smell of the sea with it, mingled with the odor of seaweed and the distinctive fishy aroma of unrefined whale oil. Nat breathed it in, an addiction as powerful as alcohol. Here was where he belonged, where the masts and spars of the whaling fleet rose in a tangled forest against the sullen sky, among the stone or brick or clapboard countinghouses and chandleries and candleworks. He belonged here every bit as much as the elderly gentleman in gray and black, one of the city's Quaker merchants, making a dignified progress along the street; as much as the sailor who ambled along, unshaven, unwashed, ditty bag slung over his shoulder and his walk the rolling gait of one accustomed to standing a moving deck. Never mind the past, never mind his weaknesses. He was coming home at last.

As he reached the bottom of the hill, the waterfront opened before him, with all the bustle of a working port. Nat turned toward Palmer's Wharf. The buildings were fewer here; instead there were huge casks of whale oil, laid in neat rows and covered with seaweed, waiting to be brought to a refinery. Beyond them were the wharves, jutting out into the river, with vessels of all sorts tied up to them. There a whaler had her sails out to dry, after completing the long voyage to the Arctic and back. Here a coastal schooner took on cargo for its next run, while in the river, past the long ferry terminal, the Nantucket steamer puffed and growled, squat and yet efficient among the more graceful sailing craft.

The land was no less busy. To Nat's left a caulker plied his chisel to force strands of oakum into a ship's seams and make her watertight, the thud of his mallet echoing dully across the water. A wagon piled with casks and drawn by oxen trundled by on his other side, on the way to the refinery whose buildings, farther south, rose against the sky. Ahead, a watchman nodded from the doorway of a tall granite building. The Palmer countinghouse, once thriving, now deserted. Nat's lips thinned as he passed and turned yet again, onto the wharf at last. What Palmer had done to his daughter was criminal.

The wide, splintered boards of the wharf creaked beneath him as he strode along. To either side ropes tied to stanchions creaked as the vessels moored there shifted with wind and tide. Palmer's Wharf wasn't as busy as the others, and those vessels tied up here already had a neglected look. Nat had eyes for only one ship, at the very end of the wharf, parallel with the shore. There, barepoled, abandoned, forlorn, was the *Aquinnah*.

They were a good match, he thought, stopping finally to

survey his new command. A ship no one wanted; a skipper no one would hire. On the surface all the *Aquinnah* was good for was scrap. Underneath, though, Nat suspected from the days he'd spent studying the ship, she was sound. Like all whalers, she was on the small side, a hundred feet or so, and wide enough to look tubby next to a sleek, graceful clipper. A whaler had to be sturdy, to face the varying conditions of the world's oceans; to take the strains of hoisting aboard a whale's carcass of several tons. When such a ship returned from a voyage it looked battered and yet proud, and that was how the *Aquinnah* appeared to him. Her figurehead, a carving of a Wampanoag sachem in full regalia, badly needed paint, the rigging looked slack, and he more than suspected that the hull was encrusted with barnacles. Yet she had her own distinctive look, with her finely drawn bows, her raked masts, and the carved scrollwork at stem and stern. Oh, yes, a fine ship.

There was no gangplank out to the wharf, but that was as nothing to a man who'd spent most of his life at sea. Nat leapt easily from wharf to railing, ignoring the green water beneath him, and at last stood on the deck of his new command. The masts towered above him; the deck rocked gently beneath his feet. He smiled, at peace at last. At home.

"Hey! What'cher doin' there?" a voice called, and Nat turned to see a skinny, grizzled old man limping toward him. "This here's private property."

Nat stood at ease, one hand in the pocket of his frock coat. "Are you the watchman?"

"Yeah, and what's it to you?" The man peered up at him, and his foggy eyes seemed to clear. "Cap'n Howland?"

"Yes."

"Well, I'll be a son-of-a— What you doin' here? Remember me? Peleg Tripp."

Nat looked more closely at the man and at last recognized him. They had once shipped out together. "Yes, I do remember you. What are you doing here?"

"Eh. On the beach on account of this leg." Peleg tapped his left thigh. "Mr. Palmer set me to work here. A good man, that. Don't know what I'll do now."

There was a slight question in Peleg's voice. "I've been named skipper of the *Aquinnah,*" Nat said.

Peleg drew back. "She's goin' to sea again?"

"Yes."

"Well, I'll be. Don't suppose you have room for an old salt like me?"

"As?"

"Steward. Mebbe I can't climb the ropes, but I can work. Bring you your meals, keep the cabin clean, like that."

"I'll think about it," Nat said noncommittally. He knew well what it was like to be on the beach; he knew, too, that people's careless sympathy cut to the quick. "She needs work."

"Aye, but she's sound. You might have trouble manning her, Cap'n. Ain't so many want to go a-whalin' anymore, not with the West all opened up. Things are different now."

Nat nodded. "I know."

"And there's her reputation," Peleg went on. "Nobody wants to serve on a ghost ship."

Nat turned sharply. "Do you believe that old fish story?"

"Nah. Many's the night I've slept aboard and never been disturbed. If *Aquinnah*'s got a ghost, it never bothered me."

"Something started the rumors."

"Aye. Strange noises or somethin'. You know sailors, Cap'n. Anythin' out of place and they think it's an omen."

"Men have died on this ship," Nat said, enjoying playing devil's advocate. Peleg was the first person to speak favorably of the *Aquinnah.* He might be good to have aboard.

"So haven't they on other ships. No, this one's just had some bad luck, what with the war and all." Peleg looked up at the mainmast and his face softened. "Give her the right cap'n and she'll do well."

"Hope so." Nat turned away, heading aft, toward the stern. The *Aquinnah* didn't have a raised quarterdeck as cargo ships did; her main deck was clean and straight, cluttered only with the structures peculiar to whaling. The brick hearth where the huge iron try-pots would sit was crumbling, while the copper tank for cooling hot oil was missing. The cooper's bench was in place, but like the goose pen, the fence around the try-pots, it was rotting from exposure. And she was dirty. The aft deckhouses, galley to starboard, hatchway to the lower deck and the ship's cabin to the other deck, should have been pristine white, but were instead dingy and dull. So was the hurricane house, the overhead connection between the deckhouses, which provided cover for the ship's wheel. The glass in the raised skylight set in the deck between the two structures, to let in air and light to the cabin below, was cracked and foggy. A lot of work lay ahead, Nat thought, turning into the pilothouse. He couldn't wait to begin.

From the pilothouse a narrow companionway, or stairway, led below. Nat took the stairs easily, only briefly distracted by a memory of stumbling and falling, drunk. No more of that. He waited at the bottom of the companionway as Peleg clambered down behind him, and then turned to his right. Here was a short passageway, with staterooms opening to either side—officers' quarters. And here at last was the aft cabin, dimly lit by the skylight. A table was bolted into the middle of the room, its edges lined with a railing to keep dishes and other things from rolling off in heavy seas. Benches were set to either side of the table, and against the stern wall was a padded settee. The upholstery was frayed, and the brass lamp, hung overhead from gimbals so that it would sway as the ship did, was black with tarnish, but all in all, it was as snug a parlor as he'd ever seen. "Cap'n's quarters," Peleg said. "I been sleepin' here nights."

Nat nodded, glancing at the door of the stateroom that would be his. His. There he would sleep; here he would take meals, work out the course, keep the log. Here in the long, slow reaches of the night, when they'd gone weeks without spotting a whale and everyone was going mad from boredom, was where he would be most tempted to drink. Some of his joy faded. He hadn't really thought about that before, hadn't realized the fight he'd have on his hands, coming back to old, familiar places. It was a fight he would have to win. He was not going to lose this chance.

"Shame about Miss Palmer," Peleg said, breaking into Nat's thoughts. "She selling to you?"

Nat didn't answer right away. "No."

"Hmph. Well, I expect the poor girl needs somethin' to hang on to. I was about to make myself some coffee when I seen you, Cap'n. You want somethin'?"

"Thanks, but no. I'm going to look around," Nat said.

He waited until Peleg had limped down the passageway and was again climbing abovedecks, before turning around to survey his new home again. There was a lot to do before he could set sail. He'd have to hire a crew, refit and repair the ship, order provisions, chart his course. He would also have to think about where he was going to put Abigail Palmer.

Nat frowned. He had his ship, aye, but at what cost? Not that he thought Abigail would really go through with her part of the deal. It took a special woman to stand up to life at sea, a strong woman who knew how to work and how to withstand life's storms. What storms had Abigail, daughter of a wealthy merchant, weathered? Aye, she was facing one now, he'd grant her that, and doing well enough. Maybe there was some strength under that pampered, plump exterior after all.

Plump? He frowned. Abigail wasn't overly plump. Nor did she seem particularly pampered, not with the way she'd taken charge of matters this afternoon. There was indeed something of her father in her, and yet she was definitely female. Into his mind flashed an image of her full breasts. Oh, yes. Quite definitely female.

And that could only cause problems. Women aboard ship always did. Men who'd been at sea for months, years, got to having thoughts and desires they wouldn't have on land. A man might just want to bury his face in that soft, dark hair, lay his hand on the full roundness of breast or hip, and . . .

"Damnation," he muttered, turning sharply away to pace the cabin. It wasn't his crew he had to worry about; they'd likely have little contact with the ship's owner. No, it was himself. And for what? A plain spinster who was not at all his usual type? Who looked as if she never laughed, never let her hair fly free, never dared life and the world? She'd spent her time in that mansion on the hill, isolated, insulated from harsh realities, while he had sweated for anything he got. No, she wasn't for him—but that was what being at sea did to a man. It made him want things he could never have. Add to that the fact that she still owned the ship and he was facing trouble.

Of a sudden Nat felt confined, cramped, in the spacious cabin. Grabbing his hat, he headed for the companionway.

He needed light, air, the wind in his face. He needed to be at sea, master of his fate, with no one looking over his shoulder, no one expecting him to fail. Not even himself.

Nat raised a hand in farewell to Peleg as he passed the galley and strode along the deck. It wouldn't work, he thought, jumping from railing to wharf. She'd have to see that. A captain had to make difficult decisions that an owner, caring only about profit, couldn't always fathom. It was hard enough when the owner was thousands of miles distant; having her aboard would be impossible. Damnation, he wouldn't have agreed to it at all, if not for Jared Swift.

Nat paused as the wharf met the land, looking back at his ship. Truth was, spiting Swift was one of the advantages of the arrangement. He didn't like the man, never had, though Swift was considered one of the fleet's best masters, so well liked that he could rise high in New Bedford's civic affairs if he'd a mind to. Oh, yes, Nat had taken great pleasure in thwarting Swift's wishes.

Another dray, this one loaded with provisions, trundled along the street, and Nat paused to let it pass. If he were honest with himself, and these days he tried to be, there had been more to his reaction than plain spite. As he'd stood in the hall of that grand house on the hill, dismayed at the way his plans had fallen apart, he had heard something in Abby's voice that had put him on alert. He'd seen the same something in her eyes a moment later, as Swift prowled toward her. Fear? He didn't know, but it had seemed very like it.

Huh. Picture that—Nat Howland, acting like a knight of old. A fallen knight in badly tarnished armor. He was not accustomed to riding to anyone's rescue, least of all his own. Yet that was what he had done, and because of it he was bound by a ridiculous agreement.

The skies over Fairhaven, the town to the east across the river, were still dark, but it was to the west that a New Englander looked for the weather to come, and there the sun shone. The wind had shifted into the northwest, and already the air felt less heavy on his skin. The storm was past, for now. In spite of the situation, Nat couldn't refrain from smiling as he headed up the hill, away from the waterfront and the ships, and then north onto Third Street, following a route that had become far too familiar to him in the past three years. Far ahead, past shops and businesses and houses, near the railroad line, the brick complex of buildings and chimneys that made up the Wamsutta Mill loomed against the sky. He'd hated the time spent there, but he'd had a goal. Now that goal was, in some measure, met. Because of that, today he would go to the mill with a light step. He was about to hand in his notice—and why not? He had a ship again, at last.

A week after reaching her agreement with Nat, Abby quietly let herself out of her cousin Elizabeth's house, at loose ends. Living with her cousin was sometimes stifling. Abby was glad to get out on her own, improper though it might be considered. This past week had been difficult. Each day she had been visited by another relative or acquaintance, each one adamantly opposed to her plan. Women simply did not go to sea. The only person who supported her was Elizabeth. Abby suspected that was from contrariness as much as anything else. Without that support, though, Abby wasn't sure what she would have done. There were too many moments when she thought she was making a terrible mistake.

There was another reason for her restlessness. Mr. Rodman had informed her just this morning that a good offer had been made on her former home. Everything was gone, even the Venetian wineglasses that her mother had bought on her honeymoon, and that Abby would have treasured. There was little left now to tie her to New Bedford. She had made her choice, and she was stuck with it.

Outside, the air was fresh and cool, in comparison to the hothouse atmosphere of Elizabeth's parlor. Wind from the northeast, Abby noted, as she had long ago been taught by her father. That was why the sky was such a rich, crisp blue, why the air felt so sweet. Perfect weather for a walk. Because fashion and propriety dictated that a lady be properly covered at all times, she had donned a paletot of black grosgrain with a wide ruffle about the edges, and a small black chip straw bonnet that perched just over her forehead. She had, she admitted, gone a bit too far in buying mourning clothes, but they had served as a kind of consolation for her. Now they were only one more debt she owed.

At the bottom of the drive Abby hesitated. If she continued on she would be heading toward the waterfront and the *Aquinnah*. Turn left, and she could either stroll along County Street and chance meeting someone she knew, or head west and soon find herself in open country. Neither prospect was appealing. It was with a sense of finality, then, that she took the only other choice open to her, crossing County Street to where her old home awaited, a few feet away.

After only a week, the big yellow house already had a quiet, neglected air. Someone had closed most of the inside shutters; on one window the louvers winked up, like a half-closed eye. Skirting the front door, Abby slipped instead through the back gate, feeling secure within the green board fence, and yet an intruder. Along the slate path, past the galleried back porch, and she was in the garden, already in need of trimming and pruning. At last she reached the pergola, her refuge, and sank down onto a bench, pulling off the paletot and stretching out her legs in a way New Bedford girls were taught was not proper. From here she could see the back side of the house, from basement to cupola. It was home, but it was no longer hers. She didn't want change, but inexorably it had come upon her.

Make your decision and stand by it, Papa had told her, and she'd usually found it good advice. Not this time. She wanted to stay; she knew she had to leave. She'd made a bargain with Captain Howland. More embarrassing, the entire city knew of her plans. If she went back on them now, she would be mortified. But it was her life, wasn't it? She was the one who had to live with the consequences of her choice.

The pergola darkened slightly, and she looked up. Clouds were marching in from the west, fair weather clouds most likely, but they had taken the shine off the day. Sighing, she gathered up her shawl and rose, stepping out onto the graveled path here. She looked up, and went very still. On the side verandah, watching her, was a man.

The sun chose that moment to peek out from the clouds, brightening the man's hair to silver. Abby's heart began to race. It could be Captain Howland, she thought, even as her mind registered other details of the man's appearance.

Though well built, he wasn't quite so tall, nor so broad, as Nathaniel. With a jolt she recognized him. Jared.

For a moment, irresolute, she paused in the archway of the pergola. It was likely that he would try again to convince her to stay, but she wouldn't listen. Her mind was made up. "What are you doing here?" she called, walking out of the pergola, her shoulders squared. Might as well get this over with.

Jared ran down the stairs from the back porch, smiling as he neared her. "I thought I'd find you here."

"Yes, well, I was just going back to Cousin Elizabeth's."

He nodded and looked back at the house. "It seems strange, doesn't it, that your family's not here anymore."

Abby fastened the paletot at her throat. "Yes. Yes, it does. I'm tempted to go in and take my mother's Venetian wineglasses."

He slanted a quick grin at her. "I don't blame you. All the time we spent here. All the memories."

Abby's stomach clenched, though she wasn't sure why. "Yes."

"You aren't really going to sea, are you?"

Abby hesitated. "I don't know," she admitted finally.

"It would be a mistake, Abby. You don't know Howland."

"He seems to have mended his ways. He's always been polite to me."

"Of course he has. He has something to gain from you. But at sea, with no one else around . . ."

"Jared, what are you implying?" she demanded.

"Nothing." He held his hands up, looking innocent. "Of course, you wouldn't be truly alone."

Abby frowned, troubled by his insinuation. "No."

"He's a dangerous man, Abby. Let him take a drink, and—"

"He's not drinking now."

"So he says."

"I believe him."

"Abby, Abby." He exhaled with a great sigh. "You always try to see the good in people, don't you? It's a commendable quality, my dear, if someone's around to protect you."

"Jared, I don't know why you're saying any of this. I don't know why you're trying to scare me."

"Because I won't be there to protect you, and you do need to be protected. It's one reason I love you."

"Jared—"

"No, let me finish, Abby. I never have a chance, not with Elizabeth hovering around every time I visit."

"There's nothing to say, Jared."

"Yes, there is. Abby, I love you." He grabbed her hand as she began to turn away. "I always have."

Abby tried to free her hand, to no avail. Jared's fingers were moist and oddly soft in comparison to Nat's firm, solid grasp. "I love you too, Jared, but—"

"As a brother. I know. It's enough."

"Jared, please."

"Marry me, Abby. It's what I've wanted for years. Ever since I came home from my first voyage. I'll make you happy."

A vast shudder ran through Abby, and somehow she managed to pull her hand free. "No!"

"Why not?" He followed her as she hurried toward the garden gate. "Am I really so repulsive? I have money, Abby, you know that. If you're afraid I'll go back to sea and leave you alone, I won't. I'll stay home."

"But I thought you loved the sea."

He shook his head. "Not really. I'm just good at what I do—and what else was there for me? But now people are hinting they'd like to see me more involved in civic affairs. Important people, Abby. I'm considering it."

"I don't want to marry you, Jared. Or anyone."

"Abby." He caught her shoulders. "You're not thinking straight. It's all right. I understand. You've been through too much. But if you'll marry me, nothing has to change."

Passive, limp, she looked up at him. "What do you mean?"

"You'll be able to move back here." His smile broadened. "I've bought the house."

Chapter 4

An emotion unfamiliar in its intensity filled Abby, and she whirled away. "Ooh! You would. Why did you have to—"

"Abby." Jared sounded hurt. "Aren't you pleased?"

"Pleased?" She wheeled around again. "That you've taken my home away from me?"

"At least I'm keeping it in the family."

"The family . . ." Her voice trailed off as she stared at him. "That's it, isn't it? You've always wanted it, haven't you? Always acted as if you belonged here, like . . ." Her throat closed up. "Oh, how could you?"

"I thought you'd be happy! Try to see it my way, Abby." Jared caught her arm, and she went very still. "Yes, I've always loved this house, and yes, I thought of your father as my father. That is what you were going to say, isn't it?" he demanded. "Well, I'd like to think he'd be happy to see me here."

"You were the son he never had." Her voice was steady, all accusation gone. "I knew that."

"But you were still his daughter, and this is still your home. Abby, marry me."

Very carefully Abby freed her arm. "No, Jared."

"Why not?" He stepped forward, his shoulders rising. "Aren't I good enough for you?"

"It's not you, Jared. I don't want to marry anyone."

"What will you do, then?" he challenged, his jaw jutting out. She took an involuntary step back. "Go on the *Aquinnah*, no matter what anyone thinks? No matter what I think?"

"The *Aquinnah*'s all I have, Jared," she said quietly, and turned away, toward the gate. Behind her Jared called her name, but she continued on, closing the gate softly behind her and turning to walk down the hill. She felt oddly light, clear, free. Her life as the dutiful daughter of Susan and Benjamin Palmer was over. A new, unknown life awaited her.

She turned one corner, and then another, passing on the one side neat clapboard homes, their gardens a riot of orange daylilies and pink rambling roses and on the other, the brick Quaker meetinghouse. Before her beckoned the waterfront, and the only thing she could still call her own. Jared had stolen her house. *How dare he?* she thought, but without much heat. She was angry, and yet she felt detached, distant. Odd. She never got angry. She always held back the retorts that came to her lips, always tried to see the other person's side. All she wanted was peace, and if that had sometimes put her in an uncomfortable position between her parents, it was the price she'd paid. People didn't like it when women got angry. People didn't like her to get angry. Both her father and Jared had taught her that.

"Miss Palmer?" a voice said, and she spun around, fists clenched. "Are you all right?"

"Captain Howland." She took a deep breath, forced her hands to relax. Someone else who would take her heritage away from her; someone else whom it would not be wise to anger. He was so big, taller than Jared, and broader, too. Yet as he stood a few feet away, shoulders relaxed, eyes questioning, she felt something within her unknot. "I want to see the *Aquinnah*," she blurted out.

Nat pursed his lips as he gazed down at her. Something had upset her. Her cheeks were flushed, her eyes bright, and her chin thrust forward. The angle of her head emphasized her cheekbones, made her eyes seem larger. She was, he realized with surprise, rather pretty. He simply hadn't noticed before. "You've the right."

"I most certainly do. She's my ship."

"So she is. I wondered when you'd show up."

Uncertainty flickered in her eyes. "I—aren't you going to stop me?"

"Why should I?"

"You're the captain."

"You're the owner," he pointed out, biting back a grin at her discomfiture. With her flush faded, she looked unsettled and vulnerable. "In fact, I was on my way to see you."

"You were?"

"Aye. There are things we need to discuss." He held out his arm to her. "Are you coming?"

"What? Oh, yes." She turned to walk with him, though her fingers settled on his arm tentatively, and she kept her distance from him. If he said the wrong thing, she would bolt. It was amusing, touching. Never had he seen the competent Miss Palmer so at a loss.

"The *Aquinnah* needs work," he said as they walked along. He rather liked her light touch on his arm. It wasn't that he'd been without a woman. By Neptune, no. There were women aplenty for the men who sailed the sea, and Nat had cheerfully taken advantage of their availability. Still, he didn't know the last time when he had walked these streets with a woman on his arm. "But you knew that."

"Yes. Captain, do you think I'm mad?"

"You seemed angry a few moments ago, but—"

"No, not that way. Insane. For wanting to go to sea."

"Why, do you?" he asked, intrigued.

"I don't know." She frowned, and again he noticed that her lower lip was full and red. "I can't figure it out. The *Aquinnah*'s mine, of course. And if I changed my mind now, I'd be mortified by what people would think of me."

He shrugged. "That doesn't matter."

"Oh, but it does." She looked up at him, her eyes grave, clear, earnest. "It matters a great deal. People already disapprove, except for Cousin Elizabeth. If I change my mind and stay behind it will only be worse."

"Then don't do it."

"It's not that easy."

"Abigail, you can't please everyone," he said, stopping and laying his hand on hers, and feeling her go still.

"Yes, I can." She avoided his gaze. "I should."

"No." He began walking again, shaken by that brief moment of intimacy. He could still feel the warmth of her hand under his. "No matter what you do, there'll always be someone who doesn't approve. I've learned that well."

She looked up at him then. "Doesn't it bother you?"

"Only if it's someone I care about. It's your life." He shrugged. "You have to live it for yourself."

"Hm." She frowned again, and he wondered what she

was thinking. "That's all very well, Captain, but I have friends and relatives who care about me."

"And of course I don't."

"I didn't mean that! I meant—"

"I know. Been pestering you, have they?"

"Yes. Captain, I am sorry." This time she stopped, her brow puckered. "I didn't mean to imply that you have no one—that there's no one who cares—oh, mercy—"

"But it's true," he said, calmly. "I'm alone. Most of my brothers are at sea, and the ones who aren't don't exactly approve of me. One of them turned preacher, can you imagine that? He thinks all sailors need rescuing." His face twisted. "My sister, Catherine, married a farmer in Westport, so I see her from time to time. She's glad for me to go back to sea." He looked down at her. "And that's without mentioning cousins and uncles and people I thought were friends. So, you see, I do know what it's like to have people disapprove of me. Makes me wonder why you're risking so much being seen with me."

Abby's chin was raised. "You're the captain of a ship I own. I have every right to talk with you."

"But you're wondering if going to sea is such a good idea, and that's why this is bothering you." At her quick gasp, he went on. "Never mind. Come see the *Aquinnah*. There's a lot we have to talk about."

"All right," she said after a moment. They began walking again, she with downcast eyes. "What repairs does she need?"

"More than I expected. I've had a carpenter looking her over and she's basically sound, but there is much to do. She needs to be rerigged."

"Completely?"

"Aye. The standing rigging, for sure. It's gone slack. Leave it as it is and we'll lose a mast in the first gale. The running rigging—you know, the lines to the sails—"

"I know the difference between standing and running rigging, Captain," Abby said, with a touch of her earlier asperity. "The running rigging would need replacing after the voyage, anyway."

"True. She has an old set of sails, acceptable for light weather, but not for the Arctic or for rounding the Horn."

"We're going around South America?" she interrupted.

"Why not head out past the Cape of Good Hope to New Zealand?"

"We would if it was earlier in the year. By the time all the work's done and we sail, it'll be too late for the southern whaling grounds. And we want to get around the Horn while it's still summer there."

"And then?"

"Winter over in Honolulu with the rest of the fleet, then to the Arctic in the summer."

"Honolulu." Her voice had gone soft. "Where it's warm all the time."

"If you feel the cold that much, a trip to the Arctic will be mighty uncomfortable."

"I'll manage. She needs sails. What else?"

They were nearing the Palmer countinghouse now. Abby, he noticed, was looking elsewhere. "We'll heave her down at the wharf to check her bottom. Probably the copper sheathing will need replacing. And the seams will have to be recaulked."

"Of course." They stepped onto the wharf. "What else?"

"New hearth for the trypots, and new trypots. What happened to her old ones?"

"My father needed them for another ship."

"You could have held on to them."

"It wasn't up to me."

"You're the owner."

"He was my father. I imagine she needs repainting."

"Yes," he said, backing off the touchy subject of her relationship with Benjamin Palmer. "And new pumps."

She frowned. "Does she leak?"

"All ships leak."

"But more than usual?"

"As I said, her seams need caulking, and she'll likely need new planking as well."

"Mm-hm. Mostly repairs that any ship would need before a voyage."

"Plus new harpoons, lances, and at least one whaleboat. Maybe more."

"So long as you keep an accounting." Her gaze was cool as they stopped before the ship, calculating. Nat frowned. For a fleeting moment she looked like her father, intent and businesslike. Nat's respect and caution rose a notch.

Abigail Palmer was no featherheaded female. "But she is a fine ship, isn't she, Captain?"

He smiled. "That she is. I'm proud to be her skipper."

Abby smiled at him, for the first time that afternoon. "Good. Do you know, I haven't been aboard since she was launched?"

Nat's hand cupped her elbow as she stepped up onto the rough board that served as a gangplank, and he noticed again the fineness of her bones. She wasn't tall—came up to his chin, maybe. And she'd lived her life as the sheltered daughter of a wealthy merchant. How she would survive the rough life of whaling he didn't know. "I haven't done anything to the cabin yet, but it's not too bad. Needs cleaning and new paint, mostly." He paused. "That's where you're planning to stay, isn't it?"

Abby was gazing up at the top of the masts. "Have you ever been up there?"

He followed her gaze to the lookout, high atop the mainmast. "Aye. Often."

"What a feeling it must be. I can't imagine the view." She stared upward for another moment and then turned to him. "I don't expect special treatment, Captain."

"Hah." It came out before he could stop it.

"I don't! I mean it."

"Maybe you do now, but you don't know what it's like at sea. I don't have time to pamper a rich man's daughter."

Something flickered in her eyes, something that looked like hurt. "No one's ever given me special treatment, Captain. The cabin is your parlor, is it not? And the stateroom with it is your berth."

"You're the owner," he shot back, unsettled by what he'd seen a moment before in her eyes.

"Then as owner I order you to take the cabin." Unexpectedly, she smiled. "My! I could get used to that."

"That's what I'm afraid of." He resisted the urge to run a hand over his hair. "Just so you understand that at sea I'm the one giving the orders."

"Of course."

"Huh." They'd see. She was opinionated, and not shy about expressing her thoughts. He suspected they would clash more than once, and not because she questioned his expertise. No, he was more concerned about his authority.

A ship could not have two masters. "I estimate maybe six weeks, two months, to get the work done."

"Then we'll be sailing in September." She nodded. "I'll be ready."

"No matter what other people say?"

She was quiet for so long that he thought she wasn't going to answer. "I do think sometimes that they're right."

Relief mingled with disappointment, an odd mixture. "Are you changing your mind?"

"No. Oh, no." She looked up at him then. "I'm not going back on my word. You're still skipper of the *Aquinnah*."

"And you?"

She took a deep breath. It lifted her bosom in an altogether too enticing way. "I am still going to sea."

Disappointment and relief. "It won't be easy."

"I don't expect it to be. I do expect you to get started on the repairs as soon as possible."

"Fine. I assume you can afford them."

"Yes, if I can find someone to extend me credit. The house has been sold."

"I didn't know that." He looked away. "I'm sorry."

"Thank you. Of course, that money will go to cover Father's debts. Whatever money I have will go into this ship."

He blinked. This was no halfhearted commitment on her part. "Then I'll lend you the rest."

"No," she said quickly.

"Why not? It's the logical thing. Or"—he said, thinking quickly—"we could change the terms of the agreement."

"In what way?"

"What I suggested last week. A partnership."

Abby stepped away from him and stared off across the harbor. "I cannot let go of this ship."

"It may come to that."

"No." Her lips were set. "I'll find the money. I've an aunt in New York who may lend it to me. She believes in women being independent."

"You don't need to. I told you. I'll lend it to you."

Abby's lips pursed in apparent displeasure. "I don't know when I can pay you back," she said, her gaze fixed on the spires and steeples of Fairhaven, across the river.

"When you can. We both know this is a risky proposition," he went on as she looked up at him. "We could be out four years and come back with empty holds."

"You don't believe that."

"No." He smiled. "I'm willing to take the risk."

"So am I, God help me." She nodded. "All right. I'll accept a loan, and we'll work out terms for repayment. But this isn't part of the agreement."

He nodded, disappointed but not surprised. Abby was too sharp at business to give someone an advantage over her. Still, this could be his chance. He might be able to negotiate something, might be able to change the terms in the future. He wanted this ship so much it was almost a physical craving. Like wanting a woman. Freedom, self-respect, all the things he'd lost—they awaited him, so long as he had this ship. "We're in this together," he said and held out his hand.

She looked up at him with a startled sweep of lashes and took a deep breath. "Yes," she said, and put her hand in his. In the brief moment before she pulled back, he was aware of so many things: that her hand was small and soft and yet her grasp was firm; that her eyes were steady, resolute. By Neptune, he did have a partner in business, in adventure. Something settled inside him. This would work. It had to.

And in that brief moment, Abby, too, became aware of several things: that his hand was warm, strong, and yet somehow gentle; that his eyes really were the most amazing blue; and that perhaps, just perhaps, she was no longer alone. It was frightening. It wouldn't work. What had she gotten herself into?

Jared stood in the shadows of a doorway and watched as Nathaniel Howland came out of a building across the street. He waited until Nat turned east onto Union Street and then stepped out of the doorway, following from a distance, keeping his quarry ever in sight. This morning Nat had met with a ship's agent, who found crews for whalers. Probably it hadn't gone very well, Jared thought and smiled to himself. Not since he'd put out the word that taking a berth on the *Aquinnah* was something he'd rather no one did.

Jared knew many, many people in New Bedford. Though

his father had been nothing but a common sailor and his mother an invalid, Jared had managed to overcome all obstacles to rise to the top of a difficult profession. He was one of the most successful, most sought-after skippers. Owners trusted him to bring in a profit, no matter what. He was on friendly terms with the Morgans and the Rotches and even George Howland, who had had the good sense not to hire Nat, though they were cousins. People were talking about him running for office in the city, or the state, or possibly even nationally. Jared had power. He intended to use it.

Ahead of him Nat paused, staring across Union Street at a brick building with a sundial set into its southern face, checking his watch and then snapping it shut. He then turned and went into a shabby-looking frame building. Jared's hopes soared. A tavern. Well, well. And wouldn't this be a bit of news to tell Abigail, that the man she trusted to skipper her ship was slipping back into his old ways?

A few moments later, however, Nat was outside again, pushing his cap back on his head and talking with a man who accompanied him. Jared recognized him as another ship's agent. By their gestures and postures, the two men appeared to be arguing. Maybe Howland hadn't had time to take a drink; maybe that was too much to hope for. It certainly looked, though, as if he were having trouble rounding up a crew, and that was good. Jared had never liked Nat, not when they'd been young, not as Nat's first mate, not since. He wasn't going to let Nat go through with his plans, not without a fight. Abigail was his.

Ahead was Front Street, and beyond that the wharves and buildings of the waterfront. Jared rounded the corner where Nat had turned a few moments before, and then stopped, frowning. Before him were Quaker merchants bustling into countinghouses and workmen going about their trades. Of Nat, however, there was no sign. It was as if the man had disappeared.

"Swift," a voice said behind him, and Jared whirled to see Nat stepping out of a doorway. In an instant, hunter had become hunted. "Looking for me?"

Chapter 5

Nat leaned against the clapboards of a grocery store, hands tucked into pockets. Swift had been following him for several days now. "Well?"

"No." Jared stepped back. He recovered quickly, Nat would say that for him. "I have no desire to see you."

"Odd. Seems to me I've caught sight of you a few times lately. Always behind me."

"Someone has to look out for Abby."

"Ah." Nat nodded, now that Jared had stopped pretending. "What is it, Swift? Afraid to challenge me to my face?"

"I'm not afraid of you," Jared said softly. "I know too much about you."

Nat's lips tightened, and it took an effort for him to relax. "Past history, Swift."

"Not all of it. Abby should know who she's hired on."

"Miss Palmer is smarter than you think."

"Abby is naive. She's been sheltered from scum like you. Someone has to look out for her interests."

"Has she asked you to?"

"She didn't have to."

"Then she doesn't know. Hm." He pushed himself away from the building. "I don't have time for this. I've a ship to refit," he said curtly and walked away.

"Are you having luck finding a crew?" Jared taunted.

Nat turned slowly. In the past week he'd spoken to everyone he knew about raising a suitable crew. Oddly enough, there seemed to be no men available. Not for him; not for the *Aquinnah*. Until today. "Yes, as it happens." He smiled. "Mr. Wing is rounding one up for me."

"What!" Jared took a step forward and then went still. His anger showed in his eyes, however.

Interesting, Nat thought. He had been right. Swift was behind his recent difficulty.

"He told you he wouldn't, right? Well, he's changed his mind. And I wouldn't suggest going after him," Nat went on, as Jared's fists balled. "It's me you want, isn't it?"

"I want you to leave Abby alone." His voice was soft, even. "I will do whatever it takes to make you do so."

"And stand behind a woman's skirts to protect yourself."

Jared smiled thinly. "Better than what you do with a woman's skirts."

Nat chuckled. "For God's sake. You're no innocent, Swift."

"I haven't debauched myself the way you have. Going into taverns, being seen with low women—"

"Better that than some other things." All trace of humor left Nat's face. "I was on a whaler with you for two years. More than enough time to find out what kind of man you are."

"The kind that saved your neck when you wrecked your ship. If I hadn't been there to get the crew off, they'd be dead now, and you with them."

"And we both know that's what you would have liked, if you could have gotten away with it."

Jared smiled. "Prove it."

"I don't have to. I know that if you could have left me to freeze, you would have. I also know that you like native women, the younger, the better."

"Abby won't believe you."

"Maybe not," Nat said, though he had no intention of ever telling Abigail anything about Swift. God alone knew why, but she actually liked the man. "And maybe she will." He turned. "I'm busy. Go find someone else to pester."

"We're not done, Howland," Jared called after him. "I'll do what I have to, to keep you from skippering that ship."

"Do so," Nat snapped over his shoulder and stalked away.

Abby laid down her steel-nibbed pen, clenching and unclenching her hands to stretch her cramped fingers. In the guttering candlelight the row of figures she had been studying danced before her aching, scratchy eyes. The price of rope. The cost of copper. The expense of replacing not two but three whaleboats, with all their gear. The numbers were adding up, higher and higher, while her precious store of money dwindled by the day. It was an expensive undertaking to refit a ship. She only hoped she was doing the right thing.

It was late at night, and all about her the city slept. In the past Abby would have argued that she had not led a leisured life. Even though she'd lived in a mansion, she'd still had her duties, her tasks. She was discovering, though, that there was a vast difference between occasionally playing her father's hostess and making all the decisions necessary to run a business. She couldn't just sit at a desk and authorize payments, not without knowing what those payments were for. And though she trusted Nat—to an extent—still it was her ship, her money. It was her responsibility to see that all repairs were done properly and yet efficiently.

Far off she heard a noise. Odd. It sounded like the front door knocker. She frowned, rising, as the noise came again. Who could that be at this hour of the night? Elizabeth was abed, as were her aging servants, leaving Abby the only one to cope with a nighttime intruder. Lighting a candle, she headed toward the hall, hesitating in the doorway as the flesh on her back tightened in involuntary, reflexive shudders. Something was wrong. Without giving herself time to think, she snatched up a poker. Thus armed, she went to face whatever trouble lay ahead.

The door knocker sounded again as she went downstairs, candle in one hand, poker in the other. Thank heavens she was still dressed, though her hair was down and held back only by a ribbon. "Yes, yes, I'm coming," she muttered, more irritated now than frightened, and paused before the door. "Who is it?"

"Miss Palmer?" A voice came faintly through the solid oaken door. "It's me. Peleg Tripp."

Abby's skin tightened again. Tripp, the ship's watchman. Dear God, had something happened to the *Aquinnah*? "Wait." She fumbled with the lock and flung the door open. "What is it?"

Peleg didn't waste time on apologies or greetings. "There's a fire, miss."

The poker clattered to the floor. "The ship. Is she—?"

"I don't know, miss, but you'd better come."

"Yes. There's a fire," she said, turning to speak to Elizabeth, who was bending over the banister. "I have to go. Does Captain Howland know?"

"Aye, miss," Peleg said as they hurried down the front stairs. In the drive waited on old cart, pulled by a tired-looking nag. "He's been sleepin' there nights."

She cast him a sharp look as she clambered into the cart. "I didn't know that."

"Aye, miss. Takes his duties seriously, does the cap'n."

And he doesn't have to pay for lodging, she thought, gripping the edges of the bench as the cart jolted into motion. Unworthy thought, she knew, since he'd been working so hard these past weeks, but still, there it was. Jared had warned her during one of his increasingly strident visits that Nat would try to take advantage of her. He was that kind of man. Smooth on the outside, but the devil within. Why, he'd been seen with low women and other unsavory types. And if she found he'd had a woman aboard the *Aquinnah,* Abby thought grimly, she would sack him. The *Aquinnah* was her ship, and Nat was her captain.

Palmer's Wharf was bustling with people and vehicles. Abby was relieved to see the fire department already there, with men holding the hose from the steam engine. Beyond that an orange glow lit up the spars and masts of the *Aquinnah,* towering into the night. Abby jumped down from the cart and ran even before Peleg had come to a stop. "That's my ship," she said tersely as a fireman held out a sooty hand to detain her. The smell of burning wood was pungent, almost pleasant, like woodsmoke in the fall. From here it looked as if the hull was afire. If that were so, the ship was doomed.

"Abby." Another hand reached out, this one landing on her arm. Abby wrenched away, to find herself staring up at Nat's grimy face. "Easy, there. You'll only be in the way."

"The ship—the fire—"

"There's no damage."

That stopped her. "What? But the fire—"

"Is almost out." Nat looked grimly back at the ship, and she followed his gaze. The flames had lowered in the few moments since her arrival; she could see now that they were actually on the wharf itself. "It didn't touch the ship."

She grasped his forearms. "She's all right?"

"Aye. She's fine."

"Oh, thank God," Abby said and sagged against him. He went absolutely still, and after a moment she straightened. Mercy, what had she just done? "But what happened?"

"The lumber we had stacked for planking went up," he said, looking toward the fire. He seemed unaffected by the brief embrace; indeed, he'd kept his arms at his side and hadn't touched her, while she— Well, she could still feel the strong, solid warmth of his chest against her cheek, a reassuring bulwark against the world. "Part of the wharf caught, too."

"It's a miracle that the whole thing didn't go up." She shuddered. A fire on the wharves, fed by combustible wooden ships and fueled by whale oil, would be disastrous.

"Aye. I was aboard, and so was Tripp. He smelled it first and raised the alarm. There was someone on that schooner, there," he pointed, "and he came to help. Tripp rang for the city watch and then went for you."

"I'm glad he did." She shivered. Now that the worst of the crisis was past, she was aware of other things; that the wind off the water was damp and cool, and that Nat's shirt, open at the throat, exposed strong neck muscles and short, curling hairs that glinted in the light. Uncomfortable, she looked away. "Whatever started it?"

"We don't know yet." He took her arm as she stepped hesitantly toward the still-smoking pile of lumber. It was good money gone up in smoke, and yet all she felt was vast relief. Lumber could be replaced. Her ship was safe. "Careful here, the wharf's been weakened. If it had happened during the day I'd say maybe someone was careless smoking. But who was around in the middle of the night?"

Abby stared at the embers. "Are you saying it was set?"

"Do you smell anything?"

She wrinkled her nose. "Yes. Charred wood."

"Try again."

She sniffed, and frowned as she caught an elusive scent. "There is something. What is it?"

"Kerosene," he said grimly.

"Kerosene!"

"Aye. The smell was strong when the fire first started."

"Someone set it," she said numbly. "Why?"

"I don't know. She's supposed to be hove down tomorrow to start work on the bottom," he said, indicating the ship. "Actually, we were going to do it today, but the workers got delayed on another job."

Abby frowned a bit. To heave down a ship meant to use ropes to tilt it onto its side, so workers could repair the bottom. "So?"

"If this had happened tomorrow night, she likely would have gone up. There'd have been no one to call the alarm." He looked down at her. "Someone wants to cause you trouble."

"Me?"

"You're the owner."

"You've antagonized more people than I have," she blurted, and was instantly sorry. "I'm sorry. That was uncalled for."

He nodded, seemingly unoffended. "It's true I've made enemies in my life, but I've friends, too." He shook his head. "I think this was meant for you."

"But why?"

"Someone wants to stop you."

Jared, she thought, and again felt chilled. Who else was so opposed to her going to sea? Yet she couldn't conceive of him, her childhood friend, doing something that would hurt her so much. "I don't know."

He glanced down at her, waited as if for her to go on, and then nodded. "Whoever it was, we'll have to put more watchmen on, to make sure this doesn't happen again."

"Mm. Another expense."

"Can't be helped, not if you want to protect the ship." Nat's face was grim. Whoever had set the fire—and he had his own ideas on that—had wanted to hurt her. It took an underhanded, sneaky sort of mind to do such a thing rather than come out and fight in the open. That made that person dangerous. Nat wasn't worried for himself. Abby, though, was another concern. "You can't do anything here. I'll take you home."

She nodded and turned, walking away, head down and arms folded across her chest. She looked young, lonely and vulnerable. He had to resist the urge to put his arm around her again as he caught up with her. He'd wanted to embrace her when she had leaned against him, earlier; he wanted to now. Instead, he walked beside her, not touching her, not talking. She was the ship's owner, and his boss. That set her off-limits. Besides, he told himself, she wasn't his type.

They both were quiet during the short ride up the hill to Elizabeth's house, which was alight from top to bottom. "Oh, dear," Abby said, shaking her head as she stepped down from the cart, just briefly touching Nat's hand. "Everyone's awake."

Nat fell into step beside her. "What did you expect?"

"It's so late, past midnight, and they're old."

Which meant they wouldn't be much protection, should the person who had set the fire decide to attack her. He'd have to do something about that. "They're concerned about you."

"I know. I've turned their lives upside down lately."

"Seems to me your cousin enjoys that kind of thing," he said just as the front door opened.

Elizabeth stepped out onto the porch, her hands held out. "My heavens. Child, is everything all right? Why, your hands are like ice. Is the ship safe?"

"Yes." Abby smiled tiredly. "There was a fire nearby, but it's out."

Elizabeth looked past her to Nat. "And how did it start, young man?"

"An accident," Abby said quickly, "and if not for Captain Howland it would have spread."

"Would it." Elizabeth nodded. "Then it's a good thing you were there."

"I plan to keep my eye on that ship," Nat said, meeting Elizabeth's gaze. Her eyes were dark and fierce and concerned. So. She had her suspicions as well. "You can be sure of that."

"Good." She nodded again. "It's high time Abby had someone on her side."

"Captain Howland wants to be certain he has a ship."

"And an owner to pay the bills," he retorted, smiling.

She looked back at him, her eyes uncertain, and then returned the smile. "True. We do need each other, don't we?"

"Yes, Miss Palmer. We do."

"There'll be plenty of time to discuss this in the morning," Elizabeth interrupted, putting her arm about Abby's shoulders and turning her toward the door. "Captain, thank you for everything. Good night."

"Good night," he answered and turned back to the cart, his mouth pursed thoughtfully. Someone was so opposed to what he and Abby were doing that he would apparently go to any length to stop them. Not that Nat would let that happen. The *Aquinnah* was his. He'd do what he had to to protect it, and Abby as well. It wasn't what he'd bargained for when he'd signed on as skipper, being as concerned about one young woman as about his future, his goal. It changed things. What, he wondered uneasily, had he gotten himself into?

Out in the stream of the Acushnet River, the *Aquinnah* stood at anchor, gaily decorated with colorful pennants, with the house flag snapping proudly from the mainmast. The sails were loosely furled, just waiting to be released, the rigging was taut and clean, and her paint shone brilliantly. Against all odds, she had been refitted and repaired and was now as ready to sail the seas as any ship. The pump organ from the Seaman's Bethel had been trundled down and was in place to play hymns of farewell; the chaplain was ready to give his blessing. Now the final test had come. It was sailing day, at last.

On Palmer's Wharf, near a shed, Nat scowled at the large gilded cage he held aloft. Within the cage was a bird, mostly gray with some red on its tail, returning his stare balefully. "Miss Palmer's," someone had said a moment ago, thrusting the cage at him, so that he'd had no choice but to take it. Damnation! If ever he'd needed proof that Abigail Palmer was going to disrupt life aboard ship, he had it now.

The weeks since the fire had been relatively calm. Jared Swift was still around, still stalking Nat, but there'd been no more attempts at sabotage. Nor had the man he'd hired to keep watch over Abby, without her knowledge, reported anything out of the ordinary. Swift visited her every day, and was otherwise busy refitting his own ship. Nat was still on guard, however. He would not feel easy until they left New Bedford.

Now that time was almost here. As promised, Mr. Wing

had delivered the crew, a raucous group with bleary eyes
and the odor of rum hanging about them. After much effort
and some not-so-subtle persuasion, they were now on the
ship, with family and friends to see them off. The ship had
been provisioned with vegetables and flour and water; live-
stock in pens would provide fresh meat for a time, while
the chickens would give eggs. Cabins and staterooms had
been refurbished and were now comfortable, if not elegant;
he had stored his charts and his sextant and his other navigational tools in a cabinet. His precious chronometers, the
timepieces set always to New Bedford Time, held in a mahogany case under his arm, would go aboard only when he
did, and he would board last. He awaited only the arrival
of Miss Palmer and her party.

The bird squawked. Nat looked back at it, frowning, to
see it regarding him with small bright eyes. A bird, God
help him. In the past days Abby's belongings had come
aboard gradually. First, a colorful quilt for her stateroom,
and then her trunks. These were followed by a sewing
table, an artist's easel, and a parlor organ. Nat had gladly
consigned all these articles to be stowed, though there
wasn't much he could do about her collection of books—
poetry, of course—in a bookshelf in the aft cabin. Now
there was a bird. It was too much. If he weren't careful,
Miss Palmer would turn the *Aquinnah* into a hen ship.

"Tripp," Nat called as his steward hurried by on his way
to the whaleboat that would bring him out to the ship.

Peleg turned toward him. "Yes, Cap'n?"

Nat thrust the cage at him, and the bird, disturbed, ruffled its feathers and squawked. "Do something with this."

"A parrot!" Peleg's face brightened as he took the cage.
"An African Gray, Cap'n. Know how rare they are?"

"No, and I don't care. Just get it out of my sight."

"So that's why Miss Palmer wanted me to put a hook in
the cabin overhead. I wonder if it talks. Oh, yes, you're a
fine fellow," he crooned to the bird.

"Good God. Don't go getting soft on me, Tripp."

"No, Cap'n. But it might be fun, havin' this here bird
aboard. You know, times when there's no whales to be
found."

Nat looked at Peleg from under his brow. "Mr.
Tripp . . ."

"I'll take care of him, Cap'n," Peleg said hastily and hurried across the wharf.

"I do apologize for that," a soft voice said behind him. Nat turned to see Abby, lips twisted in a rueful smile. She had apparently just descended from a carriage a few yards away. "My cousin Elizabeth's idea."

She was small, he thought again, looking down at her face, shaded by her black silk bonnet. "I didn't see you arrive."

"No, you appeared busy with Harold."

"Harold?"

"Cousin Elizabeth's—"

"Idea," he finished for her.

"Yes. She seems to think I'll be bored."

"Bored? With a sewing box and an easel and an organ to entertain you?"

Her face brightened. "Do you like music, Captain?"

"I had it stowed. I had to," he went on, as the brightness faded from her face, making him regret his abruptness. "At sea it would likely be tossed around and damaged."

"Of course." She smiled mechanically. "I should have thought of that."

"It can be set up when we're in port."

She nodded. "Of course," she said again and turned slightly away, scanning the group of bystanders who crowded the wharf. "There are more people here than I expected."

"We have a reputation to live down. The *Aquinnah* and me," he added, as she looked up at him with a quick sweep of lashes. Damnation, he was being uncommonly clumsy with her. "Do you have family coming?"

"Yes, Elizabeth will be here soon. I decided to come ahead of her to make sure everything is all right." She paused. "I also see some cousins in the crowd."

"Strange they haven't greeted you."

"They don't quite approve of me, Captain."

"Or me, most likely, but that's no reason to snub you."

"Where is your family, Captain?"

"Not here," he said, with more lightness than he felt. Sailing day should have been a festive occasion. A whaler leaving port was common enough not to attract much notice, but usually friends and well-wishers gathered around

to offer congratulations and to wish them Godspeed. Not
so this crowd. It was curiosity that had drawn them, the
novelty of a long-abandoned ship being skippered by a man
most owners wouldn't trust, combined with the scandal of
a young woman's sailing aboard, unchaperoned. They kept
their distance, the good people of New Bedford, even those
he'd once counted as friends, even those who were related
to Abby. Until this moment he hadn't realized quite how
ostracized he and Abby were.

Well, let those people think what they would. He had
paid for his mistakes, and he knew his capabilities. He
could, and would, skipper the *Aquinnah* successfully. Four
years hence, such success would change their attitudes. Not
so for Abby, though. People being people, it was likely
they'd still shun her.

He glanced down at her, noting again the fineness of her
profile, silhouetted against the brim of her bonnet, as she
gazed out toward the ship. He preferred bright colors on
women, not black, but he had to admit that it suited her
in some way, enhancing the color in her cheeks and giving
her dignity. He liked the gown, too, in that new style with
the skirt flat in front and bustled behind. It changed her
shape, made her look trimmer and more attractive.
Damnation!

Abby looked up at him, and he glanced hastily away,
embarrassed at being caught, chagrined at the direction his
thoughts had taken. "My cousin is arriving," she said quietly. "She'll come aboard as my guest, if that is all right
with you."

He shrugged. "You're the owner."

"But you're the captain."

"As long as you remember that."

"I'm not likely to forget if you keep reminding me, am
I?" she snapped, and with her back very straight, stalked
away, toward the carriage that had just stopped on the
wharf. Nat watched her, his good humor mysteriously restored. Doubtless she'd irritate him again in the months to
come. If he could return the favor, so much the better.
Besides, with her shoulders thrown back like that her
bosom jutted forward even more than usual . . .

Damnation! His hand tightened on the box that held his
chronometers. This was new, this attraction he felt toward

her, and he didn't like it. Maybe it was because he was facing months of abstinence, though he'd tried to make up for that in the past days. This morning he'd thought himself satisfied for a time. He had to get his mind onto other things besides the red lushness of Abby's lips, or the gentle curve of her hips. He had to. The last thing he needed was any sort of feelings for his ship's owner. Restoring his reputation was more important. Somehow he would have to discipline himself.

Abigail and Elizabeth had been helped into a whaleboat and were being rowed out to the ship, where a chairlike contraption would hoist them aboard in relative comfort and modesty. Everyone—crew, officers, and now owner— was on the ship. It was nearly time to sail. The only person missing was himself.

Nat stepped away from the shed as the men in the whale-boat, having delivered the two women to the ship, began to pull for shore. The organist had finished, and the chap-lain was giving his blessing. Almost time. Nat could feel it tingling in his bones, in his fingertips. All his life seemed to lead up to this one moment. He was going to skipper a ship again. And though he was glad of it, anyone leaving home for a voyage of three or four years' duration would feel a tug of sorrow at departure. Nat strode across the wharf and stood at ease, waiting for the whaleboat to tie up, aware of people watching him. Ignoring them, pres-enting to the world a confident, determined front, he looked back at shore. One last look, at the brick and gran-ite and wooden buildings huddled together near the wharves; at the white church spires piercing the sky; at the trees, mostly green, though one or two showed scarlet or orange, heralding the changing season. Then he faced for-ward, aware as he did so of something seen out of the corner of his eye, something wrong, out of place. Casually he glanced back and locked on the source of his unease, the lone figure that stood apart from the crowd. Jared Swift, hands bunched into fists, face expressionless, stared back at him. For a long, long moment their gazes held, measuring, unfriendly, until one of the men in the boat spoke to Nat, distracting him. He was just as glad. He'd no time for such foolishness. Glancing back at Jared, he flipped him a mocking salute and then jumped down into the boat. Another problem behind him.

The rope ladder was out on the ship. Though encumbered, Nat climbed it easily due to years spent climbing rigging, his stern face hiding his elation. The deck was crowded and rowdy, with people milling about the try-works, the cooper's bench, the ship's wheel. "Let's get under way, Mr. Martel," he said tersely to his first mate and strode toward the deckhouse that opened to the lower decks. Behind him Gerald Martel began bawling commands, ordering the landlubbers ashore and cursing those who didn't move quickly enough. Nat bit the inside of his mouth to hide his grin, but then grew serious. There was still much to do. The steam tug that would tow them out from the harbor was nearing; soon a line would be cast from the tug to the *Aquinnah,* and they would be under way. Chain rattled and thudded as the crew, singing a ragged chorus of "Away to Rio" to help them work the windlass, labored to bring the anchor aboard. Not "Shenandoah," though that was traditional; Nat would never allow that chantey to be sung aboard any ship he skippered. Pausing in the doorway of the deckhouse, he smiled at last at the mixture of sounds, all overlaid by the creaking of timbers and rope. He was finally home.

He didn't know how long he stood there, listening to the music of his ship, before a squawk from below broke him out of his absorption. That damned parrot. Brought back to reality, Nat turned and made his way down the companionway. At the bottom of the stairs he turned, to enter the passageway leading to the aft cabin. One of the women was walking toward him, but his vision hadn't yet adjusted enough from sunshine to shadow for him to see who it was. Politely he stepped aside, just as the ship, under tow, jolted forward. To Nat, the motion was negligible. Not so to the other person. "Oh!" a voice said. *Abby,* he thought, as she stumbled. He threw his arms out to break her fall; one hand caught her arm, and the other fell onto something unexpectedly warm, soft, yielding. Abby's startled gasp confirmed what his body already told him with a surge of heat. *Good God!* His palm was filled with her breast.

Chapter 6

Abby went still, her mind blank, her limbs frozen. Help was nearby, with Cousin Elizabeth in the cabin and Mr. Tripp bustling around somewhere. Not here, though. Here there was only Nat, looming up before her, and his hand on her—person. She should cry out, she thought detachedly, or at least move, but she couldn't. She couldn't.

"I beg your pardon." Nat pulled back, sounding surprisingly normal. An accident, she thought, breathing again. She had stumbled; he had caught her. "I didn't see you."

"I got in your way," she said, her voice breathless, while he seemed not in the least affected. But then, he likely had more experience in this area than she did. "I was just going to find out what's going on."

"The towboat's hawser is aboard. We'll be out of the harbor soon."

"Oh. That's why the ship moved as it did."

"Best get used to it, Miss Palmer. You'll face worse than that. Excuse me." He held up a box. "I need to stow this."

"Oh. Of course." Abby stepped back to let him pass, aware of his arm brushing her sleeve, of his leg against her skirt. In this confined space, it would be difficult to avoid touching. She'd have to keep her distance.

"Miss Palmer," Nat said, turning suddenly from the cabin doorway. Abby, still rooted in place, looked back at him. "Have you ever been on a ship leaving the harbor?"

She forced a smile. "No. Not even on *Aquinnah*'s maiden voyage. I don't suppose the Vineyard ferry counts as a ship?"

"Not quite. It's a sight you don't want to miss. I'd like you and your cousin to join me on deck."

"Thank you," she said, and he disappeared into the cabin. Abby groped at the wall behind her, finding at last the latch to her stateroom door, and stumbling into the tiny room. Finally alone, she crossed her arms protectively over her chest and stood still for what seemed like a very long time.

"Abigail?" a voice called somewhat later. Cousin Elizabeth, Abby thought, straightening and putting a hand to her hair. "Where are you, girl?"

"In here." Abby opened her stateroom door and forced a smile. "I was just checking my hair."

"Well, put your bonnet on and let's go. The captain's invited us up on deck."

"Yes, I know." Abby stepped toward the companionway. "Careful on these stairs, Cousin."

"Skirts are so impractical," Elizabeth grumbled behind her. "I hope you will wear your bloomers."

Abby looked down from the top of the companionway. "What?"

"I packed bloomers for you."

"Oh, Cousin, you didn't!"

"I did. Please move aside, Abby, you're in my way. There, that's better." Elizabeth joined Abby on the deck. "They're practical. I expect you'll use them frequently."

"But what will people say? Bloomers are so scandalous."

"Hmph. Don't let that bother you."

Abby shook her head as they reached the bulwark, the high, sturdy side of the ship. Over the railing to the right—starboard, she reminded herself—was New Bedford, the wharves and the ships and the oil refinery giving way to green space, with the lighthouse at Palmer's Island glowing very white in the sun. To the left—*port, Abby, port*—in Fairhaven was the old Revolutionary War fort, its flag snapping in the breeze. Abby's eyes stung with tears, surely from that same breeze. Her home was slipping past, looking almost like scenery in a play. She was making a dreadful mistake.

"I will tell you, I had my doubts about this, Abigail," Elizabeth said. "With the work the ship needed and the man's reputation. But I find him to be pleasant, and he seems steady enough. I've no doubt you'll have a marvelous adventure."

Abby looked back and bit her lip. Nat, standing on the platform that straddled the two deckhouses, was watching them, his mouth tucked back in what looked suspiciously like a smothered grin. Oh, mercy—he'd overheard Elizabeth's evaluation of his character. Thank heavens he seemed to have a sense of humor. "Yes," she said faintly.

"I know mail is not a regular thing when you are at sea, but I expect you to write to me, Abigail, and put the letters aboard any homeward-bound ship you see."

"I will."

"And do keep a journal. Your adventures would make a splendid book."

Abby nodded. "Yes."

"And if you wish to come home with me, you can."

Abby looked at her in surprise. Nat seemed not to be listening, but she was still aware of his presence. Likely he thought this was a mistake, too. "I think I—"

"Not that I imagine you'll want to," Elizabeth went on. "The Russell women don't give in to fear."

This Russell woman might, Abby thought morosely, except that the road to escape seemed to be blocked. "Of course not."

"And you're much too young to stay with an old lady like me. I think you will enjoy yourself." She turned. "You'll see to it, won't you, Captain?"

Abby felt herself coloring. Nat had approached them without her being aware of it and now stood next to Elizabeth. His face wore that same look of suppressed amusement it had earlier. "Well, Miss Russell, I can't say I've ever heard a whaling voyage described as a pleasure cruise." He smiled. "I imagine Miss Palmer will get what she expects from it."

"And I can look after myself," Abby murmured, annoyed and embarrassed. Just what did Captain Howland think she expected from this voyage? More to the point, what *did* she expect?

"Of course you can. You are a capable young woman, but you have never been to sea before." Elizabeth glanced forward. "Your crew looks a villainous lot, Captain."

"Aye, that they do," Nat agreed easily, as Abby followed Elizabeth's gaze. In the forward part of the ship, the crew scurried and stumbled to follow the orders shouted by Mr. Martel and Mr. Taber, the ship's officers. "Hard to get a good crew nowadays. Most of them are green and are likely wondering what they're doing here. But they'll shape up."

"I hope so. And things are quite disorganized, Captain." She waved her hand toward the gear that littered the deck, the coils of rope, the mattresses and baggage and ditty bags of the crew. "Shouldn't all that be put away?"

"Cousin, this is all quite normal for sailing day," Abby said through clenched teeth. "Papa told me so once."

"Miss Palmer is right," Nat put in affably. "Once the officers choose the crew for their watches and we get them trained, things will get sorted out."

"Hmph. I hope so. But I do imagine you know what you're doing, Captain."

"Yes, Miss Russell, I do." He glanced back at the deck-house. "We'll be getting under sail shortly, and then I hope you will take supper with me in the cabin."

"Thank you, Captain, that sounds pleasant," Elizabeth said, turning and dismissing Nat completely. "I think he'll do, Abigail."

Behind Elizabeth, Nat was openly grinning. Abby clenched her teeth. She didn't think she'd ever been so embarrassed in her life. "Would you please lower your voice?"

"Why? I'm complimenting the man, aren't I?"

Nat had turned away at last, Abby saw with relief; he was squinting critically up at the masts, while his inexperienced crew was fumbling to set the sails. "In a backhanded way."

"Nonsense. He's really quite kind," Elizabeth went on, her voice softening.

Abby blinked. "Kind?"

"Yes. A nice young man. He kept his manners, even though I provoked him."

Abby stared at her, aghast. "Are you saying you behaved that way on purpose?"

"Of course I did. I wanted to test the man to see how he'd react. He was quite thoughtful of me, both here and in the cabin."

"You're not the one sailing with him."

"Abigail, if I thought for one moment you weren't safe with him, I would never have agreed to this."

"I'm on my own ship. Of course I'm safe." Nat's reputation wasn't for safety, or kindness, for that matter, but Elizabeth was right. No matter the provocation, he had behaved like a gentleman. Except for one brief moment in the passageway, and that had been an accident. Hadn't it?

"It's not too late to change your mind," Elizabeth said, her eyes serious.

Abby glanced away. The deck was chaotic, true, but above her, sail blossomed from the yardarms and bellied with the wind. The *Aquinnah* seemed to be straining at the towboat's hawser, or cable, wanting to fly. Home was already behind her. "Yes, it is," she said, and turned to her aunt, forcing a smile. "Come. Let's go down to supper and toast the ship."

The towboat's hawser had long ago been cast off, leaving the *Aquinnah* on her own at last. Night had fallen; the deck was lit by the glow of lanterns, streaming golden light across the waves. In the foc's'le someone was playing a harmonica, badly. Nat leaned against the aft deckhouse, arms crossed on his chest, enjoying the moment, enjoying the peace. His ship rode easily in the swells of Buzzard's Bay, with the mainland a dark bulk to starboard and the offshore islands, Cuttyhunk, Naushawena, Naushon, just visible to port. His ship. Sailing day was over. The voyage was about to begin.

Off the starboard bow a whaleboat made steady progress toward the waiting pilot boat, its passenger a solitary old woman who sat with back very straight and, presumably, dry eyes. Not so Abby, standing just a few feet from him near the bulwark. Her shoulders rose and fell, and even from where he was, Nat could hear her breath sigh out. Damnation. If she was going to cry, the best place for him was elsewhere. Somehow, though, he found himself crossing the deck to her.

"We can lower another whaleboat," he said, fetching up behind Abby, his elbow resting easily on the rail.

Abby didn't turn. "No, we can't."

"I'm the captain, and I say we can."

"I'm the owner, and I say we won't." She looked up at him, smiling a little. It took the wind out of his sails. He'd been braced for an argument or for tears, and instead she was smiling. "If I go, who will take care of Harold?"

"Harold? Oh. The damn—excuse me—bird." He grimaced as he leaned his forearms on the railing, looking out toward land, now hidden by darkness. "Tripp seems to have taken a liking to it."

"I thought of asking Cousin Elizabeth to take him back, but I didn't want to hurt her feelings."

"I like your cousin."

"So do I." Her chest rose and fell again, capturing his attention. Instantly his memory flashed back to that moment in the passageway this afternoon, when he had briefly and accidentally fondled her breast. And a nice bit of flesh it had felt, he thought, his hand tingling with the tactile memory of her shape, her softness. Damnation. Such thoughts were dangerous. He'd have to get over them, and quickly.

Abby was looking up at him, and he realized she'd spoken. "I beg your pardon?"

"I said, are we taking in sail for the night?"

Nat glanced up at the masts. The ship was hove to, with the yardarms backed at an angle to each other, acting effectively as a brake. Since leaving the harbor the mates had chosen their men, and now the port watch, led by Mr. Martel, were in the rigging, furling the sails. "All whalers do."

"I know. I've often wondered why."

"Speed's not important in whaling, not like in a merchant ship, or we'd be fitted for steam."

"The coal would be too expensive."

"Spoken like a true owner."

In the dimness he saw her frown. "It just seems to me that the longer we take getting to the whaling grounds, the longer the trip will be."

"I do know what I'm doing, Miss Palmer."

"I'm not implying that you don't, but—"

"The whales are migrating south," he interrupted. "What good would it do us to hurry to the grounds in a ship not built for speed, with an inexperienced crew, and putting more strain on the gear than necessary? In all likelihood we'd get there before the whales and have to waste time waiting."

"I wasn't questioning you, Captain," she said, in a small voice.

"Believe me, Miss Palmer"—he glanced away, still annoyed, in spite of her meekness— "I know how to run my ship."

"Your ship," she said, and now she sounded amused.

"Yes." His voice was clipped. "My responsibility, my ship. Even if the owner is aboard."

"This is all very novel."

" 'Novel'?" he mocked. "What is novel about it?"

"I've never been anyone's boss before."

"You are not my boss, Miss Palmer."

"I am if you think of me that way."

"Ha. Are you saying you won't try telling me what to do?"

"I hired you to do a job, Captain. I expect you to do it."

"And I will." He looked down at her, his face grim. "But I will not have my authority questioned."

Abby glanced away, her shoulders hunched. "This voyage will be long enough as it is, without our sniping at each other."

"I don't want to argue with you," he said, his annoyance fading because of her mild response. "But we need to agree that there's only one captain on this ship."

"You."

"Yes, me."

"Then start acting like it," she snapped and turned away. He caught up with her with one quick stride. "Excuse me?"

"You have your authority, Captain. You also have your ship's owner aboard." She paused in the doorway of the deckhouse. "Get used to it," she said and went in.

"I am," he snapped in return, following her in time to see her slip and miss her footing on the last two steps of the companionway. "Are you all right?"

"Yes." She sounded annoyed. "Good night, Captain." A moment later Nat heard her stateroom door close with a defiant, definite click. He started down the companionway after her and then stopped. No good continuing this tonight. She was a woman, and thus irrational. Thank Neptune she'd gone below.

Alone again, he stalked back to the railing. Get used to it? As if the situation were his fault. He wasn't the one who'd asked her to come aboard, with her parlor organ and her bird and her damnably soft, rounded breast, fitting

so well in his palm, so right— *Damnation!* He turned
abruptly away and began patrolling the deck in an attempt
to discharge the restless energy within him, the sudden,
unexpected need. If only she hadn't stumbled that afternoon. If only he hadn't caught her, then maybe, just maybe,
he wouldn't be quite so aware of her as a woman. Maybe
he wouldn't mind so much that she was the owner. It always came back to that.

You're fooling yourself, lad, a voice said inside his head,
and he stopped short. Nearby some of the crew, not now
on watch, lounged on hatch covers, watching him. Without
acknowledging them, he turned away. He would not let his
crew see him in any sort of turmoil because of a woman.
Because of a woman that he couldn't—shouldn't—want
but did.

He exhaled in a short, sharp puff, fetching up against the
bulwark again and staring out at the whaleboat, returning
from the pilot boat. He wanted her. That was the real trouble. He wanted her, and she was right. It was his problem.
He had to deal with it.

"Whaleboat's back, Cap'n," a voice said behind Nat, and
he turned to see Mr. Martel. "And all sail taken in."

Nat nodded. "How's the crew?"

"Rough, but we'll work 'em in. There's one we'll have
to watch." Mr. Martel stepped closer. "He's a common seaman, served on clippers. I overheard him bragging he was
part of a mutiny once."

"A bully boy? That'll change. Send him aloft and keep
him there. I don't care if he turns as green as the sea."

"Aye, Cap'n."

"Anyone else I should know about?"

"Not yet. But we'll keep an eye on 'em all, see if we can
sort out the troublemakers."

"Good. There'll be no mutiny on this ship. And between
you and me, Mr. Martel, I'd rather not use the lash if we
don't have to."

Mr. Martel nodded. "Aye, Cap'n. We'll watch for anything, Taber and me."

"Good." Nat stepped away, suddenly tired. The real
work of the voyage was just beginning. "I'm going below.
I want to be informed of any problems."

"Aye, Cap'n. Good night."

"Good night," Nat said and walked toward the deckhouse. A rough, green crew; a ship that had earned an unenviable reputation; his own worth to prove. He had his work cut out for him, and he was eager to get to it. Just having a ship beneath him again was enough.

Belowdeck, he paused for a moment outside Abby's cabin and then turned away, heading toward his own stateroom. The problems of his ship were manageable—familiar, almost comfortable. His other problem, though, was anything but. He would, indeed, have to get used to it, he thought, sitting on the edge of his bunk, one shoe off, the other temporarily forgotten. If he didn't, the voyage would be very, very long.

The *Aquinnah* was four days out of New Bedford, with land long ago left behind. Each day they sighted other sails or the plume of smoke from a steamship, but as they went farther southeast, the sightings were rarer. When Abby went on deck, she saw only water surrounding them: sparkling sapphire or dull gray or clear green, depending on the weather. No land, no ships, no people. She'd thought she was prepared for life at sea, but now she had to admit the truth to herself. It wasn't at all what she'd expected.

Sitting at the table in the aft cabin, her journal set before her, Abby rested her check on her hand and pondered that. What had she expected? She wasn't sure. She knew quite well that she was not on a pleasure jaunt and that this was a working ship. What disconcerted her, though, were the long hours of quiet monotony, with only Tripp and the unresponsive bird to keep her company. She saw little of Nat, though perhaps that was just as well. The last time they'd talked he'd picked a quarrel with her, something she still found puzzling. She had no intention of interfering with his work; heaven knew she wouldn't want the responsibilities he had, of running the ship and keeping the crew in line. And the voyage was just beginning. The work was only going to get harder.

The cabin door opened and Nat marched in, slate in one hand and sextant tucked under his other arm. He paused for a second and then handed her the slate. "Hold this, please," he said, crossing the room to the cabinet where he stored his navigational equipment and taking it out.

Abby frowned at his brusqueness, though she understood the request; the seas were rough today, and if Nat had placed the slate on the table it could have slipped off and broken. She glanced down at it. It was covered with numbers, figures he'd gleaned from the sextant as the sun approached its apex. She couldn't make them out. Another reason to be glad she wasn't running the ship. "It's rough today."

"Aye," he agreed absently, unrolling a chart and spreading it out on the table before sitting down across from her. "Swells are a good fourteen feet."

"So when we go from crest to trough to crest, it's like climbing hills."

"In a way. Thank you." He took the slate from her, frowning down at the figures.

"Are we in for a storm?"

Nat glanced up at the barometer, hanging on the inside bulkhead. "Barometer's holding steady, but we're likely on the edge of something. It's hurricane season."

"I know." Chin propped on her hand, she watched as he set out dividers, parallel rulers, a volume of navigational tables on the chart. Each day at noon Nat used the sextant to sight the sun against the horizon; numbers etched on the sextant's arc would tell a mariner its apex. Using that number and the navigational tables, he would then make a series of calculations to find the ship's latitude. Longtitude was easier, a matter only of comparing the chronometer, set always to New Bedford Time, to local time. "The sun is getting higher."

"We're heading south," he answered, and then looked up. "Is that something you've just noticed?"

"No." She tapped the slate. "The zenith is higher each day."

The sun, streaming through the skylight, gilded Nat's hair as he sat back. "You know how to navigate," he accused.

She wrinkled her brow at his tone. "Yes. My father—"

"Taught you," he finished for her, his mouth set in annoyance.

"Yes. Is there something wrong with that?"

He held the slate out to her. "Would you care to calculate our position, then?"

"Me? Heavens, no. I'm no good with numbers." She

forced a smile, still puzzled by his animosity. "I can add the same column three times and come out with three different sums. Sometimes I transpose numbers and don't even know it. Jared does that, too."

"Fortunate for us, then, that this is my job, or who knows where we'd end up," he said dryly.

Ah. So that was it. He felt threatened again. Abby bit back a smile. "You're welcome to it."

"Thank you."

"Besides, I have enough to do," she went on as he bent his head over the chart. "I tried pressing my clothes yesterday. Have you ever used a flatiron at sea? No? It's hard enough keeping it hot—I had to keep going back and forth to the galley. Then when I was using it I kept losing my balance. I'm lucky I didn't hurt myself. Mr. Tripp said he'll help me next time."

Nat had put down his pencil and was staring at her. "Miss Palmer, do you always talk so much?"

"No." She rested her chin on her fist, aware that she had been babbling. "Aren't I allowed to talk to you?"

"Most people don't."

She frowned. "Why not?"

"Because I'm the captain," he said patiently.

"I understand that. I realize you can't be friendly with the crew because of having to give them orders, but does that mean no one ever talks to you?"

"No. Just not very much."

Her frown deepened. "That sounds lonely."

"It's the way things are. You'll have to get used to it."

"Me? Oh. No. I wasn't talking about myself. I meant it must be lonely for you."

Nat looked up, surprised. Lonely? Him? Ridiculous. "I assure you, Miss Palmer, this is where I want to be."

"I'm aware of that, Captain. But sometimes we pay a high price for what we want."

"Usually it's worth it." He gave up all pretense of calculating the navigation figures. The task had to be done, but it could wait a few minutes. "Isn't it?"

"Mm." She rested her chin on her hand, and he was again aware of the delicate structure of her brow, her nose, her chin. Her plumpness had kept him from noticing before. "I don't know. At least, not yet."

"Why did you want to come to sea?" he asked, the question that had bothered him since she had first suggested their arrangement. "You knew the life is hard."

She nodded. "Though it's different when you actually experience it. I don't know, Captain." She let out her breath. "Maybe I was lonely, too."

Her gaze caught, and held, his. He was lost for a moment in those gray-green depths, drowning as surely as if the waves had closed over his head, and her plumpness didn't matter a jot. *Damnation!* "Then you've chosen a difficult course," he said gruffly, staring down at the chart as if his life depended on it. Damnation, what had just happened to him?

"I don't think so," she said, surprising him. He looked up again. "I don't really know why I wanted to go to sea. I wanted—want—to hold on to this ship."

"You could have stayed ashore and done that."

"No. I couldn't, somehow." She looked around the cabin, before returning her gaze to him. "I belong here, I think. Besides, there's no one for me in New Bedford anymore."

"You have your cousin," he said, while into his mind flashed a sudden, vivid image of the wharf on sailing day. All those people come to see them off, and not one was there for him. There was no longer anyone for him in New Bedford, either. When he thought of things that way, they did seem lonely. "And Swift, of course."

Abby's fingers, until then tapping a light rhythm on the railing that edged the table, went still. "He's a friend."

"He warned me away from you."

"He what?"

She'd gone pale, he realized. "Told me if I didn't give up skippering the *Aquinnah*, he'd make me regret it."

Abby rose, arms folded about her middle. "I didn't know."

Nat leaned back, studying her. Something was going on here, something he didn't understand. "I can handle him."

She bit her lip. "It wasn't because of you. You do realize that."

"Swift and I go back a ways," he said easily.

"Mm." Abby sat down. "He won't let things rest."

"I can handle him," he repeated, watching her closely. "Why are you so scared of him?"

"Scared? Of Jared?" She smiled, and it seemed genuine enough. "I'm not scared of him. He's an old friend. 'Distressed' might be a better word. We didn't part well."

"I think he'd like to be more than that to you."

"Well, he isn't." She rose, shoulders squared, smiles and vulnerability both gone. "I believe you have work to do, Captain. I'll leave you in peace," she said and slipped out of the cabin. If that wasn't just like a woman, he thought, engaging him in conversation and then blaming him for it. He'd be more careful the next time they were together. And what did it matter to him if Swift viewed Abby as more than a friend? Nothing. The hell of it was, though, that it did.

"Damnation," he muttered and applied himself at last to his task. The calculations finished, he transferred his figures to the chart, thus setting the ship's course for the next twenty-four hours. Maintain current heading, he thought, looking up through the skylight at the compass mounted on deck, visible both to him and to the man at the helm. Within a week they would reach the South Atlantic whaling grounds.

Satisfied with his work, Nat rose to stow his equipment. Chronometers, there; dividers and rulers, there. Everything was in place, including the bottle of brandy.

Nat stilled, his hand on the edge of the cabinet door. He knew the brandy was there, had stored it there himself for medicinal purposes, along with a variety of other remedies. None of those potions beckoned to him, though, called to him with a siren song promising pleasure and peril in equal amounts. None of them ever invaded his dreams. If ever he'd needed a drink, it was now. Slowly, watching his hand as if it belonged to somebody else, he reached into the cabinet and brought out the brandy.

Chapter 7

The deck beneath Nat's feet rose and fell, though he barely noticed it. Brandy was not one of his favorite drinks. If he had a choice he'd prefer good aged whiskey, the taste sharp, bracing, and yet mellow; the feeling of it in his veins powerful, invigorating. Ah, yes, he'd prefer whiskey, but he had only brandy, or the rum kept for the crew, as his choices. Or neither.

Taking a deep breath, Nat set the bottle back in the cabinet, very carefully, very quietly. Only when he'd locked the door and was walking away did he let his breath out. He'd faced the enemy and won. This time.

"Hold her steady," Nat said quietly to the helmsman as he came out on deck, and then paused to get his bearings. To an outsider, what was happening on the ship would look like chaos. Some men were in the whaleboats, still suspended from davits, with others scampering in the rigging, while all the time the mates barked orders and yelled and cursed. Whaleboat drill, Nat thought, leaning against the deckhouse and watching everything with a critical eye. The men of the port watch, now in the whaleboat, had to learn how to pull together as a single team, against the day when the boats would actually be lowered and the hunt for a whale begun. They had to know when to strike oars, when to pull, when to keep quiet, as sound carried all too well over the water and a whale could be spooked. They had to learn how to hold the boat steady for the moment when the boatsteerer would plunge his harpoon into the whale, and then how to pay out the line so that it wouldn't kink or foul, should the whale, enraged, frightened, decide to make a run for it. And they had to learn to hold the boat steady yet again, when the mate in charge struck the killing blow with a sharp lance. The rest of it they could not know

yet—the arduous task of towing the whale's carcass back
to the ship, the long process of cutting in, the greasy, dirty
work of trying out the blubber in a smoky inferno. All that
came only with experience, and God, how he envied them.
There were times he wished he were a young man again,
green, eager, with all of life's possibilities and perils still
before him. As captain, though, he had responsibilities instead. But he'd wanted it, he reminded himself, stepping
out from the shelter of the deckhouses. He had a ship beneath him again, and if he'd sacrificed something for it,
well, then, he'd gained as well.

"How are they shaping up?" he asked, stopping beside
the first mate and looking up at the rigging.

"Better," Mr. Martel said briefly, pushing his cap farther
back on his head. "You there, Slocum! Tighten up on that
line! They're not quick enough," he added in a more normal voice to Nat. "Bunch of green hands who don't know
anything about sails. But they'll learn, Cap'n. I'll make sure
of it."

Nat nodded, lingering for a moment. The crew *was* green,
he thought detachedly, some of them literally so at this
point. The motion of the ship, already strong with the sea
running so high, would be intensified up in the masts and
shrouds. He'd experienced that himself. Again, though, the
men had to learn how to handle themselves. If a squall blew
up suddenly, the ship's survival could very well depend on
their skill. He wondered if Abby, secure below, had any
idea of just how much work was being done on this ship
she owned.

"Carry on," he said to Martel and turned away, prowling
the deck, very much annoyed with himself. For a few moments it had been like it used to be, until he'd thought
about Abby. Trouble was, that seemed to happen a lot
lately. Of course he worried about her status as owner. It
was likely that they'd clash about something. When they
did, would she still sit in the cabin and talk with him, distracting him from his work, as she had today? Probably
not. Probably she'd learn to keep her distance, owner to
captain, and that was how it should be. It would also be
lonely. Until she had pointed that out, he hadn't let himself
admit it. He was the one in command, the one who had to
keep discipline and authority and could not allow himself

friendships among the crew, with his officers. Sometimes being the captain was a heavy burden.

Grimacing, Nat turned back from the bow of the ship, consciously forcing himself to notice every little detail, and then started down the companionway to the cabin and the danger that awaited him behind a locked cabinet door. Brandy, with its seductive siren call. The long days when no whales were spotted, with little to do, were hard on everyone. It was only human nature to want to ease the boredom by reaching for a bottle, and so he had. He would not do so again, no matter how the thirst came upon him, no matter the memories of the liquor seeping warm and soothing into his veins. And, he acknowledged grimly as he reached the bottom of the stairs, it was going to be damned difficult.

Nat paused in the passageway, though he could see that Abby wasn't in the cabin. It should have been a relief. If nothing else, she would act as a check on his drinking. It might even be pleasant to talk to her occasionally. That was all he felt for her, though. It had to be, he told himself, stepping at last over the high coaming into the cabin. A captain ran his ship alone. He must never forget that. Nor should he forget that Abby was more than a companion. She was the owner. Like liquor, talking with her was a pleasure in which he could not indulge.

The parrot squawked as Nat walked into the cabin, and Nat made a face at it. No, it had been better before, when he ruled his ship alone. For only now, as he sat at the table, did he realize all of the complications Abby's presence could cause. What had he gotten himself into?

"Pretty bird," Abby cooed to the parrot, standing on tiptoe so she could see into the cage. "Pretty bird, won't you talk? I have a cracker here for you." She held out a bit of sea biscuit between thumb and forefinger, while the bird regarded her with its customary narrow, suspicious stare. African Grays were supposed to be good mimics, but so far Harold had yet to say anything. "It's good, Harold. If you'll just say one word. Say 'hello.' " She held the morsel closer. "Hello—oh!" She snatched her hand back as the bird, lightning quick, lunged for the biscuit, nipping her finger in the process. "You bit me, you damned bird."

A low chuckle behind her made Abby whirl, to see Nat, leaning against the doorjamb and grinning. "My sentiments about him as well, Miss Palmer."

Abby's cheeks felt hot. "I didn't know you were there." She wouldn't give him the satisfaction of seeing her touch her face to see if she indeed were blushing.

"Obviously." Nat ambled across the deck, standing just scant inches from her. He smelled of tobacco and salt and compellingly fresh sea air. "Not a talkative thing, is he?"

"No," she said, avoiding his gaze, fighting the urge to move to the side, away from him. He was standing much too close. That didn't bother her so much. What she minded was her own reaction. She rather wished he'd move closer.

It was loneliness, that was all, and boredom, she told herself, backing away from the cage. Eight days out of New Bedford, with the weather growing warmer by the day as they headed south, and she was unexpectedly seized by ennui. There was no one to talk to, except for Peleg, who treated her exactly as an owner should be treated. That reduced her to conversing with an uncommunicative bird. She'd seen little of Nat lately, except at meals with the ship's officers or when she was on deck. Never alone, just the two of them in the cabin, as now. That was how it should be, of course. He had his work, and she went on with whatever she could find to keep herself busy. She didn't need him for company. She didn't. It galled her, though, that he apparently felt the same way about her.

"Well, it's just as well he doesn't talk," Nat said, turning away from the cage. "We're near the southern whaling grounds. From now on we have to avoid unnecessary noise."

Abby tapped the cage lightly and then turned away. "I hardly think the sound of a parrot would scare away a whale."

Nat, sitting at the table, opened the logbook. "Sound travels at sea. You never know what might spook a whale."

"I suppose." Abby glanced at him, his blond head already bent over his work, the morning sun catching his hair and turning it to silver. As easily as that, he'd dismissed her. She was nothing to him, and so his casual manner shouldn't bother her, but it did. She had, she realized with sudden, stunning force, made a terrible mistake by going to sea.

Biting her lips against the cry of despair that rose, unbidden, in her throat, she turned and stumbled toward the sanctuary of her stateroom. There she could examine this revelation and decide what action to take. Should she stay aboard, where she was so clearly not wanted, or return to a place that held nothing for her? She didn't know. She didn't. She had just reached the doorway when a deep masculine voice spoke behind her. "Come on, then, give me a kiss."

"What!" she exclaimed, spinning around, thoroughly jolted out of her thoughts. "What did you say?"

"It wasn't me." Nat, holding up one hand, looked as startled as she felt. "I swear—"

"Come on, then," the voice said again. "Damnation."

"Damnation, the bird—" Nat began at the same time, stopping when Abby looked at him. "I didn't teach him that. At least, I didn't mean to."

"It sounds like you."

He rose, hands tucked into his pockets, head down, for all the world like a little boy preparing for a scolding. Abby bit the inside of her lip. "Aye, it does."

"So?"

"So—oh, damnation. I was bored yesterday, day before, I don't remember, and I said that to him. I didn't think he'd remember it."

Abby's lips twitched. "Do you often ask parrots for kisses, Captain?"

"Hell, no!"

"Just a little kiss," the bird said coaxingly, and it was too much. The laughter Abby had held back, as much at Nat's consternation as at the bird, broke free, unrestrained, carrying away all other thoughts. Through streaming eyes she could see that Nat was laughing too, his head down and his shoulders shaking as he braced his hands on the railing that edged the table. In that moment Abby felt closer to him than she had to anyone for a very long time.

Nat recovered first, straightening and looking at the birdcage. "I'll have to watch what I say," he said ruefully.

"And whom you say it to." Abby smiled. "Of all the ridiculous things!"

"Is it?" he asked, suddenly still, suddenly serious.

"Is it what?"

"Is it so ridiculous to ask for a kiss?"

Abby stepped back. "Captain—"

"When I said that to the bird, I was thinking of you." He stared straight at her, his eyes dark with an emotion that both thrilled and frightened her. "Because I think, Abby, that I would like to kiss you."

Chapter 8

Abby's breath caught. Surely he wasn't serious—was he? There was little about her to attract a man except her bosom, which she was careful not to flaunt. At twenty-four, she was no longer a young girl; she was passably pretty but no beauty; and never had she given him a sign that she would welcome his attentions. She didn't think she knew how to, and for some reason that thought made her shiver.

"Do I scare you so much, then?" Nat said. She gazed at him blankly, as if for the first time, and saw gleaming blue eyes that held mischief and kindness. Oh, yes, he scared her, but not, perhaps, the way he thought. "I didn't mean to."

"I—you didn't."

"I didn't expect to say it out loud." He leaned over the table, his gaze a fiery beacon that somehow made her lips tingle. "I managed not to before. But since I have . . ."

He had thought about kissing her before? Good heavens. "Captain, I—" she began, and at the same time there came a cry from far, far above.

"Blo-o-ows! She blows!" Nat's head snapped up and he looked at the skylight, as from the deck they heard a sudden babble of voices and a pounding of feet. "She blows!" the cry came again, the voice of the lookout, and this time Nat moved.

"A whale," he said, sounding excited as he crossed to the cabinet and unlocked it. "Ever seen a whale spout, Miss Palmer?"

Miss Palmer. So they had returned to formality, as if he had never made that amazing statement about kissing her. "No."

"Come on, then." Telescope under his arm, he caught her hand and pulled her toward the companionway, heedless of the careless intimacy. "Come see what all our work's been about."

"My bonnet—"

"You don't need it." From the top of the companionway he held his hand down to help her up. "Don't cover your hair, Abby. I like it."

"A whale, Cap'n," Mr. Taber said as Nat reached the deck. Abby followed, dazed, her hand still warm from his touch. He'd called her Abby. He liked her hair. He—God help her, but he wanted to kiss her. After all that, he expected her to stand calmly on deck and gaze over the restless sea to see a whale spout? Men really were peculiar creatures.

"Where away?" Nat called, shielding his eyes with his hand as he peered up at the lookout.

"About three miles off port quarter, Cap'n."

"Three miles." Nat raised the telescope, scanning the sea. "I don't see him—there!" He lowered the glass, his expression one of mixed satisfaction and determination. "Heave to, Mr. Taber. And lower the boats."

"Aye, Cap'n. Your boat, too?"

"No, not this time. Get to it, Mr. Taber."

"Aye, Cap'n," the second mate said again and dashed away, bawling out orders. From the chaos of men milling about emerged a kind of order, as some of the crew, trained by the ship's drills, began to work the lines that controlled the main yardarm, bringing the ship about. Nat looked after them for a moment, his face unreadable, and then turned to her, holding out the telescope.

"Do you want to look?" he asked, as the rest of the crew took their stations at the whaleboats. "Of course you do. Here." And with that he thrust the telescope at her, though she had shaken her head. The glass was heavier than she'd expected, and in her surprise she nearly dropped it. She did want to see the whale, she realized, catching some of the excitement that permeated the ship. Captain Howland was right. This was what their work had been about.

"See it?" he asked, when she had been gazing, to no avail, in the general direction he had looked a moment ago.

She squinted through the eyepiece, as if by not seeing the whale she would fail in some way. "No."

"We're in a trough. When we crest the wave—now do you see it?"

"No."

He made a sound of annoyance and impatience. "No wonder, the way you're shaking. Here." His hand reached around her from behind, grasping the telescope. The horizon immediately steadied, but it didn't matter. She was instead more aware of his chest at her back, of his arm pressing along hers. A wave of heat rose from the tip of her toes, the beginning of panic that would engulf her in a moment. She had to escape.

"See anything?" he asked, breaking into her thoughts.

"No—yes! Oh, my! There it is." And there indeed it was, a plume of spray blooming into the sky. The wonder of it almost made her forget about the heat sweeping over her. "I see one—no, there are two! Two spouts."

"Two? By Neptune." Nat pulled back, taking the telescope. Abby could suddenly breathe again, though her legs were shaky. "So there are. Let's see what our men are made of."

Abby glanced up at him as he lowered the telescope. His eyes were opaque and his mouth was set in a firm line. "You want to go with them, don't you?" she said in surprise.

"Yes," he admitted. "But someone has to act as shipkeeper."

"But the crew—"

"Is still too green. Once they're seasoned there are some who can stay behind when the boats are lowered, but not yet." He looked down at her, his face still without expression. "A whaling captain has a duty to the ship, too."

"But because you're the captain you don't have the excitement of the first chase."

He snorted. "Excitement? It's damned hard work." Abby followed his gaze as he watched men and ship. The main and foremast yards were set at right angles to each other to act as a brake. Against the familiar sounds of water slapping at the hull and wind singing in the rigging was a new one: the creaking of blocks as the boats were lowered from their davits. "Second mate's boat is the first one out," he commented, moving to the rail. "No, I'm not sorry I'm staying behind."

"Why not skipper a merchant ship, then?"

Nat glanced down at her, his brows knotted. "Miss Palmer, you ask too many questions."

"Do I? I don't mean to."

"And you talk too much. We need no unnecessary noise."

"I hardly think I'll frighten a whale." She gave him a sidelong glance. He was scowling, his gaze on the two boats, where masts were being stepped and sails raised. She supposed she did talk to him a lot, which was strange for her. She tended to be quiet, especially around men. But then, Papa had always done all the talking, and with his uncertain temper she'd found it best to keep her own counsel. Jared was his opposite, so still that she was often at a loss for words. Nat was different. He was more self-contained, yet at the same time more approachable. She had the odd feeling that she could say anything to him, without fear. "I never realized."

Nat had raised the telescope again. "What?"

"The whaleboats. They seem such a good size on the ship, but now they look so small."

Nat lowered the glass. The boats were a distance away, their sails drawing well and the men pulling at their oars. The hours of drill were paying off. "They're large enough."

"I wonder. For an animal of—how many feet?"

"Over seventy feet sometimes, but we don't see monsters like that much anymore. Anyway, men have something the whales lack."

"What is that?"

"A brain."

"How do you know that?" she asked, and he glanced down at her. She looked serious, and somehow very young. Damnation, she didn't have her bonnet on, which also explained why her nose was slightly pink. If she stayed out with her head uncovered she'd likely get heatstroke, and yet he was reluctant to send her below. Why had he told her he liked her hair?

"Your face will burn if you stay out here much longer," he said gruffly and turned away. There was work to be done. The lookout on the masthead had a weather eye out for the whales' position. As ship keeper, Nat had to use that information to set the sails in varying combinations to signal to the boats where the whales were or, if the chase became distant, to follow the boats. That way, if—when—they caught a whale, they wouldn't have too long a job of hauling the carcass back.

"You were the one who wouldn't let me get my bonnet," Abby said, and he realized she had trailed behind him to the helm.

"You'll likely want to go below anyway. Cutting in a whale's not pleasant the first time you see it."

"It's what's supported me all these years."

He glanced up at the tiny windsock. Wind holding steady. "Whaling supports a lot of people who never see it up close."

"Owners, you mean," she said, without apparent rancor. "Perhaps we should."

"Maybe," he said absently, looking down again without meaning to. She, too, was looking up, and in silhouette her profile was finely etched. Yet she'd changed. She was no longer the proper, reserved young woman who had greeted him in a silent house and made a business deal with him. She seemed younger, freer, no longer afraid. Which was an odd way to describe her. "You'll only be in the way."

"I'll keep back."

"No," he said, and at that moment the lookout called down.

"Cap'n! The mate's boat's ready to strike."

Nat strode forward, aware again of Abby behind him. "Is the harpoon in?"

"No, Cap'n, the boatsteerer, Santos, he's up, got the harpoon—*oo-eee,* there he goes! That there whale don't know what hit him."

Nat grasped the railing, wishing he could see. "Is he going after the boat?"

"No, Cap'n, but he's fightin', and—*oo-eee!* There he goes! A real Nantucket sleigh ride!"

"Swing the for'ard arm around," Nat yelled to his scanty crew, caught up in the urgency and excitement. A whale traveling at high speed could cover great distances very quickly, and a boat being towed behind it could soon lose sight of its ship. "Full and by!"

"Aye, Cap'n," a voice came back.

"Let go main sheet. Hard alee!"

"Aye, Cap'n!" the man at the helm replied and spun the

big wheel. The ship canted about, the sails going slack and, after a breath-stopping moment in which Nat feared they'd been taken aback, filling with wind. They were in on the chase.

"Headin' east-so-east, Cap'n."

Nat glanced at the compass. "Steady on," he said to the man at the helm and then looked up. "Can you see them?"

"Just about, Cap'n. That whale, he's got some speed on him!"

"It will be dark soon," a voice said quietly beside him. Nat started. Abby. In the excitement he'd almost forgotten about her. "What happens if we lose sight of the boats?"

"We'll send up flares. We won't lose them, Miss Palmer. After all, whaleboats are expensive."

"Captain—"

"A jest, Miss Palmer," he interrupted, at the mingled expression of anger and hurt in her eyes. "A bad one, apparently. My apologies."

She nodded, looking away from him. "A Nantucket sleigh ride," she said softly.

"The whale's running and he's towing the boat."

"I know what that means, Captain. I always thought it sounded like fun."

"Fun? Hmph. Not knowing what the whale's going to do, having to watch the line so it doesn't foul and take you overboard, water coming in everywhere and the boat slapping up and down and you with it—fun, Miss Palmer?"

"Yes," she insisted. "Fun."

He looked away, though the mate's boat was long out of sight. "Aye, it's an experience, though I think I'd use a different word."

"What?"

"Exciting." He grinned down at her, remembering his first Nantucket sleigh ride and how he had been both terrified and exhilarated at the same time. "And—all right. Might be fun."

"If you catch the whale."

He nodded, his smile fading. The rest of the boats were nearing the ship, apparently having failed to make their own captures. *Damnation.* "There is that."

"Forgive me if I sound like a heartless owner, Captain,

but if the mate's boat has to cut loose, we'll have lowered the boats for nothing."

"Aye. True. But you're not heartless, Abby."

That made her look up through her lashes. For a moment, just a moment, he couldn't look away, until a banging sound broke the spell. One of the boats had bumped into the hull, he noticed absently. "The boats are back," he said. "Got to get them on board."

"And the other one, Captain?"

"We'll keep after them, Miss Palmer. No need for you to stay topside."

"Oh." She suddenly looked lost. "Then I'll get out of your way."

Nat opened his mouth to speak as she crossed the deck to the deckhouses. Then he turned away. Damnation, there was no reason for him to feel so alone, not with all the work ahead. They had to get the boats stowed properly, while keeping up after the one remaining boat. Long after Abby had gone below, Nat was quite busy indeed. He could not explain, even to himself, why he could not seem to forget her.

The lost whaleboat had been sighted again just before sunset, a whale triumphantly in tow. It had been too dark to begin cutting in, and so chain secured the whale to the ship. Nat had ordered a measure of rum to be served to every man, earning him a ragged cheer, and the evening had been enlivened by music and the telling of tall tales. They had made their first catch. It boded well for the rest of the voyage.

Now it was morning, and the work of cutting in was about to begin. From his vantage point aboard the hurricane deck Nat watched the preparations, as first, part of the starboard bulwark was removed, and then the cutting stage was lowered. Though he would not be involved in the actual work, in the end he would be as dirty and greasy as every man aboard. He didn't mind. This was what he'd been trained for.

On the main deck he saw Abby in the stern, gazing over the starboard railing at the whale. It was a right whale, about forty feet, Nat judged. Its oil might not be of the best quality, but they'd get a lot of bone from it, to be used for things like buggy whips and corset stays. Abby should be pleased with her profit, he thought, even though he knew he was doing her a disservice. She was a game enough girl, seemingly undaunted by the hardships of life aboard a whaling vessel. Now she appeared ready to face the less pleasant aspects of the voyage as well, something he hadn't expected. He'd misjudged her.

The windlass, forward, groaned and chain creaked, and over the side the whale's carcass began to revolve. From the cutting stage, jutting out over the water, the mates, using long-handled spades, had made their first incisions in the blubber, the whale's thick outer covering. As the carcass revolved, the blubber peeled away like skin from an orange. All around the dead whale sharks swam in a constant circle, making the men doing the cutting, whether on the stage or on the whale itself, look lively. This was a dangerous task in a dangerous job.

Abruptly Abby turned away from the railing, the movement catching Nat's attention. He glanced down and her eyes, huge in her pale face, caught his, accusing, reproachful. Then she passed under the hurricane deck, apparently hurrying down the companionway to the cabin. Just as well. It would get very messy on deck soon, and she would only be in the way.

Soon the first long strip of blubber had been hauled high and, with the use of chain and hooks, brought onto the deck. Other men cut it into smaller pieces and tossed it into the cauldrons in the tryworks to be tried out, or melted into oil. The flames in the hearth gave a lurid glow to the men's faces, while oily soot soon covered everything. It smelled, and it was dirty. The smell of money, Nat thought. Soon the barrels in the hold would be filled, while the bone would be harvested, dried, and stacked. The *Aquinnah* had already had greasy luck, and its owner didn't seem pleased.

At noon Nat went below to have his dinner. He was a bit surprised when, after he'd sat at the table in the cabin, Abby brought him a cup of coffee. "You've been working," she explained at his inquiring look.

He took a deep sip of the coffee. It tasted better than he'd expected. "Doesn't mean you have to wait on me."

"It won't happen too often," she retorted.

Nat grinned at the note of asperity in her voice. This

Abby he was familiar with. "I figure we'll get thirty barrels from this one," he announced, setting the mug down. "Plus the bone. And the boats are already out after more."

Abby sat across from him. "Will we be staying here, then?"

"Aye. If we don't have any sightings we'll cruise back and forth. This seems as good a place as any. Lookout spotted another ship last night, boiling her oil."

"Who was it, do you know?"

"No, but we'll find out soon enough. Might even be able to have a good gam."

"Mm. And the more ships there are, the more whales will be taken."

"That's the way of it." Nat leaned back as Tripp came in with his dinner of tinned meat and plum duff. He'd thought Abby would be more excited at the prospect of gamming, or visiting, with another ship. "It's what we're here for."

Abby propped her chin on her fist, her gaze serious and unflinching. "Doesn't it bother you?"

"What?"

"All the killing."

"Of whales? No."

"It bothers me."

"I warned you that cutting in is messy—"

"No." She cut him off with a wave of her hand. "This morning I looked at the whale, before the cutting started."

"You saw profit," he said, when she didn't go on.

"No! I saw a magnificent creature that we killed, and for what? Lamp oil and buggy whips."

"Things people need," he said mildly, deciding not to let her draw him into an argument. "And maybe not for much longer, not if the petroleum from Pennsylvania is used more often."

"And who knows but that in a hundred years we'll have used that up, too," she said bitterly.

"Look." He set down his fork. "I grant you that it's stupid to hunt whales to the point where they're scarce. The whale fishery doesn't have too many years left, looked at that way. But it's simple supply and demand, Miss Palmer. People demand these products. We supply them."

"And of course the whale has no say in all this."

"The whale's an animal, Abby. Don't give it human feelings."

"How do you know it doesn't have them?" she challenged. "It knew enough to fight and run away after being harpooned."

"Instinct. Nothing likes being hurt. It doesn't mean these creatures think."

"How do you know?" She leaned toward him, intent on making her point. Abruptly he became aware of her in a different way—the soft strands of hair framing her face; the light of passion, albeit misplaced, in her eyes; her flushed cheeks. By Neptune, she was more than attractive. She was beautiful. "How do you know they don't think and feel as we do?"

"What? Oh, the whales." Nat pulled himself away from the vivid fantasies filling his mind. "Because they're animals."

"With their size, surely they have large brains."

"No. Their brains are small. Abby, look." He leaned forward. "Do you expect dogs to have feelings the way we do? Or cats? Or, for that matter, your bird over there?"

"Pretty Harold," the bird said, as if on cue.

After a startled silence, Abby smiled. "He seemed to know you were talking about him."

"I doubt it. Do you really think he feels the same about things as you do?"

Abby didn't answer right away. "No," she admitted. "I don't. Or dogs, or cats either."

"Then why whales?"

"I don't know." She shook her head. "I just know that the whale we caught was magnificent and now it's gone."

"It's the *Aquinnah*'s job."

"If I'd known, I might have converted her to a cargo ship."

"Not with me as skipper."

"Why not? The ship handling's the same. In fact," she went on, apparently warming to her theme, "it's more challenging. No shortening sail at night, for one thing. Merchant ships have to make time. I'd think you would like that."

Nat toyed with his fork. "The captain's always on duty."

"You are, anyway. You don't strike me as being afraid of work, Captain." She leaned forward, elbows on the table. "What's your real objection?"

"I have no objection." Nat went on eating and carefully avoided looking at her. "It's just not for me. Too boring."

"Boring?" She frowned, and then sat back. "It's the hunt, isn't it? You enjoy the hunt."

"Don't make that sound like a crime."

"I'm not, but—"

"The hunt, as you call it, supported you very well for a long time. It's supporting you now."

Abby glanced away. "I know," she said finally. "I know all the good and sound reasons for whaling. I know there are markets for the oil, and if we don't do it, someone else will. It's just"—she took a deep breath—"I can't help feeling we're destroying something we had no right to touch."

"Abby, it's the way of the world," he said quietly. "Everything has some use. Even people."

That made her look up, eyes wide, reminding him yet again of her hidden beauty. "I suppose you're right. But it's a hard lesson to learn."

"Aye." He nodded. "So it is."

"Even for you?" she said quickly.

"Aye," he said, after a moment. "Even for me." And how she'd known that about him, he couldn't guess. "The cutting in can be hard to watch. It might be best if you stay below."

"No." She shook her head. "If I'm involved in this business, then I want to see all of it."

"Good enough. But, fair warning." He rose from the table. "Everything gets greasy."

"Greasy luck," she said and smiled. She was a brave girl, with so much more to her than he'd once thought. It made her more appealing. It also made him realize, yet again, that he'd done her a disservice yesterday.

He paused in the doorway. "I owe you an apology."

"For what?"

"For my actions yesterday." He turned to see her watching him. The puzzled look in her eyes hit him like a blow. Aye, he'd done her a disservice, but given the chance, he would do so again, God help him. "When I said I wanted to kiss you."

"Oh." She drew back, frowning, not at all the reaction he'd expected. "Yes. I wondered about that."

"It won't happen again," he said gruffly and turned away.

"I accept your apology. But, Captain," she said, stopping

him as he was about to step into the passageway, "there's something I don't understand."

Damnation. He'd almost escaped. "What?"

"Why did you say it?"

"Why?" He turned to stare at her, with her upturned face like a flower, her lips lush, full, tempting. Didn't she know? "Loneliness, I reckon."

"Oh." She drew back again. "Of course. I understand."

"No, you don't," he said, suddenly impatient with her, with himself, for his evasive reply. "I meant it. You are a very attractive woman, Abby."

Her lips parted. "Excuse me?"

"You heard me."

"I'm not attractive."

"Don't beg for compliments."

"I'm not," she said, and he realized for the first time that she believed what she said. "It's just that no one's ever said that to me before."

"I find that hard to believe."

"Well, my dowry was always attractive," she said, with a wry frankness that both amused and annoyed him. "Until recently."

"Yes, well." He stepped into the passageway. "It won't happen again," he said and at last made his escape.

Abby stared after him, fingertips to her lips. What an odd exchange that had been. Some of it was inevitable, she supposed, striving to be sensible and pragmatic. Far from home, with only each other to talk to, it was probably normal that an attraction would spring up between her and the captain. Not that she was attracted, she told herself hastily. Heavens, no. She felt only friendship for him. Nat, though, was a man, deprived of female companionship. Under such circumstances even a plump, plain spinster like herself might look attractive.

She'd have to be careful, then. She liked Nat, but in future she would have to keep some distance between them. He was a gentleman, an honorable man. No matter what he felt, he likely wouldn't act on it unless she gave him encouragement. And that was unlikely.

Sighing, she rose, clinging to the table railing to steady herself. Disregarding the last few moments of the conversation, she had learned again that she was engaged in a business. If it sometimes seemed distasteful, it was something she'd have to adjust to. The work of whaling had been going on much the same way for hundreds of years. It was not going to change merely because her sensibilities had been offended.

Setting her lips in a determined line, Abby climbed the companionway to the deck. She might as well learn all she could about this business. And if, in the process, she saw Nat—well, that was something best not dwelt upon. Nothing would come of their acquaintance. She was determined on that.

"Land ho!" the lookout cried, and Abby, sitting in the deckhouse mending some stockings, jumped to her feet. Land, after all these weeks of seeing nothing but the ocean, everywhere! A respite from the ship, greasy from stem to stern with oil. A chance to experience life beyond the confines of the ship. A chance to rectify the mistake she only recently realized she had made. Land, at last, and the end of her adventure.

Nat was already on deck, peering eastward through his telescope. "The Cape Verde Islands?" Abby asked, coming up beside him, being careful to keep a distance.

"Aye." He lowered the glass and collapsed it. "Be another few hours before we're there."

Abby nodded. Without the aid of the glass all she could see was what looked like a cloud, low on the horizon. Cruising the southern Atlantic the last weeks, the *Aquinnah* had had a fair amount of luck, coming upon several schools of sperm whales, the best species for oil. The barrels in the hold were beginning to be filled, a good omen for the voyage.

It meant that everyone, from Nat on down to the greenest hand, had been kept busy. The work of whaling went on around the clock. At night the tryworks were kept running, fueled by scraps from whales, making the sails glow red and heating the ship so that the cabin was nearly unbearable. Nor was Sunday, previously a day for the crew to relax and to wash their clothes, distinguished from any other day, except by a quick prayer service read by Nat. It was an alien life to Abby, who found sleep nearly impossible in her stifling stateroom and who fought a constant battle against grease invading her living quarters. She had not expected to come to sea only to do continual cleaning, or to have no one to talk to save her parrot. She was lonely and homesick, and she was becoming far too eager to see Nat. Her emotions were too much to bear. As time went on, all she wanted was to escape.

Now her chance was near. As the afternoon wore on, the mountains of the island of Brava seemed to rise from the sea. Here they would take on supplies: fresh vegetables, meat, water. Here they would recruit more men for the voyage, for Cape Verdean sailors usually made the best boatsteerers. Here, too, Abby would stay, until she could find passage back to New Bedford. She was tired of whaling, tired of the isolation. Most of all, she was tired of the strain between her and Nat, and of her awareness of him. It was a dangerous situation. She would be glad—and sorry—to leave.

The harbor was filled with a scattering of vessels, looking like a still life in the warm light of evening: the local fishing fleet, tying up for the night; a few merchantmen from different nations, with paint scarred and faded from their battles with the sea; and several whaleships. Among the ships Abby saw several that had been on the whaling grounds at the same time as the *Aquinnah.* Her spirits rose a little. In those weeks when she'd gone gamming, visiting from ship to ship, and hostessing visits to the *Aquinnah,* she had made some friends. She was not the only woman who braved the seas, though she was the only one traveling without a husband. Seeing again her friends, Mrs. Parsons, Mrs. Bowen, and her dear childhood friend Sarah Hathaway, would take some of the melancholy out of her stay on the island.

The *Aquinnah* anchored at last, and everyone prepared to go ashore, leaving only a skeleton crew behind. Like her, Nat would be staying at the inn on the island for the few days it took to reprovision the ship. She had asked that her trunk be brought along and later would make arrangements for the rest of her belongings. No one knew of her plans, least of all Nat. She didn't know how to tell him.

From the whaleboat, Abby glanced back at the *Aquinnah* and then turned resolutely toward shore. One part of her life was over. She was glad she had gone to sea, but returning was the right thing to do. What she hadn't expected was how difficult it was to say good-bye to the ship. What she dreaded now was saying good-bye to Nat.

The town of Forna huddled close against the shore, with the mountains rising high in steep folds behind it. As the island was arid, the mountains were more brown than green, yet there was some color splashed against the darkness, from the orange roofs on the whitewashed buildings to the occasional flowers of a tropical shrub. A little surprised at how shaky she felt on solid ground, Abby was grateful for Nat's hand helping her into the rickety old carriage that drove them up the steep, rutted road toward the inn. He was in a good mood, suggesting things for her to see and do during their brief stay. This was the Nat she liked—open, congenial, the best of company. The man who looked at her with eyes dark with desire, or, more recently, friendly politeness, was a stranger. She wouldn't have the chance to learn more about hm, she thought suddenly, with a sharp stab of regret. It wasn't too late to change her mind. But then he was helping her down from the carriage, his broad hand solid and warm about hers, making her tremble in a way that had nothing to do with needing to regain her land legs. She had complained to herself about her isolation, about the ethics of whaling and the messiness of the business, but she knew those were only excuses. Her real need was to get away from Nat, and the tense, wary anticipation he awoke in her.

Nat took her arm to escort her inside. "The place isn't much, but it's comfortable," he explained as they passed through a low, narrow doorway and stepped into cool darkness. "It's also the only place to stay."

"Then it'll do," Abby said with a lightness she didn't feel. The hallway opened into a broader room, with a tiled floor. Waiting while Nat spoke with the innkeeper, Abby looked around. The walls were whitewashed, the furniture plain, but everything was blessedly clean, and cool. It *would* do, she realized, when of a sudden a hand clamped onto her shoulder.

"Abby?" a voice said, as she turned to see who had accosted her. But she knew. She knew even before she looked up, and her senses registered a familiar face, a well-known voice, and a grip that held her still. A grip she would never escape, a man she would never escape. It was Jared.

Chapter 9

For what seemed like an eternity Abby couldn't move, not with Jared's hand pressing on her shoulder. "Abby," he said, his eyes warm. "I was hoping I'd see you here."

Somehow that broke her paralysis. It was easier than she'd expected to slip away from his grasp, easy enough to smile. "Yes, we've just arrived," she said, gesturing across the room, where Nat stood. To her surprise he was looking back at them, his eyes opaque, his face unreadable. "We'll be staying a few days while we take on provisions."

"Abby." Jared drew back, his eyes wide and dark. "Not you and Howland—"

"What? No," she said sharply as she took his meaning. "Of course not. I'm shocked you'd think such a thing, Jared."

"I'm sorry." His mouth twisted into the wry smile that had always charmed her into forgiveness in the past. "That was unforgivable of me. But I've missed you very much, Abby, and"—he glanced toward Nat, talking with the innkeeper—"I don't like seeing you with him."

Abby retreated just a bit. "Have you had a good voyage?"

"Not as good as some, but good enough." Jared was still watching Nat. "We've taken six whales."

The *Aquinnah* had taken only four. The fierce competitiveness that flared within Abby startled her. "That's quite good."

"It's a start. Howland." He nodded as Nat joined them.

"Swift." Nat's voice was flat, and his eyes were still that odd opaque blue. "Imagine meeting you here."

"Yes, imagine." Jared bared his teeth in something re-

sembling a grin. "I expect we'll run into each other elsewhere. Valparaiso. Honolulu. Point Barrow."

"Maybe." Nat looked down at Abby. "Our rooms should
be ready. The innkeeper has promised us a view of the
harbor."

She smiled. "Oh, good. I do pine for a view of the sea."

Nat relaxed at last, his mouth twisting into a little smile.
"They'll have a good breeze, and that's what counts." He
held out his arm. "Miss Palmer?"

"Allow me," Jared said at almost the same moment,
proffering his arm as well. For a moment Abby stood between them, two tall, well-built men staring at each other
with an enmity she didn't quite understand. Then, taking a
deep, silent breath, she laid a hand on each man's arm.

"Thank you both." She smiled briefly, impersonally.
"Though I do hope the stairs are wide enough for the three
of us—but isn't that Sarah Hathaway?"

Nat had drawn closer to her the moment she touched
him. He could not shield her completely from the man on
her other side, but he could try. "I believe so," he said,
not looking at the other woman.

"Oh, I must speak with her. If you'll excuse me?" Abby
slipped away, the touch of her fingers on his almost a caress. Did it feel the same to Swift? he wondered, and again
fought back the jealousy and rage that had assailed him
when he had seen Swift with his hand on Abby as if he
owned her. This wasn't the place for a confrontation, but
someday, somewhere, the clash between them would come.
Looking into Swift's pale eyes, devoid of life, Nat knew it
with an intensity that went to his bones.

"Planning to stay long?" Jared asked.

"For provisions," Nat said shortly. He'd prefer to have
nothing to do with the man, but for Abby's safety he
needed to stay nearby. "Maybe a man or two."

"It's been a hard year. Men are looking for work. We
can pick the best of them."

Nat nodded, one whaling master discussing business with
another. "Good to know that. Any problems with
provisions?"

"None yet. Oh, they try overcharging, as usual, but I
haven't let them get away with it." He glanced over at the
two women. "Abby looks well."

"Aye, she is."

"Yet I'd say she's gotten thinner. Has she been ill?"

"No," Nat said, irritated. He hadn't noticed before, but Abby was thinner; her cheeks were finely tapered, and her dress seemed looser. Oddly enough, he regretted the change. "I think the life agrees with her."

"The question is, does she?"

He didn't know. "She seems happy."

"Make sure she stays that way." The facade of politeness had left Jared's face. "Or you'll answer to me."

Nat sized Jared up. He was a little shorter, a little slighter, but still solid of build. He was also not above trickery. "Hah."

Something flamed in Jared's eyes, something dark. Then he smiled again. "Abby loves me, you know. She may not realize it yet, but she does."

The same mixture of anger and protectiveness that had surged within Nat when he'd first seen Jared with Abby flared again. Swift was goading him, he thought, and managed to tamp down his emotions. "Maybe, but she's not on your ship."

"Yet," Jared said, and at that moment Abby returned, with Sarah Hathaway, obviously pregnant, close behind. It spared Nat the necessity of answering, and, in truth, what would he have said? That Abby belonged with him? No, that was foolishness, even if he would not allow her to go with Swift.

"Sarah has offered to come to my room and help me settle in," Abby said, looking directly at Nat, after greetings had been exchanged. "If you'll tell me where it is?"

"Of course. I'm going up, too." Nat stepped away from Jared, whose face was once again a placid, smiling mask. Odd. Abby hadn't looked at him once. "Swift."

Jared nodded. "Howland," he said, and with that the encounter was over. For now. For Nat, following the two women up the narrow stairs, knew that matters were not settled between them. Someday there would be a reckoning. Someday.

Abby stirred in her sleep, turning her head on the pillow. It was heaven to be in a real bed again, heaven to have a window open, letting in the breeze. Her body still hadn't acclimated to land. She still felt the ship's motion and had had trouble falling asleep because of it. That wasn't what had roused her, though. It was a sound, and as she thought about it, she realized it had sounded like her door latch.

Rubbing her eyes, she squinted at the door through the darkness. She must have dreamed it. Everything was quiet now, no movement, no sound. Everyone was long abed in this hardworking town. There was no reason for her to be alarmed.

Time spun out and the silence thickened, broken only by the sounds of the waves on the beach and the soft breeze. Abby gave in to drowsiness, snuggling into the feather mattress. She was nearly asleep again when there was a sudden scraping sound.

This time she sat bolt upright, her heart pounding. Who could be out there? Thank heavens she had locked her door. She was safe. Frightened, but safe.

After a time of sitting tense and alert, Abby lay down again, though she didn't relax. There was no further sound from the corridor, no sense that someone was there, but still she was uneasy. It was a long time before she slept again.

In the bright sunlight of morning, the night's fears seemed foolish. Abby dressed quickly and went to her window, taking everything in: the scents of dirt and animals and plants, smells she was belatedly realizing were missing at sea; the occasional flowering plant, bougainvillea and orchids and others that Abby couldn't identify; the low, square houses with their roofs of deep orange semicircular tile. Quite different from the wooden shake shingles or slate tiles used at home, but attractive, she decided, turning away from the window. She was suddenly eager to explore the island while there was time. While Nat was still with her.

She opened her door, smiling at herself for having been so frightened during the night, and gasped. The doorway was blocked. Someone loomed there, someone tall and broad in the shadows, making Abby step back. The person moved, and in that same instant she recognized him. "Jared!" she exclaimed, one hand to her heart and the other placed instinctively on the edge of the door, to slam it closed. "My, you gave me a start!"

"I'm sorry, Abby." He smiled. "I didn't mean to frighten you. I was just about to knock on your door to see if you're ready for breakfast."

"Yes, I am, thank you." She stepped into the dim corridor, scolding herself. It was only Jared, her old friend. She had no reason to think he'd been standing at her door for longer than he'd said, no reason for her pulse to race.

"I trust you slept well?" he went on, quite normally.

"Yes, thank you." She preceded him down the stairs to the dining room. "I'm eager to explore the island."

"Let me escort you."

"Haven't you business to do?" she asked, as he fell into step beside her.

"I've done most of what I came here to do. I can take time for an old friend."

She glanced at him over her shoulder as they entered the dining room. "When do you sail again?"

"In a few days. There are the Hathaways and the Bowens. Shall we join them?"

"Yes, let's." How nice it was to see familiar faces in a strange place. She smiled at the others and was swept into the conversation. It was a long time before she realized that Jared had been oddly vague about his plans.

That morning marked the beginning of a pleasant routine for Abby, as she found herself caught up in the social life of the other whalers. At home she had been the owner's daughter; now she was one of them, belonging in a way she never had before. Though the island was small and rural, there were some interesting sights: small, neat villages high up in the mountains; a thermal spring, said to have curative properties; carefully built terraces and dikes, for holding back water and eroding soil. The people were poor, but friendly and polite, and the donkeys ridden during these expeditions gave rise to exasperation and laughter. There was always new food to try, too, such as seafood served in highly flavored sauces or *linguica* or *chourico*, spicy Portuguese sausages. Every meal featured a rice dish called *jagasida*, or simply *jag*, while sweetbreads and *malassadas*—thick, doughy rolls—satisfied her neglected sweet tooth. She also acted as hostess aboard the *Aquinnah*, serving more familiar fare of chowder and baked beans and displaying with pride the parlor organ, which had finally been taken out of storage. It was fascinating, too, to see how the other whaling wives had turned their ships' cabins into parlors, with thick carpets and pianos and stereopticons. She had never enjoyed herself so much in her life. The only cloud on her pleasure was that Nat was never there.

Jared, though, was always available to act as her escort when she went on rides or walks with the others, and he was a genial host aboard his own ship, the *Naushon,* once part of her father's fleet. It was larger than the *Aquinnah,* Abby admitted, but not quite so fine in its detail. She was proud of her ship. She would miss it more than she had expected.

Abby finally found Nat alone some four days after their arrival, sitting by himself at breakfast. "Good morning," she said, smiling as she sat down across from him. "I haven't seen much of you lately."

"There's work to do," he answered, his smile impersonal.

"Well, if you're trying to impress the owner with your diligence, you're doing well. But I do think you could come to some of the entertainments in the evening."

"Harold has learned some new words," he said, as if on a tangent.

"Harold?" Abby frowned. "Not when I'm there, no matter who tries to make him talk. What is he saying?"

" 'Jag.' And some Portuguese swears."

Abby shook her head. "He would. He does seem to pick up the most unsuitable words."

"Influence of all this dissipation."

"Now you're teasing me," she said placidly. "Seriously, Captain. People have been asking for you. I should think you'd want to enjoy what time we have here. There's little enough left." Little enough in which to sit with him like this, to talk with him, just to look at him. Good heavens, she sounded like a girl in the throes of her first infatuation. Which she most definitely was not. She did like Nat, though, and all too soon she would have to tell him she was staying behind.

Nat had been regarding her from across the table, his eyes thoughtful. "I noticed your shadow isn't with you today."

She frowned. "My shadow?"

"Swift."

"Jared? He's not my shadow." Annoyed, she toyed with her coffee cup. "What a thing to say."

"He's wherever you are."

"No, he isn't."

"Yes, he is. The only time he's not is when I'm around."

"That's absurd."

"Walking with you, taking you for drives, showing you his ship," he went on as if she hadn't spoken. "And," his face darkened, "going aboard the *Aquinnah*."

"Yes, as my guest."

He sat back, remote, distant. "You are the owner."

"Are you saying that if it were up to you you wouldn't have him aboard? You are, aren't you?" she went on, though he had made no protest. "Of all the foolish things—"

"I do not like having him aboard my ship."

"Captain, I realize you don't like him—"

"I don't."

"—but he has always been a good friend to me."

"I don't trust him," he said bluntly.

"Well, that's silly. What do you think he'll do?"

"I don't know, but there's little he wouldn't stoop to."

She shook her head. "Not the Jared I know, and I've known him for a long time."

"But do you trust him?"

Unbidden, into Abby's mind came the memory of the morning when she had opened her door and Jared had been there. And another memory, darker, more distant. It teased at her, flirted with her, and then flitted away, leaving her oddly shaken. "He is a friend," she said again and wondered which of them she was trying to convince.

Nat gazed at her for a few moments, and then rose, tossing his napkin on the table. "Be careful, Abby. That's all I ask."

"Gracious, of course I will. What a thing to say!" She shook her head. "This is going a little far, don't you think?"

He shrugged. "If you ever need help, Abby, you can come to me. You know that, don't you?"

She stared at him, perplexed. This was the oddest conversation. It was almost as if he believed Jared to be some kind of danger to her. How absurd! "Thank you, but I doubt that will be necessary."

He shrugged again. "If you say so." He began to turn away, and then stopped. "I haven't had much of a chance to see the island. Will you take a ride with me this afternoon?" he asked gruffly.

"I'm afraid I made plans with Mrs. Hathaway and Mrs. Bowen. I'm sorry," she said, surprised at how regretful she felt. "Perhaps tomorrow?"

"Maybe." He nodded to her and walked out of the dining room, leaving her to stare after him, perplexed. What a very odd encounter that had been.

Touching her lips with her napkin, she rose, somewhat annoyed at Nat's rudeness in leaving her alone, the only foreign woman in the dining room. She did not understand the man, and she wasn't sure why she should bother trying. She would be better off going in search of other companionship. All too soon her friends would be gone; too soon she would be on her way back to New Bedford and its cold, gray winter.

A figure abruptly stepped before her in the doorway. Jared, of course. Why he must always loom up before her she didn't know. "Why do you do that?" she said crossly.

"And good morning to you, too," he said, smiling, so affable that she felt momentary guilt. "What did I do?"

"Nothing." She was aware that she still sounded grumpy, and so she forced a smile to her lips. "I was about to go out, so if you'll excuse me—"

"Is something wrong?" he interrupted.

"No. I'm not angry with you."

"Me?" He sounded surprised. "I was talking of Howland."

Abby drew back, on guard and at the same time annoyed. She was growing tired of hearing admonitions from one man about the other. "What of him?"

"Did he hurt you in any way?"

"No, of course not," she said, genuinely surprised. "What makes you think that?"

"He looked angry about something. Knowing his temper, I assumed . . ."

She waited. "Yes?"

"Nothing. At least, not something we should discuss here."

"Jared—"

"May I see you someplace, Abby? I'm at liberty today."

Abby hesitated. She really had made plans with the other women, but they were nowhere to be seen at the moment. It was far too fine a day to wait inside for them, when sunshine and azure skies lured her. "I do have plans for the day, Jared, but I would like to take a walk."

"Certainly." He held his arm out to her. She hesitated only briefly before taking it. No matter what Nat thought, Jared was almost family. Family forgave each other. Family depended on each other.

"I'll miss this," she said, when they were walking along the dusty main street, past whitewashed houses splashed with colorful tropical flowers. "There's nothing quite like it in New Bedford."

"Hm?" He looked down at her, frowning. "There are other places you'll see, Abby."

"Oh, of course." She managed a quick smile, though she was annoyed with herself. Her decision to return home was still secret. When she did announce it, she would tell Nat first. She owed him that much. "I meant only that at home it's nearly winter."

He didn't return the smile. "Are you homesick, Abby?"

"No," she said. It was true. New Bedford was behind her. And so, she thought, looking up at Jared, was the past. It was foolish of her to keep clinging to it. She loosened her fingers, letting it go, and felt a great wave of relief. She was free. "I was at first, but now I'm used to it."

"I don't like thinking of you being unhappy."

"I'm not, Jared."

"If you want to go home, all you have to do is say so."

That stopped her. "I beg your pardon?"

"I'll take you home, Abby, if you want me to."

"Good heavens, Jared." She began walking again. "I don't know what you're talking about."

"I'm talking about the fact that you spoke to Captain Holmes about passage home."

She turned, dismayed. "He promised to keep that to himself!"

"I'm rather hurt, Abby," he went on, as if she hadn't spoken. "That you'd ask him, and not me."

"You're outward bound, not on your way home." She turned, arms crossed on her chest. "Am I to have no privacy?"

"You're not happy, Abby. I know it." He took her hands in his. "Let me help you. Please."

"Jared, I'm fine." She pulled away. "Really."

"Is he cruel to you? Is that it?"

"What?" she exclaimed. "You surely don't mean Nat— I mean, Captain Howland."

The look he gave her was hard. "On a first-name basis, are you?"

"Oh, for heaven's sake. I'm tired of this. First him, and now you."

Jared followed closely behind her. "He's drinking again, isn't he?"

"No." She turned, and again he caught her hands, this time holding her fast. "Jared, you are treading on thin ice."

"I would never forgive myself if something happened to you and I hadn't spoken up."

Abby wanted to roll her eyes in disgust. Instead, she moved away. "When do you leave?" she asked, coolly, formally.

"Whenever you wish."

"I beg your pardon?"

"I meant what I said, Abby. I'll take you home."

"On what?" she demanded. "Not the *Naushon*."

"Why not?"

"You can't be serious." She stared at him. "You can't go home with your hold nearly empty."

"You forget, I'm part owner."

"I don't care, Jared. It will ruin your reputation as a master. No one will ever hire you again."

"Good."

"What?"

"Do you think this is what I want, Abby?" The wave of his hand encompassed all of whaling: the ships, the captures, the work, the tedium. "Do you think I want to spend the rest of my life on a stinking whaleship, when there are so many grander things waiting for me?"

"But I thought you loved it."

"People with no imagination love it. Like your Captain Howland."

"He's not—"

"Your Howland? Maybe not yet. But he'd like to be."

"Don't be silly," she snapped. Nat was not without imagination, was what she had planned to say. Her Nat. Ridiculous. "If you hate it so much, why do you do it?"

"How else could I get ahead? I didn't have money and I don't have family. But there are people who think I'm destined for bigger things. Think of it." He swung her around. "Mayor Swift. Congressman Swift. Maybe, someday, Senator Swift. Would you like to live in Washington City, Abby?"

"Not particularly," she said, standing passively before him. Jared had always been like this, spinning grandiose tales of his future. When they were children, she had believed in them. Now they merely made her feel tired, and sad. "But it sounds like a fine life, if it's what you want."

"For both of us, Abby." His eyes glowed with dark fervor. "We'll go home. We have the house. It'll be enough to get us started. We can entertain, meet the right people. And you'll be the perfect helpmeet. What a team we'll be, Abby!" He pulled her hand to his mouth for a quick kiss. "Together we can conquer the world."

"I don't think so, Jared," she said gently, pulling her hands free at last.

"Why not?" He grabbed her hands again, his grip this time hard, almost punishing. "Why won't you let me make you happy, Abby? Why can't we go back to what we had?"

"Oh, Jared." She closed her eyes, weary, wishing he would go away. "Anything we had is over. And, Jared—"

"Not for me, it isn't."

"Jared, it wasn't much to begin with," she finished.

"You're wrong." His hands slid up to her wrists, shackling her in what was apparently meant to be a caress. "It's never been over for me. Abby, I want to kiss you."

Her breath sighed out in a quick gust. "Jared—"

"Only if you want me to, Abby. If you've learned how to want me."

"Good heavens!" She felt detached, watching the scene unfold as if it were a play and she a spectator. Again that dark, distant memory flickered in her mind, and then was gone. "What should I say to that?"

"Say yes, Abby."

"I can't."

"You can," he urged, pulling her closer. "Or is it Howland?"

"Jared—"

"You prefer him to me, don't you?"

"Jared, let me go, now!" she commanded, and stepped quickly back as he released her. Her wrists were sore from his grip. "It has nothing to do with him. It's me. I've told you before, Jared. I don't want to marry you." She looked up at him. "I don't love you."

"But you will." His voice was soft, chilling. "I'll make you love me, Abby."

She shivered, and she didn't really know why. "No one can make me do that, Jared. Even if you could, you won't have the chance." She turned away, the decision made. "I'm committed to the *Aquinnah*."

"But, you said—"

"No, I didn't, Jared. You did." And there it was. Her plans to return home slipped away. If she stayed, Jared would stay. If she left, so would he. She had no choice. She would have to return to the *Aquinnah*. Odd how light, how good, that made her feel. "The ship's my home now."

"Well." Jared turned, hands fisted, lips grim. "You'll regret this, Abby."

"I don't think so. Why, there are Mrs. Hathaway and Mrs. Bowen. Sarah, Elizabeth. How nice to see you. Jared, I will talk to you later," she said, walking away on shaky legs, frightened by the intensity of Jared's feelings, frightened by the way he looked at her. She didn't understand what she saw in his eyes—anger, hurt, and something that resembled desire, except that it was darker. More dangerous. If she had needed proof that she was doing the right thing, that look gave it to her. Squaring her shoulders, she went to meet the other women, leaving behind Jared, leaving behind the past.

Chapter 10

It was like coming home.

Abby stood on the *Aquinnah*'s deck as they left the harbor at Forna, her body already readjusting to the dip and sway of the ship. Above her the sails were blindingly white against the azure sky, and the breeze carried with it the mingled scents of salt and tar and whale oil. The ship had been cleaned during their sojourn ashore, the decks holystoned and the stairs scoured with sand. Even the brightwork had been polished, and paint applied where needed. A week earlier Abby had been eager to escape the ship and go ashore. Now she was glad circumstances had forced her to return.

She glanced quickly back at the island, but only the reddish-brown sails of the Brava fishing fleet were visible. No other whaleship was standing out to sea. Certainly not the *Naushon*. Silly. As if Jared would be following her. He might have offered to bring her home, thus forfeiting the remainder of his voyage, but he was no fool. He, too, would try to catch as many whales as possible, as quickly as possible. His affection for her wouldn't interfere with that.

Nat gave the order for the mainsail to be loosed, and the men on deck working the sheet, or line, that controlled the big sail, heaved with gusto. The sail dropped into place with a clatter, and the ship took flight with the northeast tradewinds, a rare tropical bird. The beauty of it made Abby's eyes sting. Her ship. How could she ever have considered leaving it behind? How could she have thought of leaving Nat?

Dangerous thought, and since when had she taken to referring to him so informally, even in her mind? He was her business partner and no more. That she trusted him, had even come to like him, had no bearing on the matter.

She was the ship's owner, he the skipper. She would do well to remember that.

Glancing once more up at the sails, she slipped into the deckhouse to reach the cabin, taking the tilting, moving companionway as easily as the most experienced sailor. "Your trunk's in your stateroom, miss," Peleg said, from the forecabin, where he spent much of his time, seeing to the ship's stores and to the captain's personal belongings. "Just you let me know when you're ready to have it stowed."

"Thank you, Mr. Tripp, I will. I—what is that?"

Peleg turned to see what had caught her interest in the main cabin. "What, miss?"

"I don't believe it." Slipping past him, she walked into the cabin, bright and almost too warm from the sun streaming through the skylight. Against the port bulkhead stood her parlor organ. "What is this doing here?"

Peleg shrugged. "Cap'n's orders, miss. He had Cooper put brackets in the deck to hold it in place, as well as those straps on the side," he said, referring to the ship's carpenter, who was known as Cooper, no matter what his name was.

Abby's fingers drifted over the ivory keys. "He never said a word to me."

Peleg shrugged again. "Told me to see to it a few days ago. Is there anything else you need right now?"

Abby glanced up at the skylight, through which she could see Nat—Captain Howland, she reminded herself. "No, thank you, Mr. Tripp." She turned away. "I'll just get settled."

"Aye, miss. I'll call you for dinner."

"Thank you," Abby said again as Peleg went out. Above her she could hear Nat's footsteps and, occasionally, his voice. She'd not seen much of him on Brava, and when she'd come aboard this morning he had been little more than polite. Yet he had had her parlor organ secured in place, as if he knew how homesick and bored she had been during the first part of the voyage. Really, a most unfathomable man, she thought, turning toward her stateroom. She didn't think she would ever truly know him.

The nightmare came that night, the one that had once haunted her sleep so often, but that had been gone for years. Abby sat straight up in bed, heart pounding, mouth dry, and fumbled toward her bedside table for the lamp. But, no, she was at sea, in a dark stateroom with no table nearby, no light. There was a candle in a sconce on the wall across from her, but she was so confused, caught between reality and her dream, that she could not remember how to light it. Yet she needed light, if only for reassurance. Not stopping to think, to put on her wrapper or even throw a shawl about her shoulders, she swung out of bed and into the passageway.

The ship was quiet, with most sail taken in for the night and the men not on duty asleep. A faint glow seeped into the passageway from the lamp in the cabin. Abby followed it into the cabin feeling some of her tension ebb away. The lamp was turned down too low for her peace of mind. She reached out and turned the key, raising the wick. There. Bright, brilliant light, chasing away the shadows, banishing the darkness. She let her breath out in relief and at that moment heard a footstep behind her.

"What are you doing?" Nat asked, stepping into the cabin.

Abby turned, her nightgown swirling about her, her hair in a loose braid swinging over her shoulder. "I, um, nothing," she said, her cheeks turning pink, her eyes not meeting his. "I was just making sure the lamp worked."

Nat's gaze flicked briefly from her to the lamp and then back again. "Why? Is there something wrong with it?"

"No. I just wanted to be sure. I'll go back to bed now."

"Mm-hm." He leaned against the doorjamb, arms crossed on his chest, intrigued by this new side of Abby. She seemed uncertain, embarrassed, and very young. "So at nearly eight bells, you decided to check it?"

"Is it midnight?"

"Yes."

"Oh. It seemed later. I had a bad dream, you see."

"Oh?" he said, and she looked at him at last. Her eyes were shadowed, haunted. Any impulse he'd felt to tease her faded, and in its place surged protectiveness, a feeling he'd never quite understood. "I see. Well, while you're awake, there are some things I need to talk to you about."

"Such as?"

"Business. Expenses in Brava for the provisions. The new men. Things like that."

"Can't it wait?" She shifted from one foot to the other, and he was abruptly aware that she was clad only in her nightgown. It covered her completely, except for her toes, and yet the intimacy of her attire stirred his blood. "I'm rather tired."

"It's dark there," he said quickly, instinctively, and saw her shudder. "Sit down for a minute."

She glanced doubtfully at the settee and then sat, with a little sigh of resignation. "Very well, but only for a moment."

"Fine." He stepped into the cabin, glancing at the lamp. A waste of oil, having it so bright, but he didn't consider dimming it. Abby didn't look quite so strained as she had, but there was something about her hunched shoulders that touched him. She looked vulnerable, he thought, and stopped, realizing for the first time that he stood in front of the cabinet holding the ship's supply of liquor. The habit had a way of sneaking up on him when he least expected it. "A brandy might settle you down," he said gruffly, not looking at her.

"Thank you, no. I never did develop a taste for drink."

He dropped into his chair at the table, deliberately distancing himself from her, though he could see her all too well. Her capacious, encompassing nightgown hid everything from his view and nothing from his imagination. She wore no corset beneath it, no petticoats, no . . . "Wise of you," he said. "Drinking alone at night is a bad habit."

She looked up. "Is that how you started?" she asked with frank interest.

"Me? No. Not at first." He gazed back at her, wondering why her question didn't bother him more. "I learned young. At home. My father died from drink."

"Oh! I'm sorry—"

"It's long ago." He shrugged, ignoring the old memories, the old scars. "Drinking's something you do when you're a man."

Her brow wrinkled. "Why?"

"Why?" He considered that. "To prove how much of a man you are, I reckon. Which is stupid," he went on before she could speak, "but it's what a lot of people think."

"Hm." She pursed her lips. "I imagine going to sea just made things worse."

"Of course. Sailors drink." And he had been young, eager to prove himself. "Ships make port, the crew goes ashore, and all hell—excuse me—everything breaks loose."

Abby looked as if she were biting back a smile. "The way our crew behaved on Brava?"

He grimaced. Like sailors from time immemorial, the *Aquinnah*'s crew had managed to have a fine old time on the island, crowding into taverns, searching out women, and generally getting into as much trouble as they could. "I didn't think you knew about that."

"Oh, I knew. Even if I didn't, it was obvious today that most of the men were still intoxicated."

"There'll be some sore heads tomorrow," he admitted. "But we recruited three good men from the island for boat-steerers. That's what I wanted to talk to you about."

She waved her hand. "I'll leave those decisions to you, Captain. You know more about them than I do."

"You pay the bills."

"No, they share in whatever the ship makes, like the rest of the crew. I trust your judgment."

"Thank you," he said, unexpectedly touched. It had been a long time since anyone had trusted him. "I appreciate that."

She looked startled. "Well, I do. Oh." She nodded. "I see what you mean. Because of the drinking."

"I don't think we need to go into that anymore."

"Sailors drink," she said, as he had earlier. "But not all sailors become skippers."

"No," he said, and sat back, resigned. For whatever reason, she was determined to discuss his past problems now, when it was very late and they might as well have been the only two people on the ship. She, in her nightgown; he, with all his defenses down. Dangerous moment, and yet he didn't want it to end. "My father was a common seaman. We wouldn't see him for years, and when he did come home he'd get lured into some tavern. We learned, my brothers and I, to catch him before he drank up all his pay, but sometimes we weren't quick enough."

Abby's eyes were dark with sympathy. "How awful for you."

He rose. Somehow it was easier to talk about this on his feet. "We managed. Learned to fight young, learned what it was like to be thrown out of a tavern. But I never wanted to be like my father. So I drank. Sure. Carefully, if there's such a thing. I never drank too much, or let myself get rolled."

"Excuse me?"

"Robbed, usually by a hook—a woman and man, working together. I made myself learn, too," he hurried on, hoping she hadn't caught his reference to prostitutes, knowing she probably had. "I realized I couldn't run a ship if I couldn't do figures, or write better and such. My ma had made sure we all could read, so that was good. And I watched how a ship was handled, and I worked my way up. Finally, your father decided to take a chance on me." He smiled, glancing about the cabin. "She was an old ship— the *Edgartown*—remember her?"

She smiled. "Yes, one of my father's first ships. He sent her in the Stone Fleet to blockade Southern ports during the war. It broke his heart, though he'd never admit it."

"Mm-mm. She was a good ship. The *Aquinnah* reminds me of her. A ship no one really wanted and no one expected much from."

"My *Aquinnah* is a fine ship," Abby said, laying her hand on the paneling, as if the ship were alive and might take offense.

"I'm not saying she's not. Well, I did well enough on the *Edgartown,* and that was the start. I had what I wanted. And you know the rest."

"Not really," she said gently. "If you did have what you wanted, what made you start drinking?"

He looked away. He'd asked himself the same thing a thousand times and never had answered it to his satisfaction. "I don't know. We talked once, you and I, about the captain being lonely. I don't think I am, but could be you're right and that was it. Or going for weeks without sighting a whale and being bored to hell—pieces. Or working around the clock to try out all our whales. Or when we lost a whale. I don't know." He shook his head. "There's pressure in this job, to run the ship, to make money, all that. It's hot in the tropics, cold in the Arctic. Who knows?" He held his hands up. "When you want to drink, any reason will do."

"Yet you still managed."

"Most of the time," he agreed. "It usually didn't interfere with my work. I was proud of that. No matter how much I drank, I could run my ship. And I didn't really need the drink, no, not me. I could stop whenever I wanted. I just didn't want to." He stopped, looking away so he wouldn't see the pity, or condemnation, in her eyes. "I can tell you all the reasons, and I'd be lying. I have a need." Now he looked squarely at her. "I think people like me all have the need. My father had it, and he passed it down to us. I have the need, and the only thing that keeps me from giving in to it is that I am not going to let it win again."

Abby didn't speak right away. "What happens if the need gets stronger?"

"I'll just have to get stronger, too."

"Do you still want to drink?"

He met her gaze unflinchingly. "All the time."

"Well, that's honest, at least." She rose, arching her back, hand at her neck, unaware of the picture she made, all the more enticing for her innocence. Her throat was white, inviting; her nipples taut through the thin cotton of her gown. Nat was suddenly, instantly, hard. Dressed only in shirt and trousers, he couldn't hide his condition. He wanted her. God, he wanted her, and not just because he had been celibate since leaving home. He wanted Abby, her unbound hair swirling about him, those soft lips pressed against his, his hands finding and holding the lush fullness of her breasts. The consequences didn't matter, or that she was his employer, his partner, or that he'd worked so long and so hard to make it back to sea. He wanted only her, and nothing else mattered. "Abby—"

"Thank you for being honest with me," she interrupted, her arms lowered and her gown again falling about her in prim folds. "Not many people would be."

She was so close, just a few steps away. If he held out his hand he could touch her, caress her cheek, cup her shoulder, draw her closer. She'd said something, he wasn't sure what, but she looked at him as if expecting a reply. "Hm?"

"Most people wouldn't admit they still had a problem."

Oh, he had a problem, all right, and she could help him with it. "Yes."

"Though I think that if you'd told me in New Bedford, I wouldn't have hired you."

That brought him back to reality with a jolt. What the hell was he doing? "Excuse me?"

"I would have been more cautious. And I'd have been wrong."

"Oh."

Her brow furrowed as she looked at him. "Is that all you have to say?" she asked, and he realized for the first time that she had no idea of her effect on him. God help him, but he had almost made a colossal fool of himself.

He turned away, putting the table between them. "It's not something I talk about often." *Go to bed, Abby,* he thought. Go away and let him deal with his need alone.

"I understand." She glanced at the lamp and smiled. "Well. Now that I know the lamp works, I'll go back to bed."

Thank God. "What was your dream about?" he heard himself say, as if someone else were speaking.

She smiled, but even through his preoccupation he could see the effort it cost her. "Nothing to be bothered about."

He knew he should let her go; he wanted her to stay. "Bad enough that it scared you, though."

"Well, yes." She hesitated, poised between the settee and the doorway, and then sighed. "If you really must know . . ."

"This seems to be an evening for confidences."

She put her hand to the back of her neck again. This time he looked away, forced himself to ignore the fact that she was so very near, and so very enticing. "Frankly, it won't sound scary at all," she said, sitting down again.

Nat sat as well, relieved, uncomfortable. He wasn't sure he could bear her presence much longer, and yet he didn't want her to go. "What was it?"

"Well . . . it's silly. It's a dream I used to have a lot, when I was younger. Funny, I haven't had it in years." She frowned. "I wonder what brought it back."

"Is it a nightmare?"

"Not really." She bit her lip. "It's very ordinary. I'm in my room at home, or in some other part of the house. The music room, usually. It's dark, and I want to light the lamp, but it doesn't work. I try striking match after match, and none of them will light. Or when I do light the match the wick on the lamp won't catch, though I keep trying." She shuddered, her arms crossed on her chest. "I'm not afraid of the dark, truly, but there's this—this *feeling*—that if I don't find light something terrible will happen."

"Does it?"

"What?" She looked up, dazed, and then shook her head. "No. Usually by that time I wake up. And then I light a lamp or a candle as quickly as I can."

"So tonight you came out here."

"I needed light. I was embarrassed when you caught me." Her smile was sheepish. "This time in the dream I was in here. It must be because of the organ."

"If that's so, I'm sorry I had it set up."

"No, don't be. I'm glad, though I must say I'm surprised. Why did you change your mind?"

He shrugged. "I enjoy hearing music now and then."

"Oh. I see." Her smile faded. Good. Let her think his motives had been purely selfish; let the distance between them grow again. "Well." She rose, and he did, too, less uncomfortable now. It would be a relief when she returned to her stateroom. "It's late. I'll go back to bed."

"Yes. Abby—" he said as she brushed past him.

She went very still as his hand caught her arm. "What?"

Damnation, what was he doing? He should let her go, and yet he couldn't. He couldn't. "You know that whatever it was that scared you in your dream . . ."

"Yes?" she said again when he paused.

"Abby, I'd never let anything hurt you."

Her startled gaze flew to his. "Excuse me?"

"I mean it." Her eyes were dark, deep, as intoxicating as liquor could ever be. "Nothing will hurt you while I'm around."

She swallowed, still tense under his hand, though there was a different look in her eyes, a look of awareness. "I don't know why you'd say that."

"Damned if I do, either," he said and lowered his mouth to hers for a very brief, very gentle kiss.

Chapter 11

Abby stood very still as Nat's warm, dry lips touched gently against hers and then pulled away. Somewhere within her a small voice urged her to draw him back, but mostly what she felt was numb. "Why did you do that?" she asked.

"Damned if I know," he said, echoing his earlier statement. He hadn't released her, and yet his grip was gentle and easy. She could escape at any time. The odd—and frightening—thing was, she didn't want to.

"I don't know what you think I am, Captain, but—"

"Abby, hush." He laid his finger on her lips, and it was like being kissed again. "I know who you are. What just happened—call it friendship, call it middle-of-the-night madness—but don't think that I mean you any harm."

"That's rather what I'm afraid of," she said tartly, pulling free at last.

He grinned. "Tempted, are you?"

"No." She peered up at him. "You can't be serious."

"Why not?"

"Why not? Look at me, for heaven's sake. I'm no beauty."

"I think we've had this conversation before, Abby."

"I didn't give you permission to use my name."

"Doesn't matter." His grin widened. "I can do what I want on my ship."

"My ship, Captain."

"Mine. At sea, mine. Abby," he added deliberately.

"Captain—"

"Go to bed, Abby."

"What?"

"Go back to bed. It's late and the lamp works."

That made her blink. The lamp? Oh. Odd to think that

a little while ago she had been frightened of so small a thing as darkness. "I'll say good night, then." She stepped away, pausing at the doorway. "I'd prefer to forget about tonight."

Nat leaned against the table, arms crossed negligently on his chest. The stance emphasized the broadness of his shoulders; his shirt was open at the neck, where the lamplight glittered on golden hair. With his eyes glinting, he looked dangerous, disreputable, and altogether too appealing. "So you'd just have us both pretend that nothing happened?"

Heat surged into Abby's face, adding to her already overloaded senses. She felt upset, elated, perplexed, confused. "Nothing did happen," she snapped and swept into her stateroom, closing the door behind her with a definite click.

"Oh, but you're wrong, Abby," Nat said softly, looking at her closed door. If he were braver or less scrupulous, he would go into that stateroom and prove just how wrong she was. Something more than just a brief kiss had happened between them. *God help me,* he thought, turning down the oil lamp and going into his own stateroom. He knew what it was, and it scared him to death.

The *Aquinnah* continued south, bowling along steadily under the northeast tradewinds. There were no slowdowns now, no stopping to visit on other ships except to exchange mail. They needed speed if they were to round Cape Horn, the very tip of South America, in good time. Though it was summer in the Southern Hemisphere, conditions were always rough at the Horn. Letting the summer slip away would only make matters worse.

The stars in the sky were different now, the constellations familiar to Abby replaced by new ones, such as the Southern Cross. The ocean twinkled, too, as the ship's passing disturbed small marine animals that turned phosphorescent in its wake. At another time, Nat might have shared these wonders with Abby. At another time, Abby would have welcomed his presence. Not now, though. Since that night late in the cabin, since the kiss, they had nearly become strangers.

They talked, of course, since they couldn't avoid each other completely. They took meals together, and occasionally Abby stood on the deck near him, taking the air. Sometimes when she played the organ, he sat and listened; sometimes she asked him a question concerning the ship or business. Always they were scrupulously polite. Abby, however, never poured Nat a cup of coffee, never talked to him as he charted their course, and most certainly never left her stateroom at night. And Nat never, ever addressed her as other than "Miss Palmer."

Abby pulled her woolen shawl tighter about her as she sat at the table in the cabin, carefully dipping her pen in the inkpot for the letter she was writing to Elizabeth. The weather was quite disagreeable, she wrote, pausing as a swell lifted the ship and then continuing when she was steadier. As they went farther south it was growing progressively colder and rougher. Strange, wasn't it, when at home they always thought of the south as a warm place? But she was managing quite nicely. She stayed below, reading, writing in her journal, sewing, or playing the organ. It was high adventure, to be rounding the Horn, still one thousand miles distant, and . . .

There was no warning. One moment she was writing her letter; the next, there was a roaring sound, followed by a crash. Looking up, she saw water raging over the skylight in a torrent of greenish froth. Letter forgotten, Abby jumped up, grabbing the edge of the table to keep from falling as the ship heeled sharply. By now she was accustomed to waves breaking over the bow of the ship, flooding the deck and seeping down the companionway so that everything was damp. Never, though, had she seen one break so far aft, over the crew. Over Nat.

The thought sent her scurrying to the companionway, heart in her throat. Water was trickling down the stairs in little rivulets, and she held on tightly to the railing to keep from falling. Any injury at sea was frightening, but if Nat were hurt, if something had happened to him . . .

The door to the deckhouse refused, at first, to budge, and then suddenly flew open, pulling Abby with it. The force of the wind blew her up against the deckhouse and showered her with spray, so that even under the shelter of the hurricane deck her black merino dress was soaked. Where was Nat? She pulled herself upright, looking forward, and froze. Ahead, towering high above the ship, was a gray-green mountain of water. She couldn't think, couldn't move. She could only stare at her doom. She was going to die, and in that moment all she knew was that she'd never see Nat again.

An arm caught her about the waist. Abby cried out in surprise, even as she recognized Nat, dragging her into the deckhouse and slamming the door behind them, just in time. The ship bucked as the wave broke over her, throwing Abby against him. She buried her face against his wet wool coat, safe, as the water rushed by outside with a thunderous, roaring boom.

The ship pitched forward, held, and for a long, long moment seemed about to slip into the sea. Then, with a groaning of timbers, she righted herself again. "That—was a big one," Abby said shakily.

Abruptly Nat pushed her away. "What in damnation were you doing out there?" he demanded, gripping her arms.

"I thought you'd want some coffee." He was safe, she thought, smiling giddily at him. "You must be cold."

"Coffee," he snorted and released her, just as the ship pitched again, throwing them back together. Nat crashed against the wall, one arm flung out to keep from falling, the other tight around Abby's waist. She had not been held so close to a man in a very long time. In spite of the wet chill, it was not unpleasant. "Coffee," he said again. "You little fool, what were you thinking of?"

She looked up at him. "Is anyone hurt?"

"Yes, dammit, there's at least one broken arm. Dammit, Abby, from now on, don't come on deck without my permission."

"But—"

"If you'd gotten caught by that wave you'd've been swept overboard, and then where would we be?"

"You wouldn't have the owner to bother you anymore."

His face softened briefly, and then he pushed her away. "Don't talk nonsense. I mean it, Abby." He turned away. "I have enough to deal with without you getting hurt, too."

"Is it safe for you to go out there?"

"I have to." He looked back at her, as if surprised by the urgency in her voice. "There's work to do, and God knows how many injured men to see to. If you want to make yourself useful, tell Peleg to get the cabin ready for surgery."

"Surgery! But we haven't a doctor."

"No. Only me," he said, and went out into the roaring wind, leaving Abby to stare at the closed door in bemusement. Of course she knew that the ship's captain usually acted as doctor to the crew; of course she'd known that the sea would be rough. Nothing, however, had fully prepared her for the reality of it. This so-called cruise was not exactly what she had expected, she thought as she made her way below.

The ship was pointed into the wind to ride out the gale, thus saving it from being battered by the waves. The hapless crewman's broken bone was set, and it seemed he would retain full use of arm and fingers. When the wind finally abated some hours later, Nat and the crew were at last able to return to the deck to assess the damage. The crashing noise Abby had heard when the first wave struck had been the top of the foremast breaking off. It was in the bow that Abby, well wrapped in her cloak, found Nat, directing the repairs. "It's still rough," she said, planting her feet wide apart for balance.

Nat stared at the men working high above him. "Better get used to it. From here on it will only be worse."

"And we've still a thousand miles to go before we reach the Horn." She followed his gaze upward. "How bad is it?"

"Bad enough, but we should be able to use the extra spar as a topmast. Cooper's up there now, looking it over."

"You're not going to make him repair it now, are you?"

"Yes, Miss Palmer, I am."

"But it's so rough."

"He has a lifeline on."

She frowned. "It doesn't seem safe."

"Safe or not, the topmast has to be repaired."

"We already have one crewman injured, and he's an ordinary hand. Who will make casks if the cooper is hurt?"

Nat's voice was very quiet. "Miss Palmer, are you questioning my judgment?"

Abby paused for just a moment. It was true that Nat knew what he was doing. It was also true that, in the rough conditions, the men who were aloft were in danger. The ship was important, but people had to come first. "Yes,

Captain." She stood a little taller, held her head a little higher. "I am."

"You don't know anything about the matter."

"I know that I don't want those men's lives on my conscience! I want them to come down, Captain."

Beside her Nat was very still, his face tight, his eyes as stormy as the sea. He was, she realized, very angry. "Is that an order, Miss Palmer?"

"Yes, Captain." She kept her voice quiet as well, though the contest of wills was no less fierce for being conducted so softly. "I believe it is."

"You believe so? Is it, or isn't it, Miss Palmer?"

She faced him then, her muscles tight with resolve and strain, astonished by her daring and defiance. "Yes, Captain. It is an order. Will you give it, or shall I?"

Nat jerked away. "No, I will. Cooper! Bates!" he yelled, his hands cupped about his mouth. "Come down."

The cooper yelled something back, his voice lost in the shrieking of the wind, and Nat gestured impatiently. "Now! Come down now!"

Abby let her breath out in silent relief as the two men fumbled their way into the ratlines, the part of the rigging that resembled a ladder, and began coming down. Thank heavens, they were safe.

"That's better," she murmured.

Nat swung toward her. "It would be best if you returned below," he said, and Abby blinked at the look in his eyes. Oh, yes, he was angry. "Or I won't answer for your safety."

Somehow she knew he was not referring to the weather, or to the sea, or to any of the crew. Dear heavens, what had she done? "Of course," she squeaked and looked away, mortified. She'd thought she had better control of herself than that. "I shall be in the cabin if you wish to speak to me."

"Not anytime soon," he muttered. She turned away, realizing for the first time that there had been witnesses to the confrontation between her and Nat, that in spite of their lowered voices the crew knew what had happened. Several looked at her speculatively as she crossed the deck, and her heart sank. She had just done the one thing she had promised Nat she would never do. She had undermined his authority.

Damnation—she'd just taken over his ship, Nat thought, glaring after Abby. Even now, angry though he was, he had to be sure she made it to safety. He couldn't help it. But, damnation, she had presented him with an enormous challenge. It was going to take all his strength and all his will to control the crew if she ever did such a thing again.

There was a thud as the cooper jumped from railing to deck. "Bad up there," he commented. "Like freezing rain. There's ice on all the lines. Matter of fact," he paused as his helper joined him, "we was just going to come down when you called us."

Nat nodded. Likely these two were the only men on the ship who didn't know what had just happened between him and Abby. They soon would. "How's it look?"

"Not bad. If the ice lets up we can get the spar in place and start repairin' the rigging."

"We wouldn't be spreading that sail in this weather, anyway." Nat nodded again at the two men. "Go get yourselves some coffee and then join your watch."

"Aye, Cap'n," the cooper said, and they turned away. Nat was alone again, as he always was, as he usually preferred to be. Alone, and facing a challenge. What the hell was he going to do about Abby?

The gale moderated, allowing the crew to finish repairs to the foremast. The waves, though still big, never quite reached the heights of the ones from the storm, and the sun shone on a clear world. The work of running the ship went on as usual. It was frosty topside, but below, in the cabin, it was positively icy. Nat had not spoken to Abby since their confrontation, and the stove, blazing away, couldn't ease that chill.

It was a new experience for Abby, who expected Nat to explode at her at any time. She deserved it. She'd been in the wrong, even if the men on the mast had been in danger. Yet with other people Nat was much his usual self. He simply didn't acknowledge her. If they met in the passageway he would step aside to let her pass, his gaze fixed on some distant object, while on deck he ignored her completely. If they happened to be alone in the cabin he would not look at her at all, and meals, when the ship's officers were present, became a tense ordeal. Abby soon learned not to address anything to Nat; he would simply pretend not to hear, while the officers were leery of choosing sides. The ship was tense and unhappy, and for the life of her Abby didn't know what to do about it.

Nat's type of anger was new to her. Papa's temper might have been unpredictable, but he'd never kept his anger hidden. Though Abby never had grown accustomed to his shouting, at least she'd known that when he cooled down he would behave as if nothing had happened. Jared's anger didn't intimidate her as much. They'd squabbled as children, after all, and that made him less fearsome. No, she'd never encountered such cold, silent anger as Nat's, and she didn't know how to handle it.

A pounding noise made her look up from the table, where she sat trying to write in her journal. Across from her Nat was working out their course, behaving as if she weren't in the room. Above her, on deck, crew members were busy nailing boards and stretching canvas over the skylight, to protect it from the large waves to come at the Horn. Abby had known this was coming. She knew, too, that soon the cabin stove would have to be shut down, no matter how cold it got. She had accustomed herself somewhat to the discomforts of life at sea, but suddenly it was all too much. Most especially, she could not bear the cold silence that lay between her and Nat.

Abruptly she rose, journal in hand, and paced away from the table. "I'm sorry," she said, her back turned to Nat. "I shouldn't have overridden your order."

For a long moment the silence was disturbed only by the sounds of the hammers. Then: "I shouldn't have had men aloft," Nat said.

Abby turned, startled. Her father would never have admitted to any fault. "Maybe, but I shouldn't have said anything in front of the crew."

"That could have caused trouble." He leaned back, hands clasped behind his head. The cabin was warm enough that he had taken off his frock coat, and the sight of him in shirtsleeves did funny things to her breathing. "Fortunately you've been quiet since, so there's no harm done."

"I've been quiet!" She stared at him. "You've acted as if I don't exist."

His brow wrinkled. "I have, haven't I?"

"Oh, yes, you most certainly have. And how do you think that makes the crew look at me?"

He rose swiftly. "No one's insulted you, have they?"

"No. But you can see that the mates just don't know which of us to talk to." She braced her hands on the back of a chair. "Like it or not, Captain, I am the owner of this ship."

"Aye, I know." And how could he forget that? He had come to terms with the facts, that this ship was not his own and that his employer was a woman, until she had interfered in his job. That she had been right only made matters worse. He had then done what he always did when he was seriously angry. He withdrew into himself and brooded, and in the process discovered something that made matters much, much worse. He missed Abby. He was, in fact, in love with the wretched woman.

He didn't know why, no matter how he tried to figure it out. He found her beautiful, even if in the beginning he hadn't thought so. Nor was she at all pliant, yet he found their discussions and arguments stimulating. At the same time, he'd seen vulnerability in her eyes, in her posture, making him want to protect her. She was womanly, too, warm and caring; her figure might be slimmer than it had been, but it was still rounded enough to drive him mad. He thought of her constantly, on deck, in the rigging, in bed. Oh, yes, often in bed. He wanted to hold her, touch her, possess her, body and heart and soul. He had never felt such things for any other woman, and it scared the life out of him.

Abby shifted. "Why are you looking at me that way?"

He stirred, shaken from his thoughts. "What way?"

"Like you're a tiger, and I'm the prey. Are you still angry?"

"Angry? No. No. Not anymore." Good Lord, what was he going to do? She had no idea of his feelings, not if she could mistake his hunger for anger. No matter her age, she was damned innocent. Lord help him, even that was appealing. Damnation, he'd better get his mind onto a different topic. "But we have to settle this, Abby."

Abby sat across from him. "I know. I do understand why a ship can have only one captain. Frankly, I wouldn't want your job. But . . ."

"But sometimes you interfere."

"I wouldn't put it quite that way." She frowned. "When I see something that needs doing, I want to take care of it. I can't help it. It's how I was brought up."

"Hm." He nodded, a little surprised. The more he learned of her life, the more curious he became. Even if her father had been a wealthy merchant, she wasn't at all spoiled, as he'd feared. She'd make someone a good wife. Hell, he'd promised himself he wouldn't think of that. "All right, I understand that," he conceded. "But I'd rather you told me first."

"Yes, I—oh, dear." This as the cabin abruptly darkened, making them both look up. The canvas had been securely fastened to the skylight. "How dismal."

Nat grinned as he rose and struck a match. "At least the lamp works."

"You won't let me forget that, will you?"

"Never." He sat again, regarding her in the golden glow. She was still looking at the skylight, and the curve of her throat was softly white, enticing. He swallowed and shifted in his chair. "Tell me something, Abby."

She glanced back at him. "What?"

"What are you going to do with your life when this voyage is over?"

"I don't know, but as that's a long time off I'm not particularly worried. I'm hoping you'll make me enough profit to live on, at least for a while."

"Do you think you'll marry?" he asked, elaborately casual.

"Probably not."

"Why not?"

She gave a little laugh. "I didn't exactly have suitors lined up at my door when I left."

"Except for Swift."

"I'm not marrying Jared," she said quickly.

He leaned back. "He seems to think you are."

"Well, I'm not." She rose, her skirts twitching as she strode across the cabin. "I'm not."

Nat twisted in his seat to watch her. She was standing with her back to him, gazing at the bookcase as if it held the secrets of the world. Her head was up, her color was high, and her shoulders were braced. She looked both angry and utterly desirable. Swift wasn't good enough for her, he thought, giddy with relief as he got up. "Well, I'm glad to hear that."

"Why?" She turned, and now her anger seemed to focus on him. "Do you think I don't deserve to marry?"

"I think you deserve better."

Abby's shoulders dropped. "Jared is only a friend," she said yet again. "A good friend, but nothing more."

A scraping noise made Nat glance at the table, where the motion of the ship was scattering his dividers and parallel rulers across the charts. "Wasn't there anyone else?" he asked, gathering up his equipment so it wouldn't fall and be damaged.

"Not lately, no." Abby sat again and watched as he stowed charts and equipment away. "I'm not a terribly attractive prospect for marriage. Not since my father died."

"Strange thing to say." He, too, sat on the settee, not close to her, and yet near enough to touch, if he held out his arm. "That all anyone would want you for is money."

"Money is attractive, Captain."

"But it doesn't keep a man warm at night."

"Depends on the man," she said dryly, startling a laugh out of him. "It's all beside the point now, anyway. I've made a new life for myself."

"A life without a family."

"Like you," she countered, so swiftly that he might only have imagined the flash of sadness in her eyes. He'd best watch himself. Abby had a quick tongue in her own defense, though he hadn't meant to attack her. "What about you, Captain? Why have you never married? Or aren't I allowed to ask?"

"No, it's a fair enough question. I reckon I just never found the right woman." *Until now,* he thought. He still couldn't quite believe it.

"No? In all the years you've traveled the world, and all the women you've met—"

"Not the kind a man marries."

Her cheeks pinkened, but she didn't turn away. Instead she faced him, more curious than uncomfortable. "Not at home either?"

"Oh, no." His laughter was mirthless. "Definitely not at

home. All those proper young women, going about doing good works—too serious for me."

"We're not all like that."

"'We'?" He grinned at her. "Are you offering yourself as a candidate now?"

"Don't be foolish." Her face was very red. "I simply think that you haven't tried hard enough."

He shrugged. "Maybe not."

"So tell me." She shifted, laying her arm casually across the back of the settee. If he leaned back, his shoulder would rest against her hand. Tempting prospect. "Who would be the right woman for you?"

He pursed his lips. Funny, he'd never thought about that before. He'd just known that no woman he'd ever met was right. Except, perhaps, Abby. "I don't know. But I'd know her if I met her."

"A beauty, I imagine."

"No," he said swiftly. "Definitely not."

Her look was skeptical. "You'd choose someone plain?"

"I'd choose someone whose looks please me. She doesn't have to be what anyone else would call a beauty, as long as I think she is."

"Oh." Her face softened. "How very lucky she'll be."

"I'm not so sure about that." He looked away, across the room. Whatever he was going to do about Abby, he'd have to make a firm decision and stick to it. She was not the type for a brief affair, not just because of her upbringing but because it wasn't in her. Abby was a forever kind of woman, the kind a man made a home with. The kind he had children with. "I've never really thought of marriage," he said finally. "I'm not so sure it works."

"Are you afraid of giving up your freedom?"

"No." He shook his head, ignoring the sarcastic edge to her voice. "If I decide to marry, I'll do things right. But I've seen bad marriages, Abby." He looked at her. "I grew up in one. I've seen friends and family who are miserable, women as well as men."

"My parents were happy."

"Then why aren't you married?"

She opened her mouth as if to answer, and then closed it again. "I really don't know."

"You must have had suitors, Abby, even if all they did want was your father's fortune."

"Yes, and I saw through those quickly enough. Yes, I had suitors." She frowned, fingertips to her lips. "I think I didn't want someone who would forever be telling me what to do, having control over me. I'd like children, but not a husband."

He grinned. "One's difficult without the other."

"Oh, mercy." Her hands flew to her cheeks. "This is a most improper conversation."

"It wasn't, until a minute ago."

"Well, I'm not the one who started it!"

"Why do you dislike men so much, Abby?" he asked, suddenly serious.

"I don't dislike men."

"No? Have you ever been kissed?"

"Mercy! What a question."

"I know." He held her gaze with his. "It's rude and improper. But there it is. Have you, Abby?"

"Of course I have."

He should leave it there, he knew he should. After all, he'd kissed her himself, and would not mind doing so again. Now. Right this minute. "That's right. I've kissed you."

"You're not the only one," she snapped, goaded, as he'd hoped she would be. "So you needn't look so smug."

He couldn't help it; he grinned. "How did I compare?"

"How did you—ooh!" She stormed to her feet, putting the length of the cabin between them. "I will have you know, and you may tell this to any other male, that I consider kissing to be a vastly overrated experience."

"Do you?" He rose, slowly, easily, keeping his distance. For now. "It mustn't have been done right, then."

"Not right!" she exclaimed, and then closed her mouth. "I don't want to talk about this anymore."

He ambled over to the cabinets and leaned his arm against them. "Why not? Scared?"

"Of what?"

"That I'll kiss you again, and that I'll do it right."

"Don't be foolish."

"Or are you scared that I won't?" He advanced another pace, enjoying the look of wide-eyed shock on her face, enjoying the anticipation. Never had he worked so hard for a kiss. Never had he wanted one so much. "Which is it, Abby?"

"Neither." Her voice croaked, and she blinked. "I'm not scared," she said, sounding more resolute, but looking small and vulnerable, and utterly desirable.

"No?"

"No."

"Then I dare you." Another careful step, so that now he stood next to the table. She was near the door. If he made a mistake, moved too fast, she would run. "I dare you to try."

"Dares are for children, Captain."

"Oh?" Damnation, he'd thought he had her. "Then let me suggest this. A bargain, just as you once suggested to me."

She was standing with her back to the door, her hands braced behind her. "Which would be?"

"I'll kiss you. If you like it, you'll say so. If not, we'll never speak of it again."

"We shouldn't be speaking of it now."

"Maybe not." He leaned over, propped his hand on a door panel. "But we are."

She swallowed, though her eyes never left his. "Why are you doing this?"

"I want to kiss you, Abby." With his free hand he reached out, stroked his fingertips along her jawline, felt a shiver run through her. "But it's your choice."

She stared up at him, her eyes huge. "We'll never speak of it again? You promise?"

"You seem certain of the outcome." Again he caressed her, this time along the side of her throat; again she shivered. "I promise."

"Oh, all right, then!" Her head snapped up, proud, defiant. "Do it and get it over with."

He chuckled. "Abby, Abby." His fingers slipped around to the back of her neck. "You do know how to entice a man," he murmured and lowered his head to hers.

Chapter 12

O h, mercy! What was she doing? Abby wondered as Nat's head bent. She couldn't allow a man to exert such power over her. For she had lied to him. Kissing and being kissed by other men had been pleasant, unremarkable experiences. Being kissed by Nat, though, had fueled her dreams. Frantically she turned her head away, and his lips, slightly parted, warm, dry, landed on the angle of her jaw. He didn't seem to mind; his lips slid along the line of her chin, moving upward in slow, nipping progress. The sensation made her stomach jump, her breathing speed up, and he was only at her jaw—no, good heavens, he was taking her ear into his mouth, his tongue stroking the contours. Her knees trembled, and she pressed her hands harder against the door to stay upright. This was more than just kissing, and far more than merely pleasant. Just what it was, though, she didn't know. "Nat—"

"Yes, sweetheart," he murmured, his lips brushing her cheek, her temple; his hands framing her face, holding it still. "I know."

Did he? Did he know how her pulse raced, that the touch of his lips on her forehead, usually such a chaste, innocent gesture, made her feel anything but? How could he, when these feelings were so new to her, so fresh? Her eyes drooped closed as his lips fluttered upon them—mercy, who would ever have thought eyes could be so sensitive—and her head tilted up when his mouth moved down her nose. Now was the moment. Though his hands held her still, they were not imprisoning. She could break free if she wanted to, but she didn't. Oh, she didn't.

And so she let her eyes close all the way, let her lips part, feeling his breath so warm against her. His mouth was on hers again, soft, easy, and yet with enough pressure that she raised up on her toes to meet him. It still wasn't enough. Somehow she knew there had to be more.

When he pulled back, she met his gaze squarely, all defenses and pretenses gone. His eyes asked a question; she answered by raising her chin. His arm slipped down, down, along her shoulder, her back, to her waist, pulling her to him, while his other hand curled about her neck, holding her still for him. Again she felt his breath against her face; again her lips parted, more widely this time, and—

And there was a sudden, sharp knock on the door.

Nat jumped away from her as if the sound had been a bullet shot. "Damnation! What is it?" he barked.

Abby looked away as the door opened, wondering if her face looked as warm as it felt, wondering if their activity would be obvious to whoever the intruder was. "Lookout says he sees a squall line coming," Mr. Martel, the mate on watch, said. "Thought you should know."

Nat's hands gripped the back of a chair. "Where from?"

"West, Cap'n."

"And the winds?"

"So-west, Cap'n."

"Likely we're in for it, then. Take in all sail except for staysails and batten everything down. I'll be topside soon as I get my storm gear."

"Aye, cap'n," Mr. Martel said and went back out.

"We're in for heavy weather." Nat reached into a locker for his oilskins, glancing back at Abby, who stood where he had left her. "You'll be safer in your stateroom."

Abby nodded and cleared her throat. "Yes," she said, her voice very small.

"Good." He strode across the cabin, stopping before her. His fingers stroked along her jaw, and she looked up at last. Then he opened the door and was gone.

Her knees suddenly a-tremble, Abby staggered over to the table and fell into a chair. Good heavens, what had just happened to her? She had never felt anything like this before, this deep, spreading warmth that defied the weather's frigidity—and he hadn't even really kissed her. But she wished he had. Oh, she very much wished he had, and that was the most astonishing thing about the interlude.

Abby gazed sightlessly down at her journal. She thought she knew herself well; she thought what she had told Nat was true. Since she had received her first, stolen kiss at the age of sixteen, she'd considered the activity pleasant at best. Always it had baffled her when other girls had giggled about their experiences and the rapture they had felt. One or two of her married friends had even hinted at more pleasures to come. Abby didn't quite believe any of it. Maybe such feelings happened to other women, but not to her. She did not crave a man's touch and had never thought she would. Not until Nat Howland had threaded his hands into her hair and explored her face with his lips. Until duty to the ship had taken him away, leaving her shaken, aching in unexpected places, and very confused. Something had begun today, here in the cabin. How she would deal with it, she did not know.

The first strong waves of the storm lifted the ship as Abby reached her stateroom, after helping Peleg stow away anything loose in the cabin. How bad it would be she didn't know, but she settled herself on her bunk and reached for the ropes attached to either side, tying herself down with the knots Peleg had taught her. She had barely finished when the wind struck, heeling the ship over so far that the deck was nearly vertical. Only the ropes kept her in the bunk. She cried out in surprise and fear, clutching at the sides of the bunk, as slowly, slowly, the ship settled again. Dear God, it was going to be a terrible storm. What would happen to the men on deck? What would happen to Nat?

The wind abruptly shrieked louder and as abruptly quietened. In the passageway outside her stateroom Abby could hear men's voices, all in a jumble and indistinct, except for Nat's. "I'm not hurt, for God's sake!" he said, sounding shaky. Dear God! She struggled with the knots, swearing softly in impatience as they held. Was Nat hurt?

With the ropes at last loosened, Abby rolled to her feet, bracing her hand against the bulkhead. Though the wind roared as loudly as before, the ship rode easier; they were headed into the wind now, instead of across it, and could ride the storm out. Staggering from side to side in the passageway, she made her way to the cabin.

Inside, two of the crew were just easing Nat into a chair at the table, while Peleg leaned over them, peering at Nat's head. Water ran off Nat's oilskins and dripped from his hair, but it was the bleeding gash near his temple that made her breath catch. He had been hurt.

Nat looked up at her gasp. "What are you doing here?" he demanded.

"You're hurt." She stepped into the cabin, ignoring his anger. Maybe it was her imagination, but the storm seemed to be easing. Or maybe it didn't matter so much anymore.

"I'm not hurt, and if these bas— idiots would let me up—"

"He fell when the wave struck," one of the crew volunteered, holding Nat down by the shoulder, while Peleg held a cloth to the wound. "Hit his head on the deckhouse. He was out for a couple o' minutes."

"Unconscious?" she asked, sounding calmer than she felt.

"Yes, ma'am."

"Are you needed topside?"

"No, ma'am, Mr. Martel told us to go to the foc's'le once the cap'n was safe. We got to ride this one out."

She nodded. "Go on, then. Mr. Tripp and I will see to the captain."

Nat raised his head. "Don't give orders on my ship," he snapped.

"Then give them yourself," she snapped back, as the men hesitated near the cabin door. "No one's going to be doing anything until this blows over, and you know it."

Nat paused, and then raised his hand. "Go on," he said to the men, who looked relieved as they escaped. Damnation, but she could be a termagant. Why was it that he loved her so?

"This may sting," she said at the same moment, and touched something wet and fiery to his forehead. His nostrils filled with the pungent scent of alcohol; his eyes watered, and yet what preoccupied him wasn't the pain of his injury. The depth of his feelings for her stunned him. "Can you see all right?"

"I can see fine," he growled, blinking first to clear his eyes, and then in surprise. Abby's breasts were at his eye level, as fine a quartet as he'd ever seen—no, a pair, he thought, forcing himself to focus. He began to feel better.

"No double vision?"

Not of the kind she was talking about, but he didn't

mind. "I can see just fine," he repeated, briefly mesmerized by the view, and then pulled back. They were alone in the cabin. "Why are you doing this? Where is Peleg?"

"Someone else is injured. He's gone to see to him. Here, hold this a moment." She pressed a cloth against the wound. He reached up to hold it, and his fingers brushed hers. She paused, and then pulled back. "Don't you remember?"

"Yes, yes," he said, irritably. The last thing he wanted was for Abby to think of him as weak, though his memory of recent events was hazy.

"You must have a headache."

"Nothing a whiskey wouldn't cure," he said frankly.

"Well, you're not getting one." She turned away, heading toward the cabinet where he kept their medical supplies. "What about damage to the ship?"

"Nothing drastic." He propped himself on his elbow, watching with undisguised interest as she stretched up into a cabinet for more supplies, her bodice pulling taut over her breasts. For the first time he realized she wasn't wearing a skirt. Instead she had on—well, he wasn't sure what it was, but it looked more like underdrawers than anything else. It was voluminous, and it covered her from waist to ankle, but it was still one of the most enticing sights he had ever seen. He closed his eyes. How much was one man supposed to take? "What are you wearing?" he demanded.

Abby turned from the cabinet, apparently startled at his tone, and then her cheeks pinkened. "Bloomers." She raised her chin. "My cousin gave them to me. They keep me warm."

"They're unsuitable."

"I like them."

So did he, but he wouldn't give her the satisfaction of saying so. "Go change."

"No," she said calmly, closing the cabinet.

"Dammit, Abby—"

"Please don't swear at me, Captain." She stood with hands folded, as prim as a schoolmarm. The combination of her posture with her costume was so incongruous that it only heightened his desire. "I have the right to dress as I choose."

"Not when the men haven't seen other women in months," he ground out.

"But they won't see me, will they?" she said patiently. "Only you will."

Dear God. He closed his eyes again, but the image of her in that ridiculous outfit remained. Ridiculous and voluptuous and totally desirable. "And do you think I'm so trustworthy?"

For the first time she looked uncertain, but she raised her chin, a sure sign of defiance. "You had best be, Captain, or someone else will have to bandage your head."

"I'll do it."

"Your hands are shaking too much." The reproof was gentle, but, as she bandaged the wound, he sat fuming and aching. Was she implying that a little knock on the head rendered him helpless? "I'm glad there wasn't much damage."

"Who said?" he muttered, hands fisted on his knees.

"Then there is damage to the ship?"

"I'm not talking about the ship, Abby." He rose, though she was in the middle of tying off the bandage. He'd had enough. "I'm talking about me."

"Oh." She stepped back at something she saw in his face, and lost her balance as the ship lurched. At the same time his arm shot out, catching her about the waist. He seemed to be recovering quite well. "I'm—not going to fall," she said, holding herself stiffly. "But thank you."

He didn't release her. "As I recall, we were in the middle of something when we were interrupted. Would you please sit down?" he added, irritated, as the ship heeled again.

"If you'd let me go."

He patted his knee. "There's a seat right here."

"Captain—"

"Miss Palmer." He grinned at her.

"Will you please let me go?"

"Time is too short sometimes, Abby," he said, suddenly serious.

She frowned, not straining to escape but not leaning against him either. "What do you mean?"

He shook his head, an action he instantly regretted. "Nothing." Nothing he could quite put into words. The ship had to come first, but in that split second when he'd been lifted off his feet and thrown against the deckhouse, it wasn't of the ship he had thought. It was of Abby, and of missed opportunities. It didn't matter why he loved her, or how it had come about. It mattered only that he did.

"You're pale." She twisted gently out of his grip. "You should rest."

"Aye, I will. Abby."

She turned from the doorway. "What?"

She was beautiful, he thought again, seeing her through a light-headed daze. The angle of her jaw, the swell of her breasts, all beautiful. He had been blind. "Nothing. Thank you."

She smiled quickly and left the cabin, trailing behind her only a faint scent of lavender, a scent that would forevermore remind him of her. He was in love with her, and just what was he going to do about it?

Nat didn't see much of Abby as the *Aquinnah* made its difficult progress around the Horn. With the seas high and the winds blowing easterly it was difficult to make westing, and so it was nearly two weeks before they reached the Pacific. During that time he was kept constantly busy running the ship, with sleep caught in snatches on the settee in the cabin. Abby sensibly kept to her stateroom; from Peleg he learned she was coping with the discomfort well enough, with few complaints. She was a brave woman, and she'd make a good whaling wife. For he had decided, somewhat to his bemusement, that that was what he wanted. He, who had cared so long only for his career and for what he had lost, now dared to want more: a home, a family, someone to call his own. He'd missed her during their long passage around the Horn, thought of her during the long, cold watches of the night, when the deck was washed with icy water that could sweep a man to his death; and he'd realized at last that there was more to life than work. He wanted Abby, for more than one thing, one night. He wanted her with him forever.

The sun slanted in warmly through the skylight, illuminating the chart set before Nat on the table. Their next port of call was Valparaiso, for supplies and a brief liberty for the men, and then on to Hawaii, where they would meet up with the rest of the whaling fleet. The large casks in the hold were filling nicely with oil, and they had also stored the beginnings of a fine cache of whalebone. He'd had better voyages, aye, but he'd seen worse, too. If they continued with the luck they had had so far, they would make a tidy profit.

From high above came the lookout's cry, of whales spotted in the distance. Charts and profit forgotten, Nat bounded to his feet and ran up to the deck. Right whales, the lookout thought, a good-sized school, making it worthwhile to lower all boats. Nat was intensely aware of Abby watching from the cooper's bench, and yet he gave no sign. His feelings would have to wait. But he could do something to increase her future security. He would go catch her a whale.

Sometime later, Nat's boat bumped back against the *Aquinnah*'s starboard hull. Disgruntled, he climbed the rope ladder to the deck. Mr. Martel's boat had won the informal race to the whales and had harpooned a fine catch, a large female. Mr. Taber's boat had had similar luck a few moments later. By then, though, the remaining whales had taken flight. Keeping the ship in sight, looking for the signals that indicated the whales' location, Nat at last admitted defeat. He'd take no whale today.

Nat dropped lightly onto the deck from the railing. He couldn't participate in the hunt, but this was still his ship. Now, which of his crew was that standing on the port rail, hand shading his eyes—*Good God!* Not a crewman. It was Abby.

"Good God," he said, and she looked back at him. At once her face flushed, but she showed no signs of climbing down. Instead, she stood easily, holding to the rigging tightly. That was surprising enough, but she was wearing— damnation, she was wearing her bloomers again, and the crew were giving her covert, astonished looks. He had to get her down, before any of the men got ideas. Before he hauled her into his arms.

"What do you think you're doing?" he asked, his voice low and fierce as he crossed the deck to her.

"Watching the capture," she said calmly. "Mr. Martel has just put in the lance."

"And Taber?" he said in spite of himself.

"I can't see his boat without a glass. The whale's fighting—no, he's going belly-up." She sounded both regretful and satisfied. "Looks a good size."

"It is. Damnation, Abby, what are you doing up there?"

"I was bored," she said, echoing his earlier thoughts. "It didn't seem fair to me that you men should have all the fun, and then I remembered." She looked down at him. "I do own this ship."

"And you remember that when it suits your purposes."

"Of course. I suppose you'd rather I came down."

"If you would," he said, elaborately polite.

"It's not fair," she repeated, jumping down without his aid. "I used to climb trees when I was a girl."

"You're not a girl anymore." He kept his voice low. "You're a damned attractive woman on a ship filled with men who are as randy as goats. I don't need you encouraging them."

"Oh, pooh. I like my bloomers."

So did he, but he wasn't going to give her the satisfaction of saying so. "Go below and change, Abby, or I won't be responsible for the consequences."

"Whose? Yours, or the crew?" she asked, as if she knew what he was feeling.

"Go change," he repeated tersely. "We'll talk later."

"Later you'll be busy cutting in."

"We'll talk, Abby," he promised her and turned away, not waiting to see if she followed his command. If he looked at her a moment longer he would, indeed, pull her close and make her suffer the consequences, and that wouldn't do. Not yet.

It took nearly two days for the whales to be cut in and tried out; longer than that for the oil to cool enough to be stowed in the huge casks belowdecks. Once that was done, the crew got busy cleaning, scouring deck and companionways with sand and holystone until they were spotless again. Not until she was certain she could walk on deck without falling did Abby come out of her self-imposed isolation.

In the evening's dimness, she walked to the taffrail in the stern of the ship, gripping it lightly. Overhead the Southern Cross, a recognizable formation in a sky of unfamiliar stars, glittered like diamonds on velvet, and the air held just a hint of soft warmth, though the weather was still chilly. It was all so different from what she'd grown up with, different from what she'd expected. She loved it. She loved the breeze that ruffled her hair and the way the ship rocked her to sleep at night; she loved, even, the majesty and terror of a storm. Something leaped in excitement within her whenever they spotted a whale, and if she still didn't like the process, at least she had come to terms with it. This ship was where she belonged, and she would never have known it if she hadn't left New Bedford.

A slight smile curved her lips. "Something funny?" a voice said beside her, and she looked up to see Nat, lounging with his elbow on the taffrail.

"Not particularly, no. How many barrels did we get?"

"Thirty-two from the first, forty-six from the second."

She did some quick mental calculations. The holds were well on the way to being filled. "We're doing well."

"Aye. We might want to think of transshipping some of the oil home when we reach Honolulu."

"Do you think that's a good idea?"

"Depends on the cost, but aye. That way we'll have more room."

"And no guarantee of luck."

"We'll have luck. I can feel it." She could sense him studying her in the dark, and kept her head resolutely turned away. "So what were you smiling about?"

Persistent man. Why should it matter to him? "Nothing very much. I was just thinking that I might never have left New Bedford if not for Jared."

Nat turned so that he, too, faced outward, his profile oddly stark. "So that's why you came aboard."

"Excuse me?"

"You're following Swift."

"Heavens, no!" She laughed, startled. "No, if I'd wanted to go to sea with him I had the chance—"

"The hell you did!"

"—but it wasn't what I wanted. No, it's because he bought my father's house."

"Your house, you mean."

"No." She shook her head and looked up to see him studying her. Odd. She didn't think she was particularly fascinating. "Now that I'm away I can see it never really was my home. It was my father's. He wanted to show how successful he was." She let out her breath. "And in the end, he lost it."

"So did you."

"No. I was set free." She smiled at him, wanting to share her newfound sense of peace, of joy. "No matter what happens, I'm glad I came. I think I'll remember this voyage for the rest of my life."

He didn't speak right away. "All of it?"

"Yes, all of it." She frowned, puzzled by something in his voice. "Are you referring to something in particular?"

"Aye." He gazed out across the sea again. "To an evening in the cabin, and a certain wager that we never settled."

Abby could feel herself growing red. That near kiss, he meant. "Oh."

"Had you forgotten?"

"No." Oh, no. Not a minute of it, of his fingers in her hair, his body solid and strong and so close to hers, and his lips, warm, dry, slipping along her cheekbone, causing odd fluttering sensations in the pit of her stomach. No, she hadn't forgotten. "But I thought you had."

He grinned, making her instantly regret her words. "No. Did it bother you, thinking I had?"

"Don't be silly." She glanced behind her. The deck was dark and quiet, but she well knew that the ship never really slept. "This isn't the place to have this conversation. Someone might overhear."

"Shall we go below, then?"

"No! I think we should let it pass."

"Do you?" She could feel his scrutiny, though again she wouldn't look at him. "You know, Abby, I've thought a lot of things about you, but I never took you for a coward."

She gripped the railing harder. "You may call me all the names you want. It won't work."

"My mistake. Perhaps what I should have said is that you strike me as someone who honors her wagers."

That went home. When she gave her word to something, she kept it. She shouldn't, though, for something so outrageous as this. Should she? "I really don't want to discuss this any longer," she said and turned away, slipping past the helm to reach the deckhouse.

He followed close behind. "Why not? We've nothing else to do."

For some reason, that angered her more than anything he'd said so far. "If it's nothing to you, why do you keep on so?"

He shrugged. "Why not?"

She stared at him for a moment. Then she whirled and went into the deckhouse. Nat grinned as he fell in behind her, following her down the companionway. So that had gotten to her. He'd known something would. He'd known, too, that she remembered that almost-kiss as well as he did. He'd seen it in her face, heard it in her voice. For that reason, he couldn't let this moment pass.

Abby turned when she reached the bottom of the stairs. "Why are you following me?" she demanded.

"We're not done."

"Yes, we are."

Nat stepped down, crowding her, making her move back. "Mm, no, I don't think so. We never settled the wager."

"As far as I'm concerned we did." She put up her chin. "I didn't enjoy it."

"Liar." He advanced toward her again. Again she stepped back, just out of reach. "If we hadn't been interrupted you would have been in my arms."

"If we hadn't been interrupted I would probably have slapped your face."

"I don't think so, sweetheart." He grinned as he stepped toward her. Her back was to the wall. She had no place to escape. "I really don't think so."

"Please." Her voice was breathless. "Please don't . . ."

"What?" he prompted. "Don't what?"

"Crowd me."

"I'm not," he said, but as he did so looked down at her. There was fear in her eyes, making him take a quick step back. "I'm sorry. I didn't mean to."

Some of the color returned to Abby's face. "Now who's lying?"

"No lies, sweetheart." He brushed his finger quickly down her cheek. "Don't you know I'd never hurt you?"

"No." Her gaze was steady. "I really don't know that."

He propped his hand on the wall behind her, bending

his head to hers. "It's a risk, isn't it? For all I know, you could break my heart."

"Ha!"

"You could. You have power you don't even know about."

Surprisingly, that made her laugh. "Is that what you say to all your women, Captain?"

"What women? The only one I see here is you."

"I'm not a toy, Captain."

"I'm not playing, sweetheart."

She frowned. "I really don't understand you."

"It's very simple, Abby." He lowered his head. "I want to kiss you."

"Oh, for heaven's sake." She slipped away from him, into the passageway. "You're not going to give up, are you?"

"No."

"Very well, then," she said, and, turning, walked into the cabin. "You might as well get it over with."

He followed her, grinning. "The last time you said that, I took you up on it."

"You're not going to be satisfied until you badger me into this, are you? So." She raised her face. "Do it, then."

Nat bit back a smile as he looked down at her. Her eyes were closed and her lips were tightly pursed. What a contrary, contradictory woman he had chosen to love. It would take him the rest of his life to figure her out. He was rather looking forward to it. "It's not that easy, sweetheart," he murmured, tracing the outline of her lips with his fingertip.

She shuddered. "Yes, it is," she said and, reaching up, pressed her lips against his.

Shock held Nat still for a moment, but then his arms came around her, pulling her against him. She stiffened and, ever conscious of her, of the sweet woman in his arms, he let up the pressure, instead nibbling lightly on her upper lip. Little by little she relaxed, her head tilting a bit more, her body softening, though she didn't respond. Not quite yet. And though earlier he had promised himself he wouldn't rush her, he suddenly very much wanted her response, wanted her to acknowledge that he was the one holding her, kissing her. Making love to her. And so he slipped his tongue between her lips, not quite so tightly closed as they had been, silently urging her to open for him. She stiffened slightly, but then, with a sigh, her mouth parted and her arm slid around his waist.

Triumph mingled with the desire that surged through Nat. He pulled her closer, his lips no longer soft, but urgent, demanding. She shuddered and went limp, her mouth moving ardently against his. Yet she didn't seem to know what to do as his tongue darted within her mouth, and that filled him with another kind of joy. Her untutored kisses were far more heady than any he had ever received from the most experienced woman. Teaching her the pleasures of lovemaking would be ecstasy.

When his lips moved to explore her face, Abby pulled back. Nat retained just enough wisdom to loosen his grip, though his body urged him to finish what he had started. Her eyes were huge and dazed as she looked at him. "I . . ." She licked her lips, already swollen, and desire shot through him again. "What is the outcome?"

"Of what?" he asked, looking at her mouth, craving its taste again, always.

"The wager."

The wager. He'd forgotten that. He suspected that for a moment she had too. "I think we call it a draw, sweetheart."

"What does that mean?"

"It means we'll have to try it again," he said and pulled her back against him. There was no tentativeness between them this time, no coaxing. This time she opened to him immediately, meeting the caress of his tongue with her own. He groaned. He wanted her, far more than he'd ever wanted any woman, and for more than just this one evening. For more than just her body. He wanted her, heart and soul, forever.

"Abby." He wrenched his mouth away, wrapping her in an embrace to hold her to him for all time. This wasn't what he had planned, but the time was right. "Marry me, sweetheart."

Chapter 13

A bby pulled away from Nat so unexpectedly and with so much force that he released her. "What did you say?"

"I asked you to marry me, Abby," he said very calmly, annoyed at himself for speaking before she was ready. Her eyes were wide and her face pale. "Nothing so terrible, is it?"

She leaned on the table. "You want the ship," she accused him.

Nat couldn't help it—he laughed. He pulsed with need for her, wanting her, and she believed such foolishness. "No, Abby. What I want is—"

"You don't have to laugh at me." Her face was stark. "You're not the first man to try to win his fortune through me."

"Damnation, is that what you think of me?" he roared, leaning forward, his face inches from hers.

"It's the truth. I know men. You all think alike. You think I'll marry you and turn the *Aquinnah* over to you, just like that. Well, I won't."

"I don't want the damned ship."

"Don't swear at me."

"Dammit, Abby, you're not being fair. Whoever those other men were, they're not me. I wouldn't use you like that."

"Then what—"

"Do I want? You." He stabbed his finger downward, saw her eyes follow the gesture, saw by her sudden stunned expression that she was aware of his desire for her. "I want you."

"No." Her fingers gripped the table railing; her face was chalky. "I don't believe it."

"Why? You think someone could prefer a ship to you?

What is a ship, Abby? Just wood and rope and metal. Doesn't keep a man warm at night. Only a woman can do that. You."

She took a deep breath. "I'm not that much of a woman."

"You're all woman, Abby." Leisurely, deliberately, he raked his gaze over her straight, slender shoulders, the full curve of her breasts, her round hips. "Any man would want you."

"That's beside the point," she said crisply, her shoulders back, her head up. "Because I don't want you."

"Oh, but you do, Abby." He didn't move, yet she pulled back as if he had. Odd. "A woman doesn't kiss a man the way you did without feeling something."

"It was madness."

"It was desire," he said baldly. The time for teasing, for flirting, was over. "We had a wager. You lost."

She raised her chin. "No, I didn't."

"Are you going to stand there and tell me you pretended to like kissing me?"

There was an odd little smile on Abby's face. "Surely, Captain, I'm not the first woman to do that."

He swore, quietly but with great force, deeply angry, deeply hurt. If she were closer he would grab her, and—what? Shake some sense into her? Or drag her against him and kiss her until she admitted that, yes, her feelings for him were as strong as his? Neither would do any good. "I know you're lying," he said more calmly than he felt. "If I thought it would work I'd kiss you again to prove it. But," he went on as alarm flared in her eyes, "I want you willing, Abby. You have to admit on your own that you want me as much as I want you."

She stared at him. "Are you serious?"

"Very."

"Then you have a long wait ahead." She straightened, calm, in control again. How could she be so cool while his emotions churned and rioted? "Because I won't."

"You will."

She shook her head. "No. If you'll excuse me, Captain, I would like to go to my stateroom." She stepped forward, stopped. "Or am I likely to be molested by you again?"

He moved aside, hands held out. "Far be it from me to dare to touch you."

"Good." Head high, eyes averted, she slipped past him. It was hard, but he managed not to reach out as she passed, not to touch her hair or her cheek. God help him, but her rejection didn't matter. He wanted her still. "I shall bid you a good evening, then," she said and went into her stateroom.

The click of her latch was like an explosion in the silent cabin, making Nat lurch forward from his seemingly comfortable lounge. What had just happened? He had proposed to Abby in all sincerity, and she acted as if he'd insulted her. As if he wanted only her ship. He snorted. There were easier ways to get a ship than to marry for it, especially to a woman so contrary, so aggravating . . . so warm and yielding and soft, and so very, very scared.

His temper finally cooling, Nat sat down, frowning into space. He didn't understand the fear. Certainly he'd never done anything to hurt her. But then, maybe that was the problem. A woman of her age, a spinster with no experience of men, would probably be scared by her unfamiliar emotions. Aye, that was it. He had a frightened virgin on his hands, a rare phenomenon. He could handle it, he thought, leaning back with his hands linked behind his head and a small smile on his face. Not yet, because he didn't want to face rejection again, but eventually, when she got over her fright, when she realized that she could trust him. Then, then she'd come to him.

Nat's smile broadened. He would give her time and space, and love, and see what happened. She would come to him. He was certain of it.

Abby sat on the edge of her bunk, shaking, fists clenched. The worst of the panic had passed: the nausea, the waves of heat, the feeling of impending doom. Still, the fear remained. What had she done? What had seemed like a safe, innocent flirtation with Nat had turned into something else, something deeper, more—tempting. Dear God. For he had been right. She wanted him every bit as much as he wanted her, but only disaster awaited her should she give in to her desire.

Wonderingly, she raised her fingertips to her lips, startled to find them puffy and swollen. She'd never known. In his arms she had felt yielding, soft, and yet alive, so alive. For that alone, she should be grateful. No other man had ever stirred her in such a way. It wasn't their fault, she had concluded long ago, as she saw some of her suitors marry other women. Somehow she knew that the lack was in herself, and she had come to terms with it. Lately, she'd even been a little glad of it. Such feelings could be uncomfortable, and improper, for a spinster.

Nat attracted her. He always had. Yet when they had decided to become business partners, she had been relieved. Chagrined that that was all he wanted, but mostly relieved. Only now did she realize that his attitude toward her had made her relax in his presence. Just as he regarded her, so she had come to see him: as a person first, and not a man. She'd even come to consider him a friend. That was how she'd rationalized the kissing. A teasing kiss between friends was allowable. It wouldn't lead anywhere, except to satisfy her curiosity.

But it had. It had led to feelings she'd never before known, feelings that frightened and exhilarated her. Even those she could have handled, though, until he had proposed to her. Until for one mad moment, she had been tempted to accept.

Abby pounded her fists on her knees. She didn't love him. She couldn't. Love was dangerous. It could take a woman like her mother and tie her to an erratic, unpredictable man like her father. But then, most men seemed like that to her. Jared was, and so was Nat. True, he'd set himself a goal, to return to sea, and had worked steadily at it; true, he was a superb shipmaster. But a man who roamed the sea was by definition undependable to a woman. Abby's adventurous streak had sent her to sea. It did not extend to risking the rest of her future. So just what was she to do?

You could marry him. Oh, tempting thought. It sent warmth into her cheeks, into the pit of her stomach. For a moment, she imagined herself living as other women, normal women, did, with a mate by their side, and found it unexpectedly appealing. Perhaps there would even be children, the daughter she'd always yearned for. Would it be enough, though? She didn't know. Her life now was far from perfect, but at least she knew who she was. As a wife, she could lose her sense of self, so hard-won. A man would take it from her.

Abby rose and began undressing. Difficult though it would be, she would have to talk to Nat about this. They had to work together, after all. Personal considerations would have to be set aside, else their partnership, already shaky, would fall apart. And then where would she be?

She owned the ship. It always came back to that. She could hire another skipper, though the very thought made her stomach churn anew. It wouldn't happen, though. Nat had as much at stake as she did. If he wished to keep his position, he'd have to accept her decision. But she wondered, as she drifted off to sleep, just what being married to him would be like. And she wondered, in the freedom of half-consciousness, if she weren't making the biggest mistake of her life.

"There she blows!" the call came down from the lookout. Abby, sitting in the deckhouse and desultorily working at a piece of embroidery, rose and crossed the deck to the railing. They were back in northern waters, having crossed the Equator a few days previously, and were nearing the Sandwich Islands. Hawaii. She'd heard tales of the islands in the dead of a New Bedford winter and had wondered what life was like in a place where summer never ended. It was spring back home, she thought almost irrelevantly. The daffodils would be out, and the forsythia. She was sorry to miss that sight this year.

A shadow fell across her vision. Nat stood beside her, telescope in hand. "Aren't you lowering the boats?"

He shook his head. "No. We're too close to the islands. These waters are where the whales have their young. We'd be foolish to go after them and scare them off."

"Others have."

"We don't."

She nodded. "Good."

"Good?" He looked at her, with eyebrows raised. "Do you mean to say you aren't going to argue with me on this?"

"Since when have I argued with you, Captain?"

He snorted, but he was smiling, which pleased Abby inordinately. In the last few days a line of squalls had kept her confined belowdecks, and so the chance to talk to him hadn't yet come. She was anxious about that. She wanted things said, done, out in the open and finished. At the same time, she had to admit that this moment of companionship was pleasant. She didn't want to lose it.

"I don't think we should transship the oil home," he said unexpectedly.

Abby came out of her thoughts. "Excuse me?"

"We discussed shipping the oil and bone home to make room in the hold. Remember?"

"Yes." As if that were all that mattered. They had other things to settle. The trouble was, she wasn't quite certain how to broach the subject. "It might be a good idea."

He shook his head. "Maybe next season, after we've been in the Arctic. We don't have enough to justify the costs of shipping. Not yet, anyway. If we have a good season, fine, we'll make room. If not, we'll have saved money."

Abby nodded. "That makes sense."

"That's twice."

"Excuse me?"

"Twice you've agreed with me. You feeling all right?"

"Yes. Fine. Nat—Captain . . ." She faltered as he turned to look at her, his eyes very blue, very bright. "What happened the other night—"

"You're not ready," he said calmly. "I'm aware of that."

"No! I mean, it won't do. You must see that?"

He hadn't looked away. She wished she could find a way to escape from that keen blue gaze. He could see into her soul if she didn't shield herself. "Why not, sweetheart?"

Something swelled in her chest. "Because—that. I'm not anyone's sweetheart."

"No. Only mine."

"Nat—"

"At least you used my name." He grinned. "I like it."

"We're partners." Her lips felt stiff. "That's all."

"Aye, but in more ways than one, Abby." He turned so he could lean back against the railing. Abby looked away. All about them the everyday work of the ship went on: the cooper knocked together barrels; a sailor spliced rope; another crew member, not on watch, torturously carved a traced design onto a whale tooth, making a piece of scrimshaw. No one seemed to be watching her and Nat, and yet she knew that anything they did would be noticed. What was said here and now could influence the delicate balance of power between them.

She looked out to sea, not wanting to face him. "I don't want to marry you."

"So I gathered."

That made her look at him. "You sound calm about it."

"You sound annoyed."

"I am not annoyed!"

A slight smile played about his lips. "Miffed, maybe?"

"No." With great effort, she held onto her temper. "We have to settle this, Nat."

"No, we don't."

"We do. Why can't you see it?"

"Oh, I do, sweetheart. At least I see that you think we can't work together if it's not settled. Am I right?"

Her throat was dry. "Yes."

He nodded. "Thought so. Well, you're wrong." He looked directly at her. "I have no trouble working with you."

That threw her. "You—don't?"

"No. Do you have trouble working with me?"

"I don't know," she said honestly. "Everything's changed."

He nodded again. "Fair enough. Well, for what it's worth, Abby, I won't try to kiss you or anything like that, not when you're not willing. And I won't propose to you again."

"Oh." The breath went out of her. It was what she'd wanted, so why did she suddenly feel so bereft?

"But the offer stands." His gaze held hers. "The offer is open."

She couldn't breathe. Surely he couldn't be serious, after the way she'd treated him. Surely she wasn't relieved. "I won't change my mind."

"If you do, come to me." He pushed away from the railing. "Time to take the sights," he said and walked away, leaving Abby to stare after him, baffled. She didn't understand men. It seemed that once they got an idea into their heads, it was impossible to get it out. She would not marry him, and he should know why. He, of all people, should know how much the ship meant to her and how she feared losing it. Didn't she?

Abby pursed her lips, her fingers resting lightly on the railing, the wind off the water riffling her hair. Eight months ago the *Aquinnah* had been the most important thing in the world to her. When had that changed? Its success mattered, and the profit she would eventually make, but it was only wood and rope and metal, as Nat had said. Not a living person. Not her father. He was gone, she admitted finally, and felt something settle into place within her. He had ruled her life and continued to influence her beyond the grave, but he was gone. Any decisions she faced were now her own. She was free.

What that meant for her future, she wasn't sure. The thought of returning to New Bedford and quietly setting up a home no longer held any appeal. At least she didn't have to worry about it yet. The *Aquinnah* would be her home for a while to come, she thought, turning from the rail, and then went still. A few feet away, sextant raised to his face, was Nat.

She shouldn't have been so startled at the sight of him, but something quivered in the pit of her stomach. Matters between them were far from settled, she thought as she carefully skirted around him to reach the deckhouse. Every time she saw him, she remembered. Every time she watched his hands, whether navigating or holding the wheel or simply at rest, she thought of his touch. And every time he spoke, she looked at his lips and remembered just how they had felt on hers, just how she had felt when he had finally, finally kissed her.

A little giddy, wanting to giggle, afraid she'd cry, she stumbled down the companionway and into her stateroom. There she'd have privacy. Nat Howland, the man who had always reminded her of a Viking god, had proposed to her. Her! Quiet Abigail Palmer, who had thought she would remain a spinster forever. It didn't change anything, but the knowledge of it warmed her clear to her toes. No matter what else happened in her life, she would always remember this.

Elation fading, she sat on the edge of her bunk. Memory was fine. Reality was different. If she married Nat, she would surely fail him, and she couldn't bear it. Her future was still uncertain. What, she wondered, was she going to do?

"Let go the anchor," Nat called, and with a mighty splash the anchor hit the water, the length of chain rattling and clattering behind it. At the same time the yards creaked as sail was taken in, and the man at the helm gave the wheel an expert twist, pointing the bow into the wind. The ship's forward motion made her surge ahead, until she was brought up short by the anchor, now holding fast. The *Aquinnah* was moored at last, after the long passage from New Bedford and Brava.

From her vantage point in the whaleboat being rowed ashore, Abby looked wide-eyed at her first glimpse of what was surely paradise. They'd reached the Sandwich Islands two days ago, passing first by Hawaii, the biggest of the island chain, with its tops shrouded in mist, and then Maui, where once the whalers had tied up. Now they stood off Oahu and the town of Honolulu. Abby repeated the names to herself, liking their musical, exotic lilt. She had wanted to leave New Bedford. For the first time, she knew she had.

Or had she? She frowned as they neared land. Certainly the waterfront didn't look so very different from any she'd seen in New England. Wharves extended out from the shore, where buildings of wood and stone clustered, in lines and angles that she recognized. Warehouses and counting-houses, she thought. Ship chandleries and repair yards. More than likely, too, brothels and taverns, which meant they'd have problems with the crew. It might have been just another port, except for the mountains behind the town, forming the island's spine. Before even setting foot on land, Abby somehow knew that Hawaii was not like any other place she'd known.

The mountains rose steeply in folds and valleys of earth, vividly, achingly green: deep emerald, bright peridot, pale celadon. She had never seen such foliage before. Closer to shore were trees with long, tall trunks and a canopy of broad leaves. Palm trees, she imagined. Interspersed among them were the riotous colors of flowering bushes, crimsons and purples and golds, flowers whose names she could only guess at. And though the air carried with it the aromas of human habitation, she fancied she caught as well the perfume of those trees and flowers. She was suddenly eager to reach the shore.

The pilings of the wharf loomed above her, blocking the sun, the water dark in the shadows. A seaman tossed their line up; it was caught and the boat secured. Then hands were helping Abby up the wooden ladder, until she stood at last on land again. The air was warm, the breeze soft, and the sun strong. Paradise, and yet in an odd way she already missed her ship.

A dark-haired, dark-skinned man approached her, smiling, and before she could react dropped a garland of fragrant blossoms around her neck. Startled, she stepped back, into something solid. Nat, she knew immediately, without even looking around. Nat, as patient and even-tempered as always, smiling, not pressing her about marriage or anything else. It was what she wanted. It was also maddening. Here on land perhaps she could somehow manage to avoid him occasionally.

"It's called a lei," he said, reaching out to finger the necklace before she could move away. "A custom for greeting people on the islands."

"It's very nice," she said inanely, stepping away.

"Yes, I've always liked getting lei'd."

"Excuse me?"

"Nothing." He helped her up into a waiting carriage. "That is the royal palace over there. Iolani Palace."

"Iolani," she repeated, trying to force her tongue around the strange syllables. "My heavens."

He glanced down at her as they drove along—past the fort, flying the Hawaiian flag with its broad stripes; past grocery stores and dry goods shops and, as she'd suspected, taverns; past larger buildings built of a porous-looking stone that Nat had told her was coral. "What?"

"It just struck me what an adventure I'm having. Is that a Hawaiian woman?" she asked, looking at an older, heavy-set woman crossing the dusty street before them. She was dressed in a long, full cotton-print gown, with leg-o'-mutton sleeves. "I thought they wore grass skirts, and—well, grass skirts."

He grinned at her discomfiture. "So they did, and a fine sight it was—"

"Captain."

"They dress that way because of the missionaries. The men make fine sailors," he added, glancing at a tall man passing by. "We'll likely take on a few, when we see who's jumped ship."

"You think we'll have deserters?"

"I'm surprised the farm boy from Lakeville has lasted as long as he has."

"But he signed the ship's articles."

Nat shrugged. "Not much we can do about it, if he decides to take off. Oh, hell."

"Nat," she said reprovingly. Then she glanced in the same direction. Ahead of them rose a fine building of stone and wood, with a galleried verandah and a sign proclaiming it to be the Hawaiian Hotel. Standing at the top of the broad flight of stairs on the verandah, thumbs hooked in vest, was Jared Swift.

Chapter 14

Something lurched within Abby. "I didn't think he'd be here yet," she said.

"Didn't you?" Nat said grimly, helping her down from the carriage. "Since he is, we might as well play out the game."

"What game?" she said, but Jared was already approaching, hand outstretched. Abby's fingers tightened on Nat's arm.

"Abby." Jared's smile widened. "Well, look at you! Life at sea seems to agree with you."

"Yes," Abby said, a little startled, letting Jared take her hand. He pressed it only briefly before releasing her. Nor did he try to claim the brotherly kiss their relationship allowed him. "It's good to see you again, Jared."

"Good to see you, too, Abby. Captain Howland."

Nat inclined his head. "Captain Swift. Have you had greasy luck?"

Jared waggled his hand back and forth. "Tolerable, but I've seen better. How did you find it in the South Pacific?"

"We had a fair cruise."

"Seven whales," Abby put in, wondering why Nat was being so modest. "Almost three hundred barrels of oil."

"Good for you. We had some trouble off Chile." Jared's face sobered. "You'll be hearing it soon enough, so you might as well know the truth. One of the men went berserk."

Abby gasped. "Was anyone hurt?"

"No. He made for me. I had to shoot him, I'm afraid."

"Mutiny?" Nat asked, not smiling now.

"No. It never got that far. But I'll tell you, things looked tense for a time. Didn't help that we couldn't seem to raise

whales." He rolled his shoulders, looked out at the bay.
"I'd like to send out a boat in these waters."

"Jared, not to get the babies," Abby protested.

"No, that would be foolish. Too much work for too little
oil. But if we did catch a baby whale, you can be sure that
mama whale would be close behind." He smiled quickly at
her. "Wishful thinking, Abby. Of course I wouldn't do it."

"Of course not," Nat said, with absolutely no inflection.
"If you'll excuse us, Swift, we'd like to get to our rooms."

"Certainly." Jared stepped aside, tipping his hat. "You'll
like it here, Abby. More than enough to see, and there's
to be a reception at the palace on Friday."

"That sounds nice." Abby smiled at him and then let
Nat lead her into the hotel. "How very odd."

Nat looked down at her as they stepped into the shadowy
coolness of the lobby. "What?"

"Nothing." How polite Jared had been, she thought, as
Nat went to secure rooms. Pleasant and friendly, as if those
moments on Brava had never happened. But then, she had
just arrived. She shivered.

"Cold?" Nat said, returning to her.

"No. Oh, there's Sarah!" Abby pulled away, tired of men
for the moment. "I haven't seen her since we left Brava."

"Abby!" Sarah Hathaway held out her hands to Abby,
and the two women touched cheeks. "How good to see
you, and how well you look! The sea agrees with you."

"Yes, it does, and you, too. You're blooming, Sarah."

"More like exploding." Sarah glanced wryly down at the
bulk of her stomach. She was obviously not far from giving
birth, and the thought gave Abby an unexpected pang. To
have a child. Nat's child. *Heavens!*

"Yes, though Isaiah and I are arguing about it." Sarah
took her arm as they walked out onto the verandah. "He's
put me on the beach for the duration."

"Here in Hawaii? But that's wonderful!" Abby looked
past the streets and buildings to the vista of glossy dark
palm leaves and glittering blue water. "It's heaven here."

"It is, and there are other ladies staying as well. You
should consider it, too."

"The *Aquinnah* is my ship," Abby said, but she was
tempted. There'd be no Jared to deal with, once the fleet
left. No Nat. That strange pang went through her again,

stronger this time. "And, cold or not, I think I would like to see the Arctic."

"Brrr. I think I'm glad I'm not going. Summer at Point Barrow is—well, think of November at home."

"Oh, dear. But I'll manage, I think." She leaned forward, smiling mischievously. "My cousin Elizabeth gave me a suit of bloomers."

Sarah's hand flew to her mouth. "She didn't!"

"She did. And"—the pause lengthened—"I've worn it."

Sarah let out a laugh that attracted attention from the other people on the verandah. "Oh, Abby, you didn't!"

"I did." Abby grinned. This was almost like old times, when she and Sarah had attended Friends' Academy together. Both of them had been good students and dutiful daughters, but both had also been called on the carpet for mischief more than once. "Nat—Captain Howland—caught me wearing them."

Sarah's hand fell, and a different look came into her eyes. "Hmm."

"It wasn't like that," Abby protested, sorry she'd brought the subject up. Sarah had a matchmaking gleam in her eye. "It was cold. They were practical."

"Mm-hm."

"Well, it was."

"Mm-hm. And what did he think?"

"He ordered me to change," she said ruefully.

"Yes, but did he like it?"

"Sarah."

"He likes you, Abby."

"I know." Abby glanced out to sea, serious. She was not going to tell anyone, not even Sarah, about the situation between her and Nat. "I like him, but not the way you mean."

"Well, I think that's a shame. He's a good man."

"What about his drinking?"

"Shame on you, Abby. He's overcome it, hasn't he? Else you wouldn't have hired him."

"Well, yes." It had been a rotten thing to say, Abby admitted. "I hear there's to be a party this Friday?"

Sarah brightened. "Yes, at the royal palace. Did you ever think, Abby, that someday we'd meet a king?"

"Never. What is he like?"

"Oh, very pleasant, though he can be stern when he wants to be. I think you'll find him interesting."

"I'm sure I will."

"Is Captain Howland going to escort you?"

"I have no idea." She frowned. "Sarah, no matter what you might think, he and I are nothing but business partners."

"Mm-hm."

"I mean it!"

"Mm-hm. Are you seriously telling me that after all those months at sea, nothing's happened?"

Abby recoiled. She would not—would not!—remember that shattering, devastating kiss. "What are people saying about me, Sarah? That I've become a loose woman?"

"No! Oh, no." Sarah's hand fluttered out to rest on Abby's arm. "I am sorry, I never meant that. No, of course no one's saying any such thing. I'm just being nosy."

"Oh."

"Everyone has the highest regard for you, Abby."

Abby relaxed. No one suspected, thank heavens. "Good."

"But I do think he's handsome. I wonder why he hasn't . . ."

"What?" Abby asked, as Sarah regarded her speculatively.

"You really should wear the bloomers more often."

"Sarah!"

"He won't pay attention to you when you dress like that. Black isn't your color, Abby."

"I'm aware of that, but I'm in mourning. What will people say if I start wearing colors before the year is done?"

"You didn't let that stop you when you went to sea."

"That's different."

"Oh, yes, far less important," Sarah said dryly.

"Sarah." She spoke with forced patience. "I owe my father the respect."

"Do you? After what he did to you?"

"Yes."

"You owe it to yourself to get on with your life. Oh, there's Isaiah." Sarah turned as she saw her husband. "And Captain Howland. Do think about it, Abby."

"Think about what?" Nat asked, as Sarah and Captain Hathaway strolled away.

She shook her had. "Nothing. Are the rooms ready?"

"Yes. They're bringing your trunk up now."

"Good." She walked beside him back into the hotel. "I'm looking forward to washing in fresh water again."

"Don't get too spoiled."

"I intend to enjoy myself." She stopped at the bottom of the stairs as her conversation with Sarah whirled through her head. Why had she not married? Not for lack of chances, even now, when she was a spinster with no fortune. She just must not want to, she concluded once again. She didn't have to behave as if her life were over, though. Going to sea had proved that. And what would Nat think if she wore something besides black?

"Why are you looking at me like that?" Nat asked, leaning forward with his hand on the newel post.

"I'm sorry." Abby stepped back, her fantasy of wearing a crimson silk ball gown dissolving. Silly. "I was woolgathering."

"Hm." Nat held out his arm. "I'll see you to your room."

"Thank you." She let her fingers rest lightly on his arm. Through the wool of his sleeve she seemed to feel the very pulse of him. Strange, and intriguing. Her life was hers to do with as she chose, she thought, enjoying this moment of awareness, knowing it wouldn't last. She could let the current take her, as she always had, or she could chart her own course. With Nat beside her, the world suddenly seemed filled with possibilities. Where would events lead her now?

Jared strode down Fort Street toward the harbor, his handsome face twisted into something so ugly and forbidding that even tall men stepped out of his path. Just as well. His mood was as ugly as his expression, as ugly as the demon rioting inside him. Oh, he kept close watch on that demon, a mixture of anger, jealousy, and pride, and who knew what else. He'd learned early enough that it was dangerous, had seen it at work in his father, battering at his mother until she took refuge in illness. Never enough, never good enough. Jared had vowed long ago that no one would ever say that about him. To his knowledge, no one had, or had even thought it, except perhaps himself. He had it all, did he not? Success in his career, a fine home, a promising future. He needed one thing more for his life to be complete, a wife from the proper background. He needed Abigail, but she wouldn't cooperate. She seemed to prefer Howland instead.

Fury rose in him, rode him hard as he continued on his way. In the harbor the ships of the whaling fleet rode at anchor; he found his own, the *Naushon,* without so much as a second glance, so familiar was it to him. His ship, his girl. That was how it was supposed to be. Had the man been anyone other than Howland, maybe he wouldn't have minded so much. Howland acted as if he owned Abby, taking her arm, smiling down at her. What made it worse was that Abby seemed to like the man's attention. Jared would have to do something about that.

Carefully, though. If he attacked Howland openly, Abby would take the man's side and act as if he, Jared, were in the wrong. All that, when he was only looking out for her. Howland was a sot. That he had dried out didn't matter. Jared had seen it before. Once a drunkard, always a drunkard.

The thought made him stop suddenly in the middle of the street, causing a man driving a cart behind him to swerve. Now *there* was a thought. There might just be a way to discredit Howland. Once he had, once Abby knew what kind of man she had hired, then he could step in, taking care of her as he'd always wanted. He would best Howland at last.

His good mood restored, Jared began walking again, aware at last of his surroundings. Here, near the fort, clustered small buildings housing inns and taverns and brothels, all to service the seamen who stopped here. In the windows of one building several girls with bright flowers in their hair looked out, their dusky skin proclaiming them to be of Hawaiian or mixed ancestry. Jared rather enjoyed the native women's hospitality; he liked a woman who was built like a woman. Like Abby, before she had slimmed down. Today he was in a mood to celebrate. Had he not discovered a way to best his enemy?

"You, there, *wahine,*" he said, using the Hawaiian word for "woman" and snapping his fingers at the middle of the three women. She was a little older than the others and fuller-figured. "You come with me."

"You come in, sailor," the woman said, her smile promising mysterious delights. "Come in and let Leila take care of you."

"Oh, I will." His smile was grim as he stepped into the brothel. He'd let her take care of him. And then, he'd take care of Howland.

"There." Sarah stepped back and nodded. "I knew there was a way we could get you into another color."

"I still don't know—oh." Abby fell silent as she turned to face the mirror. At Sarah's insistence she had agreed to visit a dressmaker's salon, though she was certain she wouldn't find anything appropriate. Besides, she had gowns, day dresses and morning dresses and even a black satin evening gown. Too many gowns for sea, she'd long ago admitted, but she thought the evening gown would be fine for the reception at the Iolani Palace. So she'd argued, until she'd seen the model of lilac silk in the shop. It wasn't particularly stylish. The bustle was smaller than those shown in *Godey's Lady's Book,* and it wasn't terribly beruffled. But it suited her. Her back end was quite large enough, thank you, without adding a contraption of wire and steel, while her bosom need no improving from ruffles. And lilac was close to the shade for half-mourning . . .

Lilac also suited her brown hair and fair skin, bringing color to her cheeks and sparkle to her eyes. The gown, which was, fortunately, not extremely low-cut, fit tightly in the bust while the front of the skirt fell straight to the floor. The bustle was definitely there, but instead of emphasizing her anatomy, it flattered her. The entire gown flattered her as nothing else ever had. "I've lost weight," she said inanely.

Sarah patted her stomach. "And I've gained."

"I knew my clothes were loose, but I never realized." She smiled. "And there I was at sea, wishing I had chocolates."

"The gown looks better on you than chocolate does."

Abby turned to look at her reflection from another angle. "Yes, it does, doesn't it?"

"It needs some adjusting. It's much too long. How long will it take for you to alter it?" Sarah asked the dressmaker.

The dressmaker glanced toward the back of the shop. "You would want it for the reception?"

"Yes," Abby said, before she could change her mind.

"Well—certainly. It will be done before then."

"Is there a problem?" Sarah asked.

Again, the dressmaker glanced toward the back. "No, no problem. My best seamstress, Malia—but it is nothing to concern yourselves about. She can do her work."

Abby and Sarah looked at each other in concern. An illness of some unknown nature could be dangerous, especially to Sarah. "Is she ill?"

"No, not, nothing like that. Malia's daughter was hurt rather badly last night."

"Oh, dear. Was it an accident?"

The dressmaker set her lips. "No. But these things happen sometimes when girls take up with sailors."

"A sailor hurt her?" Abby exclaimed, turning.

"Yes, though she can't say who. Her jaw is broken."

Sarah and Abby both winced in sympathy. "The poor girl. I'll see what I can find out about it."

The woman looked skeptical. "You may try, but these things do happen."

Abby squared her shoulders. "Not aboard my ship," she said, very much aware of her responsibilities. She wasn't really surprised that seamen consorted with the island girls, or that trouble sometimes resulted. There was no God west of Cape Horn, whalers were fond of saying, as a way of justifying their behavior after months at sea. She knew the men needed the liberty ashore as much as she did. If she learned, though, that the sailor who'd beaten the island girl was in her employ, she would do something about it. No one in her crew would be allowed to do such a thing without facing the consequences.

"Will you take the gown?" the dressmaker asked.

Shaken from her thoughts, Abby looked in the mirror again. She shouldn't. It wasn't a mourning gown. It wasn't even half-mourning. A proper New England woman would keep to her blacks for the full year. New England was behind her, though, and Papa was gone. No amount of mourning outfits could bring him back. "Yes," she said, nodding, and decided at that moment that an entire new wardrobe was called for. "I'll be happy to."

Sometime later the two women emerged into the dazzling sunshine, onto a street lined with bushes flowering with unfamiliar blossoms. Bird of paradise, Sarah said, pointing to an oddly shaped orange plant, and hibiscus, and, of course, orchids everywhere. She would have missed this had she listened to all those sane, wise people who had counseled her to stay home. "It's paradise here," she said, as she and Sarah set off toward the hotel.

"Yes, it is. You'll be staying, won't you?"

"When?"

"When the fleet goes north."

"Please, let's not start that again." After Hawaii's warmth, the Arctic would be a frigid hell. "I don't want to leave my ship." Or, if she were honest, the ship's captain.

"The ship will do fine without you."

"Maybe, but it's all I have."

"That's not true," Sarah chided. "Your friends care. And if you're not interested in Captain Howland—"

"Sarah—"

"—here's someone else for you."

"What?" Abby followed Sarah's gaze, and her heart sank. For just a moment, she had expected to see Nat. "Jared." She mustered up a smile. "How are you this morning?"

"Well, thank you." He stood before them, smiling, handsome. "You're about early."

"We had an appointment at the dressmaker's," Sarah said. "We thought Abby needed something special for the reception."

Jared frowned. "I wasn't aware Abby was going to the reception."

"Why shouldn't I?" Abby said, annoyed at his assumption, annoyed that he would discuss her as if she weren't even present. "I am a ship's owner."

"It isn't seemly."

"Seemly?"

"I see Catherine Bowen across the street," Sarah said hastily. "I must go speak with her. Will you excuse me?"

"You don't have to go because of us."

"Of course," Jared said at the same time. "A pleasure to see you again, Mrs. Hathaway."

"And you, Captain," Sarah said and walked away with an admonishing shake of her head at Abby.

Abby frowned as she turned to walk with Jared. "I shall have to apologize to her. We were rude to argue in front of her."

"I'm not arguing with you, Abby."

"No. Just ordering me about."

"I don't mean to," he said, suddenly earnest. "But I wonder if you've thought this through. You're still in mourning."

"Not anymore," she said, reckless now. "You told me about the reception yourself, Jared. I won't wear black, either."

Jared's face hardened. "Yes, you will."

Abby's lips twitched in annoyance. She was trying hard to be patient with him, but it was difficult. Thank heavens they were at the hotel. "I beg your pardon?"

"You'll wear black," he said, steering her into the garden.

"I don't want to go here," she protested.

"We need to talk. If you're so bent on ruining your reputation—"

"Jared, it's none of your affair."

"Oh, but it is," he said and pulled her roughly against him. "For once, Abby, you'll do as I say."

Chapter 15

Abby tensed. The hotel shielded them from view, and Jared was larger and stronger than she. In the past months, though, she had discovered within herself unknown reserves of strength. "You can't do that, Jared."

"Do you have such disrespect for your father's memory, then?" Jared accused.

Her face softened. "Oh, Jared, is that what this is about?"

"Consider how it looks." He stared stonily ahead. "Ask yourself how your father would feel."

"He's gone, Jared." She spoke gently. "Nothing can change that."

He frowned. "I know that."

"We have to go on. I can't live in mourning forever. And we have more important things to discuss."

"Abby." He stopped and turned toward her, his face lightening. "About us?"

"Jared," she said, exasperated, though still gentle, "that's past as well. No, I was referring to the incident last night."

Beside her Jared scuffed a toe at the dirt, like a little boy. "What incident?"

"The island girl who was hurt. I wonder if—"

"How do you know about her?" he demanded.

"Her mother is employed by the dressmaker. It's a terrible thing, Jared. Have you heard who did it?"

"It's not something for you to be concerned with."

"Of course it is, if it's one of my men."

"Then let Howland handle it."

Unbidden into her mind came the memory of Nat, his hands on her arms, his lips sliding, oh, so softly, so sweetly, along her jaw, to her lips. Oh, yes, Nat could handle anything. Including her. "If it is one of my men, of course

Nat will handle it," she said coolly. "But I do bear some responsibility."

"Why?"

"Jared, really. Because I'm the owner."

"Abby, I'm a skipper, and I can't be responsible for everything my men do. We can pay reparations if necessary, but it probably won't be. After all, the girl is only a pros— a woman of ill repute."

"I'm well aware she's a prostitute, Jared," she said tartly. "I'm also aware that sailors can be wild. But I see no need to allow any of my men to go without punishment."

"Leave it to us, Abby."

"Oh, yes, let you handle it, and perhaps another girl gets hurt."

He frowned. "But who else can you trust?"

"Nat, of course."

"Really? After last night?"

Abby stopped. "Are you implying—"

"The man is trouble, Abby. You know that."

"No, I don't know any such thing. Are you saying he's the one to blame for what happened to that girl?"

"No. Even I don't think that poorly of him. Though . . ."

"For mercy's sake, Jared, if you have something to say, then do so!" she snapped, suddenly impatient. "If you're going to accuse Nat of something—"

"Admit it, Abby. The man has an unsavory past."

"He's been nothing but a gentleman to me," she said, feeling her face go stiff in an effort to keep her memories from showing again. Oh, yes, he'd been a gentle man. He hadn't tried to force her, or persuade her to do anything she didn't want to. What he had done instead was infinitely worse. He had shown her a side of herself she had never known existed and in doing so had turned her world upside down.

"Of course not. You own the ship. Which he wants."

Abby shrugged. Nat had never made a secret of that. But would he really use her as a way to get what he wanted? No, she wouldn't believe that of him. Nor could she believe he'd beaten an island girl. "And because he wants it he'll take care of this problem," she said and pulled away, stepping out of the garden. "Thank you for your escort here, Jared."

"I won't leave you alone, Abby, until you're safe inside."

"But I won't be alone." She raised her hand. Nat was

walking toward them, his bearing confident, easy, his face somber. Something unclenched inside her, startling her. Jared was her longtime friend, yet she could depend on Nat. No matter what happened between them, that much was true.

Nat halted a few paces away. "What's wrong?" he asked, looking from one to the other, his eyes narrowed.

Jared started to speak, but Abby, tired of the animosity between the two men, stepped forward. "We were discussing what happened to that poor island girl last night."

Nat's face was grim. "It's a bad business. I've been trying to find out the whereabouts of the crew."

"Oh, have you?" Abby exclaimed, more relieved than she cared to admit. Jared's insinuations had, after all, made her uneasy. "Have you learned anything?"

"No. So far none of our men seems to be involved."

"Thank mercy for that."

"George Pickens is missing. The hand from Lakeville."

"Do you think he's jumped ship?"

"It's likely."

"Maybe he's the guilty party," Jared put in. "Which would be convenient."

Nat glanced at him and then away, dismissing him. "I'll keep looking into it, Abby, unless you don't want me to."

"No, please do." She slipped her hand through his arm almost without thinking. "What do the others think?"

"Same as us." He nodded to include Jared. "That we can't let this sort of thing happen."

"Excuse me," Jared said curtly and stalked away.

"Mercy." Abby stared after him. "What was that about?"

Nat shrugged, but there was an odd smile on his face as they walked toward the hotel. "What's got him so riled up?"

"Oh, silly things. Mostly he's angry because I'm going to wear a lilac gown to the reception Saturday."

"Instead of black? Good for you."

"You don't think I'm showing disrespect for my father?"

"It's almost a year since he died, Abby."

"Yes, and I don't think he'd want me to behave as if my life had ended too."

"Don't you?"

She glanced up at him as they climbed to the hotel's wide verandah. "No. Why? Do you?"

"I think he'd enjoy it, yes."

"Captain—"

"Your father liked to have people toe the line, Abby. He also liked things to revolve around himself."

She frowned. "Do you think he'd disapprove of my being here?"

"Yes."

"And wearing colors."

"Yes."

"You make him sound like a tyrant."

"It's your life to live now, Abby." His hand slipped down to grip hers; his gaze was steady. "Your choices to make."

Abby swallowed, her throat dry. Yet again her memories returned her to the cabin of the *Aquinnah,* where Nat stood before her, kissing her sweetly, making her feel things she'd never known. Her choices? Maybe. Nat hadn't forced her into anything; he didn't have to, and that made the threat he posed even more potent. And Jared wanted to handle everything for her. Even her father was trying to control her, from the grave. She was suddenly weary of all of it. "Fine. Then you may as well know right now that the *Aquinnah* is not for sale."

He frowned. "What are you talking about?"

"I'm well aware that you want the ship, Captain. I think you should know that I've no intention of selling."

"Not now, no. But when we get home—"

"Not then." She cut across his words, her voice dry, decisive. "My life, Captain. My choices."

He studied her for a moment, his eyes puzzled. "You may find that the best choice is to let her go."

"To let men control things, you mean. Maybe. Maybe not. I do know that I have no intention of marrying you just so you can get the ship."

His eyes went frosty. "You insult both of us, Abby," he said quietly, and dropping her arm, turned on his heel. Abby opened her mouth to call him back as he stalked away, aware that what she had said was indeed an insult of the highest order, and then sighed. She didn't understand anyone anymore—not Jared, who was so often more a stranger than her old friend, not Nat, and certainly not herself. All she knew was that her life was vastly different from what she had ever expected, and just now that was dismaying. The future suddenly seemed fraught with unknown perils.

Friday evening, Nat stood near a window in the reception room of Iolani Palace, glass of punch in hand, trying not to tug at the neck of his shirt. The palace was grandly named, being in reality a long, low building, with the pitched roofs typical of island architecture. The windows were tall and open to the breeze, which was a relief. More accustomed to the casual attire of shipboard, Nat was finding his white shirt with its stiff collar and his black wool frock coat uncomfortably warm. When he'd so longed to return to sea, he'd forgotten about moments like this.

Leaning against the wall, he scanned the room. Swift stood with other whaling captains, all of them laughing at some joke, while of Abby there was yet no sight. At the last moment she had chosen to come to the reception with Captain and Mrs. Hathaway rather than with him, a decision that still nettled him. But then, she'd acted cool toward him for quite some time now, ever since he'd proposed to her. Nat took a large gulp of punch, wishing it were stronger. Whiskey, brandy—hell, it wouldn't matter. Just one drink, to get him through the night. The last month, wanting her, knowing she didn't feel the same, had been hell. His feelings hadn't changed. If anything, he wanted her even more. It was all too easy to imagine her in his bed, her hair loose, her eyes warm and liquid with need for him. Nat closed his eyes at the feeling of that same need within him. How would he get through the next three years with her aboard ship, so close, yet so very far?

There was no special sound to make him open his eyes, but he did, in time to see a small party of people enter the room. Captain Hathaway and his wife, and—good God. Abby, in her gown that wasn't really lilac, or even purple, but instead a mulberry satin, shimmering and shining as she moved, cut so it left her shoulders bare and hinted at her cleavage. Abby, with her hair dressed in a soft, loose way he'd never seen, curls framing her face and bringing a sparkle to her eyes. Abby, with her soft white skin and the sweet, full curve of her bosom. The need he'd felt a moment before returned, stronger, more intense. How in God's name had he ever thought her plain?

Instinct made him set his glass down somewhere and cross the room, to claim her. Abby was his. He didn't know how to convince her of that, but he would. She belonged to him, and he wanted to possess her utterly, body, soul, heart. He wanted her in his bed, yes, but he wanted her by his side, too, sharing their lives, running the ship, raising children, growing old. It wouldn't happen if he didn't do something about it.

"Abby." He held his hand out to her, certain she must hear the pounding of his heart. "You look well."

Abby's hand rested lightly and briefly on his. "Thank you," she said. Her brow was slightly furrowed, making him bite back a smile. Good. So she had neither liked, nor expected, such lukewarm praise from him. "So do you."

He shrugged. "Necessary evil." This close, her gown, dear God, more than hinted at cleavage. She was magnificent. Not the plain girl he'd once thought; not the shy spinster. She was a woman, and she was his.

"Everyone looks splendid, all dressed up. Jared."

"Abby." Jared had come up to them without Nat's realizing it, so concentrated had he been on Abby. Swift wasn't frowning exactly, but his eyes·held a curious mixture of emotions. Disapproval, certainly, and—desire? Nat tensed. The thought of Swift setting his sights on Abby was repulsive.

"You should be presented to the king," he said, taking Abby's arm before Jared could make a move. "He's probably never met a female whaleship owner before."

Abby seemed to gather herself together. "Yes, of course," she said, a bit startled, as if she had forgotten about business. Nat's lips quirked in regret. She had obviously looked forward to this evening. It was a shame that his strategy to gain her trust was taking away some of her pleasure. Before this night was over, though, he intended to let her know how he really felt. "How should I behave? Should I curtsy?"

Nat entertained a brief fantasy of the cleavage a curtsy would reveal and let out his breath. "No. Just be polite. Swift." He nodded at Jared over his shoulder. "He's more concerned with the old ways, though he tolerates foreigners."

"I never thought I'd be meeting a king."

"You look grand enough for it. There he is," he said, indicating a large, heavy man in military uniform, standing across the room. "King Kamehameha."

"Kamehameha," Abby repeated, stumbling a bit on the pronunciation. "Who is the woman with him?"

"His sister-in-law, Queen Emma. He's never married. Do you want me to introduce you?"

"Yes." Abby raised her head. "Please do."

He nodded and led her across the room, watching as she talked easily with the king about the state of the whale fishery. Amazing, the transformation in her. It wasn't just external, though that was obvious; it was within as well. He'd seen her raise her head in just that way many times— when she had made the decision to go to sea, when she had agreed to his dangerous wager on kissing. Only now did he realize that the gesture meant she was gathering her courage. To confront something one feared took real bravery. Abby was more special than he'd known.

"She's holding her own," a voice said beside him, and Nat turned to see Jared.

"Aye, and then some." For once in agreement with the man, Nat took a sip from his glass, which he had reclaimed. "I doubt anyone knew what she was capable of before her father died. Not even herself."

"Benjamin Palmer was a good man."

"Aye. But he never let her live her own life."

"This is unseemly," Jared said, his voice a low hiss. "You know it as well as I do, but you encourage her in it."

"In what?" Nat said mildly, knowing that would only anger the other man further.

"In behaving in ways that will make her life difficult."

Nat glanced toward Abby, talking with Queen Emma, and shrugged. "She looks fine to me." He took a sip of his punch and grimaced. "Tastes as if the fruit in this has gone bad."

Jared drank from his own glass. "Mine seems fine. Of course," he smiled, "I have liquor in mine. But, excuse me. That was tactless of me to say."

"It doesn't bother me." Nat raised his glass to hide his expression. Liquor. It no longer ruled his life, but seldom did an hour pass that he didn't think of taking a drink, of the biting taste of whiskey and the warm glow that followed. Of the way it eased any pain, dulled the sharp edges of life. And Swift knew it, damn his eyes. "Stop worrying about Abby," he said abruptly. "She's doing fine."

Jared still smiled, though his eyes were cold. "But what happens when she returns to New Bedford, and she finds that people cut her because of what she's done? She'll need help then, but not from you. No. She'll need me then."

"Maybe." Nat set his empty glass down. The orchestra in the gallery was starting up the first measures of a Virginia reel. "But that's three years away. Right now she needs someone to dance with. Excuse me," he said and walked away, feeling good, feeling strong and confident and in control, as he hadn't in a very long time. He could almost feel Swift glaring at him, and that only made claiming Abby's hand and leading her into the dance that much sweeter. Abby was his, he vowed as he stood across from her in the line of dancers. He would not let Swift have her.

"Thank you." Abby smiled up at Captain Bowen, who had just escorted her to the row of chairs lining the wall. "I enjoyed the dance."

"Which one?" Sarah asked, sitting down beside her. "You haven't missed one yet."

"I'm sitting this next one out. I'm warm, not to mention how my feet feel!" She glanced at Sarah. "I still haven't forgiven you for telling the dressmaker to make changes to my gown. The lilac silk would have been much more suitable. And as for lowering the neckline—"

"But you look so well in it. I think you're the most popular woman here this evening."

"I doubt that. Silk would have been cooler, too."

"Stop complaining," Sarah said cheerfully. "You're enjoying yourself and you know it."

"I know." Abby's mouth quirked back. "I wonder what everyone in New Bedford would think if they saw me now?"

"They're thousands of miles away, Abby. You don't need to worry about them."

"But she should," a voice said, and they looked up to see Jared. He smiled as he held a glass of punch out to her. "Here. I thought you looked thirsty."

"Thank you." Abby took the glass, grateful and annoyed

at the same time. She wished Jared would stop hovering over her. She wished Nat would—what? She didn't know. What she wanted from Nat was a vast, confusing mystery to her. "Where is Nat?"

Jared glanced around the room. "I don't know. I saw him go out some time ago."

She frowned. "I wonder why."

"I wouldn't worry about him. Would you care to step outside for some air?"

That Nat was gone was vexing. Strange, when she'd found his presence an irritant earlier. That didn't have to stop her from enjoying herself, though, and getting out into a cool breeze sounded pleasant. "Yes, I would. Sarah, do you mind?"

"No, of course not." Sarah's eyes were bright with interest and what looked like anticipation, deepening Abby's annoyance. Why, she didn't know, except that she was tired of people's abiding interest in her life, no matter how well-meaning they might be. "Do enjoy it."

"Thank you." Abby hoped her smile was cool as she rose and placed her fingers on Jared's arm. His gaze never strayed below her chin, whereas Nat's eyes had been admiring and frankly appraising. Again she was vexed, and again, she didn't know why. Or with whom. "I must warn you, Jared, my mood seems strange tonight."

"You're not used to this life." Jared spoke calmly as they stepped out onto a wide, shadowed verandah, overlooking sweet-smelling darkness. The garden, Abby presumed. "You were brought up to live quietly."

"Yes, I was, but that life is gone."

"It doesn't mean you have to change into something else."

She considered that, thinking of the past months, thinking of the years spent living under her father's thumb. Nat was right. Papa would have wanted her to stay in mourning, and not get on with her life. Maybe that was why she was so uncomfortable tonight, so unsettled. "I'm not sure I have, Jared," she said finally. "I've always been what my parents wanted me to be. Now I'm finding out who I am."

"You're fine as you are, Abby. I care for you, just as you are."

"As I am now, Jared, or as I was before?"

"As you really are," he said gently, disconcerting her. "Sweet, kind, gentle." He held her hand in a tight grip. "You can't deny you're all those things."

"No, but—"

"No buts." He laid his finger on her lips, and she went instantly still. "I love you, Abby. Don't you know that yet?"

"Oh, Jared." This time she did pull back, the spell broken. "I know you think you do, but—"

"Allow me the courtesy of knowing my own feelings," he said coolly.

"Of course! I'm sorry, I didn't mean to insult you. I do care about you, Jared, but as a friend, or a sister. After all, we grew up together."

"But we're not brother and sister, Abby." His grip on her hand tightened. "We never were."

Abby's mouth went dry. "No."

"There is no reason we can't love each other as adults. As man and woman."

The verandah railing was hard at her back. Until this moment, she hadn't realized that Jared had pressed her backward. "I don't feel that way, Jared."

"I don't care."

"What!"

"I've had a long time to think about it, Abby, and I've decided that whether you want me or not is unimportant. I'll make you love me, but what matters is that I want you."

"Let me go, Jared." She pushed at his chest, but he was implacable, immovable. "Jared—"

"I should have finished what I started eight years ago," he said and bent his head to hers.

"Jared, no!" she exclaimed, panicked in a way she could not explain. All she had to do was cry out, and help would be at hand. Eight years ago, she thought, twisting her head away from his. What had happened eight years ago? "Let me go."

Jared's hand caught her head, his fingers twining into her hair, holding her painfully still. "Not this time," he said as his mouth slammed onto hers, hard and wet, not at all like Nat's. She imagined she heard Nat's voice, and that only added to the unreality of the moment. Jared's kiss did not at all affect her the way Nat's did—and why should that matter?

Of a sudden the awful pressure was gone from Abby's face, from her body. She could breathe again. Shaking, she raised her hand to her mouth, rubbing away the taste of the kiss, and only then realized what was happening. Nat had Jared pinned up against the wall of the palace with one hand, his other drawn back and bunched into a fist. Oh, thank heavens! He'd seen what was happening and come to her rescue. Jared deserved it, but she knew that if they fought, what had happened here this evening would become common knowledge. "No! Nat, no," she said, grabbing his arm. "Please."

He looked at her, still holding Jared by the throat. He must be very strong, she thought dimly. "Stay out of this, Abby."

"No." She clung to his arm, though he tried to shake her off. "If you two fight, what do you think will happen?"

"It won't be a fight." Nat's speech was clipped, precise. "I'm going to kill him."

"Nat, think of what people will say."

"I don't care what anyone says about me—"

"Not about you, Nat. About me."

That seemed to penetrate. His hand relaxed. "No one would blame you, Abby."

"Of course they would. When something like this happens, people always blame the woman."

"They won't know you were involved. Shut up." This to Jared, who was making a peculiar gurgling, gagging sound.

"Nat, you're choking him!"

"Good," he said, but he eased the pressure. Jared pulled in a deep, tortured breath. "He deserves it."

"Let him go, Nat. Please."

"I can't. Abby, he was trying to molest you."

"Abby." Jared's voice was hurt. "I'd never hurt you."

"Watch it." Nat glared at Jared, his grip tightening just a bit. "I haven't deshided— decided—to let you go."

"He's drunk." Jared pulled back. "Abby, he's drunk."

"No, he isn't," Abby protested, and at the same time Nat suddenly let go. Jared stumbled a few paces away, hand to his throat. "He isn't."

"By God!" Nat looked stunned. "I *am* drunk."

"What!" Abby stepped back. "How can you be?"

He rubbed the back of his hand over his lips. "Damned if I know. All I drank all night was punch."

"Now he's lying, too." Jared's voice sounded more normal. "You can't trust him, Abby. He's a drunk and a liar."

"There must be some reason." Abby stood firm. Her mouth throbbed unpleasantly, and her arms were sore from Jared's grip, but she had to face this. "There has to be."

Jared laughed harshly. "Of course there's a reason. He's a drunk, and he saw liquor. It's all the reason he needs."

She turned, looking beseechingly up at Nat. "Nat?"

He shook his head and winced. "I can't explain it, Abby. I'm sorry."

She stepped back again. He had promised her he'd stay sober. Why did that broken promise hurt so? "Nat—"

"I warned you of this, Abby." Jared's face was calm, as if nothing had happened. Did he not realize what he'd done to her? "You can't trust him to skipper the *Aquinnah* now."

Coldness settled like a lump in Abby's stomach. If she let Nat go, what would she do? What would he do? He would never be given another command. "That's not your concern."

"Oh, but it is, Abby." Jared captured her hand again. "I love you. I do," he went on at Nat's derisive snort. "Marry me."

"No." Abby pulled back her hand. "For the last time, no."

"I'm not going to let you go. You're mine, Abby. I love you. Be quiet." This last was to Nat, who had snorted again. "Marry me, Abby. I won't let you go until you say yes."

He meant it, she thought. Not just for tonight, but for tomorrow, and next month, and next year. Wherever she went, there he was, whether on Cape Verde or Hawaii. Where she would go, there he would be, and she would always feel a little uneasy in his presence, a little frightened. She didn't know why, not when their friendship spanned so many years, but neither could she deny it. He would not let her go, and she would again live her life under a man's dominion. "I can't marry you, Jared." She placed her free hand on Nat's arm, linking them in an odd embrace. "I'm already engaged to Captain Howland."

Chapter 16

Jared dropped her hand. "I don't believe it."

"Oh, but it's true." Abby looked up at Nat, dark and silent beside her. "Isn't it?"

Nat was quiet for so long that she feared he wasn't going to answer. "Aye, so it is," he said finally. "Though you made me wait long enough for your answer, sweetheart."

She smiled at him, as if they were indeed lovers. "I know, and I'm sorry, but we'll have the rest of our lives."

"I don't believe this," Jared interrupted.

Abby turned to him. "Excuse me?"

"You can't marry him." Jared scowled. "He's a drunk."

Abby linked her arm tighter through Nat's. He wasn't defending himself against Jared's charge, but then, he couldn't, could he? "That's between him and me."

"You can't marry him, Abby," Jared said again, taking a step forward. "I love you."

To Abby's surprise, Nat's arm snaked about her waist. "Be careful what you say to my fiancée."

"Jared, I'm sorry," Abby put in, as Jared's face darkened with anger. "I should have told you about this earlier."

"I wouldn't have believed you then, either. You're mine."

"Not anymore." Nat's grip on her tightened. "Why don't you go find yourself another woman? An island girl, maybe?"

"Nat," Abby protested.

"To hell with you, Howland." Jared stood with fists bunched. "And you, Abby . . ."

Abby could feel Nat's muscles tensing. "Jared, I'm sorry, but you must accept this. Nat and I are going to be married."

"Better listen to her. Before you say something you regret."

Jared stared from one to the other. "This isn't the end of it," he said and, turning on his heel, was gone.

There was silence in the wake of his leaving, awkward and heavy. Abby had just betrothed herself to a man she didn't love, and possibly could never love. What was she going to do now? "I won't hold you to it," Nat said quietly, pulling away.

She turned. "Excuse me?"

"The engagement. I know why you agreed to it."

"Nat—"

"If you want to pretend to it while we're in Hawaii, I'll go along with it, but I won't hold you to it after that."

"I thought you wanted to marry me."

He turned toward the garden, his back to her. "Not this way, sweetheart. Not this way."

"Nat, I didn't do this just to get away from Jared."

"Didn't you?" He turned his head. "Seemed like it to me. He ever done that before?"

"No. He tried to kiss me once, but it was a long time ago." When she was sixteen. Eight years ago. Abby frowned. Was that what Jared had meant? "Nat, I want to marry you."

"Why?"

"I don't know," she said honestly. She didn't know why, but the prospect of spending her life with him was enormously appealing. "Maybe I'm tired of having to be proper all the time. Maybe I want to live my own life at last."

"You don't love me, Abby."

"No." She was quiet a moment. "Are you going to tell me now that you'll make me love you?"

"Sweetheart, I don't have that much power. And I'm not stupid enough to think my feelings will be enough."

"What are your feelings?" she asked, curious.

He gave a bark of laughter that held no humor. "You don't want to know right now."

Timidly, tentatively, she laid her hand on his arm. These were uncharted waters indeed. "I know we like each other. I know we get along well. And there's the ship."

"Ah, yes. The ship. That's why I want you, of course."

"Don't be silly. Nat, if we don't straighten this out, one of us will have to go."

"In other words, me." Again he laughed mirthlessly. "You are just like your father."

"What do you mean?"

"What you're saying is blackmail, Abby."

"I would never—oh. Oh, Nat, I didn't mean it that way." She pulled back. "I've made a botch of this."

"The *Aquinnah*'s a fine ship. You'll have no trouble finding a skipper for her. Hell, for that matter, Martel's ready for command."

"She's your ship, Nat." She paused. "If we can't resolve this, I'll stay behind."

He was quiet for a moment. "You really want to marry me?" he said finally, his head turned away from her.

Abby let her breath out. "Yes. I'll be a good wife to you."

"In all ways?"

Another breath. "Yes. All ways."

Again he was silent, and then his hand came out. Their fingers met, clasped, and instantly Abby felt enveloped, cocooned, and very, very safe. "Then we're engaged, God help us."

"Yes."

"We should be married here," he said, turning to face her.

"Here? In Honolulu?"

"Aye. It'll be bad for your reputation if we sail together engaged but not married."

"I don't really care—"

"I do."

"Then I could stay behind—"

"No. Here, Abby, and soon. Or not at all."

"Very well." She raised her chin. She'd gotten herself into this; she would have to see it through. Wasn't it what she wanted? "You're right, of course. It's just—"

"What?" he prompted.

"Nothing." *Frightening,* she had nearly said. Scary to make so major a change in her life, without taking time to think about it. But that was how she had decided to go to sea, and it had worked. So far. "No, you're right. But, Nat?"

"What?"

She hesitated. "The drinking."

His fingers tightened on hers, and then relaxed. "Looks like we'll have to take that day by day."

"I need to know I can depend on you," she said, and it wasn't just the ship she meant.

"You can, Abby." He let his breath out. "It's not the way I wanted things to be, but I'm glad we're marrying."

She turned her hand in his, tentatively clasping his fingers. "I am, too."

"We'll stand together and tell the rest of the world to go to hell, shall we?"

To her own surprise, Abby laughed. "Yes. Let's do that."

Nat sat on the edge of his bed, arms dangling loosely over his knees, head bent. Tell the world to go to hell. Aye, last night that had sounded fine. This morning, with his head pounding and his mouth tasting like bilgewater, he had his doubts. Maybe if he had a drink, to ease the hangover? No. He'd promised Abby. He'd promised himself. Yet here he was, beginning the battle all over again. Day by day, he reminded himself. Just get through today. Hell, getting through the next hour would be an accomplishment.

Rising at last, he splashed cold water on his face. It didn't make him feel any better, but at least he looked more presentable. He had some amends to make to Abby, and the hell of it was, it wasn't his fault. Oh, yes, he'd been drunk last night, but he hadn't set out to get that way. Someone had done that for him, and he had a very good idea who it was.

In the clear light of morning, it was easy to see how it had happened. He'd left his glass unattended several times. He was still annoyed that he hadn't recognized the taste of liquor, even if the punch had been strongly flavored. Funny, it hadn't taken much to get him drunk. Just three glasses. In the old days he'd have tossed that amount back like nothing and not felt a thing. Last night, though, he'd had trouble walking, and his speech had been overly precise. He was more susceptible now. He'd have to be cautious, on guard. One more slip, and he'd likely slide back down the high, high slope he'd climbed toward sobriety. It would mean the end of all his dreams. And there was only one person who would benefit by his failure.

Ignoring his ringing head, Nat continued to dress. He might feel like hell, but, by God, he wouldn't let anyone know it. Particularly not Swift. Who else would have wanted to see Nat drunk, and thus discredited, before Abby? Likely the man had managed to bribe someone who worked at the palace. Nat had known Swift was his enemy, but he had never really expected him to use such tactics. But then, his treatment of Abby last night had been ruthless. Nat's mouth firmed into a grim line as he finished tying his cravat. Good thing he'd come along when he had, drunk or sober, or God knows what would have happened to Abby. Swift deserved to be horsewhipped for that. He'd do it, too, except that Abby would be hurt by the resulting scandal. He had to protect his woman. His future wife.

He smiled. Damnation! Of all the things that could have happened last night, the very last thing he'd expected was that Abby would accept his proposal. Not quite willingly, true—but when he'd given her a chance to escape, she hadn't taken it. He wasn't sure if that were due to her sense of honor or to some other motive, but there was one thing he did know. She cared for him. Maybe not in the same way that he cared for her, but the basis was there. It was enough for a start.

Feeling marginally better, he left his room. Last night was past. If he complained that the punch had been spiked he would sound weak and unbelievable, even to Abby. Better to keep silent, no matter what she might think. He'd damaged her trust in him, and he would have to work to repair it. And, he thought grimly, going downstairs for a breakfast he didn't relish, he would have to do something about Jared Swift. Very soon.

Sarah was, predictably, delighted about Abby's engagement. "But why didn't you tell me?" she asked, as she and Abby sat in wicker chairs on the verandah the following morning.

"I didn't know how I was going to answer Nat." Abby looked out over the street. She hadn't thought she'd ever agree to marry anyone, let alone someone so vital, so virile, as Nat. What in the world was she doing? "I couldn't say anything."

"I understand, Abby, but I am your oldest friend."

"Yes, and when have you ever been able to keep a secret?"

"True," Sarah said without rancor. "It would have been a delicious piece of gossip. And I would have been so happy for you."

"Aren't you happy for me now?"

"Yes, but we have work to do. There's a wedding to plan."

"Nat and I are thinking of something quiet—"

"Oh, never! This will be the social event of the season."

"But I don't want any fuss," Abby protested.

"Abby, everyone is dying for something like this. Particularly the women. When the men sail away, it will be very quiet here. Not that you'll have a chance to find that out."

"No, it's my ship."

"And you'll be newly married." Sarah's face softened. "Are you scared?"

"Terrified," Abby admitted, knowing that she could pour out her innermost secrets to Sarah and they would be safe. For all that she loved gossip, Sarah was actually a good confidante. "I think I'm making a terrible mistake."

Sarah waved her hand. "Oh, that's normal."

"It is?"

"Yes. Sometimes I look down at myself"—she patted her stomach—"and wonder whatever made me think I can be a mother! Good heavens! I felt the same way about getting married. One day certain I was doing the absolutely right thing and the next terrified I was making a mistake."

"But you're happy. Aren't you?"

"Oh, yes. It works out, though it's not always what you expect, and it's not always easy. Men!" Sarah rolled her eyes. "They bellow, they give orders, and they can be positively stupid. I don't know why we put up with them."

"I dealt with my father for a number of years," Abby said.

"So you did." Sarah looked at her. "Captain Howland should be easy by comparison."

"Why is it everyone knew what my father was like but me?"

"You were too close to see. And he did love you."

"Yes, I know. That's what makes everything so hard."

"Captain Howland loves you, too."

"Oh, I don't know—"

"Of course you do! Haven't you ever noticed how he looks at you? No? Sometimes he looks so proud of you that you'd think he's going to burst. He did last evening, when you were talking with the king. Sometimes he looks as if he wants to take all your troubles on himself."

Abby blinked. "He does?"

"Oh, yes. When a man feels that way, you can be certain he cares. And sometimes when he looks at you, he wants you."

Abby's cheeks flamed. "Sarah!"

"It's normal, Abby. You don't look at him like that—"

"Sarah!"

"—but that's normal, too." Sarah leaned back, appraising her. "You don't know what to expect."

Abby put her hands over her eyes. "I cannot believe we're having this conversation."

"Someone has to talk to you, since your mother's gone."

Into Abby's mind flashed a memory that had always puzzled and warmed her simultaneously, of an ordinary evening at home, when her mother had looked at her father in a certain way and he had looked back. Good heavens! Her parents had wanted each other. "She—told me some things," she said in a strangled voice, reeling from the revelation.

"Did she?"

"Yes. I know what happens on a wedding night, Sarah, so you can spare us both the embarrassing details."

"Oh, I'm not embarrassed. Did she tell you it hurts the first time?"

Abby bit her lips. "It does?"

"She probably meant to. When Isaiah and I were married—"

"Sarah, I really don't want to hear this."

"Remember my wedding?" Sarah's smile was soft. "Oh, what a party that was! All the lamps in the house lit, and everyone we knew there—and the music. My grandfather was angry, you know, though I don't know if he minded the wasted oil or the music more. Pious old Quaker that he is."

"Your grandfather's toe was tapping from time to time."

"Was it? That old fraud." Sarah sounded delighted. "I must tease him about that when I see him. If I have the chance."

"You will." Abby laid her hand on Sarah's arm in sympathy. Home was so very far away. Anything could happen to people they cared about, and they'd not know for months. Sarah herself faced the risks of childbirth, far from her family. "Everything will be well."

"Yes. Well. As I was saying. It was such a party and it went on so late that when Isaiah and I left we were exhausted. So nothing happened that night."

"Sarah, please—"

"And then in the morning it didn't seem quite decent, in the daylight. We were inexperienced then and didn't know different. So we waited until that night—and it did hurt."

Abby's face was in her hands. The conversation was mortifying beyond belief, but she could not have walked away had her life depended upon it. "All of it?"

"No, not the parts before or after, the kissing and touching. Those were quite nice. Just the—well, you know. And even that wasn't so bad after a few minutes."

"Oh."

"But after that, it just kept getting better, and—"

"Better?" Abby interrupted, intrigued in spite of herself.

"Better," Sarah said firmly. "I quite like it, as a matter of fact. So you have no reason to be scared."

Abby took a long time answering. It wasn't that she was scared, precisely. She just knew that matters would not be the same for her as for Sarah. She was different. "Actually, I'm more concerned about what you're planning for the wedding."

"Oh, that." Sarah waved her hand. "Leave that to me."

"That's what worries me."

"Abby, you'll only marry once." Sarah was suddenly serious. "It should be something you'll remember forever."

"I hardly think I'll forget it."

"Well, we should make certain of that. Emma!" Sarah waved at another whaling wife who had just come onto the verandah. "We're planning Abby's wedding. Do help us."

Abby sighed as the other woman came to sit with them, and the discussion turned to flowers and music, silk and champagne. Her wedding, like so much of her life, was out of her hands. The only thing she could do was resign herself to Fate, and to trust Nat. If, after last night, she could trust him.

The wedding plans were proceeding apace, leaving Nat rather bemused. Had it been left to him, he and Abby would have married quietly. Once Sarah took charge, though, nothing either he or Abby said made any difference. There would be the ceremony in the Stone Church, with a breakfast after at the Hawaiian Hotel, and no arguing about it. Being only the groom, Nat escaped most of the fuss, but sometimes when he saw Abby her expression was despairing and stunned and amused, all at once. He didn't envy her the planning, especially since the other ladies seemed to take it so seriously. He would be glad when the whole ordeal was over, and he and Abby were alone.

Heat went through him at the thought. Alone with Abby, with no one to interfere, he would be free to do all that before he'd only imagined. To kiss her, touch her, stroke her breasts, and—*damnation*. Thank God his frock coat, though too warm for the climate, hid the results of such thoughts. He wanted her, now, and to hell with any ceremony. Abby was his.

Captain Bowen, across Fort Street, raised a hand in greeting and called his congratulations as Nat passed on his way to the waterfront. Nat, still striving to rein in his unruly libido, nodded and went on. It was odd. If anything had completed his return to respectability, it was the wedding. Not that anyone had been overtly hostile before. No, the other skippers had always treated him cordially. What had happened to him could happen to any of them, and that was frightening. He was a reminder of all that could go wrong. Since the news of the engagement had gotten out, though, he'd met with more genuine friendliness than he'd encountered in many a year. It wasn't enough, apparently, to skipper a ship. A man needed to succeed in other areas as well.

There was one notable exception. Jared Swift had not proffered his congratulations. Nat expected instead to receive a fist to his nose or, more likely, a knife in the back. He wasn't overly concerned. He could handle Swift. What did worry him was the man's attitude toward Abby. There was something wrong about it, something that went beyond love or even lust, though he couldn't quite pinpoint what. Maybe it was a good thing that she was so preoccupied with the wedding plans. Because of them, she was never left alone, an easy target. Nat would have to make certain Swift never had a chance with her.

Ahead of him, near the wharf, stood a small group of men, Hawaiian or of mixed blood. Just who he was looking for. Another hand had jumped ship. Rumor had it he'd found a native girl and was living with her on the other side of the island, which meant that Nat had to replace him. He had changed his direction slightly, intending to recruit at least one of the men, when of a sudden a figure stepped in front of him. He stopped dead, every instinct alert, every nerve on edge. It was Jared.

"Swift," he said curtly.

"Howland," Jared said, and much to Nat's surprise, he smiled, his lips barely moving, his eyes cold. Still, a smile it was, and it made Nat even more wary. "I haven't congratulated you on your engagement."

That startled a laugh from him. "You can't be serious."

"Smile, damn you," Jared said through gritted teeth. "If you don't have a care for Abby's reputation, I do."

Nat's amusement quickly faded. Jared was a danger to more than Abby's reputation. "I find that hard to believe, too."

"Why? Her reputation is priceless to me. She will be my wife someday."

"Hah. Over my dead body."

"But that's the idea." Jared's smile was chilling. "Because I am going to kill you."

Chapter 17

Nat went very still. The fact that the threat was uttered with a smile made it all the more menacing. Even the surroundings, the blue sea, the deep green palms, the soothing, warm breeze, heightened the danger. "If you can," he said coolly.

"Oh, I can, and I will. Perhaps not today, perhaps not tomorrow, but soon. Abby's mine."

"Abby belongs to herself."

"She's mine," Jared repeated, "And you always have coveted what is mine. First the *Nantucket,* and now Abby."

"The *Nantucket* was never yours."

"Abby has always been mine. And the *Nantucket* should have been. Palmer was considering me for master, but he chose you instead." He laughed mirthlessly. "Bad choice."

"You would have had us answer the *Shenandoah*'s distress signal," Nat retorted, referring to the lure the Confederate raider had used to trap so many New Bedford ships. "We'd have been burned to the waterline."

Jared sneered. "Coward, running away to save your own skin."

Nat merely smiled. To this day he didn't know what instinct had kept him from answering the distress flag, something no mariner ignored. Maybe it was because he'd heard in Honolulu that the *Shenandoah* was using that tactic; maybe it was the hours he'd spent poring over pictures of the ship, until every detail of line and rigging had been engraved on his memory. For whatever reason, he had decided to change course, ignoring the signal, in spite of Jared's vehement protest. His instincts had been proved right when the lookout had spotted a thin trail of black smoke: a steamship, coming up fast behind them. Under ordinary circumstances a whaleship, tubby and lumbering, could never hope to outrun the sleek raider, but that day, Nat had, slipping away under cover of darkness. If he had been drunk that night, it had been with excitement and accomplishment and pride. He had saved his ship.

Now he had bested Jared again. "I am the one marrying Abby in three days' time."

"Maybe." Jared's smile had stiffened into a grimace. "And maybe not."

"Marrying her," Nat repeated, "and making her my wife."

Jared laughed, an oddly disconcerting response. "Much joy I wish you of that. Tut, tut, mind your manners." This as Nat, goaded at last, surged forward, hands bunched into fists. "Remember Abby's reputation."

"You are a son of a bitch," Nat hissed.

"And you're a dead man." Jared turned on his heel. "Watch your back," he said, and strode away.

Nat stared after him, hands still clenched, rage pounding within him. If he didn't exactly discount the threat to himself, it didn't worry him much either. He'd handled the likes of Swift before. No, it was the insult to Abby that angered him, the implication that Jared had already possessed her and found her wanting. Oh, he knew it wasn't true. At least, he didn't think so. Abby behaved toward Swift as a friend, not a former lover, and her kisses aboard the ship had been shy, untutored. Nat's fists relaxed. Jared had said that simply to goad him, and he had succeeded. He had chosen his weapon well. It made him more dangerous than Nat had realized.

Nat turned back toward the hotel, his former intention of recruiting crew members forgotten. Swift fought dirty. Instead of using his fists like a man, he employed weapons like spiked punch or a slur on a woman's reputation. Nat didn't think that way. If he had to fight, then he would fight, openly and honestly. He could not fathom the workings of Swift's mind. God alone knew what the man would do next.

What he did know was that he would have to keep watch over Abby. She was unprotected, thinking of Swift as a friend. A friend, by God! No, he thought, taking the steps at the Hawaiian Hotel two at a time, he was going to protect his Abby, his future wife. And he would, indeed, watch his own back.

*   *   *

Abby stood in the foyer of the Kawaiahao Church, more familiarly known as the Stone Church because it was made of blocks of coral. She clutched a small bouquet in one hand, while nervousness clutched her stomach. Here she was, about to walk down the aisle of a crowded church, to marry a man she felt she hardly knew. "I can't do it," she said.

"Of course you can." Sarah rearranged the veil of white netting more carefully over the wreath of plumeria that covered Abby's coiffure of braids and curls. "Captain Howland is a good man, and just right for you. You'll be happy with him."

"Mm." Abby had her doubts. She thought her father would have, too. What would he say, could he see her now, in her gown of white peau de soie? Oh, it was a lavish gown, with a lacy V neckline, a tight waist, and a softly gathered skirt trimmed with pleats and bows of white silk. Papa would tell her she looked silly and send her off to change. That gown wasn't appropriate for someone who hadn't inherited her mother's beauty, and as long as he was paying for this wedding—

But he wasn't. Abby straightened as the organist began the processional music. Papa was dead and could no longer resent somebody else being the center of attention. She wished—oh, how she wished—that he were here to give her away, yet it was a relief not to have to deal with his domineering ways. Nat wasn't like that, she thought, watching Jane Ashley, daughter of one of the captains, step into the sanctuary, proud of her role as flower girl. At least, she hoped he wasn't.

Catherine Bowen, her matron of honor, turned to give Abby a smile and then followed Jane, leaving Abby alone. Then the music changed to the "Wedding March." It was her turn.

He was mad. Absolutely mad, Nat thought, standing ramrod-straight at the head of the aisle. He knew how to hide his emotions, and so he was sure that no one suspected his feelings. They gazed at him from the enclosed pews, the women in extravagant bonnets, the men in dark frock coats, like his. He could almost be back in New England, except for the warm breezes blowing in through the open windows.

And if he were, would he be doing this? The nervousness that danced in the pit of his stomach coalesced into a great lead ball. He was marrying a woman who didn't love him. God, he wanted a drink.

The processional started on the organ; no turning back now. He would have to go through with this crazy wedding and make the best of it somehow. He watched, as if in a fog, as Abby's attendants moved solemnly down the aisle, the little girl scattering some kind of flower petals before her. And then he saw Abby . . .

Nat was holding out his hand to her. Somehow Abby had made it down the aisle, pulled, it seemed, by the force of his blue, burning gaze on her. Of the people gathered to see her wed she had only a blurred impression, with few faces standing out. There was only Nat, tall, compelling, willing her to come to him, willing her to want him. Heaven help her, but she was powerless against this strange force. It was frightening, exhilarating. And then Nat's fingers folded over hers, strong, solid, warm, and everything was suddenly all right.

It would be all right, Nat thought, turning with Abby to face the minister. Her fingers, threaded through his, felt natural, as if they belonged there. This would work. Maybe she didn't love him the way he loved her; maybe she was marrying him for the wrong reasons. It didn't matter. He had love enough for the two of them, and a lifetime to make it work.

A voice penetrated his consciousness, filled with the woman standing beside him. Time to speak the vows; time to exchange rings. "With this ring . . ."

The wide gold band slipped onto Abby's finger and settled there. She belonged to somebody else now. It should have terrified her, but it didn't. Her nervousness was gone, leaving in its place a calm, sure certainty. She didn't think she loved Nat, though what she felt for him was likely as close to love as she could get for any man. She was marrying him partly for protection from Jared, and maybe to hold on to the *Aquinnah,* but it didn't matter. This was right. Whatever else she did in her life, she doubted she would ever truly regret marrying Nat.

"With my body I thee worship . . ." Carnal words to speak aloud in a church, but for Nat they rang true. He had wanted Abby for what seemed like forever, and yet what he felt now was almost holy. Tonight when they truly became man and wife, when he at last kissed her and held her and made her his own, the act would be much more than the merging of bodies. It would be the merging of spirits as well, he and Abby becoming one. Never had he felt this way. Never would he feel this way for any woman but Abby. Whatever else he did in his life, he doubted he'd ever truly regret marrying her.

"I now pronounce you man and wife." Abby and Nat returned to themselves at the same time, to realize they were holding each other's hands, searching each other's eyes. Something had happened between them that could not be fully accounted for by the marriage service. They were bound together, indissoluble, and nothing else, no one else, mattered. Only the two of them, and this moment of perfect, complete union.

Then Nat was bending to drop a gentle kiss on Abby's lips, and she startled herself by raising her head, her lips clinging to his for just a moment. There was a soft murmur in the congregation, enough to break through Abby's absorption. She returned to reality, aware that she and Nat were not the only two people in the world. Yet, as he tucked her hand through his arm and they turned to walk down the aisle, she knew somehow that he was as awestruck as she by the vastness and the seriousness of what they had done, and as determined to make their marriage work. Her last doubts fled. She wasn't alone any longer. She and Nat would get through this together.

In the church foyer they stood to receive the best wishes of their guests, no longer holding hands, yet close enough that his sleeve brushed her arm, her skirt whispered against his leg. Close enough to feel each other's warmth, even though Nat was shaking hands, even though Abby was allowing people to kiss her on the cheek. Only when she saw Jared, hand outstretched and a smile upon his face, did her uneasiness return. She'd seen little of him since that night at Iolani Palace. Just as well. That he was hurt she knew. That she could do nothing to ease his pain she knew as well.

"Jared," she said, as he took her hands, tilting her face to let his kiss fall on her cheek. "I'm happy to see you."

"Are you, Abby?" His smile was enigmatic; his eyes watchful. "On a day when you've married another man?"

"Jared." Her voice was chiding. "You know that you and I will always be friends."

"Friends." He spat the word out, though his chilly smile remained. "We're more to each other, Abby, and you know it."

Abby looked quickly at Nat, but he was speaking to another guest and seemed not to hear. "This isn't the time or the place, Jared."

"I know." His smile faded. "It may surprise you, Abby, but I do wish you well. I care for you enough for that."

"Thank you, Jared."

"And I want you to know I'll be around."

"For what?"

"For when you're alone again." He raised her hand to his lips. "Soon, Abby," he said, his gaze holding hers. "Soon."

Abby drew back, and Jared at last dropped her hand. Without a backward glance he turned and walked out of the church, leaving Abby shaken. It felt as if the first winds of winter had touched her, and though the day was warm, though her new husband stood beside her, she shivered. The future, so bright and promising just a moment ago, now was tinged with menace, and all, she suspected, because of her own actions. What terrible events had she put into motion?

Eight hours later the dark cloud had lifted somewhat from Abby's consciousness. Glad of an excuse to celebrate, the members of the whaling fleet had turned her wedding breakfast into a wonderful party. There had been music and dancing and even champagne, though when she and her new husband toasted each other, his glass had held only water. It was natural to have doubts and fears, she told herself as she brushed her hair. She had been nervous before going to sea, and look how that had turned out. Marriage was another sort of journey. She tucked the brush away in a bureau drawer. Take it day by day, Nat had said. It was good advice.

Abby turned, looking again about her new home, the captain's cabin aboard the *Aquinnah*, where they would spend their wedding night. Unlike her old stateroom, this room was as spacious as a ship could afford, with the straight stern bulkhead providing a padded settee for her to sit upon. The paneling was pristine white and elegantly carved, while the oil lamp above had a cut-glass shade. Everything was neat and tidy; hooks held clothes, while built-in drawers provided space for other belongings. And then there was the bunk, wide and spacious and suspended on gimbals, to sway with the ship's motion and give the captain undisturbed rest. She decided not to contemplate that particular furnishing just yet.

"Abby?" Nat's voice was accompanied by a knock on the door.

"Yes," she answered, lifting her hair and then letting it fall. She should probably braid it, but a contrary feminine impulse made her leave it loose as she moved toward the door. Tightening the sash of her frilly wrapper, of softest, delicate peach silk, about her, she opened the door, took a deep breath, and stepped out into the cabin.

Nat turned from the table, where he was pouring a ruby liquid into two fine-stemmed glasses. With a jolt, Abby recognized them. "My mother's Venetian wineglasses!"

"Aye." He held one out to her, his gaze raking her over appreciatively. "Did I ever tell you I like your hair?"

"Once. Nat." She looked at the glass. "Should you—"

"It's fruit juice, Abby," he interrupted. "I thought we'd probably both want to have clear heads tonight."

"Mm." Abby sipped at the juice, feeling just the slightest bit guilty at her assumption. Except for that one evening at Iolani Palace, she had never seen Nat the worse for drink. She would simply have to trust him to remain that way. "These glasses meant so much to my mother. My father bought them for her on their honeymoon, you know."

"Aye." His eyes met hers over the edge of her glass, and her gaze skittered away, nerves and something else dancing in the pit of her stomach. "I know. Elizabeth told me when she gave them to me."

"Oh." Abby's spirits returned to earth with a thud. His seemingly romantic gesture of producing the glasses on their wedding night was actually nothing more than a present from her cousin. "When did she do that?"

"Before we sailed. She said they meant a lot to you, and I should decide when to give them to you."

Abby's lashes swept up. "Do you suppose she thought—"

"That someday we'd marry? I think she hoped for it."

"Why, that conniving old woman!" Abby lowered her glass, smiling. "All the time talking of women's independence, and going so far as to give me bloomers—"

"I like your bloomers, Abby."

Color bloomed in her face. "You do?"

"Aye."

"Oh." She looked down, taking refuge in annoyance. "And all the time she was plotting against me behind my back."

"Against you, Abby?" he said almost gently.

"No," she said, and setting her glass down, went to him in an instinctive gesture of homing. His arms settled around her as she rested her head against the soft cotton of his shirt, breathing in the mingled scents of starch and sea and male. So different from anything she'd known, from her father's bear hugs or Jared's clutching embraces. He was so broad, strong, solid. Something stirred to life within her, so long forgotten or ignored that it was almost alien. Why, she liked being held by him, and not because of any protection he might provide, not because she needed comforting. Quite the opposite. This feeling was heady, reckless, and exciting.

She raised her head to see him regarding her seriously, his eyes for once unfathomable. Shyness overcame her, and so she turned her attention to the garlands of flowers that festooned the cabin. They were looped from bulkhead to bulkhead and draped from the skylight, wreathing the bird-cage, their scent filling the air with a rich, heady perfume. "I can't believe Mr. Tripp went to such trouble for us," she said breathlessly.

"Aye," he said again, and she could sense, actually feel, that his gaze had not for one moment left her face. The power of it compelled her to look back at him at last. There was no force in him—just strength. "I've waited a long time for this, Abby."

She swallowed, her mouth gone dry. "I know."

"I'll do my best to be a good husband to you."

"I know that, too." She leaned back, confident that he

would not release her, yet also would not entrap her.
"Nat—"

"Shh." He shook his head, laying his finger on her lips,
and she went absolutely still. This was what they'd both
been anticipating all day, she admitted at last, hooking her
arms about his neck. This was something she wanted. And
so when his mouth came down to hers, she raised up to
meet it, tentatively, for this was still new to her, but eagerly.
No hesitation this time; no doubts, no wagers. Once she
had held back, aware of who she was—Benjamin Palmer's
daughter, a proper New England girl who didn't feel such
unseemly emotions. New England was thousands of miles
away, though, in spirit as well as in physical distance. She
was no longer the same person she had been when first she
set sail. She was Nat's wife, and in his arms was a haven
and a heaven, far beyond the sea.

Then his lips were on hers, hard, questing, and there was
no more room for thought in the riot of emotions within
her. Her fingers clutched his neck, curled into his hair, finding it unexpectedly soft; his cheek, firm against hers, was
faintly scented with bay rum. It delighted her deep inside
that he'd thought enough of her to shave; it eased her mind
that here was the only place she smelled or tasted rum. No
hint of it on his mouth or lips or tongue, only pineapple
and papaya and passion. It made her thirsty for more. She
pressed up against him, her own lips searching, and of a
sudden his arms crushed her about her waist, lifting her off
the deck and full against him. For the first time she felt his
desire, hard and pulsing against her, and it set up an answering pounding within her. She let her tongue tangle with
his in a tantalizing mating dance; let him pull at the tie to
her wrapper; let his hand grasp her hip and hold her tighter.
Though never before had she felt such fire, though never
had she acted in such a way, still she knew this was right.
Married or not, they belonged together.

Nat's grasp loosened, just a little, and she found herself
swaying against him, her bare feet balanced precariously
on his, their lips still locked together. Dazedly she opened
her eyes, to see him regarding her, so close that his eyes
merged in a brilliant blue blur. Amusement welled up
within her, and before she could stop it erupted in a snort
of laughter. Nat jerked his head back, and then he was

laughing too, holding her against him and rocking her with
the sway of the ship. Oh, but it felt good to let her emotions
go, to laugh without fear that it might be inappropriate.
Not to walk on eggshells for fear of awakening a man's
temper. Nat had his faults, she knew, but inconsistency apparently was not one of them.

Her laughter faded first, as it had sparked first. In its
wake the air felt clear, fresh, as if there had been a storm.
His grip on her was easy, sure, the muscles in his back
relaxed. She traced them lightly with her fingertips, and to
her delight felt them bunch, contract. The amusement in
his eyes darkened into something more elemental, new to
her, but that she nevertheless recognized. Desire. Need.
Wanting. Why, she could affect him with just a touch. She
had never before known she possessed such power. She felt
a quick impulse to tease, to test herself, but then brushed
it away. This moment was too important for teasing.

Serious now, she stretched up and kissed him the way he
had taught her, lips searching, moving, tongue seeking. His
hand clamped on the back of her head and held her immo-
bile as he responded, with need and tenderness. There was
no rush. They knew now that what was between them
would last a lifetime.

At length Nat drew back, leaving her feeling thoroughly
kissed, with her lips swollen and her breath ragged. "Shall
we go into the stateroom?" he said, his voice low.

"I suppose." She came back to herself and her surroundings. How perfectly appropriate that they were on the
Aquinnah to begin their lives together. Her wrapper was
open, she noted detachedly; she had only a vague memory
of that happening. And when had the top button of her
nightgown come undone? Goodness. She was certain her
hair was mussed, and though Nat had loosened his grip,
she could still feel the hard, contoured imprint of his body
against her. "We wouldn't want Mr. Tripp to come in on
us."

"If he does I'll throw him overboard," Nat growled, and
swung her up into his arms.

Abby dropped her head against his shoulder as he carried her into the cabin. Soft lamplight spilled onto the colorful quilt spread neatly on the bunk. Her quilt, she
thought, as he set her down with excruciating slowness, so

that she slid against his hard body. She could contemplate the bunk now and not feel skittish. Silly of her to have been that way earlier. Why, this was Nat, she thought, turning in the circle of his arms. "I'm glad we're here, and not at the hotel."

"Mm." He gripped her shoulders through the silk wrapper. "This is very pretty, sweetheart. Will you take it off?"

Her mouth was dry. "Yes," she whispered, and shifted her arms so that he could pull the wrapper off her. He flung it across the room, where it landed in a puddle on the deck. Her face rose in anticipation of being pulled close to him again, but instead he rested his knuckles against her midriff. They stayed there a moment, and then trailed up, between her breasts, onto her chest, to the second button of her nightgown. She shivered, and this time it was not entirely from desire.

"Silk again." His voice was rough velvet as his knuckles brushed back and forth on the button. "Shall I?"

"Yes." Her voice sounded very far away. She felt very far away as he slipped the button free, and the next, and the next. He would want to touch her breasts, of course, she thought, as if her body belonged to someone else. Men liked that, or so she'd been told in giggling midnight sessions with her friends, long ago. Perhaps this time she would like it, too. She closed her eyes, parted her lips, as his fingers slipped under the silk, touching her skin, gliding against her until they rested on the upper slope of her left breast.

She waited as his fingers moved on her, and felt nothing. No fire from his kisses, no tingling from his touch. Just nothing.

Abby's breast was beneath his hand. God, he couldn't believe this moment had actually arrived, couldn't believe that she responded to him as she did. Who would have guessed she had such passion in her, the seemingly plain, seemingly prim merchant's daughter? But there was nothing plain about her, not in the delicate lines of her face; nothing prim in the riotous abandon of her hair. Her breast was full and round and heavy in his hand as he palmed it, his fingers questing deeper as her nipple tightened. *Ah.* He thought at that moment that if he died he would surely go to heaven.

Reverently he slid the silk nightgown off her shoulders, down her arms, down her breasts. It caught briefly on her nipples, until with a light flick of his fingers he freed it, to fall to the deck as the wrapper had. Her skin, pearly in the lamplight. The indentation of her waist, and the slight roundness of her stomach. The taste of her shoulders, throat, breasts; his hands spanning her waist. Her legs, slender, shapely. Her eyes, downcast so that her lashes made spiky shadows on her cheek as he slowly lowered her to the bunk and hastily shed his own clothes. Her arms, reaching up as he came to her. He loved her, he loved her, and his hands swept down her body, searching, seeking. The curls below were as soft and riotous as those about her face, and slightly damp; he closed his eyes in relief and thanksgiving. He didn't want to rush, not this first time, and he didn't want to hurt her, but, God help him, he could wait no longer. His need was pulsing, mindless, an instinctual urge to be within her, to be one with her. Clamping his mouth on hers, he rose above her, his hands caressing her in a long sweep, neck to hips; his knees prodding her legs apart. She stiffened a little, but he expected that. She drew back when he entered her, and winced, but he'd expected that, too. He noticed it with one part of his brain, and went on, powerless to stop. So long he'd wanted this, so long he'd wanted her, his Abby. He heaved above her, lost, in love, and when his climax took him, he yelled out her name.

Later, though, when they had exchanged sleepy kisses, when Abby had turned onto her side so that they were spooned together, he remembered the hesitation, the wince, her stillness beneath him. Abby lay quiet in his arms, but not asleep. He could feel the tension in her muscles, and the pretense bothered him. If she were awake, if she were as content as she'd seemed, why turn away from him? Certainly this first time had hurt her, but he had reassured her it wouldn't hurt the next time. Yet he couldn't help thinking that her lack of reaction had little to do with pain. For hadn't she been still when he'd caressed her? When he'd touched her body and kissed her glorious breasts, hadn't she been quiet? The response he'd felt when he kissed her was absent, and that bothered him.

It had been her first time, he reminded himself again,

closing his eyes. Things would get better. But he couldn't shake the troubling thought, as his wife lay quiet and awake beside him, that there was already something wrong with his marriage.

Chapter 18

Jared was angry enough to kill. He stood ramrod still at the end of the verandah of the Hawaiian Hotel, looking toward the group of women seated together in wicker chairs. In the center was Abby, glowing the way a new bride should. Jared's hands curled into fists, before he remembered to relax them. Careful, careful. No one knew of the rage within him, eating away at his very soul. Let them see him instead as the man who had been a good friend to Abby for so many years. If they knew how he really felt, they'd stop him, and he couldn't let that happen. He would have his revenge, and he would have Abby.

Jared watched as Nat bounded up the stairs to the verandah and crossed to Abby. Her eyes lit up, Jared noted with seeming dispassion, and she smiled when the man laid his hand on her shoulder. *God!* Jared's fingers curled again. How could she stand his hands on her? How could she allow him to—no, he wouldn't think about it.

The funny thing was, he'd thought seeing her with another man wouldn't bother him. After all, she was his. She always had been, and always would be, no matter what. From childhood on he'd loved Abby. Not as a brother, though they had been so young and he'd been careful to keep his caresses innocent, chaste. Only when he'd returned home from a voyage, when he was nineteen and she sixteen, had he felt the time was right. She'd grown up, matured from a child to a beautiful young woman, with curls dancing about her face and a shapely figure that had entranced him. He had tried acting on his feelings then, but events conspired against him. She was too young and skittish, and he too poor. He could wait if he had to. He was moving up in the world; his next position would be as second mate. Soon he would captain his own ship, and then he would ask for her hand.

So he had thought, Jared remembered, coming back to himself, but he had been wrong. Circumstances had worked against him, and now, seeing her so obviously content and fulfilled fueled his rage. He couldn't eat, couldn't sleep. His rest was tortured by dreams of Abby being pleasured by another man, and an all-pervading sense of failure. Most humiliating of all, though, was that when he'd bought himself an island girl, nothing had happened. It wasn't his fault, of course, but the girl's. He'd punished her appropriately. Though that had been satisfying, he couldn't do it every night without being found out. He had to be careful. A man with his future must have a spotless reputation. He would have to wait for Abby.

Across the verandah the group was breaking up. The sun had dropped below the horizon, and night was coming on with tropical swiftness. Golden lamplight fell on Abby as she walked into the hotel, serene, beautiful in her fashionable new gown of primrose yellow—and unattainable. Howland followed, his hand at her waist, sparing Jared only a look filled with triumph and mockery before disappearing inside. Jared was left alone with his hatred and his craving for revenge.

Nat adjusted the wick of the oil lamp and then straightened. The lamplight was mellow gold on the high oak bedstead, the polished wood floors, the woman who stood at the bureau, removing her earrings. She had changed, his Abby, since their marriage, become outgoing, talkative, even a little frivolous. He didn't know her. He wondered if he ever had.

Her reflection in the mirror smiled as he approached her. "It was a pleasant evening, wasn't it?"

He watched her without touching her, though he very much wanted to. "Very."

"I shall miss this when I'm gone." The fabric of her gown strained over her bodice as she reached up to take down her hair, and his body reacted predictably. Still, though, he didn't move. "To leave this warmth for the Arctic."

"You could stay here."

"What?" She turned to him, her face filled with shock

and dismay. In her eyes, though, there was just a tiny bit of relief. "But I can't do that, Nat."

"Why not? The other wives are staying."

"Don't you want me?"

Oh, Lord. Did he want her? More than she knew. "I'm thinking of your comfort."

"Not all the wives are staying," she argued. "Sarah's close to her time, so of course she's not going, but we're newlyweds, Nat. How would it look if you left without me?"

Nat's fingers clenched. "Is that all you care about?"

"No, of course not, silly." She had taken up a wooden-backed hairbrush and was pulling it through her hair. That glorious hair that he'd once fantasized about washing over his body like sea-foam. "The *Aquinnah*'s my ship."

"And I'm your husband."

In the mirror her gaze met his again, serious now. "And skipper. Are you going to start ordering me about, Nat, now that you have double authority?"

He released a breath he hadn't even realized he was holding. "No. Would it do any good?"

She frowned. "You're in an odd mood tonight."

"Am I?"

"Yes. There you go again, not really answering me." She turned, her face serious. "Is it because of that girl?"

"What girl?"

"The second girl who was hurt. Everyone knows about it."

He nodded, pacing away from her toward a grouping of chairs. Behind them were the floor-length windows, shuttered now for privacy, with their louvers open to let in the breeze. Abby was right, he thought irrelevantly. Who in his right mind would leave this place for the frozen reaches of the Arctic? "It's a bad business. The girl was severely beaten."

Abby still stood by the bureau. "By the same man."

"Probably, but no one knows." Nat peered through a slat in the blind, seeing nothing, and then turned back to her. "He terrorized her so she wouldn't say anything. And now her family's taken her away someplace on the island. No one knows where she is."

"But it was an American, wasn't it?"

"Probably. No one actually saw them meet."

"One of us."

"Aye," he said, and the silence fell heavily in the room. For Abby didn't know the worst of it, he thought, that the poor girl had been cut, apparently with a broken bottle, and would probably never fully heal. And she didn't know the one fact that terrified Nat, and at the same time gave him a strong suspicion of who the culprit was. Before the beating, the girl had borne a passing resemblance to Abby. "One of us."

She shivered again and turned her back. "Would you unhook me, please?"

"Of course." He crossed the room to work on the tiny, intricate hooks that ran up the back of her gown. Funny, the intimacies she allowed him, after five days of marriage. Except for some natural modesty, she didn't seem to mind if he saw her unclothed for brief intervals. She let him hold her, kiss her, touch her, taste her, and she never turned him away when he sought release in her body. What she withheld from him was more subtle. He had her body; she kept from him her soul.

He gazed down at the nape of her neck—white, soft, vulnerable—and on a sudden impulse planted his mouth there. She shuddered, and relaxed against him. Her easy compliance puzzled him. Sometimes her response seemed real. At other times he might have been making love to a doll, so still was she.

His hands, at her waist, crept up to cover her breasts, and though his head was still bent, though his mouth was busy with her neck and ears, he knew the exact moment her eyes opened, the moment when any magic between them died. He lifted his head to see her looking at him in the mirror, her eyes dark, unreadable. Not the look of a woman lost in desire.

Abruptly his need for her fled, and he stepped away. In the past, all that had mattered to him was that the woman be willing. Now he wanted more. He wanted a partner, someone who was his equal in passion and in bed. Until their wedding night, he'd thought Abby was that woman.

"Nat?" Abby said behind him, her voice tentative. "Is something wrong?"

He opened a shutter, staring blindly out into the flower-scented night. "No."

"Then why did you stop?"

"Why do you keep pretending?" he snapped, turning back and slamming the shutter closed.

She recoiled. "What?"

"That you want to make love with me."

"But I do."

"Don't deny it. I touch you and you're as stiff as a statue."

She was very still, her eyes wary. "I've never denied you anything, Nat," she said quietly. "I never will."

"Is that what you think I want? Your compliance?"

"I'm your wife. I know what my duty is—"

"Duty!" He almost shouted the word. "Loving me is a duty?"

"No, Nat, of course not." Her voice was maddeningly cool. "I simply meant that I realize there are certain things expected in marriage."

He looked up at the ceiling. "I don't believe this."

"Nat, I'll never refuse you."

His lips tightened. She was calm, in control, while his emotions seethed and roiled. He was furious, and he felt oddly cheated. If there'd been whiskey available, he'd have drunk down an entire bottle. "What do you feel?"

"What?"

"When I touch you."

Her lips parted. For the first time she looked rattled. "You're my husband, Nat."

"That's not what I asked." He prowled toward her. She stood her ground, he'd grant her that. "When I touch your face." His fingers, soft against her cheek. "Like this."

She swallowed. "I like it."

Down to her neck, the curve of her shoulder. "And this?"

"Yes. I—it feels right."

"Does it? Good." He hauled her against him. "And when I hold you?"

Her words were muffled against his chest, their soft vibration tickling him. "I like it. I feel safe."

"Safe!" He pushed her away. "For God's sake—"

"I can't help it, Nat. It's how I feel. Safe." She reached

up to feather her fingers through his hair, and everything was almost, almost, all right. "You've always made me feel that way. Like nothing could ever hurt me."

Good God. He was rattled now. Safe? He was the most dangerous man she knew. Too much responsibility; too much pressure. "And what do you feel," he whispered softly, "when I do this?"

His hand covered her breast. Her eyes closed, opened again, looked into his, candid and a little sad. "Nothing."

It rocked him. He snatched his hand back. "What do you mean, nothing?"

"I mean—I feel your skin, of course, and it's warm, but that's all."

He couldn't help himself; he plucked at her nipple, all the time seeking a response in her eyes. "And this?"

She shook her head. "It's sensitive, but—"

"Nothing." He reared back. "I've been loving you, and you don't feel a thing."

"Nat, I'm sorry." She laid her hand on his arm as he turned away, and he shook it off. "I am—I'm sorry! I like it when you kiss me and when we're first touching, but then . . ." Her words trailed off. "I don't know how to describe it."

He faced her again, his voice icy even to him. "Try."

"I can't." Tears filled her eyes. She might have stopped then, but this was too important, for their future, for their happiness. "It's as if there are two of me. One is with you and the other is watching, and—I want to feel something, Nat! Don't you think I want to? But all I can do is be there and try to relax and wonder . . ."

"What?"

She shook her head. "I don't know. Am I supposed to feel something, Nat? Am I?"

Some sympathy diluted Nat's anger. If her lack of response bothered him, how must it be for her, to be intimate with a man and yet take no pleasure from it? "Wait a minute. You're always aroused."

Her eyelashes flickered down. "I—am I?"

"You're wet," he said bluntly, laying his hand at the juncture of her thighs, and watching her face take flame. "Here. Wet and warm."

"I know," she whispered. "It's embarrassing."

More sympathy, still unwanted, but insistent. "It's natural, sweetheart."

"It doesn't feel like it." Her eyes, raised to him, were wide and miserable. "You tell me I should feel something, Nat, and I want to. I just—don't."

He closed his eyes, let out his breath. How could he answer that? On the surface she was all a man could want in a wife—willing, obedient. It was his curse that he wanted more. "Then I'll leave you alone," he said in a low voice. "I won't touch you again."

Her breath drew in sharply. "But, Nat—"

"Not until you want me to. All or nothing, Abby."

"Just like that?" A temper he hadn't known she possessed blazed in her eyes. "Am I to have no say in our marriage?"

"Why did you marry me, Abby?" he asked quietly.

Her eyes widened again, and then her lashes flickered. "I don't honestly know," she said after a moment.

"For your ship, Abby. For the *Aquinnah.*"

"That may be part of it, but—"

"Part of it?"

"I don't know why, Nat! My life has changed so much in the past year, and I don't know what I want or what I'm feeling. I don't know who I am! Not anymore."

"You're someone who pretends well."

She winced. "That's unfair."

"All your friends think you're happily married."

"I thought I was happily married. Nat." She raised her hands. "Tell me what to do to fix this. I want our marriage to work. I'll do anything I can. I promise."

"There's nothing you can do." He gazed at her for a moment and then ran a hand over his face, tired now that the energy of his anger was gone. Damnation, how had they come to this? He'd been so sure that what he felt would be enough for them both. Only now did he realize how wrong that was. "I'm the one who made the mistake, not you."

She glanced away, biting her lower lip. "What are we going to do?"

"I'll sleep on the sofa for tonight," he said, eyeing that particular piece of tufted horsehair furniture with distaste. "Tomorrow we'll move back to the *Aquinnah.* No one will have to know then who sleeps where." Or that there were any problems in the marriage. Particularly not Swift. He wouldn't give the bastard the satisfaction, and he wouldn't leave Abby unprotected.

"You have it all thought out, don't you?"

He shook his head. "No. Abby—"

"I'll stay behind," she said dully, looking at him. He seemed so far away already. "When you sail, I'll stay here."

He was very still. "That might be best," he said finally.

"It makes sense. I'm tired." She turned away. "I'd like to go to sleep. But you don't have to sleep on the sofa."

"That's for the best, too."

She nodded, feeling her hair brush against the naked skin of her shoulders. A few moments ago she had put herself into his hands willingly, because that was what was expected of her. Now she merely felt exposed. "Good night, then, Nat."

"Good night, Abby," he said, and turned away, leaving them both very much alone.

Abby found Nat in the aft cabin several mornings later, standing with hands braced on the table, frowning down at a chart. The skylight was open, letting in the soft breeze with its scents of land and aromas of civilization. The flower garlands from her wedding night had long since wilted and been discarded, along with her optimism about her marriage. "Is there a problem?" she asked softly.

Nat looked up and his frown disappeared, to be replaced by a polite smile. All relations between them were polite now. They dined together, joined excursions to various places on the island, and spent their nights aboard the *Aquinnah*. There, any pretenses about their marriage ended. As before, they went their separate ways, Nat to the stateroom that had once been Abby's; she to sleep in solitary splendor in the captain's cabin. Already she missed the feel of his hard, warm body next to hers. She missed the security of having him near. She was also relieved that she no longer had to pretend to something she didn't feel.

"No, no problem," Nat said, rolling up the chart. "Just hoping the whales will be plentiful near Point Barrow. There's been talk of having to go farther north to find them."

Abby settled on the bench, chin in her hands. "Do you think we—the whalers—are chasing them away?"

"Maybe. They're smart enough creatures to know when to escape." He finished rolling up the chart. "Or we could be killing them all."

Her eyes widened. "You don't really think that, do you?"

"I don't know, Abby. All I know is it's different this time." He sat across from her, close but removed. "When I started, whalers didn't need to go so far afield. We've been lucky this cruise, compared to some of the other ships."

"Thank heavens."

"Yes. Some of the skippers are saying they might have to go as far north as Point Belcher just to make expenses."

"If we're killing all the whales, Nat—" Abby said slowly.

"—We're killing whaling," he finished for her.

"Something's got to be done."

"What? Tell people they can't go to sea anymore? No whaler worth his salt's going to accept that. And what about the foreign fleets? No." He shook his head. "We'll keep on, until something happens to make us stop."

"I can't imagine New Bedford without whaling."

"Why do you think your father invested in textile mills?" He leaned back. "I imagine he made the other investments to get out of whaling, even if they turned out bad."

"He'd have managed to save them, had he lived," she murmured, still stunned by the idea of an entire industry shutting down. No more sailing days, with their ceremony. No more long voyages to every corner of the Earth, from Cape Verde, to New Zealand, to these warm, welcoming islands. She was going to lose, and miss, a lot. "I wish I could see it."

Nat was carefully lighting his pipe, the one vice he seemed to allow himself. "What?"

"The Arctic."

"You wouldn't like it."

"Why not?"

"It's a miserable place. Frigid."

She shuddered, as that dark, distant memory fluttered through her mind again. It did so more often these days, since she had lost Nat. "So is winter at home."

"Well, then." Nat's voice was almost gentle. "Are you prepared to share my bed?"

She gazed at him steadily. "You know that the way things are between us wasn't my idea."

"No. Just that you caused it."

"That's not fair."

"Will you come back to my bed, Abby? Willingly?"

There was a large lump in her throat, in the pit of her stomach. "I can't," she whispered. "Not the way you want."

"Then that's that." He waved out the match. "There's nothing for us to talk about."

"Nat." She held her hand out, though he hadn't actually moved away from her. "I don't want things to be this way."

"No?" He did lean back then, his gaze cool. "You're the only one who can change it."

"Nat, please. I know you're angry, but it isn't just my problem. I need help. And there's no one I can talk to."

Nat gazed at her and then put down his pipe, letting out his breath. "I don't know what to tell you," he said, his tone milder. "I want a real wife, Abby, someone who's with me all the way. Not someone who goes through the motions."

"I'm not like that, Nat."

"Not most of the time, no," he conceded. "Only at an important time."

She gazed straight ahead, seeing nothing. She had thought about this—oh, she had thought about this, and yet she could find no answer. In the past she might have discussed matters with Sarah, but not this. How could she? How could she tell anyone that when her husband kissed her she felt all warm and trembly inside, that her knees went watery and her stomach weak? That she felt flushed and sensitive all over, even in parts of her body she hadn't quite known existed? She couldn't. Nor could she add that, when things went further, when her husband touched her, as he had every right to do, those warm feelings shriveled up and died. She couldn't tell anyone that she was such a failure. "I don't want to be like that, Nat."

"Then why are you?"

"I think it's the way I am." She sat back, hands folded primly in her lap. "It's just me."

"So you're telling me you're not willing to change?"

"I don't think I can." Because she had tried. She didn't like the emptiness she felt, or the way she seemed to split into two people. And it was uncomfortable. She had been prepared for the burning pain of the first encounter, but not for the continuing discomfort. Still, she would endure it. Nat was her husband. "What am I supposed to be feeling?"

He looked down at her. "Don't you know?"

"How can I?" She spread her hands. "This is all new to me."

"Yet you had suitors."

"Nat, are you implying—"

"No." He rubbed his hands tiredly over his face. "No, of course not, Abby, and I apologize for it. God!" The oath was quiet but explosive. "Why must women be kept in such ignorance?"

Because men like you want virtuous wives," she shot back. "If I'm supposed to learn how to feel certain things, who is supposed to teach me?"

"Are you saying it's my fault?"

"Why are you so determined to fix blame?" She leaned forward, hands clenched. "There's no fault in this that I can see." Though heaven knew she felt guilty enough, both for the pleasure she took from his kisses and for the deadening lack of sensation that followed. "It's a problem of both of us. I don't know." She leaned back. "Everything's happened so fast."

"I asked you to marry me months ago."

"And before that I went to sea for the first time"—she held up a finger—"I lost my home"—another finger—"and my father. I need time, Nat," she begged, suddenly certain that, given a chance, she could find a solution to this problem.

"Time's what we don't have. Not with you here and me in the Arctic."

Abby gazed at him steadily, her mind whirling but her purpose sure. She wasn't happy, true, but if she let Nat sail off without her, she would lose any chance of happiness. Perhaps she was not the only one who wanted time. "Nat, I'm going to give you an order."

He looked up from relighting his pipe. "What?"

"An order," she repeated. "Owner to captain."

"Damnation, Abby—"

"This is my ship." She held his gaze with her own. "My ship, and I will be aboard her when she sails."

Nat's eyes were icy. "I always knew you'd do this."

"Only when necessary." She took a deep, quick breath, fighting for calm. This issue had nothing to do with the ship. What chance would her marriage have if she didn't do something? "Well, Captain?"

"Damnation." He repeated and turned away. "Does it bother you that people will know we sleep in separate rooms?"

"No." She faced him squarely. "Does it bother you?"

"Damn right it does," he shot back. "It's not just the people we know, Abby. It's the crew. How can I control them if I can't control my—"

"I don't give a damn about the crew," she said, rising. "That's not what this is about, and you know it."

Nat was silent for a moment, his eyes flat, unreadable. "Then say it, Abby. What is it about?"

Abby took a deep breath. How could she answer that? Power, control, safety—love? She didn't know. The only thing she was certain of was that if she let Nat go, she would lose her only chance at contentment. "Sanity, I think."

"Sanity." He frowned. "I don't understand you, Abby."

"Don't you? If we leave everything so unresolved, how long will it take you to start drinking again?"

"You fight dirty, Abby."

She gazed at him. "You know it's true, for both of us."

"You are set on this? It's an order?"

"Yes, Captain," she said softly. "It's an order."

"Damnation." He slammed the pipe down on the table so hard that the stem cracked. "All right, you win. But don't expect me to be happy about it," he growled and stalked out of the cabin, leaving Abby alone with her hollow victory.

Chapter 19

Nat strode along Fort Street that afternoon, so angry at Abby that he wanted to shake her, throttle her, do all the things a man didn't do to anyone smaller and weaker than himself. Yet Abby had taken her best weapon and used it against him. Damnation, how had things gotten so out of hand? A man had a right to expect a wife who was willing, even eager, not someone who would use her power to bring him to heel. If he hadn't given in, he would have lost it all. No ship for him to sail; no marriage worth saving. Not that he was so certain he wanted to save it now. Except that he kept remembering things he shouldn't, not if he wanted to salvage his pride from this mess. Her lips against his, her breasts in his hands, her soft body under him; her laughter, her sympathy at his loneliness, her unexpected strength. She had looked like her father just now in the *Aquinnah*'s cabin, and that, paradoxically, only increased his regard for her. Her strength might not be comfortable in a wife, but it was admirable in the woman.

So what was he supposed to do now, he wondered as he neared the Hawaiian Hotel, his anger burnt away into weariness. He'd given in, but he couldn't let her best him. If she were going to the Arctic, she would have to come as his wife, in his bed. How he would manage to make that happen in the five days before sailing, though, he hadn't the slightest idea.

"Something's wrong," Sarah Hathaway said flatly as Nat climbed the stairs to the hotel's verandah. Sarah spent most of her time here now, in a capacious rocking chair, awaiting the imminent birth of her child. In spite of himself Nat found his gaze drawn to the great mound of her belly. How would Abby look, swelling with his child? The image filled him both with desire and a yearning he'd never before felt. To have children. A family.

Sarah spoke again. "Captain?"

Nat shook himself out of his reverie. "Nothing's wrong." He forced a smile to his lips. "Why do you think that?"

"Because I know Abby. Sit." She patted the arm of the chair next to her, a command rather than a request. "She was here earlier. Oh, she put a good face on it, but I know her. She's miserable."

In spite of himself, Nat snorted. Abby, miserable? Hardly. Though they'd ignored each other as they were rowed back to shore, he hadn't sensed unhappiness in her. And why not? She had won. "Abby's fine."

"You're blind," Sarah said bluntly and hit the arm of the chair again. "Sit down, or must I go after you? I warn you, watching me try to get out of this chair is not a pretty sight."

The stray bit of humor caught Nat. He also knew that Sarah could be relentless. "All right, all right." He sat stiffly beside her. "I'm here. What do you want to say to me?"

Sarah didn't answer right away, so that he finally turned to see her studying him. "But you're unhappy, too, aren't you? Oh, I don't expect you to admit it," she went on as Nat opened his mouth to deny her statement. "You're a man, after all."

"What's that supposed to mean?"

"I haven't met a man yet who'll discuss his emotions."

"We do have them, you know."

"Yes, I know, but you won't admit it. Why is that?" She regarded him with bright eyes. "It's not weak to have feelings."

Nat shifted uneasily in his chair. "Sarah, I have business to see to, so if you don't mind—"

"You're both unhappy," Sarah interrupted, "and yet you love each other."

This time he knew his surprise showed. Abby didn't love him. "This is none of your business."

"Now, really. Is it so hard to admit you care for her?"

"This is private, Sarah."

"She's my friend." Sarah reached over to lay her hand on his arm. "I hate to see her so unhappy."

Damnation. He looked away, touched by her concern. "I

do care for Abby," he said. "What you're wrong about"— and this was, indeed, hard to get out—"is that Abby cares about me."

"Of course she does!" Sarah peered at him. "Doesn't she?"

"She married me to get away from Jared Swift," he ground out.

"Oh, nonsense."

"He's been pursuing her since her father died. At home, in Cape Verde. Here."

"Abby can handle Jared. I've seen her."

Remembering the incident at the royal reception, Nat wasn't so certain. "I appreciate what you're trying to do for Abby, but you're meddling in things you know nothing about."

"So I gather." She gazed at him, her fingers tapping on the arm of the chair. "She doesn't love Jared."

"She did, once."

"Oh, no. Maybe when we were children, like a brother, but not since."

"No?" He looked at her skeptically. "Are you telling me he wasn't one of her suitors?"

"No. I'm saying you have no reason to be jealous of him."

"I'm not," he snapped.

"No?"

"No." He wasn't, he realized. He knew well Abby didn't love Swift. But there was the way Swift had behaved toward her, and the unresolved question of who was beating up island girls; there was something about the way Abby acted around the man. "Damnation. I don't know what to do."

"Could you tell me about it?" she said gently. "Maybe I can help."

He looked away, teeth clenched. "Maybe." Though not all of it. Now he understood what Abby had meant that morning, when she'd said this was something she couldn't discuss with anyone, even with her oldest friend.

"Adjusting to marriage can be hard. Especially for the woman."

"Could you talk to her?" he asked, still looking away.

"I did, before your wedding."

That made him look at her. "You did?"

"Someone had to, with her mother gone." Sarah rocked for a while in silence. "Everything's happened so fast for her."

"That's what she said." Unconsciously he set his own chair into motion. "She says she needs time, but she doesn't want to stay behind." He frowned, baffled. "What does that mean?"

Sarah pursed her lips. "You're a considerate man."

"What?"

"Nothing," she said, shaking her head, but Nat thought he knew what she meant. He was a considerate man, and so he would be careful of his wife in bed. As he had been. "Abby loves you. Oh, I know you don't believe that, but it's true." She looked up at him suddenly. "But that's it."

"What?"

"You have to make her fall in love with you."

"You just said—"

"Yes, yes, but I don't think Abby realizes how she feels. She's been through a lot this past year, enough to confuse anyone. Tell me something."

"What?"

"How did you propose to her?"

He frowned. "I asked her to marry me." When she was in his arms, having lost their wager.

"Yes, but did you say why?"

Considering how shaken they had both been from kissing, he'd thought his reasons were self-evident. "Yes, but—"

"And how did you ask her?"

"I didn't get down on my knees," he said dryly. "Sarah, say what you mean and get it out."

"Men! Very well. Abby's never really been courted. Oh, she's had suitors," she said, forestalling his protest, "but they were after her fortune and she knew it. Or if she didn't, her father made sure she did."

"Did he want her to marry?" he asked, curious.

"Yes. No. Hm." Now she frowned. "Do you know, I don't think he did. It must have been convenient for him, to have someone to run his house and adore him while doing so. Of course, he did love her."

"You sound like you didn't like him much."

"I never knew where I stood with him. One day he'd be

pleasant, and the next, remote. He was like that with Abby too. She did everything she could to win his approval. No, I didn't like him much." She looked directly at him. "Did you?"

"I respected him." He gave a brief laugh. "Abby's a lot like him, you know."

"Not like that. Or she won't be, if someone helps her."

"How?" he asked, abandoning any pretense that matters were fine. "I care for her, but I've never met anyone more confusing in my life."

"She's never been courted," Sarah repeated.

"So?"

"So court her."

He blinked. "How?"

Sarah waved her hand. "Oh, if I have to tell you that, you're not the man I think you are."

"Flowers?" he suggested. "Poetry? That kind of thing?"

"Yes, for a start." Sarah laid her hand on his arm again, her eyes softer. "She has to know you care for her for herself. Not for her ship."

Nat looked toward the ocean. *My ship,* Abby had said, and wasn't that part of the problem? Didn't he sometimes think of the *Aquinnah* as his alone? No wonder he so resented her giving him orders. No wonder she felt she needed to. She couldn't know that if he had to choose between the two, he'd choose her. How could she? Until this moment, neither had he. "I suppose giving her flowers would be a start."

Sarah's eyes sparkled with, he suspected, suppressed laughter. "Yes, it would."

"But I'm not going to read any damned poetry," he growled.

This time Sarah did laugh. "No, I don't think that would suit you. But, Captain?"

He looked down at her as he rose. "What?"

"Go gently with her. And don't blame her."

He frowned. "I don't," he said, perplexed, and stepped away. "Do you know where she is?"

"In the garden, I think. Good luck," she called after him.

"Because I'll need it," he muttered to himself, striding toward the hotel garden. Sarah had given him a lot to think about. One thing stood out, perhaps because he found it puzzling. What could he possibly blame Abby for?

In the garden a small group of people were gathered, mostly talking and ignoring the brilliant display of scarlet and pink and orange that surrounded them. Except for Abby. She was staring at an orchid with such absorption that he suspected her mind was far, far away. They'd parted badly that morning, he thought ruefully, ambling toward the knot of people. His fault, partly, but hers, too, because of her order. Yet, as he neared her, he admitted grudgingly that she was right. If she stayed behind in Hawaii, they would never mend the rift in their marriage.

"Hello," he said quietly.

Abby blinked, coming out of her abstraction. "Oh. Nat. I thought you were busy."

"Done. I recruited two more men for the crew."

"Oh, that's good news," she said with forced enthusiasm.

"Mm." He reached up and broke off the orchid. "Pretty," he commented, and before she could move he tucked it gently into the hair covering her left ear.

"Nat." Abby pulled back, coloring, her expression a mixture of embarrassment and pleasure. "What are you doing?"

"Nothing." Branding her. He knew it, and so did the others. For if Abby wasn't aware of the meaning of what he'd done, they were. On the islands, a woman who wore a flower behind her left ear belonged to one man. "It looks pretty."

"Thank you." Flustered, she turned away, and Nat bit back a smile. Sarah was right. He hadn't taken the time to court Abby, assuming as he had that she knew how he felt. Yet, he realized for the first time, he never had declared himself. Maybe his actions would do so. Maybe he'd enjoy it.

Abby turned away from him, rattled. It wasn't like him to make so tender a gesture in public, or to look at her as he was doing, with kindness and mischief, combined with a darker emotion that both thrilled and alarmed her. "Are they good men?" she asked, taking refuge in the ordinary concerns of the ship and avoiding the knowing, amused glances of the others.

"Who? Oh, the Kanakas. Seem to be. Strong, anyway."

He put his hand under her elbow, and the grip of his fingers was almost caressing. "The trouble with hiring on islanders is that they're not used to the cold in the Arctic."

"But I am." She swung around to face him, instantly challenged. "Anyone who's lived through a New England winter—"

"Abby." He laid his hands on her shoulders. She glanced around and was startled to see that they were the only two people remaining in the garden. "I'm not arguing with you."

"Then why are you here?"

"Maybe I wanted to see you."

That took the wind out of her sails. "Really?" she said, peeping cautiously up at him.

He smiled, amused, tender. "Really."

"Even though I gave you an order?"

He frowned, and she went still. Her entire future hinged upon the next few moments. "I'm not happy about it, Abby—"

"I'm sorry, but I thought—"

"—but I think you were right."

She stared up at him. "You do?"

"Aye. I think you should come along."

She almost closed her eyes in relief. Her marriage was still intact. "I didn't know how to get you to agree."

"You could have asked," he said, taking her arm as they turned to leave the garden.

"We weren't talking to each other. It is my ship, Nat."

"So it is." He frowned again. "You're a lot like your father, Abby."

"Am I?" She looked up at him. His fingers no longer stroked her elbow, and yet their prosaic linking of arms seemed as sensual as an embrace. "I'm not sure if that's good or bad."

"It's good in a businesswoman."

"But not so good in a wife."

"Abby." This time he was the one to turn. "Let's not start that again."

"All right," she agreed after a moment. They had time. Perhaps she could figure out how she had failed him and what to do about it. If she didn't, she thought as they reached the verandah, she would regret it for the rest of her life.

Late in the afternoon a few days later, a group of people set out on horseback and in carriages from the Hawaiian Hotel. Their destination was Diamond Head, the extinct volcano rising high in the distance, so called because early visitors had seen glittering flecks of minerals they had thought were precious gems. Servants from the hotel had gone ahead to prepare a luau, the traditional Hawaiian feast. Abby was looking forward to it. The whaling fleet would be sailing in a few days, and everyone was determined to enjoy this last excursion. All too soon it would be back to work, and separation from loved ones.

Nat's horse shied under him yet again, causing him to utter a curse under his breath. Abby, a few paces ahead, turned in her saddle. "All right?"

"Fine. And stop looking at me like that," he growled, catching up with her. "I may be no horseman, but you don't have to call attention to it."

"Oh, Nat." She smiled at him, something that had become easier lately. "No one cares. And most of us don't ride well."

"But at least they ride."

"What?"

"I haven't ridden at all lately," he said and winked.

Abby's stomach lurched, though she wasn't sure why. "When would you have had time to learn? You went to sea."

"Aye, and so did every man here," Nat admitted. The sly, teasing look had left his eyes, but Abby didn't trust him for a moment. In the past few days he'd taken to doing odd things, unexpected things that started a new yearning inside her. If she were sitting, reading, he sometimes dropped a kiss on her forehead. For no reason, except that he'd wanted to, he'd say, and walk away, leaving her confused and rattled. At church on Sunday, he put his fingers over hers on the hymnal they shared, all the time watching her. Only when Abby had pulled away did he let up the pressure, so that her own movement made the touch feel like a caress. She had not been able to concentrate on the sermon after that and was still a bit ashamed at the path her thoughts had taken. In a church, of all places!

Then there were the gifts—just trinkets but unmistakable in their intent. A flower lei, dropped casually over her head one evening when she sat talking with the other women, drawing knowing, amused looks from them. A sailor's valentine, a pretty, sentimental creation of seashells glued to a board and bearing a message of love eternal, proffered carelessly at breakfast. He'd missed the real St. Valentine's Day, Nat had said by way of explanation, and then entered into a discussion of the Arctic weather with another skipper. Finally, there was the scrimshaw corset busk, a long, flat piece of whalebone etched with flowers and an intimate poem about the giver's regard for the woman who would wear it in the center of her corset. At least he'd had the sense to give her that particular item in private, though still in the same offhand way. And every night he tucked a flower behind her left ear. Abby didn't quite know what to make of any of it.

"Except Swift," Nat said, and Abby blinked.

"What?" she said, jolted back to the present. She still seemed to feel Nat's fingers stroking the sensitive skin behind her ear. It was as disconcerting now as it had been then.

"Swift." Nat indicated Jared, several lengths ahead, with a lift of his chin. "He found the time to learn."

"He learned with me when we were children," Abby said in gentle reproof, and Nat's eyes grew opaque. For the life of her, she did not understand the animosity between her husband and Jared. The situation made her uneasy, and the fact that she was part of the cause didn't help matters. "At my cousin's farm on Clark's Point."

Nat grunted in answer, his gaze still fixed and cool. Suddenly annoyed with him, Abby dug her heels into the horse's side and trotted forward next to Jared. "What a lovely evening for a ride," she said lightly.

Jared looked at her in undisguised surprise. "Is your husband actually allowing you to ride with me?"

"He'll catch up if he can."

"Cruel, Abby. It's not his fault he doesn't ride well."

"I know." Abby made a face, annoyed with herself. Whatever was between her and Nat, as her husband he deserved her loyalty. "I just—oh, never mind, it doesn't matter. Remember when we learned to ride?"

"At your cousin's farm." Jared's eyes lit up. "It was good of them to take me in."

"I wish you'd stop talking like a poor orphan boy."

"I was, in a way. But you're right." He glanced at her. "It sounds like I'm feeling sorry for myself."

"Aren't you?"

"You're waspish this evening, Abby."

"Yes, I know," she said contritely. "I am sorry. I don't know what's gotten into me."

He leaned toward her, eyes sympathetic. "Things aren't going well, are they?"

Abby drew back. "What do you mean?"

"Between you and Howland. It's obvious, Abby. I'm sorry, but it is."

"No," she said quickly. "Everything is fine." Better than it had been, but confusing. What was Nat up to?

She glanced over her shoulder to see Nat watching her. Something about his face, still expressionless, goaded her. "I'll race you to that tree."

"What?" Jared looked ahead. "That royal palm, there?"

"Yes."

"Then let's do it," he said and slapped his reins on the horse's neck. Abby was quickly left behind, though she managed to keep close to her competitor, her head bent low. The horses' hooves dug into the turf, throwing up clumps of rich, black volcanic earth, while their breathing came harsh and labored. Abby felt the horse's coarse mane whip against her face and wanted to laugh aloud. This was glorious, glorious! When had she last ridden like this, not caring what anyone might think or say, not even her father? When had she last felt this way, reckless, a little wild, and so very free? In Nat's arms, she thought, pulling up with a jolt, remembering with sudden intensity his lips on hers. In her husband's arms.

"Good race," Jared called back to her, apparently unaware that she had dropped out of the running. "I haven't done anything like that in a long time."

"I know." Abby walked her horse under the shifting shade of the palm tree and patted its neck. She was still reeling from her revelation. "New Bedford stifles us."

"It's our home," he protested, falling in beside her.

"Yes, but we're expected to behave a certain way. To be a certain thing, whether it's what we are or not."

"I don't feel that way."

"Maybe it's different for a man."

"I don't think so."

"Jared, you know men are allowed much more freedom than a woman is."

"But, of course."

"You think that's right?"

He seemed to consider that. Nat, she thought, would have come back with some teasing rejoinder about male superiority. She suddenly very much wished he was beside her. "Last year I would have said a woman needed to be protected."

She glanced at him curiously. "What's changed your mind?"

"You. No, don't move away, Abby, I'm not going to force my attentions on you. Or my feelings."

She eyed him warily. "Then what do you mean?"

"I wouldn't have thought you could survive at sea," he said candidly. "I would have kept you at home, safe with your roses and your poetry."

"Safe, maybe, but stifled too, Jared."

"I'm not saying I approve. Just that you've stood it well."

"Thank you," she said tartly, urging her horse forward.

"I seem to do nothing but offend you lately." He caught up with her. "I don't mean to."

"I'd like to believe that."

"Then do. I don't want to lose our friendship." he fell silent. "Those were good days at Clark's Point."

She nodded. "Yes, they were."

"Riding the way we just did, flying kites—remember? And your cousin Joshua teaching us how to sail."

"I remember. Remember digging for quahogs and how my mother would always pretend to be upset that I'd gotten my dress wet?"

His teeth flashed in a grin. "Yes, and the clambakes on the beach, and listening to the grown-ups telling stories about the sea. It was a good time, Abby."

"And long past.

"But do you know what I liked the most?"

"No. What?"

"Your family. I envied you them, Abby, all those aunts and uncles and cousins. And all of them good to me."

"Why shouldn't they have been, Jared?"

He didn't answer right away. "They knew something about me that you apparently don't."

She frowned, caught by the memories in spite of her wariness of him. "I can't imagine what."

"My mother wasn't ill."

"But of course she was. I saw her myself, lying on a sofa."

"With a little brown bottle beside her. She took laudanum." He looked full at her. "That's what everyone knew."

"Good heavens. But why?"

"I've figured it out since." Jared sounded grim. "She wasn't healthy, and she couldn't manage well with my father at sea. There must have been days it just seemed easier to sleep. Then after a while, she couldn't stop using the stuff."

"I had no idea." Abby reached out her hand and then let it drop. No matter her sympathy, she could not make herself touch him. "I'm sorry, Jared."

"Yes. Everyone was." He stared moodily ahead. "My father never rose above being a common seaman, for all the years he shipped out. I decided I wasn't going to be like them, Abby. I'm not going to be a failure."

"Well, you're not. I've never seen you fail at anything you try, Jared."

"I've failed with you, more than once. And I don't understand it," he went on, as she opened her mouth to protest. "I did what I set out to do. I'm successful, Abby. I have a fine reputation and a house on the hill. But you married someone who uses a bottle, too. So I failed."

"Stop feeling sorry for yourself," she snapped. "What you did, you did for yourself. And Nat does not drink anymore."

"He will. At first my mother could go weeks without laudanum. She always promised me she wouldn't take it again, but she always did."

With a little jolt, Abby recognized Nat's own declaration. But Nat really didn't drink, she told herself. Just that one night at Iolani Palace. That, however, was not something she wanted to discuss with Jared. "We're each responsible for what we do. I could have stood up to my father," she said, and as she did so knew it was true. It simply had never occurred to her. "You've broken away from your past. But . . ."

"But what, Abby?" he cut in, eyes hard.

"But you've behaved badly toward me," she said in a rush. She could not let this pass. If she'd had the courage to change her life, surely she had enough to confront Jared. "You have, you know, and never a word of apology. I don't care if you didn't want me marrying Nat. You behaved badly."

He didn't answer right away. "I suppose I did."

"You scared me, Jared."

"I didn't mean to." He turned to look at her. "I'm afraid my passions got away from me."

What nonsense, she thought, and again, disconcertingly, remembered her reactions to Nat's kisses. If only . . . "I don't know if I can trust you anymore."

"You can, Abby," he said earnestly, reaching over and laying his hand on hers. "I promise you'll never have anything to fear from me. Please forgive me."

"Quite a sight," a voice drawled from behind, and Abby, about to pull away from Jared, instead turned to see Nat.

"Oh!" she exclaimed, freeing her hand. "Nat, I—"

"I didn't know you could ride like that," he said easily, coming up on her other side and nodding cordially enough at Jared. Between the two men Abby felt almost trapped. "I felt like I was standing still."

"I'm sorry. I didn't mean to leave you behind."

Nat's gaze traveled quickly over Abby, as tactile as a touch, making her blush. "Quite an edifying sight from behind, actually. You and I will have to ride like that sometime."

"But you told me you couldn't ride—"

"Excuse me. I would like to speak with Captain Bowen," Jared cut in and wheeled his horse away. *Damn him, damn him,* he thought, keeping the animal, and his emotions, under tight rein. If Abby had missed the innuendo in Howland's statement about riding, Jared hadn't. Damn the man, not only for taking Abby away but for being so blatantly possessive. He would pay. *And soon,* Jared thought, looking back and smiling grimly. Nat would be dead and Abby would be his.

Chapter 20

Nat wanted a drink more than he had for a very long time. He could almost taste the whiskey on his tongue, feel its fumes sharp in his nose. Damnation, he wanted a drink—and all because of a woman.

Abby looked at him questioningly, making him realize he'd muttered something. "Nat?"

"Nothing." He shook his head.

"I know I made a spectacle of myself, but—"

"You're old friends." A bond he would never have with her, childhoods shared, the same background. It hadn't mattered before. Seamen respected a man who made it to the cap'n's quarters on his own, a man who fought against the odds and won. The businessmen of New Bedford had respected him, too. But never before had he dared do anything so bold as to marry one of their daughters. "Did your father want you to marry him?"

"Oh, stop it," she said, and digging in her heels, galloped a few paces ahead. Nat's self-pity evaporated. She was his wife. He wasn't going to sit by and let Swift steal her away.

"I'm sorry," he said quietly, catching up with her again. She eyed him sideways. "I'm tired of having to defend myself for something I didn't do."

"I know." He would have rubbed a hand over his face, except that he wasn't secure enough in the saddle. "We keep letting the past come between us, don't we, Abby?"

"I don't think we do," she said, surprised. "I know it made me who I was, but I've changed."

"I know. I'm not saying you haven't."

"Then, what?"

He turned to look at her, silhouetted against the azure of the bay and the paler blue of the sky. His Abby—so close, so distant. If he reached out to touch her, how would she react? She felt nothing, she'd said, and the memory still rankled. Yet when first he'd held her, kissed her, there'd been something between them. The problem was making that something grow. "Maybe we have to go back to the beginning."

"Of what?"

"Of wagers and consequences."

She frowned. "Nat, I don't understand you tonight."

"Good." He grinned and held out his hand, more confident now. Woo her slowly; dare her and arouse her fighting spirit. "Let's catch up with the others," he said and rode forward.

Much later, with the sun gone and the sky above sprinkled with stars, Nat sprawled back on the grass, at peace. Beside him Abby sat more circumspectly on a blanket, her arms about her bent knees. Her back almost, but not quite, rested against his chest. He was aware, from her rigid shoulders, of the effort it cost her to keep that distance between them. If she would relax, lean against him, perhaps he could take matters between them another step tonight. Or, he thought, looking at the nape of her neck, left unprotected by her elaborate braided coiffure, he could do something about the situation whether she related or not.

Since the group had arrived at their destination, a secluded grove of trees, the evening had been pleasant. Swift sat with others, and Nat was unexpectedly enjoying the outing. While the ladies admired the lush foliage or sat talking under canopies of green-and-white-striped canvas, some of the men had decided to climb Diamond Head, looming high beside them. Nat made it, out of breath but triumphant. In the old days, the drinking days, he would never have had the stamina for such a feat. Now he did, and more. He had regained the respect of his companions, the fleet's captains, by again proving his competence. What he had never realized he missed, though, was their friendship. He thought that now he had that too. If his luck held, he would never lose either again.

Back on the shore, he sat beside Abby as preparations for the luau continued. Staff from the hotel had worked all day at this site, used only for the traditional feast, to prepare the pit where a huge pig was roasted. Though Nat had been to luaus before, including some that had become wild without the presence of ladies, he sat beside Abby and watched everything with interest. Something primal shivered down his spine when, just as the sun slipped below the horizon, a blast sounded from a conch horn, melodic and mournful and compelling. As darkness fell and the torches were lit, Abby turned to him, whispering that she could almost imagine what Hawaiian life had once been like. That brought to Nat's mind an image of her wearing a grass skirt, a flower lei, and little else. It was an image that recurred more than once that evening.

Now, with the meal of roast pig, sweet potatoes, corn, and pineapple consumed, everyone sat back, relaxed, sated. Some of the men had rum or spirits, Nat noted, seeing a bottle being passed surreptitiously around, but oddly enough his urge to drink was quiet. When someone brought out a guitar, he joined in singing old, well-loved songs. And now he was looking speculatively at Abby's neck.

They were in darkness, the two of them, just where the shadows of two torches merged, away from the main group. Nat had managed that simply by scanning the site and choosing the spot most likely to be private. After that, it had only been a matter of being near Abby when it was time to eat. He was rather proud of himself for his foresight. Being devious occasionally had its merits.

Abby shifted, changing position, and for just a moment leaned back. The chance was too good to pass up. Nat bent his head and pressed a brief but warm and damp kiss on the nape of her neck.

Abby's head jerked up, and she turned. In the flickering light her eyes were great dark pools, confused, intrigued. "What did you do that for?" she asked softly.

"I wanted to." His voice was equally low. "Did you think I'd stopped wanting you, Abby?"

She licked her lips, from nervousness, he knew, but the action sent a shaft of pure desire arrowing through him. "I—don't know."

Nat pressed against her back, reaching past her for one of the flowers scattered in profusion before them. "This belongs here," he said, tucking it, as always, behind her left ear.

"Thank you." Abby's voice was shaky as she glanced away. "Nat, we're not alone."

"Scared?"

"Of being seen? Yes."

"What if no one was around, Abby?"

That made her look at him again, and Nat, for the life of him, could not look away. He was drawn into the depths of her gaze, falling, seeing into her heart, her soul. For the first time since he had confronted her with the truth of their marriage, something eased inside him. Whatever their problem was, they could solve it. He knew they could.

"I don't know." Abby had turned away, and the distance between them loomed as a chasm.

"Scared?" he taunted again, though gently.

"Yes." She turned, glanced at the others, and then looked at him. "Nat, this isn't the place."

"Then we'll take a walk."

"In the dark?" she protested as he pulled her to her feet, a hand under her arm. "No one will believe that."

"We won't tell anyone. Careful, there's not much light here," he said, guiding her away from the luau site. Palm fronds rustled above them, and the air was heavy with the scent of flowers. He slipped his arms loosely about her waist, and though she stiffened, she didn't try to pull away.

"I thought you said you'd wait until I came to you."

"Aye, but I never said I wouldn't help you along."

Abby's mouth quirked. "Do you always take what you want?"

"If I did, Abby, we wouldn't be here, would we?"

She glanced away, absorbing the implications of that. He wouldn't force her. She must know that. "Nat, I don't know what to tell you."

"Tell me what scares you, Abby."

"I can't." She kept her gaze on his cravat; her hands rested loosely on his forearms. "I can't."

He bent forward, his lips grazing her temple. "Is it this?" She shuddered. "N-no."

"Good. Good." His lips slid across her forehead, slowly and easily and carefully. That was how to win her. "Then it's no different here."

Abby's fingers tightened convulsively on his arms. "No, Nat, I—"

"Shh. Shh." Down along her cheekbone, now, to take her ear into his mouth. She shuddered again and abruptly sagged against him. Triumph surged through him. She was his.

He forced himself to keep it slow, parting his lips and sliding them along her jaw. Her head tilted back, and he took advantage of the invitation she offered, pressing warm, wet kisses on her throat, dipping into the hollow with his tongue. Her arms were around his neck, her hands clasped and her back bent, jutting her bosom forward. He wanted to kiss her, as he had never wanted to kiss any woman, so much so he could feel it down to his toes. He wanted to plunder her lips with his, spear his tongue into the warm wetness of her mouth, feel her body go pliant and soft against him. He—damnation, he wanted her, and so it was only by a great effort that he pulled away.

"Don't stop." Abby's voice was quick, breathless.

"We have to." He kept his hands on her waist, loath to release her just yet. "I have to."

"But—oh." She drew back. He could feel her retreating into her dignified shell. This time, though, he knew what had prompted the retreat. Fear, though of what he didn't know.

"Do I scare you, Abby?" he asked in a low voice.

"No." Her voice was equally low, and she stared fixedly at his shoulder. "Not you."

"Who, then?"

"No one." She looked up at him in surprise. "Nat, you surely don't think there's been another man? Of all things—"

"No." He stopped her with his fingers to her lips. "No, I knew you were a virgin. Is that why you're scared?"

"I shouldn't be by now, should I?" She paused. "This feeling you expect me to have—Nat, do women really feel it?"

"Aye. But not all women," he added, compelled by honesty.

"Oh. Then maybe I can't—"

"No." This time he did kiss her, quickly but firmly. "You're one of the warmest people I've ever known. No, sweetheart. The feeling's there."

"I can't find it," she said, pounding lightly on his shoulder. "I try, and I can't. And I don't want you to be disappointed in me." She looked up at him through the dimness. "That's what really bothers me."

"Sweetheart, I could never be disappointed in you."

"Never's a long time."

"Never," he repeated, and raised his head, listening as other noises at last began to penetrate his consciousness. Someone, somewhere, was saying his name. "I think everyone's about ready to return to the hotel."

"Oh!" She stepped back from him, her hands rising quickly and futilely to her hair. "I must look a sight."

"It's dark. No one will notice."

"Yes, they will."

"So let them. It doesn't matter."

"Doesn't it, Nat?" she asked, and he knew she was talking about more than her appearance.

He drew her back toward the others. "No," he said firmly, and prayed it was true.

The carriage drive back to the hotel seemed longer than the ride out had been. Abby was glad to climb down when they reached their destination. She was more tired than seemed warranted. But then, the encounter with Nat had been draining, so emotional that now she was empty. It scared her. Nat thought her capable of feeling, but she feared he was wrong.

Voices broke out in excited chatter up on the verandah. Abby, climbing the stairs with Nat beside her, looked up curiously. "What is it?" she asked one of the women.

"Oh, the most wonderful thing!" The woman turned to her. "Sarah Hathaway has a little girl."

Something twisted inside Abby—pain, regret, jealousy. "Yes, that is wonderful! Are they well?"

"Yes, Captain Hathaway says they're sleeping now. I'm dying to see the baby."

"Yes, when Sarah's ready. Good night," Abby said and stepped into the hotel, where they had decided to stay for this one night. She hoped her face didn't reflect her emotions. She wanted a normal life. But, as she settled into bed, as Nat turned over on his pallet on the floor, she knew that normality was more out of reach than it had been. Tonight she had failed to breach the barrier that remained between her and Nat. Her marriage was empty and barren. Barring a miracle, it appeared that it would stay that way.

Captain Hathaway stopped by the table where Nat and Abby were just finishing their breakfast the following morning, his rugged face beaming with pride. A fine, healthy girl, he told them in answer to their congratulations. A little small, maybe, but her lungs were good, and he wouldn't trade her for all the sons in the world. "How is Sarah feeling?" Abby asked, smiling. His obvious happiness took away the sting of envy she had felt last evening. "Is she up to having visitors?"

"Maybe later," he said. "She'd like to see you, but don't tell anyone. I don't want her to tire herself out."

"Of course not. Please give her my best."

"I will. Oh, and have you heard the other good news?"

Nat took a sip of coffee and set down his cup. "What news?"

"The authorities caught the man who hurt those island girls."

Nat and Abby looked at each other in surprise. "No, we hadn't heard that."

"I didn't sleep much last night," Captain Hathaway said, as if by explanation. "They caught him with another girl."

"Then it's good they got him," Nat said, voice grim. "Was it one of us?"

"Aye, but I didn't hear the name. Swift," he said, turning as Jared walked past, "do you know the name of the man who was arrested last night?"

Jared, who had been smiling, went somber. "Yes. But this isn't something that should be discussed before a lady."

"I'm a shipowner, Jared," she reminded him crisply and was aware of Nat nodding in agreement, backing her up. "This affects all of us."

Jared looked from her to Nat, his eyes filled with an odd expression, part reluctance, part something she couldn't quite identify. It looked like satisfaction. "Very well. I'm afraid he was one of yours."

"What?" she exclaimed.

"Who?" Nat demanded at the same moment.

"A man named Pickens. Do you remember him?"

Nat swore under his breath. "Yes. He jumped ship when we dropped anchor. I thought we'd seen the last of him."

"Apparently not. Not if he was in town last night."

Dear heavens. One of their own men had been responsible for those terrible crimes. "How did they catch him?" Abby asked, managing to sound calm and businesslike.

"The word's gone around the past few days that he was the one. He was seen near the broth—house that night, it seems."

Nat frowned. "That's not much evidence to go on. Has either of the girls identified him?"

Jared spread his hands in an apparent display of ignorance. "No one knows where they are, except maybe their families. You can't blame them, of course."

"Convenient," Nat muttered, and Jared shot him a look. "Is Pickens being held at the jail?"

"Yes. He's to appear before a magistrate this morning."

"Then I'll be there. I suppose you want to come?" he asked Abby as they both rose.

"No." She shook her head. "I'll let you handle it. But you'll let me know what happens?"

He nodded. "Aye. This could be bad, Abby," he said, his voice lower as they left the dining room.

"I know," she said, her voice as low as his. Jared was only a few paces ahead, and the angle of his head suggested that he was trying to hear their discussion. It was annoying. "One of our men. Will we be held at all accountable?"

"No, but it doesn't look good. Damnation." He ran a hand over his face. "Why did it have to be someone from our ship?"

"I'm just glad they caught the man."

"If they have."

"Excuse me?"

He shook his head. "Nothing. I'll see what the situation is and let you know."

Abby watched him go, brow furrowed. Something was going on here, something she didn't quite understand. There were undercurrents between Nat and Jared that scared her, though she thought that Nat sometimes exaggerated the extent of Jared's enmity. Heavens, but she would be glad when they were at sea again, away from other people. Away from Jared. In the meantime, though, she was going to see if Sarah needed her.

Sarah's baby daughter proved to be as beautiful as her father had boasted, albeit rather red and wrinkled. Abby carefully held the baby as she sat beside Sarah's bed, surprised at the heft of this seemingly fragile bundle. Sarah looked tired, but otherwise well, and they spent a pleasant time chatting and admiring the baby. Abby even managed to overcome her embarrassment to broach the delicate topic of her marriage and to confess the depths of her ignorance. Sarah, bless her, was sympathetic and blunt, telling Abby some startling things about the more intimate side of marriage. When, later, Nat told her that though Pickens proclaimed his innocence he was apparently guilty as charged, she only nodded. Upsetting though it was to think that one of their crew was capable of such violence, the matter was settled. The things she'd learned that afternoon loomed larger in her mind.

A baby girl, she thought, lying in bed that night, letting the ship's motion lull and rock her. A daughter. Her eyes burned with tears she was determined not to shed. Until now she hadn't known just how much she wanted a baby. The problem was that it required intimacy with Nat, and facing that strange and baffling barrier that kept her from feeling true closeness with him. She had to figure out how to breach that barrier; she had to plan what to do, should she fail. Unfortunately, failure seemed far more likely to her than success.

Sitting up, she pushed her hair back from her face. If she could discuss her marriage with Sarah, surely she could face her problems herself. Last night, shaken, a little frightened, she'd let Nat think that the physical pleasures of love were foreign to her. They weren't, though matters were safer this way; he wouldn't pursue her for something she feared she couldn't deliver. She did feel things for him, strong things, physical things. When he held her, when he kissed her, she felt sensations such as she'd never known existed, and in the oddest parts of her body. Oh, yes, she wanted him, but not all the time. Sometimes she felt dead inside. That was what scared her. She could not overcome it, though, without making an effort. The events of the past months had proved that to her.

So. She would face it, starting from her wedding night. Beginning with the kissing, which had been exquisite and had left her feeling both languorous and alive. Going on to the moment when Nat untied her wrapper, sending a shiver of anticipation and nervousness through her; so daring to be nearly unclothed with a man. The taste of him on her lips; the feel of his hair, his skin, the crisp cotton of his shirt. His scent—heady, intoxicating—and his hands, stroking her back, urging her closer, until she was pressed so intimately against him that she could feel his need for her. Her own answering need, urgent, making her twist against him. His hand, sliding upward to cup her breast. That, she thought, eyes snapping open as she returned to reality and the realization that her body was tingling, was when the feeling had gone. When he had claimed her breasts. Stopped cold, as it had now, leaving her distant and detached. That was where the problem began.

She frowned into the darkness. She could remember feeling that way before, the observer and the observed, though not often. When her parents died. When she learned she'd lost everything. When she—this was odd—but when Jared had told her he'd bought her house, before anger had overwhelmed her. Now, this. In some fundamental way, she had failed. And, tangled up in it all was that dark, fleeting memory.

Lying back, she frowned into the darkness. Lately the memory had become a little more insistent, a little more clear. It involved the music room and darkness and a crashing chord from the pianoforte, all overlaid with a feeling of such shame that even now she wanted to squirm. But why? In that room she had practiced scales and diligently perfected her fingering on pieces of music; there her parents had entertained on warm summer nights, the long windows open to admit the heady scent of roses from the garden. No hurt had come to her in that room, and yet she couldn't shake the sense that it was far more important to her than she knew.

The question now was, how to keep that memory from ruining her marriage. Going back to sea would help. Away from other people, other distractions, maybe she and Nat could find each other again, could talk and relax. Until they went off to their separate staterooms, and nothing would have changed.

No more, she thought, scrambling out of the bunk and stalking through the cabin toward Nat's stateroom. She was no coward, by God. The time had come for action, and she was going to take it

"Nat." She knelt on the deck beside his bunk, reaching out her hand to his shoulder and disconcertingly touched skin. Before they'd returned to the ship he'd worn at least a shirt for sleeping. His skin was warm and taut, stretched over firm muscle, and if she moved her fingers just a little bit, there, she could feel the beginnings of the crisp golden curls on his chest. Her hand moved and then paused, her courage suddenly deserting her. Perhaps this wasn't such a good idea after all.

Carefully she drew back, and at that moment Nat made a noise that was half snore, half snort. Startled, Abby rocked back on her heels, but too late. Nat's hand gripped her wrist, holding her there. "Damned ice—what—Abby?" he said, his voice gravelly with sleep.

"Yes." She tugged on her hand, and his grip tightened. "I'm sorry I woke you."

"Is something wrong?"

"No. You were dreaming," she improvised.

He yawned hugely. "I was dreaming we were in the Arctic. Did I wake you up?"

"No."

"Then what is it?"

"I . . ." Abby's mouth went dry. Now was the moment of decision, to follow through on her original intention or to leave. It would be safer to leave, and surely she could try again tomorrow? No matter that her hand was now clamped to his shoulder, making her painfully aware of his nearness and warmth. "I—want to ask you something."

He yawned again. "Couldn't it wait until morning?"

"No. No," she said again, with more resolve, and straightened her spine. "It can't. Nat, I want you to come back to bed with me."

Chapter 21

Nat sat bolt upright, aware that his spine wasn't the only part of himself that had stiffened. "What did you say?"

"Come back to bed with me, Nat."

Dear God. All his hopes, all his dreams, come true. He didn't quite believe it. "And do what?"

Abby paused. "I don't know."

"You don't know." He shook his head. "Go back to bed."

"This isn't working, Nat." She settled beside him, cross-legged. "We're not growing any closer sleeping apart."

"Hell, Abby. If I go to bed with you, you know what will happen. I want you." He gazed directly at her. "I haven't made any secret of it."

"I know."

"Are you ready for that?"

She looked away. "Couldn't you just hold me for a while?"

"Just hold you." He gulped. "And then what? Kiss you?"

She didn't answer right away. "Maybe."

"And then stop. You don't expect much, do you?"

"I know it's a lot to ask, but I was thinking . . ."

"What?"

"I don't know much about all this." Her words came in a rush. She'd learned a lot from Sarah that afternoon, and though she was stunned about the audacity of what she was going to suggest, it excited her too. "But isn't there something I could do for you? I mean—well, you know."

Nat groaned and dropped his forehead on her shoulder. "Hell, Abby. I don't think I can stand this."

Her hand slid onto his thigh, jolting him. "Maybe I can help you," she said, and hesitantly moved her hand upward.

"Hell. No." He caught her hand before it could reach its destination. This wasn't right, somehow. He wanted to feel her touch, and he wanted to teach her how to pleasure him, with her hands, her mouth, her body. But he couldn't. He wanted a true joining, and this wouldn't be it. He would, he thought grimly, regret this in the morning. "Stop, Abby."

"Why?"

"It doesn't solve anything."

"You'll feel better."

"Not without you, love." He pressed a kiss into the palm of her hand. Her fingers flexed around his, reminding him briefly of what he had just refused. Dear God. Was he mad?

"Nat." She slipped her hand free, her voice regretful. "I never meant things to be this way. I never meant for the two of us to be so far apart."

Nat gazed at her through the dimness. Under other circumstances he might have found it amusing that she was the one entreating and he the one holding back. Go slowly, he had been advised, and so he had. It had worked, to an extent; some of their earlier closeness had returned. Maybe, then, this was the next step. "I'll share a bed with you, Abby," he said quietly, knowing that what he was about to say would consign him to a living hell. "But that's all."

"Oh? Oh." Abby glanced away, disappointed, relieved. He was not like any man she'd ever met. Her suitors may have wanted her fortune, but they had also expressed an interest in her person, glancing at her bosom, touching her hand, stealing a kiss. Nat's refusal confused her. Yet in some way she understood it. They had gone far beyond the point where stolen kisses were enough. "But you will come?"

"Not the way I'd like."

"Excuse me?"

"Never mind for now, but you've got some things to learn."

Abby's breath caught as he heaved himself to his feet. Briefly she caught a glimpse of taut backside and firm thighs, leaving her feeling unsettled; eager and apprehensive at once. Then he wrapped the sheet around his waist. "Will you teach me?"

"Oh, yes." He held his hand down to her. "But not to-night, Abby. There's only so much a man can stand."

"This will do for now." Together they returned to the larger stateroom. She climbed into the bunk, waiting as he climbed in beside her. The sheets rustled and the bunk swayed, almost making her roll toward him. Well. This had been her idea, hadn't it? She lay as still as she could, almost as if he weren't there. There was space between them, and yet somehow she could feel his warmth, his firmness. If she wanted, she could reach out to him, but some instinct warned her against it. She'd asked enough of him tonight. She'd asked enough of herself. The question now was, just what had she done?

"She blows!" the lookout's cry came from far above. In the aft cabin of the *Aquinnah,* Abby held her pen poised, listening to the sudden flurry of movement on deck. A week out of Honolulu, and already she was back in the rhythms of shipboard life. The only difference was that Harold, who would never survive in the Arctic, had been left behind. She ran her life by the ships' bells, marking the change of watch. She read, wrote in her journal, did laundry or mending, and when a whale was sighted, she ran up on deck, as excited and hopeful as any man aboard. Sometimes she missed the warmth and leisurely pace of the islands, but she knew she was where she belonged, in her true home, with Nat.

She was closer to him now than she had ever been, even in the first few days of their marriage, when she had thought she was happy. They took their meals together, and though the conversation usually centered around whales and the ship, Abby now knew much more than she had and could take part. At noon she stood beside him on deck while he took the sights. Later, in the cabin, Nat would teach her the use of a sextant, using the hanging oil lamp as the sun and the top rail of the paneling as the horizon. This entailed his putting his arms about her from behind, ostensibly to help her hold the heavy sextant steady. Both of them knew the real reason, though. Both of them knew why they often brushed up against each other in the passageway; both of them knew why he sometimes leaned over her while she played the parlor organ, though he claimed to be turning the pages of her music. They were flirting, dancing about each other in a kind of mating ritual. But then, at night, when they at last retired to the captain's cabin, they both lay still and silent and distant in the wide bunk, until at last sleep took them.

Stowing her journal away, Abby took up her shawl and went on deck. Already the weather was cooler; soon she would take out her bloomers again, no matter what Nat might say. "Where are they?" she asked Nat, as he lowered his telescope.

"North, about two miles. A school of sperm whales."

"Are you lowering your boat?"

"Aye. Sloan will act as shipkeeper."

Abby nodded, looking wistfully at the rigging. "I wish I could see for myself."

"Go out in a boat? Don't be silly."

"Not in a boat. From the rigging."

He frowned. "Abby, I don't have time for this now."

"I know." She stepped back as he handed the telescope to Peleg. "Greasy luck, Captain."

"Aye. We need it," he said, and headed for his boat.

In the boat, Nat shaded his eyes with his hand and peered into the distance, where the whale's back humped against the sky. It was still a good mile away, he guessed, looking back at the ship, already far behind. He fancied he could still see Abby at the rail. But then, he seemed always to see her. Sleeping beside her at night, knowing she was there and not touching her, was slowly driving him insane. Matters couldn't go on as they were. Somehow they were going to have to solve their problems. Just now, facing down a whale seemed easier.

The boat's sail was drawing well, and the men pulled at the oars with quiet determination. Not too far now. He'd get this one, Nat vowed. In the bow Tony Arruda, the boatsteerer, braced his knee in a cleat, harpoon at the ready. Easy, now, with the oars, because a whale's hearing was acute and if he heard them coming he'd run. Not a man spoke; not a man moved but to breathe and to row. The great bulk of the whale rose higher, closer, and then they were upon him. "Stand by your iron, Tony," Nat hissed, and the whale suddenly heaved up. No time for subtlety now. "Give it to him!"

Tony lunged forward, and the harpoon went home. Instantly the whale sounded, its flukes rising high in the air and then hitting the ocean with a splash that soaked everyone in the boat. The line suddenly went taut, and the boat sprang forward at great speed. "Peak your oars, dammit!" Nat yelled, stumbling forward in a crouching run as the boat rocked from side to side and water sprayed in a sheet over the bow. Tony passed him, grabbing the steering oar in the stern, and Nat settled in the bow, soaked, triumphant, exuberant. "Get out of the way of the line!" This as the rope attached to the harpoon spooled out at dizzying speed, smoking and whistling from the friction. A real Nantucket sleigh ride, by God, and though they were in imminent danger of tipping, though the crew had to bail constantly to keep the boat from swamping, still Nat felt alive, exhilarated. This was what he had missed for so long, the thrill of the chase, pitting his skills against the largest creature on earth. He was not going to lose it again.

After what seemed like hours, the boat's speed began to lessen, at first almost imperceptibly, and then more obviously. The whale was tiring. The line went slack; coil by coil, hand over hand, the crew wound it in, towing the boat toward the still distant whale. It was hard work, thirsty work, and yet no one complained. All knew what prize awaited them at the end of the line. The whale was visible now, lying quiet upon the water, apparently exhausted, but none of them underestimated his size or power, if it turned on them. Against a whale's fury a boat and the men within it were fragile things. Carefully, now, slowly, the men towed the line; Nat rose in the bow, the sharp killing lance held high. For just a moment he saw Abby's face, her eyes reproachful, and then he struck. With a flurry of movement the whale fought death, and then, with the frothy water turning pink, went still and rolled over. The long, weary battle was done. They had won.

"Hard astern," Nat ordered quietly, when the whale had been secured to the boat. They had traveled many miles before the whale had tired. The ship was nowhere in sight, yet they still had to tow the whale back. Glancing at the sun, appreciably lower in the sky than it had been, Nat worked out a rough course. South by west, and he'd just have to hope that the *Aquinnah* was heading toward them.

If it came down to it he would cut the whale free to save his crew, but no whaler worth his salt ever did that willingly. No, he'd keep to his course

"Pull for the ship, lads," he said and sat back, oddly at peace. Somehow, during the mad, exhilarating flight, he had reached a decision. He might be lost at sea, but he knew, at last, what he was going to do about Abby.

"Three boats coming back," the lookout called from the masthead. "One whale."

"Can you see who?" Sloan, acting as shipkeeper, called.

"No, too far away. Hey! She blows! Send up a signal!"

Abby stepped up onto the cooper's bench, straining to see, but the boats were still beyond her sight. She glanced at the rigging, wishing again she could climb it, as free as any man. She envied the crew their easy ability to climb in the shrouds, even if all they saw was more ocean. She would look for more than whales, though. She would look for her husband.

"Was one of the boats the captain's?" she said quietly, approaching Sloan.

He gave her a startled look; usually ordinary seamen had little contact with her. "I don't know, ma'am. Two of the boats have gone back after the whale, so we won't know for a while."

Abby nodded. "Thank you." She turned away, looking up at the masthead, where the lookout strained to see both whales and boats. Beyond that the sun, while still above the horizon, was lowering. If the men didn't strike the whale soon, they would have to return empty-handed. She hoped the fourth boat, the missing boat, would be sighted. She only hoped it wasn't Nat's. She was more than the owner now. She was the captain's wife. More was at stake for her than merely money.

The third mate's boat reached the ship and was hoisted aboard, its crew jubilant at their catch. From the masthead the lookout reported that the other whale was moving away and that the two boats he could see were in pursuit. Outwardly calm, Abby sat on the cooper's bench, leaving only to go below for a solitary supper. "I'll let ye know when the boats are back," Peleg offered, as he cleared away her dishes, and she rose, shaking her head. Though she wasn't sure why, she needed to go back topside.

The sun was near the horizon when she reached the deck. From Sloan she learned that one of the boats had struck the whale and that the other was standing by to lend assistance in towing the creature back to the ship. That accounted for three boats. There was still no sign of the fourth.

Occupying herself with mending, Abby sat on the bench while the boats returned, the crew securing their catch and then coming aboard. Mr. Taber's boat was back, as well as Mr. Martel's. They knew now whose boat was missing. The captain's.

"Cap'n's boat struck a whale," Mr. Martel reported. "We was going after it, but he got there first, and that bastard—excuse me ma'am—took off like a bat out of—Hades." He flushed but held his ground. "I've been on some sleigh rides in my time, but this one was fast."

Abby took a careful stitch. She couldn't just send to a dry goods store for new stockings at sea; she had to repair any holes or runs herself, an exacting task. No wonder if she were so concentrated upon it. "Could you see their direction?"

"No way of tellin', ma'am, but the cap'n knows our position. He'll figure out how to get back. It's not the first time this has happened."

Abby laid down the mending, facing the inevitable fear. "And if he doesn't?"

"He will."

"It's getting dark."

"We'll send up rockets, ma'am. He'll see them."

She nodded. "There'll be a light at the masthead, too."

"Yes, ma'am. We'll do everything we can to find them." He grinned. "Even if I would like to be skipper someday."

"I beg your pardon?" she said coolly.

"Sorry." He straightened. "Bad joke. Excuse me, ma'am, I've got to work out our course."

Abby nodded, and Mr. Martel stepped away. She didn't understand men. How anyone could joke at such a time was beyond her. Not that she really thought anything had happened to Nat. It was just that she didn't think she could face the future if he didn't return. As owner she would have to assume all the responsibility that Nat routinely handled now. That, and the loneliness.

The stocking fell to the deck, unheeded, as it all crashed down upon her, the burden of a life lived without Nat. For she knew that Nat's boat might not be simply lost upon the sea. It might be sunk, or dashed to pieces by a frenzied whale. If so, they would never know, and she couldn't bear it.

Frowning, she picked up the stocking. Since when had she let herself depend so on a man? Except for her father, she'd prided herself always on her independence. So it should be now, but it wasn't. There was an awful, gaping emptiness inside her at the thought of going on without Nat, making her want to howl with grief and misery. And she didn't know why, unless she loved him.

Her hands went still. She loved him. Of course. Why had she not seen it sooner? This feeling had been a long time growing, starting from the moment she'd seen him in the hallway of her father's house, as tall and splendid as a Viking god. It had grown as she watched him handling his job with admirable competence; flared when he had been hurt back before they rounded the Horn; flamed into something else the first time he kissed her. Now, when he was in danger, when it might be too late, she knew at last what she felt. Love, lust, desire—and fear. Fear that she would fail him again.

There was a sudden booming noise and a bright flash, high above Abby's head, making her look up. They'd set off a rocket. Thank heavens. If Nat saw it, he would use it as a guide. Abby, sitting on the bench with all pretense of mending put aside, could only pray that he would. She needed him, and not just as the ship's captain. She needed him as she needed breath. He had to return. If he didn't, how could she go on?

"Cap'n, there's a light there!" one of the men in the whaleboat shouted. "Off to starboard."

"Aye, I see it," Nat said calmly, though inside him a knot of tension dissolved. It had to be the *Aquinnah,* sending up flares for them. The light was still miles distant, low on the horizon, but it gave him something to steer by. They were not, as he had secretly feared, lost upon the trackless sea.

Something happened to a man when he faced the fact that he was in dire trouble. It had happened to him before, when his ship had gone on the ice. For the very first time he'd acknowledged that his reasons for drinking went far beyond relaxation or loneliness or whatever excuse he used. It hadn't stopped him, of course. There'd been the long voyage home to get through, and then the inquiry, all excellent reasons to keep his senses befogged. But, aye, he'd seen in a moment of clarity, so pure it stood out from all else, that if he went on as he was everything he had, everything he was, would be lost.

So it had been today. Hard work, willpower, and something mystical, something he didn't always understand, something beyond luck, had brought him back to the life he wanted. Yet a twist of fate had nearly taken it away from him again. He'd heard tales of whaleboats separated from their ships; they all had. He knew what lay ahead if they were truly lost: days spent under a merciless sun, with no food, no water, though the ocean surrounded them. They faced not death alone but madness as well. The prospect was terrifying.

There were no more lights, but the location of the flare was fixed in Nat's memory. With occasional glances at the stars above, he guided his boat. Soon another light, this one dimmer, appeared, glowing steadily as they rowed toward it. The *Aquinnah*'s masthead, he thought, peering forward for the first glimpse of his ship. They were nearly home.

"Ahoy, the ship!" he called when they were closer.

"Ahoy, Cap'n!" Mr. Martel's voice came back. "Did you take a pleasure sail?"

"Aye." Nat scrambled up the rope ladder that dangled over the ship's side. "Is all well?"

"Aye, all aboard and accounted for, and two whales taken. I thought I might end up being skipper."

"Not this time," Nat said without resentment. "And we have three whales." He had gambled, keeping his whale in tow when he thought they were lost, and he had won. "There'll be work to do in the morning."

"Aye. Tripp has supper for you in the cabin."

"Thanks. See that the others are fed once the whale's secured." Nat strode to the companionway and went below.

It was good to be back. Only now, alone, could he admit even to himself that he had been scared.

Abby rose from the settee as he entered the cabin and, before he quite knew what was happening, slipped her arms about his waist and pressed against him. "You're safe. Thank God."

For a moment Nat stood still in surprise, the warmth of her, her softness and sweet smell so heady to his senses that he was overwhelmed. Then his arms came up of their own volition, to hold her, just hold her, feminine and female and very, very precious. He'd nearly lost everything. He'd nearly lost her. "What are you still doing awake?" he asked.

She rubbed her cheek against his shoulder and then pulled back. "Waiting for you," she said, breaking free at last and going to stand by the settee. In the dim light he could see that her cheeks were flushed. "I was worried, so I stayed up."

Nat stared at her. If she were up, so was he, from her unexpected greeting. Damnation. He didn't know how much more of this he could handle. "Do you care for me so much, then?" he went on, sitting down and pulling his plate toward him.

"No, of course not," she said waspishly. "I was worried about who to name skipper. Mr. Martel's not quite up to it yet."

"I damn well am," he muttered.

"Oh?" She rose from the settee and crossed to him, her gait swaying in a way that told him she finally understood his innuendo. Dear God. His mouth went dry as she bent over him, the tips of her breasts brushing against his head. "Then we'll have to do something about that, won't we?"

Chapter 22

Nat's head jerked up, brushing against her breasts, making her feel warm. It wasn't pleasure, exactly, but it was more than she'd felt before. "What do you mean?" he asked hoarsely.

For answer she bent down and kissed him full on the mouth, using lips and tongue as he had taught her. His hand instantly gripped her head, holding her still as he responded, sucking at her lips as a man thirsty for her essence. His intensity frightened her for a moment, but then warmth spread down to her stomach. Desire, she knew now, and she welcomed it.

"Abby." He pulled back suddenly, his eyes searching her face. "Do you mean it?"

"Well." she looked down. "I do, but there's a problem."

"What?" He sounded apprehensive, and not for the first time she regretted all she'd put him through.

"It's—well, it's the wrong time of the month."

He was still. "I see," he said finally.

"But couldn't we still hold each other, Nat, and kiss?"

"No, sweetheart." He put her away from him and rose. "I couldn't stand it. You'd better just go to bed."

"I don't want to leave things as they are, Nat."

"Hell." He scrubbed his hands tiredly over his face. "We might go too far. Are you ready for that?"

She hesitated. How could she know, unless they tried? "I don't know."

"Well, then. No man likes being rejected, Abby."

"I wouldn't reject you!"

"You wouldn't feel, either."

"Do you think I like that?" she retorted. "I don't want to be that way, Nat. I want our marriage to work. I lo—"

"Go to bed," he interrupted, before she could tell him

what she had discovered during the long, long hours when his boat had been missing. "We'll discuss it another time."

It was an order, not captain to passenger, but husband to wife. Abby regretted having promised to obey in her wedding vows. "All right. Later," she said and then went into the stateroom. Later might just come sooner than he thought.

A fair amount of time passed before Nat came in, very quiet. He undressed just as quietly and then slipped into bed beside her. Abby, lying still, took an involuntary sniff. No smell of alcohol on him, she noted, and then berated herself for her lack of trust. Still, there it was. He'd promised her once before and broken that promise. She had also given him a lot to bear. Any man might give in to such stress.

Not her Nat, though. She was immensely proud of him for that, and even more determined to go through with her plans. She murmured, as if in sleep, and rolled over, so that she was pressed against him.

Nat went stiff, in every part of his body, she noted with amusement and pride. Her earlier apprehension vanished. If she could so affect him with such little effort, what might she do if she tried? "Mm." She nestled closer, felt him press momentarily against her and then, slowly, draw back. She immediately followed. Poor man. She was really testing him.

"Abby," he whispered after a moment.

"Mm?" she murmured into his shoulder. "Nat?"

"Well, who else would it be?" He sounded both annoyed and amused. "Turn over."

"I like it here, thank you."

He drew back again, his hand on her arm preventing her from following. "You're not asleep," he accused.

"Mm-hm. No."

"Then—"

"I think we've talked enough, Nat," she said, and winding her arms around his neck, kissed him as she had in the cabin. He responded instantly, rolling her over onto her back, so that she could feel every part of him imprinted on her body. A flame started low in her belly, and she gloried in it. The time wasn't right, but she was ready. She knew it instinctively. She might never feel exactly what Nat

wanted her to, but the coldness that had been inside her
for so long was gone. She could respond to him, after all.

With a groan, Nat wrenched himself free and rolled off
her, onto his back. "Abby—"

"Be quiet, Captain, and that's an order."

He jerked back as she rose up over him. "What did
you say?"

She smiled, though she knew he couldn't see. "I'm giving
you an order. Owner to captain, or wife to husband."

"Oh, are you?" He sounded amused.

"Yes."

"So what am I supposed to do?"

"Just lie there, Captain." She pressed her lips against his
throat and felt him shudder. "Just lie there."

"Abby—"

"Shh." She stopped him with a quick kiss on his mouth,
and then went on with her exploration, fascinated. His
mouth, his strong nose, his broad forehead—all familiar,
well-loved territory. The rest of him, though, she knew only
by touch, and then not that well. High time she changed
that. He groaned and shifted under her as she trailed kisses
down the solid column of his neck, to the shoulders that
so often shielded her, to his chest and the soft curls there.

"Abby." His voice was half groan, half laugh. "Do you
know what you're doing?"

"Oh, yes, Captain." She dipped her tongue into the hollow of his throat, as he had done to her, and let her head
drift lower. Oh, yes, she had a fair idea of what she was
doing, just from the way he moved against her. Heady, this
feeling of power over a man, when far too often in her life
she had been powerless, but it was a benign domination.
She hesitated and then, taking a deep breath, opened her
mouth over his nipple, touching it briefly with her tongue.
He jumped, and she felt an answering leap of triumph and
desire. He was hers.

Nat didn't protest again, not when she turned her attentions to his other nipple, not when she tugged lightly on
his chest hair, not when she explored the taut muscles of
his stomach with her fingertips. He groaned, shifted, sucked
in his breath, but he didn't protest. Emboldened, she continued her explorations, to truly new territory. And here,
for the first time, she faltered.

"It's all right." Nat seemed to sense her sudden nervousness, covering her hand with his. "It's all right."

"I—know." As much conquered as conqueror, she let him guide her hand to his manhood, though her fingers curled around it of their own accord. Velvet over steel, she thought, rubbing her hand over him as he taught her, warm and pulsing and mysterious. What startled her more was the answering pulse inside her, as if she were the one being pleasured. For the first time she understood what Nat wanted from her. It wasn't enough for her merely to cooperate. She had to be fully with him, as he was with her, or there would be no true closeness between them. Without the closeness, there would be no marriage.

Nat's breathing quickened and harshened as her hand moved; hers did, too. They were rushing to something she didn't fully understand but wanted to know, and so she deepened the pressure, increased the pace. He groaned and jerked beneath her, and there was a sudden, warm wetness on her hand. She felt briefly empty, alone, wishing his seed had been spent inside her, and then a rush of joyful triumph that overwhelmed all else. She had made love to her husband, and though they were not joined, for the first time she felt truly his wife.

Afterward they lay on their sides facing each other, knees bent and touching, faces a scant breath apart. His thumb idly stroked her cheek; her hand rested on his side. "Why?" he asked, after a few moments.

"I wanted to." *I love you,* she thought, and wondered why the words wouldn't come.

He gathered her close. "I don't know what I did to deserve you."

"I'm not all that special, Nat."

"I think you are." He stroked her arm, back and forth. "To me, you are."

"Nat." She rose up, pushing her hair back over her shoulders. "When the time is right—"

"Yes, love." He stopped her with his finger to her lips. "When the time is right." And he pulled her down to him, secure in the knowledge that, very soon, they would, indeed, be truly husband and wife.

* * *

Two days later, and Nat thought he could still feel the aftermath of what Abby had done to him. Good God. For once he had been the seduced, and he had thoroughly enjoyed every moment of it. Untutored though she was, still she was capable of drawing a response from him far more intense than any he'd ever experienced. Though they had not actually joined, she had made him very much hers. He would never have predicted, that hot summer's day last year when he had gone to her with an offer to buy her ship, that she was capable of such passion. He was anticipating heightening that passion still further, for her, when the time was right.

For now, though, he had to go on with the business of the ship. Yesterday had been spent cutting in and trying out, today cleaning the ship and stowing the oil in the hold. He was sitting down at last with some paperwork—necessary in his job, but the part of it he liked least. Abby was not a demanding owner, but even she would want to see an accounting of ship's expenses to be applied against income.

In Hawaii they'd spent a fair amount restocking the ship for the long cruise to the Arctic, in addition to taking on new crew members. As an eager young sailor he hadn't realized that the captain was so involved in such mundane matters as obtaining meats and vegetables and other provisions. From one invoice, he listed the number of casks of beef bought and the price of flour; from others, potatoes, carrots, flour, coffee. One invoice listed a price incorrectly, with the numbers switched around. Good thing he'd caught it. Abby transposed numbers, he thought, entering the correct figure, and Swift as well. Only once had Nat made a similar mistake, writing "51" for "15." That one little mistake had caused Nat's ship to go on the ice and changed his life forever. Fifteen feet of water under their hull, as measured by the plumb line, but he had written down fifty-one feet from the paper—

Nat dropped the pen, spattering drops of ink onto the account book. Most of that fateful day was shrouded in his mind, but for some reason one moment stood out clearly. He could see Swift, face ruddy from the cold, having just come in from using the lead sinker to measure the depth of the water in the channel. He could see the figure written upon the slip of paper Swift had handed him, as clearly as one of the invoices now before him. Fifty-one, not fifteen. He'd never seen that paper again, not on the ship, not among the evidence presented against him at the inquiry, but he remembered it. *Good God.* The mistake hadn't been his. It had been Swift's.

Agitated, he rose. Abby, sitting across the room from him with a book in hand, looked up at him and smiled. "Did we spend too much?" she asked teasingly.

"No. No." He brought his fist to his mouth, staring unseeing out the porthole. Swift's mistake, and what was more, he suspected the man knew it. Yet Swift had been quick enough to accuse Nat, quick enough to condemn him. Of course. In so doing, he had not only covered up his own wrongdoing but had made himself a hero. He was the one who had come out of the debacle with an enhanced reputation, while Nat had nearly been destroyed. And all because of one simple mistake. "You said once that you transpose numbers."

Abby looked up from her book. "Imagine you remembering that. Yes, once in a while I do. I have trouble doing figures."

"And Swift."

"Yes. Why do you ask?"

Nat continued to stare out the porthole. If he so much as looked at her he would pour out the whole story, and he didn't want to do that. Not yet. Not until he could find some confirmation other than his memories. "No reason."

Abby gazed at him for a moment, opened her mouth as if to speak, and then returned to her reading, leaving him to brood. Swift had destroyed his life, he thought again, and then shook his head. No, he'd done that himself. He'd been the one to drink, the one to chart the course that had wrecked the ship, wrong figures or not. Never mind that he might have averted disaster had the number not been transposed. Sooner or later, drink would have made him incompetent, forcing his removal from command. Swift's action had merely hastened his downfall.

And had it really been such a disaster? A year ago he would have answered a wholehearted "yes." A year ago, though, he hadn't known Abby as he did now. Yes, he had lost his command; yes, he had worked at menial jobs just to survive. He had also taken a good, hard look at himself.

He had fought against the bottle and had, so far, won. He had taken a ship no one wanted and, with the owner's cooperation, brought her back to life. In the process, he had fallen in love with the owner and married her. He wasn't happy about his fall from grace, but he was proud of his long climb back. The events of several years ago, though difficult, had served a purpose. They had brought him to peace, and happiness.

Not if he didn't watch the man, though. He turned to look at Abby. She didn't know of the threat Swift had made against his life, and if all went well, she never would. Nat would be on his guard. He would not, he vowed, sitting down again at his work, let Swift destroy everything again. He would do whatever he had to, to protect Abby.

Abby stood at the rail of the *Aquinnah*, watching land slip away again. They had made a quick stop at Seattle, in the Oregon Territory, to refill their water casks and obtain more fresh vegetables. It was summer in the Pacific Northwest; the air was crisp and clean, the sky a rich blue. Abby promptly fell in love with the country. In many ways it reminded her of New England, with its pine forests and sparkling bays and emerald islands. It had a sense of freedom, though, that New England, long settled, lacked. Here people could be whatever they decided to be, free of the past. Though much of the land was rugged, though she had been warned that the weather could be miserably damp and rainy, still she was drawn to the place. She thought she might like to live there someday, unlikely though that was. She doubted Nat would ever leave the sea.

With the wind whipping strands of hair onto her face, she turned to watch him, standing easily at the helm, trusting no other man to take his ship out of unfamiliar waters. He radiated a calm self-confidence that she realized had been missing last year. He was where he belonged. She wasn't sure she was, but that didn't matter. If she wanted to stay with her husband, this was the life she would have to lead. She would, she knew, have to do so as his wife. His real wife.

The sun was sinking, casting a golden glow over the ship. Night would fall soon, and her moment of decision would be upon her. When she had made love to Nat the other night, it had seemed easy to promise that soon she would be his wife in reality. If it had happened then, things might have been all right. Since then, she had had several days to think about her actions of that night, several days to wonder if she should have committed herself so definitely. In spite of the satisfaction she had taken from their encounter, in spite of their new closeness, still her old fear was there. What if she couldn't respond to Nat in the way she wished?

She was sitting at the cabin table, writing in her journal when he came in, having checked the ship for the night. "All right and tight," he said, lounging on the settee with his long legs stretched out, watching her. Her mouth went dry. Heavens, but he was a handsome, appealing man, clad as he was only in shirt and trousers. She was lucky to have won him. Why she had chosen this night, then, to put on her flannel nightdress and braid her hair, she didn't know. "The way you write in that thing, you'll have a book."

She smiled, closing the journal. "Cousin Elizabeth thinks I should write one. I certainly have had some adventures."

"Aye, and more to come."

She licked her lips. He was looking at her much as his Viking forebears must have looked at the women they captured on their raids. It was frightening. It was thrilling. "Such as?"

"Depends."

"On what?"

"If the time is right."

"Oh." She looked down. Here it was, then, the moment she'd dreaded. She knew what she had to do; if she didn't at least make an attempt, she'd never have a chance at a real marriage. She just wasn't quite sure she could make herself do it. "You're a romantic sort of fellow," she blurted out.

He looked startled. "Abby, we discussed this."

"Yes, but maybe I'm not ready."

"Abby—"

"And maybe if you talked to me a little, it would help."

"Talk." He rose, rubbing his hand over his face. "Abby, you are driving me mad."

"I know." Her voice was small. "I'm driving myself mad."

He turned, smiling wryly. "Are you, sweetheart?"

"I don't know what I want!" she wailed. "I want to be your wife, Nat, but I'm so afraid— "

"I thought we settled that."

"I'm afraid I'll disappoint you."

"Sweetheart." He went down on one knee, startling her. "You could never disappoint me. Don't you know that?"

"But if I don't feel what you think I should . . ."

"You will."

"You sound more certain of that than I am."

"Forgive me, Abby, but I know more about this than you do. The feeling is there already, inside you."

She looked down at his hands, holding hers. "This isn't what I expected."

"What isn't?"

"Marriage."

"Things usually aren't what you expect."

"I know. Oh, I know, and I know that some of the things I thought about when I was a girl were hopelessly romantic."

"Such as?"

She smiled. "I think every girl dreams of a man who will sweep her off her feet."

He returned the smile. "I can do that."

"You know what I mean, Nat."

"Sweetheart, I'm not a romantic person. You should know that by now."

"No?" She looked up at him. "Whose idea was it to decorate the cabin with flowers on our wedding night? Surely not Mr. Tripp's. And why did you keep putting flowers behind my left ear—yes, I do know what that means—in Hawaii?"

His smile broadened. "You've caught me out. But—" he grew serious—"I do know what you mean. You said it to me once. Everything happened so fast."

"Yes."

He rose, crossing the cabin to a cabinet and unlocking it. "I bought you something in Hawaii."

"Nat, you didn't have to get me anything."

"Oh, yes, I did, and I should have given it to you then, too. I guess I was angry about the way you accepted my proposal."

She frowned as he knelt before her again, calmly offering her a small box. "What does that have to do with it?"

"Open the box, Abby, and see."

"All right." With fingers that trembled, from tension or fear or anticipation, she opened the small box. Inside, nestled against a bed of midnight blue velvet, was a diamond ring. Set in gold, it sparkled with fire. "When—did you buy this?"

"When we first landed."

"Oh." Before she'd accepted his proposal. She looked up at him, meeting his eyes, bright blue, candid, defenseless. "It's beautiful, Nat."

"Will you wear it?"

"Yes." The ring slipped down her finger, resting snugly against her wedding ring, making her feel somehow more married than she had before. Nat had taken a huge step to show his sincerity. She could do no less. "Nat."

"Yes, sweetheart?"

"I think—no, I know—the time is right."

Chapter 23

Nat's hands gripped hers. "Are you sure?"

"As sure as I can be." She held his gaze with hers. Now that the moment was here, her nerves had flown. This was it. There was no going back.

"I won't be able to stop."

"I know."

"Ah, Abby." He swooped her up, bringing her to him. "I'll make this good for you, I promise."

"And for you," she said, a little shaky now, because of the feelings beginning to riot within her.

"If I do something you don't like, tell me, and I'll stop." She gave him a quick, hard kiss. "And if I do like it?" He grinned. "Tell me that, too."

"Nat." She looped her arms around his neck and swayed in his embrace, gazing at him with wonder. Never had she thought she was capable of this.

"What?"

"Nothing." She shook her head. "Just—Nat."

His arms tightened about her waist, urging her closer. There was no coercion in it, and yet she was drawn to him by a force she couldn't resist. When his mouth came down to hers she welcomed it, parting her lips, seeking his tongue with hers. When he angled his head to nip at her throat, she arched her head back, to give him freer access. And when he began to pick at the buttons of her nightdress, she stayed still, allowing him. Even when he slipped the night-dress off her shoulders, even then she was willing, if passive. Her real test was before her. What would be, would be.

Her nightgown fell to her waist, and she stood before him, exposed, vulnerable, reveling in his warm gaze. She closed her eyes as his hand cupped her breast, hoping for sensation, pleasure, anything. Instead, part of her seemed to slip away, to stand aside and watch, while the warm, liquid feelings inside her solidified. "No."

Nat's fingers stilled. "No?"

"Not there, Nat."

His brow furrowed. "Why not?"

"I don't like it." She looked directly at him. "You said that if I didn't like something to tell you."

"So I did." He looked regretfully down at her breasts. "They're beautiful, Abby. You're beautiful."

The words resonated in her mind, as if she'd heard them before, a long, long time ago. "Kiss me, Nat?"

He sighed, resting his forehead against hers. He had, after all, promised her to stop when she wanted him to. His gaze flicked down to her breasts, pearly in the lamplight, rosy at the tips. He could almost taste those tips in his mouth, feel them against his tongue; since he couldn't, he poured his frustrated longing into the kiss he slanted across her mouth.

She met him eagerly, on her toes, so willing that he decided he didn't mind forgoing one special pleasure. For now. Instead, he explored other parts, her waist, her hips, her full bottom. He squeezed it in his hands, and she jerked back.

"Oh!" Her eyes, startled, flew to his. In them he saw, not fear or distaste, but a dawning awareness. "My heavens!"

"Do you like that?" he asked, voice low, keeping his fingers still by a great effort.

"I—don't know." Her gaze was candid, vulnerable. "Do it again?"

He grinned, suddenly more sure of himself than he had been in many a day. "Gladly," he said, and let his fingers press into the soft, round globes. Her breath gasped out of her and her eyes closed, the first true sign of response he'd evoked from her. Oh, yes, she liked it, he thought, fondling and molding her bottom and feeling her squirm against him. Her belly rubbed against his manhood, making him ache, demanding that he throw her down, now, and make her his. Only a small remaining shred of common sense prevented him from doing so. Responsive or not, she still needed to be brought along slowly. He was also rather enjoying this.

Leisurely he opened his hands, let his thumbs rub along her hips. She shuddered again, but not so hard, and smiled. So. She liked that too. Of a sudden he pulled her close, still cupping her, wanting to feel again her softness against his hardness. "Abby," he said, though he didn't know why.

She moved against him, wringing a groan from him. "Yes," she answered, as mindless a response as his question, and as meaningful. She was giving herself to him willingly, at last.

In a spasm of joy and need he squeezed her buttocks and parted them, drawing his finger along her cleft, through the soft fabric of her gown. Abby's legs abruptly collapsed, so that she would have fallen if he hadn't caught her. Then her arms were around his neck and their mouths were locked together, wide open, lips pressing, seeking, suckling; tongues tangling in an intricate mating dance. He wanted, needed, to have her naked in his embrace. Without ceremony he pushed her nightgown down her hips and then reclaimed the territory that made her his. Her leg rubbed against his, and he knew he had won. He could take her now; he, still fully clothed and fully aroused; she, naked, and the eroticism of the idea was nearly his undoing. To put her up against the wall and bury himself in her, her legs around his waist, her body convulsing about him—oh, dear God. His hands moved firmly on her thighs, parting them further, and again she gasped, again her knees buckled. Fire shot through him and, at the same time, a fiercer need than his own drive for completion. A need to pleasure her as much as he could, to bring her to the same heights of arousal as he had reached; to feel her shatter under his hands, in his mouth, about his body. Not on the floor, not against a wall. Not this time, at least. This time would be in a bed, their real wedding night.

Before he could give in to his body's urges, Nat swung her into his arms and carried her into the stateroom, dropping her unceremoniously onto the bed. She landed with her legs parted, her knees bent, ready for him, making him fumble hastily at his clothes. She rose up on her elbows, pushing her tangled hair off her shoulders, watching him, not shy, not demure, and when he came to her at last, her hand curled around his manhood.

She had never felt anything like this, Abby thought dazedly as Nat knelt between her legs. Never felt this abandonment, this freedom, the elemental urge of nakedness and desire that had her in its grip. His organ pulsed in her hand and his breathing came in quick, shallow gasps. For just a moment, she had the power, and then his fingers were squeezing her buttocks again, shooting that flame of desire through her. She raised her hips in response, and in that moment he came down to her, filling her with one, sure stroke. He was within her, but, wanting him closer, she wrapped her legs around his waist. Oh, heavens, oh, heavens. Her hips bucked as he arched and withdrew, arched and withdrew, until she found his rhythm and moved at last with him. No detachment now, no feeling of being two people. She was gloriously here, loving and being loved by her husband at last, feeling the unfamiliar pleasure and pressure build up within her at last. She didn't know what it was, she didn't know where it led, but she wanted him never to stop. She wanted this feeling never to stop, even as it grew within her, until there was nothing else in the world but him, within her, around her. For just a second she split in two again, frightened by the intensity of the feeling. But then she was whole, only to shatter as waves of brilliant light and sensation flared through her, to her toes, her fingers, the tips of her breasts. She felt him jerk against her, heard him yell her name, and then everything was dark.

Abby roused to the feeling of lips moving over her eyelids and a voice whispering urgently. "Abby. Abby. Wake up, sweetheart. Wake up."

"Um." Such a sweet dream, of pleasure and closeness beyond her imagination. She wanted it never to end. Still, she answered the urgency in the voice, opening her eyes to see Nat looking down at her, his face creased in concern. It struck her, then, what had happened between them. "Mercy!"

Nat grinned and let his head drop to her shoulder. "Thank God. I was afraid I'd killed you."

"Well, I did think I was in heaven. Mercy!"

He chuckled, his breath warm and damp against her throat. "No mercy, my love. There's no need for it between us."

"If I'd realized," she began, and then fell still.

"Well, how could you?" he said reasonably. "Good God, I've never felt anything like that."

She jerked away from him, flipping onto her stomach, so that her hair brushed against his chest. "No? After—how many women, Captain?"

"None." He laid his finger gently against her swollen lips. "None that count."

"I should hope not," she said, still acerbic, but she settled against him, her head on his shoulder, her arm across his chest. "And no others from now on?"

"Of course not."

"Even if I'm not at sea with you?"

He was suddenly still. "Why wouldn't you be?"

"I don't know. Things happen, Nat." She rose up on her elbow again, and in the dim light spilling in from the cabin—had he really failed to close the stateroom door behind them?— he saw her push her hair back again. He remembered now, pulling at her braid, tangling his fingers in her hair. How he loved her. What would he do without her? "What if I should be breeding?"

"Ah." His breath sighed out. "Then we will have to be careful, won't we?"

"I'd miss you." She nestled against him, her fingers tracing patterns on his chest.

"Aye, and I, you." Because he loved her, he thought, kissing her forehead, and opened his mouth to say the words.

"Do you want children, Nat?" she broke in.

"Aye." She knew he loved her, and she obviously felt the same; surely she wouldn't have responded as she had, otherwise. "But I want you, more."

"I want a daughter. And a son. Maybe more than one." She counted them off against his chest, tickling and arousing him. "And I'll never try to hold on to them, when they should be free to lead their own lives."

"And I'll never come home drunk."

"Never?"

"Never." It was a solemn pledge. Whatever the mistakes their parents had made, they would not repeat them. "It will work, Abby. We'll be happy together."

"I know." She sounded sleepy, filling him with disappointment. He wanted her again, already, forever. She, however, was relaxed against him, nearly asleep. Oh, he could wake her up. He had no doubt of that. Tonight's lovemaking had been vigorous, though, and she would probably be uncomfortable in the morning. He wanted to spare her that, wanted to save her from any pain. Now that she was his, he could wait.

But as he held her, he felt a deep, insistent regret. For all Abby's responsiveness, he'd sensed her still withholding part of herself from him. He should have told her he loved her. He wished she had said she loved him.

Nat stood by the helm, straining to see through the fog. He'd seen some bad seasons in the Arctic, but this year was shaping up as one of the worst in memory. Since passing through "Seventy-two Pass," the 172nd latitude, around the beginning of May, the fleet had had little collective luck. Oh, the whales were here, off Point Barrow. He could hear them, under the ice. All of them could. They'd just become smart enough to stay in hiding.

Worse, the fleet had already suffered two losses. Coming up through the Bering Strait, they had been surprised to find survivors of the ship *Japan* living ashore with the Eskimos. Several of the whaleships took the men aboard and heard a horrendous tale. Whaling last year had been good, and the *Japan* had delayed its passage through the Strait until it was too late. The ship had been wrecked, and the officers and crew had been forced to winter over on the ice. It had been difficult, with not enough food to go around, yet they had lost only one man. There had been speculation in Honolulu about the *Japan*'s fate, but the fact that there were survivors was a relief.

Had that been the only disaster, Nat might not have been so concerned. In June, though, the bark *Oriole* had been caught in the ice, farther south than usual for that time of year, and been wrecked. There was no question of incompetence on the skipper's part, no indications of recklessness. The crew was portioned out among the fleet, and business went on. No seaman forgot the tragedy, though, or its implications. No matter how good a skipper was, no matter how experienced, the Arctic was a dangerous, unpredictable place.

Blowing on his hands to keep them warm, Nat checked

the compass again. Navigating in the Arctic was tricky. Currents were contrary, the compass reacted differently according to wind direction, and ice was an ever-present danger. A man needed to have all his wits about him in such circumstances. What amazed him now was not that he'd lost a ship here but that he hadn't faced disaster earlier. He had been very lucky.

"Let me know if the fog clears," he said quietly to Mr. Martel, on watch, and headed for the deckhouse and below for breakfast. These days he checked on his ship first, and on weather conditions. If they gained any visibility at all he'd set the boats out hunting walrus, though they, too, were scarce this year. Even the natives were having trouble finding enough walruses for food, let alone to boil for oil. For the first time, Nat felt just a twinge of conscience. Abby's doing, of course. She didn't see things as a whaler did; she still persisted in thinking of whales as somehow noble, and had been angry when she realized that the *Aquinnah*'s gain in capturing walrus might mean hunger for someone else. She didn't understand that whaling was a contest, man against nature, man against other men. Until this cruise he had reveled in it, but Abby's arguments were becoming persuasive. If people knew, they would say he was turning soft. In all ways except one, he thought, grinning as he opened the cabin door. Abby saw to that, too.

His smile faded just a little when he saw only Peleg in the cabin. "Mrs. Howland's not up yet?"

"Haven't seen her, Cap'n." Peleg set out breakfast: the inevitable fried fish and potatoes, and, thank God, steaming hot coffee. "Don't blame her. This is a godforsaken place."

"Let's hope not," Nat replied, tucking into his meal. He didn't blame Abby, either. She had yet to utter one word of complaint, but he knew she was feeling the cold dampness. In some ways it would have been better to leave her behind in Hawaii; in other, selfish ways, he was glad he hadn't.

Finishing breakfast, he pushed the plate away and went into the stateroom. Abby lay on her stomach in the bed, the covers piled so high about her that she was hard to see. Only her hair and the rounded edge of one bare shoulder peeked out from under the quilt. The temptation was too much to resist. He bent and planted a smacking kiss on her shoulder.

"Mmm." Abby stretched sinuously and buried her head deeper in the pillow. "Who is it?"

"Who is it, indeed." He swatted her backside, protected by layers of padding. "Get up, woman, and see to your husband."

She turned over, peering up at him through her hair. "Why? Is it another beautiful summer day out?"

"Lovely," he replied in the same mock solemn manner. "If it gets any warmer we'll have heatstroke."

"I guessed as much."

"Do you plan to stay in bed all day?"

"I had considered it, yes." She yawned and peeked up at him. "Maybe you'd join me?"

"I have work to do. I can't spend all day lolling about."

"Oh, can't you." She reached out and brushed her fingers down the center of his chest. In spite of himself, he sucked in his breath. "Do you plan to be busy catching whales?"

"No."

"Well, then?"

He was tempted. Sorely tempted. But if he got into that bed with her, Lord knew whether he'd ever get out again, and not just because it was warm. Conditions for whaling might be terrible, but his private life had never been better. Abby had proved to be an eager and responsive lover, not at all shy, in spite of her earlier difficulties. There were certain things she still didn't like and would merely tolerate; other things that, he had discovered, pleased her immensely. It almost didn't matter that he still sensed her holding a part of herself back. Almost. "I can't, Abby."

"Then I might as well go back to sleep," she said, and flipped back over onto her stomach.

That did it, as she had probably known it would. His annoyance only partially feigned, he grabbed hold of the covers and pulled them off her. Her rump immediately rose into the air, her legs tucking under her in a futile attempt to keep warm. "Nat!" she wailed. "It's cold."

"Aye," he said, his voice husky, but it was not of the weather he thought. In the clear light of morning he could see the marks their lovemaking sometimes left on her, the fading bruises on the back of her thighs, made when he became too eager and gripped her too hard. Remorse mingled with desire, and before he could stop himself, he bent to kiss one of the bruises. It was a gentle touch, meant to heal rather than arouse, but it was his undoing. His last bit of common sense was washed away in a flood of desire.

"Nat." Now her voice was husky. "What are you doing?"

His lips moved, exploringly, to another bruise, and she twisted under him. "Loving you. No, stay like that." He grasped her hips as she would have turned, holding her still.

"But—"

"Shh. Shh." His mouth traveled over all the bruises, while his hands moved to explore other territory. Again, she twisted; again her hips rose, but not from cold. The invitation was too much to resist. He fumbled with the buttons of his trousers and then, lifting her hips in his hands, plunged into her unceremoniously from behind. She cried out, but not, he knew, from pain. As he moved within her his fingers slid forward, finding the hard little bud buried in the nest of soft curls. She cried out again and bucked against him, and a moment later he followed her, into that special world where nothing mattered save their love and each other.

A few moments later, Nat lay on his back, one arm outflung, his clothing disordered. Abby was under the covers again, but her face wore a smile of almost feline satisfaction. "No one in New Bedford would believe this of me," she said.

"Then let's not tell them." He reached over to toy with a strand of hair curling about her face. "You know that I have to go back topside, don't you?"

"Isn't that just like a man. Coming and going all at once."

He grinned. "Seems to me I wasn't the only one."

"As if that excuses anything," she said, but she was smiling as she turned over. She kept the covers pressed close to her as she sat up, only, he knew, because of the cold. "How do you think we'll do today?"

"Hard to say." He took one long, last look at her and then rose, tucking in his shirt and buttoning his pants. "Best bet for us probably is to head north to Point Belcher."

She frowned. "Nat, do you really think that's wise?"

He pulled on his pea coat. "Seems to be the only thing

to do. We're not catching whales here, Abby, or walruses either."

"But the ice, Nat. You've heard the others. It's worse this year, isn't it?"

"Aye. It's true there's more ice, and farther south, too, than usual, but let's not panic. If we get a few warm days—"

"Warm?"

"In a manner of speaking. If we have a few warm days the ice will retreat. I've seen it happen before, Abby." He paused. "You don't think I'd chance us being wrecked, do you?"

"I think you might try to prove yourself," she said quietly.

"Not at the expense of the ship. Not your ship."

"Our ship."

"No, Abby, I've learned my lesson. Or are you going to accuse me next of drinking again?"

"Nat, no, of course not!" She sat up straight, looking stunned. "I'd never say such a thing."

"Oh, wouldn't you?"

"No." She got out of bed wrapped in a quilt, her anger giving her dignity even in such dishabille. "I trust you, Nat. Don't you know that?"

"Aye." He did know it, and sometimes that trust lay heavily on him. For, in spite of his confident words, he did worry about the encroaching ice pack. And, though he dreaded making another disastrous mistake, still he had to admit that she was right. He did want to prove that he could skipper a ship under such adverse conditions, to himself, if to no one else. "I'm sorry, Abby. I'm tired."

"That's no excuse." She stood firm, though her face had softened. "If you're upset about something, don't take it out on me, Nat. I had enough of that from my father."

"I know that, Abby." He drew her against him. "This is hard, but it's only for a few more months."

"I know." She sighed, more aware than ever of her dual role. She was Nat's wife, but she was also the owner of the ship. Sometimes that was difficult. "I wonder if—"

"Listen," Nat interrupted, and at the same time there was a knock on the door.

"Cap'n?" Peleg called, and Abby dove for the bed, hiding under the covers. "Wind's changing."

Nat's face brightened. "Aye, I feel it. From the northeast."

Abby peeked out from under the quilt, now that any danger of her privacy being invaded had passed. "Is it?"

"Aye. Can't you tell?"

She sat up, pushing her hair off her face. It was a nuisance, not having it braided for sleeping, but Nat liked her to leave it loose. "No."

"You'll learn." He bent to give her a brief, distracted kiss. "I told you things would get better."

"Yes," she said, but she was frowning as he bolted out of the stateroom. Men were different. If ever she'd needed any proof of that, she had it now. She might not know much about Arctic whaling, but she knew well that this was a bad season. The wrecks of the *Japan* and the *Oriole* only added to her unease. Yet Nat seemed to accept such losses as part of the risk. She had too, once, she supposed, when she had been tucked safe and sound in her house on County Street. It was one thing to hear tales of survival and danger when one was sitting in safety, but another to live them. She only prayed they would get through this season without disaster.

Sighing, she rose and began to dress, layering her warmest woolen gown over her bloomers. These days she was always cold, though not inside. That was Nat's doing, she thought, blushing as she remembered this morning's encounter. Never could she have imagined feeling the way Nat made her feel. Never, in spite of the weather, had she been so warm.

Peleg had breakfast ready for her in the cabin. There was a gale blowing from the northeast, he said. Already the fog was dispersing, and the ice pack was retreating. The cap'n had set a course north, and they'd spotted other ships doing the same. Abby's spirits perked up at the news. Nat had, after all, known what he was talking about. The Arctic was too unpredictable to take anything for granted, even bad weather. With the change in the wind they'd get out into open water, catch whales, and then head south again. She had no reason to fear, she thought, catching some of her husband's optimism at last. Her marriage was good, the ship was sound, and conditions for whaling were improving. Nothing could go wrong now.

It was late August, about the time the bowhead whales began to migrate south ahead of the encroaching ice pack, yet this year the whaling fleet was not following them. With the winds at last favorable and the fog cleared off, they had a chance to salvage the season. The prevailing mood was optimistic. Nat would be watchful, because nothing was more certain here but that the weather would change. Still, most of the ships had had luck, the *Aquinnah* among them. The worst was likely behind them.

When they could, the officers and crews of the fleet had taken to gaming aboard other ships in the evening. Abby, as one of the few women present, glowed from the attention she received. Nat watched her tolerantly. She had changed, his Abby, had grown and blossomed since last year. He could afford to allow other men to smile at her and even flirt a little. When the evening was over, he was the one she would be with.

"Abby looks well," a voice commented beside him. Nat didn't have to look to know who it was. Swift. This gathering aboard the *Emily Morgan* was the first time he'd seen Swift in a while, the *Naushon* having stayed farther offshore than many of the other ships. But then, Swift had always had a streak of caution. Or maybe cowardice. "Considering the climate."

"Abby's strong." He sipped his coffee. It no longer bothered him when others drank. He was content in his life. He didn't need to drink. "Maybe stronger than anyone thought. Besides"—another sip—"I'm keeping her warm."

Beside him Jared drew in his breath. "I've heard the fleet's had little luck this season," he said, mildly enough, considering he'd just taken what Nat knew was a direct hit.

"Conditions have been hard," Nat agreed. "But they're looking better now. Any better in the open water?"

"Some. The bowheads are shy. They make right for the ice."

Nat nodded. "So we found it."

"Thought you wouldn't want to go so near the ice again."

That was a hit too, though Nat managed not to show it. "Have to do it sometime."

"Aye. Though if I owned the *Aquinnah,* I would be concerned."

"About what?"

"The weather, the ice, things like that," Jared said vaguely. "Past history."

"Which is past," Nat said firmly.

Jared looked skeptically at Nat's mug. "Glad to hear it."

"Aye. Important, but past. Like the difference between fifteen and fifty-one. As in feet."

Jared went still. "Your navigation error, as I recall."

"An error, true." Nat set down the mug and looked directly at the man for the first time. "But not necessarily mine."

"Nat," Abby said, laying her hand on his arm at that moment. "I've just invited everyone to the *Aquinnah* for tomorrow evening, if we're still here."

Nat smiled down at her and covered her hand with his, a gesture he knew Swift wouldn't miss. "Of course. We'll see what happens." He watched as she turned to speak with someone else and then walked away, laughing. "She's enjoying herself."

Jared sipped at his brandy. "Good stuff, this. Sure you won't have some?"

"No, thanks."

"Just as well, in the ice. Actually, I'm surprised at the changes in Abby."

"Did you think I'd mistreat her?" Nat said mildly, refusing to be goaded.

"No. Just that I didn't think she had it in her."

"What?"

"Passion."

The word hung there for a moment, fraught with tension and danger. "How would you know?"

"How else?" Jared sipped his brandy again. "Do you really think you were the first man to sample her?"

"Watch it—"

"Well, you weren't, and she was as frigid as Icy Cape."

Chapter 24

"You lie," Nat said calmly. If there was one thing he knew, it was that Abby had come to him untouched.

"Do I?" Jared drained his glass, and Nat felt suddenly thirsty. "Ask her."

"I wouldn't insult her in such a way."

"It's no insult. I left her a virgin. Her choice. Seems she didn't like it much."

Nat strove for calm. Correcting Jared would violate the special bond he shared with Abby. How, though, did Swift know of her initial reluctance? "When did this mythical encounter happen?"

"Eight years ago. But it happened." Jared's smile was cold. "How else would I know such a thing about her?"

He didn't believe it. He didn't. "If you're so certain of that, why do you keep pursuing her?"

Jared's smile faded. "Because I understand her. You don't. And because I can awaken the woman in her."

Nat could not quite believe they were having this conversation in a crowded ship's cabin. With Abby, laughing and smiling and warm, just across the room. "Then you've had your chance and failed."

"I did not fail," Jared snapped. "I'm not a failure."

Nat shrugged, though he was furious. "I'm not discussing this with you, Swift."

"Scared?" Jared taunted.

"Of you? Ha."

"Not of me. Of the truth."

"Why? You've never been any threat to me."

Jared's face was red. "I took away your command."

"Aye, that you did." Nat faced him squarely for the first time. "But maybe not in the way you're talking about."

"Say what you mean, Howland." Jared set his glass down with a thump. "Let's have this out."

"Swift. Howland." The *Emily Morgan*'s captain, Benjamin Dexter, spoke. "Do you agree that we should press farther north?"

"Aye," Nat said, though his eyes never left Jared's face.

"Good. Captain Swift, what of conditions to the west?"

Jared didn't look away either. "They're frigid."

Anger surged within Nat, but Captain Dexter was leading Jared away, unwittingly averting a fight. "Tell us more," Dexter was saying, and Nat was left alone, furious, terrified. And wanting, more than he had in many a day, a drink.

"Oh, Nat, look," Abby said, as they reached the deck of the *Aquinnah* later that evening. "The Northern Lights."

"Um," Nat muttered, not looking at either her or the spectacular display of colors in the sky. But then, he had been uncharacteristically quiet all evening. Something was bothering him. "It's not as if you haven't seen them before."

"I know, but they are beautiful." She cast one last look up into the sky and then entered the deckhouse, going below to the warmth of the cabin. "If you had asked me a few months ago I would have said this was a desolate place, but it does have a kind of beauty, doesn't it?" She went on, opening the stateroom door. "The glaciers and the mirages and—"

"I want to talk to you, Abby," he interrupted.

Abby looked out from the stateroom, pausing with her hands to her head. "Is something wrong? I thought everyone agreed that the whaling might not be so bad this season, after all."

"This has nothing to do with whaling." He glanced toward the cupboard where the ship's medical supplies were kept, and then away. "It has to do with you."

"Me?" Frowning, she stepped back into the cabin. She didn't like the look in his eyes—distant, remote. Not the Nat she knew. "For heaven's sake, Nat, what is it?"

"What happened between you and Swift?"

"Tonight? Why, Nat, you were there. You saw for yourself. Nothing happened—"

"Not tonight. In the past."

She frowned again and sank down onto the settee. "I think you'd better come out and say exactly what's bothering you."

"Do you? All right. Why didn't you tell me that you and Jared were lovers?"

"Nat!" She stared at him, shocked. "We never were!"

"No?" he said coldly.

"No. I'm tired of this." She rose, her own anger building. "He and I have always been friends. That's all."

"Then what happened when you were sixteen?"

Her mouth opened and closed again. What an odd question. But then, in Honolulu Jared had referred to something similar. "Nothing," she said, but even to herself she sounded unconvincing. The darkness was back, more ominous, more pressing.

"No?" Nat turned on her. "Didn't he try to kiss you? Caress you? He would have been, what? Twenty, twenty-one?"

"Nineteen," she said, her lips frozen. "When he was nineteen he came back from his first voyage."

"I can see how it happened." Nat's voice was cool, analytical. "You were friends. He was just back from sea. You were a beauty—yes, I remember you then, Abby. Too young for me, but blossoming into a woman. Tempting for any man, but especially for someone who loved you."

Abby bit her lip. Yes, Jared had said he loved her. She remembered that. No more, though. "Nothing happened between us, Nat. I've told you that enough."

"No? You don't like me to touch your breasts."

"What in the world does that have to do with anything?"

"Maybe nothing. Maybe everything."

"I'm tired." She rose. "I don't know where you got this nonsense, Nat, but it's not true."

"He told me, Abby." Nat's voice was very quiet. "He told me you were frigid. How did he know?"

Abby turned from the doorway, shocked, stunned, sick. But why? She and Jared had never been more than friends. "Nat, for heaven's sake! Isn't it obvious that he was just trying to aggravate you? And it seems he succeeded."

"I don't think so, Abby." His voice was still quiet. "Not this time."

"Well, I don't know why you'd believe him instead of me."

"I don't want to. But can you look me in the eye and tell me honestly that nothing happened?"

She looked away, and then back. "I don't remember anything happening, Nat, and surely I would. But I can't make you believe me when you obviously don't want to."

Nat's shoulders sagged. "I believe you, Abby."

"Do you?"

"Aye. Whatever else you are, you're not a liar."

"Well, thank you very much! When I've done all I can to be a good wife—you can sleep in the cabin tonight for that," she snapped and slammed the stateroom door behind her.

Nat eyed the door for a few moments. The lock was flimsy, designed more to keep the door from opening during a gale than anything else. One kick, and he'd be inside. They could make up this fight. Maybe. He turned away. Maybe it would be best to let things alone tonight. Oh, he believed her. At least, he thought he did. They'd already said enough, though, and he doubted she would let him make love to her. Not when she knew very well how to turn cold. And how had Swift known of that?

Nat eyed the stateroom door again, and then rose, pacing across the room. He paused for just a moment before unlocking the cabinet and taking out the decanter of brandy. Not his favorite drink, but it would do, he thought, pouring a measure and tossing it back in one gulp. Ah. Just the thing to keep a man warm at night when his wife turned him out of bed. When his wife was cold. Alcohol, his old, old friend. He wondered, now, why he'd ever bothered to stop drinking.

The nightmare came again that night, the darkness and dread that always made her wake in terror. Abby rolled over, reaching for Nat, before she remembered. She'd locked him out of the stateroom. At the moment, she was sorry for it.

Sitting up, she rubbed at her temples. Light. She needed light, but that meant going into the cabin, where Nat was. Odd, the way the nightmare had returned, when she hadn't suffered through it for months. Not since she'd told Nat about it, way back before rounding the Horn. It was as if just his very presence gave her a measure of protection against the nameless terror that awaited her in the darkness . . .

Wait. Not nameless, not this time. This time there had been someone there in her dreams, in the shadows beyond the pianoforte in the music room, far away, long ago. Odd. She stared into the darkness, straining to remember, though already the details of the dream were becoming hazy. Someone in the shadows. A man. Not a stranger, but who— Jared? She frowned, swinging her legs over the edge of the bunk. Good heavens, Jared had never been in this particular dream before, and if he had been, she surely would have seen him as a savior, not a menace. But a menace he was, lurking there, smile twisted, hands cupped, as if to grasp her—

Of a sudden she remembered, and the shock of it made her fall back, gasping, onto the bunk. Long ago and far away, yes, but what Jared had insinuated tonight had happened. Dear God! Nat's accusations were correct. Once she and Jared had been more to each other than merely friends, and yet, until this moment, she had forgotten it. How in the world could that be?

"Nat," she whispered. She needed to discuss this with someone. Ordinarily Nat would be her confidant. After tonight, though, she doubted he'd want to hear anything she had to say. She'd lied to him, if not intentionally. How could he ever believe that she could have forgotten the incident, when she didn't quite believe it herself?

Rubbing her forehead again, she lay in the bed. She didn't want to remember it, but she had to. Jared had come home from sea, as she'd told Nat. At nineteen he'd gained his full height; his face was already losing the softness of boyhood, and he had been very, very handsome. At sixteen, Abby noticed such things. Boys were mysterious and fascinating, to her and to her friends, but Jared was more than a boy. He was a man, he was handsome, ambitious, and about to be promoted to second mate, and he liked her. She trusted him, so she had let him kiss her. She squeezed her eyes shut. That wasn't so bad, really; other boys had kissed her, too—quick, fumbling smacks on her lips. What had scared, and thrilled her, was that she had enjoyed it.

What was shameful, she had known even then, was that until that moment she had thought of him as a brother.

Curiosity, though, had prompted her to go on, to let him do what he would. When he reached his hand inside her bodice to fondle her, she hadn't stopped him. She'd liked that, too, she admitted, her shame deepening at the admission that that was one response she had yet to give to her husband, the man she loved. She had never loved Jared, yet she had reacted to his touch. Shameful.

It was difficult to remember it now, that pleasure and the panic that followed it. At the time, she hadn't known what to do. Frightened of what was happening, she had pulled away; she remembered scrubbing at her lips, as if by doing so she could wipe away all sensation. She remembered crossing her arms over her breasts, defensively, protectively. And she remembered Jared's look as he left, hurt, angry, and defiant, leaving her with the knowledge that matters were not settled between them. They might never be settled.

Jared had never apologized; neither had she ever referred to the incident, preferring to put it behind her. She made a conscious effort to forget it, and in time succeeded. In time, she didn't think about it anymore. She changed, though, something she only just now realized. She had become cool, as if coldness could protect her. No wonder her suitors had wanted her only for her inheritance. It must have seemed to them that she had little else to give. Only Nat had seen that the coldness wasn't real; only he had seen that she was capable of feelings, of passion, of fire. Unfortunately for him, the secret she had buried deep inside her had not died. Instead it worked away at her spirit, her life, her marriage. She might have forgotten the incident, but her body remembered. As a result, her marriage was in trouble.

The menace was there in the darkness. Not a man, as she had first thought, not Jared, but this old, old secret, shrouding everything in shadow, stealing the light she sought. She wasn't sure if she could dispel it alone. Once before, Nat had helped her find light; since then, he had helped her find fire. She rose, not caring that she would awaken him. She needed him, now, to help her understand the past and drive the darkness away. And if he didn't believe her story—well, she'd deal with that when it happened.

Somewhat to her surprise, the lamp still burned in the cabin. Even more surprising was that Nat wasn't sleeping on the settee, but was sprawled at the table, snoring. The lamp was nearly out of oil, she noted, gliding quietly over to Nat and bending over him. Odd, she thought, and then recoiled at the strong smell of alcohol. Nat wasn't lost in ordinary sleep, not with his head lolling upon his bent arms, and the wide-based brandy decanter empty on the table. Her need to talk to him was forgotten in a welter of anger and hurt. One of her fears had come true. Nat was drunk.

Nat opened his eyes to a view of plain varnished wood under his face. He stared at it uncomprehendingly, wondering just where he was. Passed out on the bar of some tavern, probably. This wasn't new, waking up in a strange place after having imbibed too much the night before. Neither was the upheaval in his stomach, which made him feel as if the entire world were rocking up and down, side to side. All this, and he hadn't even moved yet. But then he heard a ship's bell striking eight times, and he abruptly knew where he was. Aboard the *Aquinnah*. If he had imbibed last evening, he'd had cause.

Stifling a groan, he raised his head. The cabin appeared to be empty, but he didn't want to alert anyone that he was awake. Not until his head had cleared a little bit. There was only one remedy that really worked—a taste of what had gotten him into this shape in the first place. His fingers groped for the decanter, and at that moment a voice spoke behind him.

"It's empty." Abby's voice. "You finished it last night."

Startled, Nat whipped around, an action he instantly regretted. His fingers gripped the table railing as the cabin seemed suddenly to spin, and the ache in his head intensified to raging pain. "Abby, have mercy," he groaned.

"I have. That's why I haven't removed your command yet."

That cleared his head. "What did you say?"

"Mr. Tripp will bring you coffee and sea biscuit. If you think you can keep it down."

He stared at her. "You've removed me from command?"

"No. Not yet, at least."

He closed his eyes and breathed out in relief. "Thank God. I knew I could rely on you— "

"Don't be too certain," she cut in. "Mr. Martel's in command for the moment. I've told him you're ill," she added, as he looked at her. "But if this particular illness continues, I'll have no choice."

"Damnation, Abby—"

"Don't swear at me, Nat. You brought this on yourself."

"Damnation, but you're just like your father."

"Thank you." She left off any pretense of mending, setting it down on her lap. "I can imagine what he'd say to you, after giving you a second chance. Nat, how could you?"

Damnation! How could he? The question was, how could she? For if much of last evening was a blur, the important things stood out. She had had some kind of affair with Swift, and she had lied to him about it. "You lied to me, Abby."

For the first time her gaze faltered, and her hands fiddled with her mending. "Not intentionally."

"You admit it, then?"

"This isn't something we'll discuss just now," she said briskly and rose.

"The hell it isn't." He straightened, too, though it took a great deal of effort. "Not after last night."

Abby's face briefly softened, and her hand fluttered out, as if to rest on his shoulder. "Is that why you drank?"

"Why the hell else do you think?"

"I'm sorry. When I came out of the stateroom and saw you . . . " She bit her lip. "I didn't know what to think, except that you'd promised me. You broke your promise, Nat."

"Damnation, Abby, I'm not the one in the wrong here—"

"Oh, yes, you are," she interrupted. "No matter what I might have done, I'm not taking the blame for your actions."

"What have you done, Abby?"

She glanced away and then shook her head. "Have some breakfast first, and get washed up, and then maybe we'll talk."

"There's nothing to talk about, Abby." He looked up at her, sober now in spite of his hangover. "You lied to me."

She sighed and crossed to the door of the cabin, pulling her coat about her. "We could keep on with accusations, but it won't solve anything. I'll tell Mr. Tripp you're ready for breakfast," she said and slipped out of the cabin.

"Abby," he called, but she was gone, leaving him in a welter of nausea and hurt and anger. She had lied to him. She had taken away his command, if only temporarily. Damnation, she was the one in the wrong, not he. So he'd had a bit too much to drink. So what? It had happened before, and the world hadn't ended. Just his world.

That thought made him rise, his mouth set in a grim line. Aye, so he'd been drunk before, and look where it had led him. To disaster. Swift couldn't have known that Nat would react to his insinuations in this particular way, yet he couldn't have chosen a more apt weapon. For if Nat continued this way, he would lose everything again, his ship and his wife. He'd fought to become sober for several reasons. The stakes were higher now, though. He could not afford such a mistake again.

Peleg entered the cabin, a steaming cup in one hand and a small dish in the other. "Mornin', Cap'n. Feeling better?"

Nat grunted as he sat down again. He didn't doubt that everyone on the ship knew exactly what was keeping him from his duties this morning. "I feel like hell, if you must know."

"Aye, been there myself." Peleg set down the mug, the coffee unexpectedly fragrant. "Hard thing to live with, when you've sworn off the bottle, to have a slip."

"A slip?" Nat looked up at him, mouth twisted ironically. "Is that what you call what I did?"

"Aye. Unless it happens again."

"It won't." Nat took a sip of coffee and eyed the sea biscuit with distaste and determination. He would eat it, and then he would begin the long fight against the craving, the need, again. Day by day. That was all he could do. "It won't."

By afternoon, both the weather, foggy that morning, and Nat's head had cleared. Abby, standing on the deck, could tell that just by looking at him. He stood near the helm, a bit pale, perhaps, but very much in control of himself, very much in charge. The boats had been lowered some time ago to go in search of whales, and the lookout had reported that Mr. Taber's boat had met with success. They'd be busy in a little while, cutting in. For now, Nat, acting as shipmaster, was keeping careful track of their course. She could not guess what was going through his mind, but one thing she knew for certain. He would not want to risk losing another ship.

Quietly she went to stand beside him. "This place has its own kind of beauty, doesn't it?"

"Aye." He didn't look at her, but she didn't mind. He was concentrating on his ship. "Get the winds to blow away the fog, and things change. Even gets warmer."

"In a way. And it's nice not to be surrounded by ice."

He nodded. "Let the winds change, though, and it will come back. Faster than you expect, too."

"I know." They both fell quiet, thinking of the various mishaps that had hit the fleet this season. One of the worst had involved several whaleboats that had been caught in fast-moving ice. Their crews had had to tow the boats over the ice to reach their ships, a sobering reminder of how quickly conditions could change here. "Could you go below for a while?"

This time he did look at her, and she couldn't read his expression. "Aye. Until the boats come back. Call me if there's any change," he said to the man at the helm, and followed Abby down the companionway and into the cabin.

Sunlight streamed into the cabin, a deceptive sight; without the stove it would have been cold, and damp. Abby rubbed her hands together after she'd stowed her outerwear, wondering just how to begin. They had hurt each other profoundly last night. Healing that pain would be difficult.

"I'm sorry I got drunk," Nat said abruptly. "It's not something I planned to do."

She turned. "I know that, Nat. But it surprised me. I wouldn't think you'd take the risk of losing another ship."

"Or you, either."

She shrugged. "Which matters more to your pride, Nat?"

"Not fair, Abby." He sat on the settee next to her. "We have some things to settle between us."

"I know." She gazed off into space. "I didn't lie to you, Nat. At least, not intentionally."

"So you said before."

"I—what happened is—there was something with Jared. But I didn't lie to you, Nat. I—forgot about it."

"Forgot?" His voice was skeptical. "Do you really expect me to believe that?"

"No." She rested her chin on her hands. "I'm not sure I believe it myself. How I ever could have forgotten such a thing—but I did, Nat. I honestly did."

He was quiet for a moment. "What happened between you?"

She grimaced. "It was much as you said last night. He was home from sea. I was sixteen, just beginning to be interested in boys. I already loved Jared—as a brother, nothing more—and there he was, a man. So I thought," she added.

"I think I can guess what happened."

"No, I don't really think you can."

"He tried to make love to you."

"Yes," she said softly. "He did. And I let him. I trusted him. I was curious. So I let him kiss me, and . . ."

"Touch you," he finished for her.

"Yes." Even now, in spite of all they had been to each other, she could not describe that first, intimate embrace to him. "Then I stopped it."

"Why?"

"I got scared."

Nat straightened. "Did he hurt you? Because if he did, by God, I'll—"

"No. No." She laid a calming hand on his arm. "No, he didn't do anything to me, Nat."

"Then what scared you?"

"It was wrong." Her voice was small. "He was like my brother."

"Incest," Nat said bluntly.

Abby's hands flew to her face, and then she was up, running to the washroom. Only when she had lost the contents of her stomach did she straighten. Nat had put a word to the darkness within her, and she couldn't bear it.

Nat rose as she returned to the cabin. "Are you all right?"

She nodded, sitting down and covering her face with her hands. "It happened in the music room," she began abruptly.

"We don't have to talk about this now," he interrupted.

"No. I have to. In the music room, and I wanted it to. I was curious. And it was as you said. He kissed me and touched my—me." She swallowed, nausea still roiling within her. "But I got scared, and I pushed him away."

"Hm."

She turned to look at him. "What?"

"So he's been chasing you ever since."

She felt herself going paler. Jared had told her himself that he hated being a failure and that he had failed with her. "Oh, Nat!" Her fingers spasmed on his arm. "Don't let him get me!"

"I won't, Abby." He pulled her close, tucking her head under his chin. "I won't. But I don't understand how you could have forgotten such a thing."

"I don't either," she said frankly. "I had a dream last night—remember, my nightmare about darkness?—and then I remembered everything. I think I wanted to forget it, Nat. I think it was so painful I didn't want ever to remember it again." She paused. "I didn't want to think I'd let it happen."

"Abby, he was older than you."

"I knew what I was doing, Nat. I was curious. But after that I didn't really want anything to do with men."

"I can understand that," he said after a moment.

She raised her head. "Can you forgive me, Nat? I never meant to cause you any pain, or start you drinking again."

He shook his head. "That's not your fault. I knew what I was doing."

"If things hadn't happened the way they did last night—"

"No excuses, Abby." He faced her squarely. "You didn't put the bottle in my hand. I did it by myself."

"But I can understand why."

"You're more forgiving than I am." His face was bleak. "No, Abby, how I reacted last night is my responsibility."

"Well, likely it won't happen again—"

"How do you know?" he interrupted. "If you'd asked me yesterday I would have said that I would never drink again. I can't promise that now." His eyes were stark.

"Sometimes things happen. The best I can do is take things day by day."

"I won't give you such cause again." She paused. "Do you think you can forgive me?"

"Aye," he said, after a long moment, standing, and Abby let out her breath in relief. "What's happened is past. Unless there's something else you've forgotten?"

Abby rose, choosing to ignore the sardonic note in his voice. "It's past," she agreed, and placed her hand in his. Instantly he pulled her to him, and they held to each other for a long, desperate moment. Forgiveness was one thing, she thought, her head on his shoulder. She doubted either of them would ever truly forget. They had patched things up, but she suspected that the damage to their marriage would last for a long, long time.

Chapter 25

The weather changed the next day. With the wind blowing from the southwest, the ice marched inshore, capturing several ships. The rest, the *Aquinnah* among them, retreated toward shore, safe for the moment. The question was, for how long?

Because his crew had been busy boiling oil the night before, Nat had postponed any gathering of ships' officers until the following evening. It was not a festive affair. Several of the masters commented that they'd never seen the ice come in so fast. Others expected that another wind shift would free the trapped ships. No one wanted to contemplate what would happen if the ice continued its progress.

"Should we make for more open waters, do you think?" Abby asked after their guests had departed.

Nat, cravat loosened and coat unbuttoned, lounged back on the settee in the cabin. He looked tired, but normal. Tonight he'd consumed nothing stronger than coffee. She knew. She'd watched him. "No. I know the ice seems frightening, but I've seen it happen before. The weather will change again."

"For the worse, maybe." Abby sat beside him, leaving considerable space between them. For all their words of forgiveness yesterday, for all their attempts at forgetting, the damage had been done. There was now ice inside, as well as without. "It's going into fall, Nat."

"There's no need to panic, not with a channel to get out."

"And if it closes?"

"It won't."

"You sound certain."

"Abby, I am not going to lose another ship."

"I didn't say that." She paused. "Was it like this before?"

"Before when?" he asked, though she could tell by the look on his face that he knew what she was talking about.

"When the *Nantucket* went on the ice."

His mouth tightened in annoyance. Until now they'd kept the past in the past. Things had changed, though. After recent events, things would never again be the same. "It wasn't this bad. Maybe," he frowned, "I wouldn't have lost the ship if it had been."

"I don't understand."

"I would have been more careful." He rose and paced, hands in trouser pockets. "I wouldn't have gotten so drunk."

"What did happen?" she asked quietly.

"Didn't your father tell you? I thought he kept you informed of all his business doings."

"Yes." She met his gaze unflinchingly, in spite of his sarcastic tone. "He told me that it was a shame you'd let the drink get to you, that you were a fine seaman. You were lucky you had a competent first mate, because otherwise the disaster would have been worse. What happened wasn't due to the weather." She paused. "He said it was your fault."

He looked back at her. "I never said otherwise."

"He told me that, too, and said it was to your credit."

"Maybe." He shrugged. "Whatever happened, I was the captain. I was the one responsible."

"Nat, what did happen?" she asked again.

He turned away. "It was a navigation error," he said finally. "I thought we were in a channel. We weren't."

"What made you think that?"

"The depth of the water. When the plumb line went out for the sounding, I thought we had fifty-one feet. Turned out we only had fifteen."

"You switched the numbers."

"Something like that."

"Did you take the sounding yourself?"

"You know better than that. It was the mate on watch." She paused. "Jared?"

"Aye. Swift."

"No wonder you dislike him," she murmured.

"Whatever happened, Abby, I used that figure," he said quickly. "It was my fault."

"Why are you so quick to take the blame? A simple mistake—"

"That lost a ship. And a good catch of oil. I thought we had enough water beneath us," he went on. "We didn't, of course. When we grounded, it was a surprise to everyone. There wasn't any ice on the surface, you see." He grimaced. "But there was plenty below. We got off quickly enough, got the pumps going, but we saw pretty soon that we were in trouble. It was like when the *Oriole* went on the ice this year. There was too much damage to repair. We had to abandon ship."

"Was that your decision?"

His laugh was mirthless. "Mine? Not really. I was drunk, Abby. You saw me the other night. Did I look in any shape to make a decision?"

"So Jared took over, getting the crew off."

"Aye, in the boats. There weren't any other ships nearby at the time. He made himself a hero," he said bitterly.

"Well, Nat, in all fairness—"

"In all fairness, he took the sounding," he retorted.

"Are you saying it was his mistake?"

"Maybe." He sat beside her again, and she looked at him in undisguised astonishment. This was the first time she'd heard this accusation. "I don't switch numbers, Abby. Even when I drank, I didn't. There's a lot of things I can't do. I'm not romantic. I can't speak in public, the way he does. I'll never be active in civil affairs."

"No one's asking you to be, Nat," she said quietly. "You're doing what you do best."

"But I'm good with numbers," he went on, as if she hadn't spoken. "I always have been. And I can't think of any way I'd have made such a basic mistake."

"Nat, if you'd been drinking—"

"All I can do is tell you again that I don't switch numbers." He paused. "But Swift does."

She sucked in her breath. "You really do think it was Jared's fault?"

"I have no proof, of course. The paper the sounding was written on is long gone. Can't say I blame him." He grimaced. "I might have destroyed the evidence, too."

"No," she said, after a moment. "I don't think so."

He looked at her at last. "Thank you for that."

"Did you know about this at the time?"

"If I had, don't you think I would have said something? I figured it out just recently. I could be wrong about it, Abby, but I don't think I am." He gazed ahead of him. "Either way, it doesn't matter. I was the one in charge. What happened was my responsibility."

She leaned back, troubled. If Nat's accusation was true, it meant that Jared had stolen away not only his career but his reputation. "Is there anything you can do about it?"

He gave that mirthless laugh again, making her aware, for the first time, of the depth of his bitterness. "Of course not, Abby. Who'd believe me?" He looked at her. "I don't know if even you believe me."

"Last year I probably wouldn't have. But now . . ."

"Now?"

"I've learned some disturbing things about Jared since. He's not the person I thought. He transposes numbers; I do, too. And he doesn't like to fail at anything."

"He thinks he failed with you."

"I know." She propped her chin in her hands. "Poor Jared."

He snorted. "For God's sake, Abby, don't waste your pity on him, after what he's done to us both. He has what he wants."

"No, I don't think he does. I don't think he ever will, no matter how much he succeeds."

"He's not getting you, Abby," he said fiercely. "I won't let that happen."

"Well, of course not, silly," she said calmly. "I've told you before. He's no threat to you."

"But he is." Nat's eyes were serious. "He's a threat to both of us, Abby, as long as he thinks we're standing in the way of his success."

"Then we'll have to stand together, Nat," she said and held out her hand. Nat hesitated for what seemed a long time, and then clasped her hand in his.

"Aye. We'll stand together on this," he said, and there was closeness between them for the first time since their quarrel. Abby could only hope it would be enough.

* * *

Ice, everywhere. Nat stood at the helm, wearing his storm gear and watching Abby. She was at the railing of the *Aquinnah,* her cloak tightly wrapped about her, and he doubted she would be able to stand the conditions for very long. The wind was from the northwest, a very bad sign. Without constant vigilance, they would be driven toward the shore. It was also uncomfortable. Snow as sharp as needles hit his cheeks, while the seas rose, sullen gray-green, in towering crests. So far the ship had managed to stay ahead of the ice, though he didn't know how long that would last. When the Eskimos had warned the fleet, at the beginning of the season, that the weather would be unusually fierce, they should have listened. Instead, they might face imminent disaster.

The ship heeled, and Abby grabbed at a belaying pin, the line coiled around it coated with ice, to keep her balance. Though she recovered, Nat started forward. This was no place for her. "Best get below," he said curtly, reaching her.

"It's all ice, Nat." She looked up at him, her eyes huge. "Everywhere we look."

Aye, and from the masthead, too, as far as the eye could see. He wasn't going to tell her that. Not yet. "I know. Come below, Abby. It's not safe for you here."

"But it is for you?" she argued as he took her arm and hustled her toward the deckhouse.

"I'm not the one wearing long skirts."

She turned as they reached the cabin. Because of the rough seas he had had to order the stove shut down, and it was dank and cold. "Then I'll convert all my clothes to bloomers."

"Don't be ridiculous."

"I'm teasing, Nat."

"This isn't the time for that."

"I know," she said, her voice very small. "I'm sorry. It's just—are matters so very bad?"

"No. If the wind shifts again we'll be all right."

"And if it doesn't?"

"It's still early in the year. We'll wait and see, Abby."

"Until the same thing happens to us that happened to the *Eugenia,*" she said. Yesterday the ice had come down upon the *Eugenia* so thick and so fast that it had parted her anchor chain and driven her toward the shore. The crew had managed to get her other anchor to hold, just in time. There were twenty-six other ships nearby, twenty-six others all jammed close to the beach. Yet the *Thomas Dickason* had somehow managed to get into open water and was busy trying out a whale, one caught by another ship and then lost in the ice. Matters looked bad, but every master of the fleet agreed. Eventually the wind would shift again to the northeast, and the ice would go off.

"Cap'n." Mr. Martel stumbled in, his face ruddy from the cold. "One of the ships's got her ensign at half-mast."

Nat turned sharply, all too aware of what it might mean when a ship lowered her house flag. "Which one?"

"Looks like the *Comet*. Can't tell why."

"Lower a boat," Nat commander. "I'll go see."

"Nat, you can't," Abby protested, as Mr. Martel left the cabin. "It's too rough."

"I've been in worse." He opened the door to the cabin and then paused. Abby's eyes were wide with fear. She was still new to this, he reminded himself. This was her first season in the Arctic. Though she'd seen for herself how quickly conditions could change, it probably looked to her as if they were facing disaster. And she was, he reminded himself for the first time in a while, the ship's owner.

"We'll be all right," he said, crossing to her and pulling her close. "We wouldn't still be here if I thought otherwise."

"I know, but—"

"Neither would the other ships."

"They look as if they're all in the ice," she retorted, but her face lightened. "I suppose they know what they're doing."

"Aye, and so do I," he said, stung that she would believe in others, but not in him.

"I know you do, Nat. I know. But I'm frightened."

He nodded and pulled away. "I don't blame you. Just trust me on this, Abby. We'll be fine."

"All right," she said, forcing a smile, and Nat went out.

Topside, he jumped nimbly down into the whaleboat, not glancing back as he was rowed away. In his mind, though, he could see Abby. Aye, she'd agreed with him, but he knew that her trust was not quite so strong as it would have been a week ago. Nor was his in her. It would take a long time before they believed in each other again, if they ever did.

He didn't really think of Jared's actions as incestuous, since the man had evidently never regarded Abby as a relative. She did, though, and these last nights she had huddled in the bunk away from him, from any comfort he might have offered. Not that he would have. Funny, nothing about the situation was her fault, and yet he was deep down, seriously angry. He felt deceived, wounded. It was hard to believe she could really have forgotten that the incident had happened. Worse, though, was thinking that she'd lied to him. Not his forthright and honest Abby. In time he would likely come to accept the fact that she had somehow buried the memory. Time, though, was in short supply just now.

As for Jared. Nat's hands curled into fists. His feelings about Jared were far less complex. He quite simply wanted to kill the man. It was bad enough that he'd taken advantage of Nat's weakness, but using Abby as he had was unconscionable. It stirred something deep in Nat's gut, something primal and fierce. Abby was his. Swift would pay for what he'd done to her, to them; someday Nat would give him the worst thrashing he'd ever received. Not now, though, he thought grimly, as his boat reached the *Comet*. Right now survival was more important.

Sometime later Nat climbed back on the *Aquinnah*'s heaving deck, his face grim. The *Comet* was caught in the ice, wedged so tightly between two floes that she had been forced upward. By the time Nat reached the ship, the crew was already off her, in the boats. She could not be rescued. The most the crew could hope for was to salvage what they could.

Pulling off his storm hood, he entered the cabin, and then stopped short. Standing near the table, looking amazingly unruffled, was Jared. The rage he had felt in the whaleboat returned. "Swift," he said curtly, crossing the cabin to stow his storm gear. "What are you doing here?"

"Howland." Jared's greeting was equally cool. "I came to tell you of the *Comet*'s plight. Abby has told me, though, that you went to find out for yourself."

"Yes." Nat was having a hard time being polite. "We're taking several of her men."

"We are, too. Captain Sylvia told me when I was there that every timber in the ship is shattered."

"Aye," Nat agreed, unsurprised that Jared had seen the *Comet*'s situation for himself. He didn't question Jared's physical courage. Just his integrity. "So why are you here?"

"To warn me about the dangers of staying in the ice," Abby said. Her face was pale and strained, making Nat wonder just what Jared had said. Likely he'd reminded her that Nat had lost a ship in the ice before and that it could happen again. And likely Abby was remembering an incident that had occurred eight years ago. "I'll keep in mind what you said, Jared."

Jared turned to Nat. "I wouldn't advise this in other circumstances, but—"

"I told you, Jared," Abby interrupted. "We're staying."

"You have to think of Abby's safety," Jared went on as if Abby hadn't spoken.

Nat lounged against the wall. "And past history, maybe?"

"Nat," Abby protested.

"Aye," Jared said at the same time. "Now that you bring it up."

"Are you heading for open water?"

"I'm considering it," Jared said, surprising him. "You know as well as I what losing a ship does to a man's reputation."

"It makes him look like a failure," Nat said deliberately and saw to his satisfaction that Jared stiffened. "I also know that conditions can improve. No, Swift. If Abby says we're staying, then we're staying."

"I'd be happy to take Abby aboard. For her own safety."

"No, thank you." Abby's voice was icy as she moved toward Nat, standing by his side. "I'll weather things here."

"If it was my wife, I'd do it," Jared said, again as if Abby hadn't spoken.

Nat put his arm around his wife's shoulders and felt her press against him, united against this interloper. "No, thank you," he said, as icily and politely as Abby. He had to protect her. Nor had he forgotten the threat Swift had made in Hawaii. Going on the ice with him would give the man the perfect opportunity to carry it out.

"Think about it, Abby." Jared turned away. "If you change your mind, raise a flag, and I'll send someone for you."

Abby raised her chin. "Thank you, but it won't be necessary."

"Your decision." Jared shrugged and at last went out.

"Damn him!" Nat exploded into the silence Jared had left behind him, as thick and cold as the ice. "Damn him."

"I didn't invite him here," Abby said, not moving.

"I didn't think you had." Nat released her and ran a hand over his face. "But I didn't like seeing him here."

"What could I do?" she protested. "He asked to speak to you first, and then me. I couldn't turn him away."

Nat was quite certain that Swift had waited until he'd seen Nat leave before making his unwanted visit. "Mm-hm."

"I couldn't Nat. Whatever else he is, he's one of the fleet's skippers."

"I know." He turned from the locker where he had stowed his gear. "And a good one, though I hate to admit it. Maybe"—his throat clenched—"you should go."

"Nat! Are you saying—"

"Not with him." His hand slashed through the air. "Never with him, Abby."

"No," she agreed, meekly. "I wouldn't, Nat."

"I know." He took a deep breath, trying to dispel his rage. "But if we hear of another ship leaving, you should go, for your own safety."

"Would you desert your ship, Nat?"

"No, but that's a different matter."

"No, it isn't." She crossed her arms over her chest, and in spite of the situation he was again struck by her resolute beauty. "This is my ship. I stay."

"Didn't really think otherwise."

"Then why did you suggest that I leave?"

"Things look bad, Abby." His mouth tightened. "Did Swift tell you how it is with the *Comet*?"

"Yes. She's lost, isn't she?"

"Aye. And the same thing could happen to any one of us."

"Nat." She sighed. "You just told me a little while ago that we're safe."

"Aye, we are. For the moment. But things change." He paused. "If you wanted to leave, I wouldn't blame you. I wouldn't think any less of you."

"I'm no coward, Nat."

"I never said you were."

"Still, if things are that bad . . ." Her voice trailed off and her face grew still. She looked, he thought, much as her father had when he was pondering a decision. Nat felt a sudden, sharp stab of apprehension. "Maybe we should make for open water."

"No." He shook his head. "I've told you. Let's wait this out. The wind will shift."

"And if it doesn't?"

"It will."

"I'm not sure I want to take that chance." She gazed at him. "Not for the ship. I think we should leave."

"Is that an order?" Nat said very quietly.

"Yes," she said after a moment, and raised her chin. "Yes. Captain, I'm ordering you to make for open water."

"No," he replied and stalked out of the cabin.

Chapter 26

"Nat!" Abby ran after him, stopping him in the passageway at the bottom of the stairs. "Wait."

"An order." He turned, sounding calm, though his eyes were icy cold and hard. "So that's how it is."

"Yes," Abby said, knowing she sounded inane. It was a drastic step to take, but necessary. "I think it's best."

"Do you." He leaned back, still studying her. "Then I request that you accept my resignation—"

"Nat!"

"—as master of this ship, effective when we reach Hawaii."

"Nat, you can't resign."

"Why not?"

"Because—this is your ship."

"No, Abby. It's your ship. I think you just proved that," he said, almost gently.

"Oh, Nat. I never meant—"

"Didn't you? When it comes right down to it, this always has been your ship. You made it clear from the beginning."

"I haven't interfered with how you do things."

"No. You just set the conditions of my employment. No skipper likes to have the owner looking over his shoulder."

Abby looked away, not knowing how to answer. His mind was made up; the set look on his face told her that. In the past, she had always been able to persuade him around to her side. Not this time. "Nat, I don't want you losing this ship."

"Oh?" He turned, eyebrows raised. "Afraid of what it will do to me?"

"Frankly, yes."

"Don't worry." His smile was cool. "If it happens, it will

only be because we're all caught in the ice. And that won't happen, because we're all too experienced to let it."

"You won't make for open water, then?"

"No." His face was grim. "If you prefer, I'll resign now."

"No." She wasn't about to do that to him. Lord, he had integrity, no matter his other weaknesses. He wouldn't blame a woman for his own failings, whether in his work or in intimate matters. "No, I expect you to carry on, Captain."

He inclined his head. "Thank you."

"But only because the ship needs you." She could be cool, too, in spite of her hurt. "I trust you to get us through this."

He bent his head again, in ironic gratitude. "You'll have no trouble finding another skipper, after this."

"Nat—"

"And I'll likely have no trouble finding another berth."

"You have one." She faced him squarely. "If anyone's going to leave this ship, it should be me."

"Generous of you, Abby."

"Realistic. I never belonged here. I was foolish to think I did," she added.

"So what will you do?" he asked, as if her answer meant little to him. "Go back to New Bedford?"

"No. I think I'll stay in Honolulu. I like it there, and we'll be together more often than we would be if I were at home."

He nodded. "True enough. But you'll still need to find another skipper."

"Nat—"

"I can't work for you, Abby," he interrupted. "You have a choice. You can be either my employer or my wife. Not both."

Anger flared inside Abby for the first time. Until today, she'd thought she was doing a decent job in both roles. "We can discuss this in Hawaii."

"No. Discussion's over. If you'll excuse me, I have work topside," he said and climbed up the companionway.

"Nat," she called after him, though she knew it was futile. She was not going to move him. Not when she'd wounded his pride so deeply. And though the ship meant a great deal to her, Nat meant more. She would be his wife, then, and not his employer. Even though, in all but name, their marriage was over.

She drifted back into the cabin. It wouldn't appear that way to others. Likely they'd stay together, and they might even have children. They could certainly keep up the pretense of happiness, if they saw each other only a few weeks out of the year. In time, they might come to believe it themselves. But the love and the closeness they'd shared was gone—and the chance for more. She had no one to blame but herself, she admitted, sitting stiffly on the settee like an old woman. Her marriage was over, and she had destroyed it.

The anger Nat had kept hidden from Abby showed on his face as he stalked across the deck to the rail. Wind still from the northwest, he noted automatically. Abby was right, of course. They should head for open waters. That was why his anger was so fierce. If he didn't follow her order, he would lose another ship; if he did, he would lose his pride. Either way, he lost.

There was little warning of what was to come, just a slight footfall behind him. Nat, his instincts finely honed by years at sea, whirled to see a blur of movement descending upon him. Something struck his arm, shooting pain through the bone, but already his other arm was raised in defense, warding off another blow from what he now saw was a belaying pin. Good God, one of the men was attacking him. *Mutiny!* he thought, and in that split second of realization his attacker was upon him, hands locked around Nat's neck. Nat struggled, but he had only one good arm and the man's thumbs were pressing on his windpipe. Mutiny, the secret fear of every shipmaster when times were trying. For God's sake . . .

The pressure was suddenly lifted from his throat. Gasping for breath, Nat fell back against the rail, seeing bright spots dancing in the darkness that obscured his vision. "Cap'n. Cap'n!" Mr. Martel was shaking his arm. "You all right?"

Nat blinked, and the world came back into focus. Several of his crew had wrestled the man to the deck. Not his own crewman, he noted, but one of the men he'd taken on from the *Comet* when she was lost. "Damnation! What the hell?"

"Don't know, Cap'n. One minute he was standing here, and the next he went crazy. Like he was waiting for you."

"We gotta get out of here!" the man wailed as he was hauled, none too gently, to his feet. "I can't stand it, all the ice. Gotta get out."

"The man's gone mad," Nat said wearily, aware for the first time of the pain in his arm. He wondered if it was broken. If so, he was lucky. He suspected the blow had been meant for his head. Thank God, though, it wasn't a mutiny.

"Should I put him in irons, Cap'n?"

"Aye. Any others on the ship talking like that?"

"No, Cap'n, not that I know of."

He nodded. "Good. Let's keep it that way. And make sure the men know that anyone else planning this will be punished."

"Aye, Cap'n," Mr. Martel said and turned away, Nat's attacker in tow. Nat watched detachedly. Mutiny was a serious offense that struck at the heart of a captain's authority and was punishable by the lash. Nat was reluctant to enforce the penalty, though, with conditions as they were. The men knew their own survival was at stake, as well as the ship's. Use the lash, and he just might turn them against him. Besides, he suspected there was more behind this than a man's madness. He suspected that someone else was behind it.

"Nat." Abby hurried across the deck. "I just heard—"

"I'm all right, Abby." He waved her off, ignoring the look of hurt that crossed her face. "Don't make a fuss."

She stepped back, retreating into herself. He rather regretted the distance. "You could have been killed."

"I wasn't."

"Your arm? I heard it was hit."

Nat flexed his fingers, tucked into his jacket pocket. To his relief, they moved easily. "It hurts like the devil," he admitted. "But I don't think it's broken."

"You should have Mr. Tripp look at it."

"No." His voice cut across hers. "If I go below, if I show any weakness, others might get the same idea. Don't you think we have enough to handle?"

"Nat, please." She moved beside him as he turned to

look out over the railing. Ice, everywhere, as far as the eye could see. "Please reconsider making for open water."

"No."

Abby was silent for a moment and then sighed. "Very well. I'll stand by you in this, Nat, no matter how I feel."

"Thank you."

Again she was silent, and then he sensed her moving away. "Come below to have your arm seen to when you feel the time is right," she said, and was gone.

Nat remained at the railing, looking out over the ice. It was no longer merely outside the ship. It had invaded their marriage as well, and for the life of him he could see no way to set them free.

Some days later Nat regretted the pride that had made him disobey Abby's order. The wind had indeed changed, setting the ice in motion, but not away from the fleet. Instead, it had claimed another ship, the *Roman,* sinking her within a scant hour. The *John Wells* went ashore that night, pushed by the ice, though her crew had managed to get her free in the morning, and the *J. D. Thompson* was hard aground. Several mornings after that some of the fleet's captains had gone in their boats to try to find a way out. To their dismay, the only channel of open water left was too shallow for any of the ships. It was beginning to look as if none of them would ever get out of the ice again.

"It looks bad," Abby said, standing beside him at the helm. She had yet to reproach him for his decision, and though that was to her credit, it increased his guilt. She had depended on him to skipper her ship safely, and he had failed her.

"Aye," he said, more calmly than he felt. "So it does."

"What do the other captains say?"

Nat peered out over the ice, as if by doing so he could find a way to escape. "We can't winter over. Not with twelve hundred people to consider. There's provisions for maybe three months, and no shelter." He looked down at her. "You should have stayed in Hawaii."

She shook her head and, to his immense surprise, slipped her hand through his arm. "No. I wanted to learn about whaling. I have."

"The hard way."

"Mm." She gazed in the same direction as he, still distant, but closer than she had been. "So the decision is to abandon the ships?"

Nat didn't answer for a long, long time. "Yes," he said softly. He was going to lose his ship again, his fine, fine ship. Abby's ship. "I should have listened to you."

"Yes, you should have," she agreed, but without rancor. "But how could you have known this would happen?"

"The signs were there. With what we heard from the natives early this season, and the ice coming in so fast—damnation, Abby, I'm sorry."

"Let's go below." She tugged on his arm, and he let her pull him toward the cabin. "I need to know what the plans are."

In the cabin, Nat glanced longingly toward the cabinets. A drink would warm him up nicely right about now, would ease the pain of defeat and humiliation. "We're going to try to get the smaller ships out over the shoals and hope they can reach other ships farther south."

"How deep is the shoal?"

"Five and a half feet," he said bleakly.

"Oh, Nat," she said in dismay. "We draw nearly three times that empty."

"I know." He turned to look at her, his Abby, so precious and so distant. Their marriage was over. He'd known that from the time he disobeyed her command. Oh, they still shared a bed, for warmth if for nothing else; maybe, in time, they'd find a kind of peace with each other. But the closeness and trust they had nearly found was gone forever. "If that doesn't work we'll have to go out by the boats."

She drew in her breath. "Is there enough room for everyone?"

"We'll find room. It's going to be hard, Abby." His voice was very quiet. "It was enough of an ordeal going over the ice when I lost the *Nantucket,* even though I was drunk in the beginning. This will be worse."

She looked away. "Please don't drink, Nat. Not this time."

"I won't." He cast one last glance at the cabinet and then straightened. Somehow he would get through this sober. "I promise you, Abby. This time I won't."

She nodded, though her face was expressionless. "Thank you. We all depend upon you too much."

"You too, Abby?"

"Of course." She regarded him steadily. "You're the ship's skipper."

"Damnation, you know that's not what I mean!" he roared. "I'm talking about you and me. Our marriage."

"I can't discuss that now." Her spine was very straight. "We can't afford to let anything distract us."

"Not even our future, Abby?"

"We are discussing our future."

"I see," he said, and he did. There would be no forgiveness from Abby for this. She might stand with him before the crew, but in private there was no mistaking her feelings. For it wasn't just her ship that was lost. So was everything she had tried to do with her life since her father's death. So were, he reflected, the years of effort that had gone into his recovery, as well as the work and time and love he had put into the *Aquinnah*. He felt very old and very tired. He was about to lose another ship. He had already lost Abby.

"You'll make the plans, then?" she said calmly, owner to skipper and nothing more.

"Yes, with the others. Probably within the next few days. Trying to get out of here any later would be impossible."

She nodded. "You'll let me know."

"Of course." He nodded as well, coolly polite, and though they were only a few feet apart, they faced each other over a gulf as vast, and as cold, as the ice around them.

The masters of the fleet did all that they could to avert disaster. They sent out an expedition of three whaleboats to the south, to determine how far the ice extended, if there were ships in the vicinity that could lend aid, and if there were a navigable channel, though no one expected success on the last matter. Other whaleboats were loaded with provisions and sent on ahead, while on every ship the crews were busy breaking out what foodstuffs they could. Remarkably, no one lost composure during this time of waiting and watching, while the ice came in ever thicker and heavier. No one could afford to.

Abby's face was bleak, Nat noted, feeling the same way

himself. Standing with his forearms on the port railing, looking out at a sea of ice, he faced the indisputable fact. He had failed. Bad enough losing one ship; losing another went beyond unforgivable. It didn't matter that others were in the same straits. He had vowed to bring this ship back safely, and with a profit. Instead, he had made Abby, and himself, paupers.

For himself, it wasn't too bad. He was strong and could always find work. He would never skipper a ship again, though, and not because no one would hire him. No. He'd rehabilitated his reputation, and oddly enough, had gained respect as a leader, simply because he'd been one of the first captains to talk of taking to the boats. He could get another berth. He simply didn't want to. It would hurt far too much to helm a ship, any ship, after this. The *Aquinnah*—graceful, neglected, unwanted—had stolen his heart. So had her owner. Against that, another ship would mean nothing; another woman, less than nothing. If his marriage to Abby proved to be the complete failure it now seemed, he would never love again.

Abby came up beside him, coat wrapped tightly about her. "It's nearly time, isn't it?"

"Aye," he said, looking away. Underneath her coat she wore her bloomer suit, which even he had to admit was practical for the circumstances. And too damned attractive. When, he wondered, would he ever stop wanting her? When would the mess he'd made of their lives stop hurting so? "You have the copy of the letter we wrote?" he asked, referring to the document which set down the conditions under which the captains were abandoning their ships and that was signed by most of the ships' masters.

"You gave it to me yourself."

"So I did." He gazed out upon the sea. "No navigable channel, and eighty miles on the open water to reach Point Barrow. And let's pray there are ships waiting for us there."

"We have no choice."

"I don't know, Abby." He turned to face her at last, leaning against the railing. "I couldn't sleep last night, and I kept thinking there must be something we could do."

"Such as?"

"I don't know, but people at home will wonder. What if

we abandon the ships and the wind changes tomorrow and the ice blows away?"

"Then we come back."

"Oh, do we. Once we're aboard other ships, heading south? How would we know?"

"You're torturing yourself, Nat." She rested her hand on his arm, then pulled it back. "Look at it out there. Only ice, everywhere, and more every day. You said yourself that the longer we delay, the harder time we'll have getting out. Even now there are places where it's not deep enough for a whaleboat to sail. We can't afford to lose this chance."

"We can't afford to lose this ship." His eyes raked over the *Aquinnah*'s masts. "Not after all we put into it."

"We'll manage, Nat."

"I'm not talking about the money, Abby."

"I know." She sighed. "But it was a grand adventure, wasn't it?"

He looked directly at her. "No regrets?"

"Of course I have regrets. But I'm not sorry I came along. No." She, too, gazed at her ship. "She was moldering at the dock. The best I could have done elsewise was to sell her for scrap. At least this way, she's going out as a working ship. No." She shook her head. "I'm not sorry."

He looked out across the ice again, and at that moment the ship's bell rang eight times. It was noon, the agreed-upon time of abandonment. It was not the happy ending he'd hoped for. Nor could he see any hope for him and Abby. There, as she must, he had regrets.

"Look." Abby's voice was unsteady. Across from them one of the other ships had set the American flag, the signal that she was abandoned. Then another flag rose, and another. The chill at the back of Nat's neck had nothing to do with the cold. He was, he realized, watching the death of something brave and gallant.

"Time to go." He sounded prosaic as he put his hand under Abby's elbow, pulling her away from the railing.

"Yes." She was dry-eyed beside him as she climbed into the boat, clutching at its sides as it was lowered into the choppy, ice-floed waters. Nat waited while the other boats were lowered, calmly supervising. They had taken what they could of their belongings, but left behind were their books, Abby's parlor organ, their future. It was his last sad duty to the *Aquinnah* to see that the crew left safely as well.

And then, finally, it was his turn, the last man to leave the ship. He threw one leg over the railing, preparing to drop down the rope to the waiting boat, and then paused. Again his gaze took in his ship: the barepoled masts, the rigging coated with ice, the once-glistening deckhouses. Hidden from sight, but well remembered, was the snug, warm cabin, where he had charted his future, where he had fallen in love with Abby and made her his wife. All behind him now, but this was no time for sentiment. Lips set, he dropped into the boat.

Immediately the men at the oars began to pull, and within a surprisingly brief time they were away from the ship. From here he could see the ice that surrounded her hull. His fine ship floated no more, and the sight of her, so still, hurt so much that Nat turned forward, knowing that the stinging in his eyes wasn't from the fierce wind. They were now part of a ragged procession of nearly two hundred boats, filled with people making a desperate attempt to get to safety. He reached over and grasped Abby's hand, and she gripped his fingers. Ahead of them was the unknown. The *Aquinnah,* and all she represented, was behind them.

Chapter 27

The day wore on. Though there was enough of a breeze for the boats to set their sails, still progress was set by the slowest boat, to keep the convoy together. Separation could only mean disaster for the ragtag fleet.

As night came on, dark, black clouds hung over the boats, increasing Abby's feeling of doom. She was chilled to the bone, but she didn't complain. Everyone else was in the same boat, she thought, smiling ironically at the unintended pun. She was relieved when the decision was made for those boats including women and children to make landfall, though they faced discomfort at best. At least it would be a respite.

Peleg, bless him, had gone before them and had joined with other sailors to scour the land for driftwood. They'd built a scanty fire and brewed coffee strong enough to put some starch into the limpest backbone. Abby grimaced at the taste, but she forced herself to swallow it. She needed all the warmth she could get. Huddling under the inadequate shelter of a boat, dragged ashore and turned upside down, she thought longingly of her garden at home, of the tree-shaded pergola and her mother's roses. Not her home now, though. Never again her home.

She had finished her supper and was looking for Nat, when a shadow rose before her. For a moment it was so like her nightmare that her heart seemed to stop. Then she recognized him. Jared. Of course. Her nightmare, after all.

He hunkered down before her, his pea coat pulled tight about his throat. "Are you all right?" he asked.

"As well as I can be," she answered cordially enough, glancing past him for a glimpse of her husband. "When we left I decided to take my quilt instead of another set of clothes. I'm glad I did." And she had left behind all else, all the things that she had once thought so important to an ocean voyage: her sewing box, her paints, her trousseau. All that remained was her journal and, ironically, Harold, safe and warm in Hawaii. And Nat. She spied him conferring with several other men, heads lowered, faces grave, and she relaxed. He wasn't far away.

"It should never have happened to you, Abby." Jared's voice was low. "I would have kept you home, safe and warm."

"Warm?" she queried, gazing at him. Funny that at one time this man had inspired such dread in her. Now that she knew what had driven him to follow her, she felt only a kind of pity for him. How difficult life must be if you didn't allow yourself to fail. "I'm not so sure of that."

"I would have tried, Abby. I would have done anything to make you happy."

"Oh? Like that day in the music room?"

He gazed at her intently. "I've never forgotten that."

"I did. For a long time."

He rocked back on his heels. "How could you?"

"It's easy to do, when something hurts so." She wrapped her arms around her bent knees. "And you did hurt me, Jared. I didn't understand why for a long time, but now I do."

"I didn't hurt you." His voice was low. "When you wanted me to stop, I did."

"It was wrong, Jared." She faced him directly. Odd, how calm and matter-of-fact she sounded, discussing so intimate a topic. Of course, she didn't feel that way. She didn't know how she felt. Nor had she had a chance to consider the matter, when her survival was at stake. Someday she would have to deal with it, but not now. "And you knew it."

"It was never wrong, Abby."

"We were raised like brother and sister."

"I never felt like a brother toward you."

"Yes, you did. Once." She looked away, knowing by his silence that her meaning was finally sinking in. "You nearly destroyed me."

"I never meant to. Abby, let me make it up to you." He reached for her hand, but she pulled back. "You need a husband who understands you, too."

"You, you mean."

"Yes. I won't demand anything of you that you can't give."

Abby glanced around at the group of people huddled around the scanty fire and was struck again by the unreality of their conversation. "Or anything at which you'd fail."

He frowned. "What are you talking about?"

"It doesn't matter, Jared." She rolled to her feet. "I'm married now, to a man who understands me more than you ever could. You see," she paused, wondering for a moment if she should go on, "I love him."

Jared, about to touch her, drew back. "You can't."

"Oh, but I do. He makes me warm, Jared." She waited while the expression in his eyes turned first to understanding and then horror. "If you'll excuse me—"

"You can't." He grabbed her arm. "Not when I love you—"

"I'll thank you to take your hands off my wife," Nat said from behind them. He sounded calm, but Abby knew well that he was holding his temper in check.

Jared turned. "You're not fit to touch her."

"Maybe not, but she is my wife," Nat said affably.

Abby slipped past Jared to stand by Nat, who put his arm around her shoulder. She welcomed his warmth and strength. "Jared, it's been a long day, and tomorrow promises to be worse. Let's end this now."

Jared stood his ground, looking from Abby to Nat. "So you're going to stay with this failure? He's lost another ship. That's two, Abby. Two."

"This time I'm not the only one," Nat pointed out.

"No excuse. Do you think anyone has forgotten the past? First the *Nantucket*, and now the *Aquinnah*. Two ships."

Nat had stiffened, though he still held her. For the first time Abby understood his anger toward Jared. She felt it herself, healing, cleansing. "You bear some responsibility for what happened to the *Nantucket*. Or did you think I didn't know?"

"About what?"

"About the mistake you made."

Jared's laugh was mirthless. "The only mistake I made was in not taking command from you sooner."

"Careful, Swift. That kind of talk sounds like mutiny."

"At least I wouldn't have put her on the ice."

"Not when I did, no," Nat agreed. "Sooner."

"What the devil are you talking about?"

"Your mistake." Nat's smile was cold, yet Abby knew with sudden certainty that no matter what the provocation, he wouldn't drink again. If he could control his temper under these circumstances, then surely he could control his cravings. Something inside her eased. "I found out about it."

"What mistake?"

"The sounding you took. Fifty-one instead of fifteen."

"Not my mistake," Jared said quickly. "You were drunk."

"And you switched the numbers," Nat said calmly.

Jared stepped forward, chin outthrust. "Prove it."

"I don't have to. I know. You do, too, don't you? Ah. Yes. I can see that you do."

"You're mad." Jared turned to Abby. "He's mad, Abby. Raving. Losing another ship—"

"And I know what you're trying to hide," Nat interrupted. "You're afraid people will find out that you're a failure. Ha. They know, Swift. And they know you'll always be a failure—"

Jared shouted an inarticulate oath and launched himself at Nat. Abby cried out and tumbled to the ground, regaining her balance to see the two men struggling, Jared with his hands clawing at Nat's throat, Nat pulling at Jared's arms. "No!" she cried, but neither appeared to hear, locked as they were in a death struggle. This fight had been a long time building. It would take more than her protest to stop it.

Abruptly, it was over. Several men pulled Jared back; several others grabbed Nat, when he would have gone after the other man. For a moment it all hung in the balance, Nat's breath coming in harsh gasps, and then he straightened. "Abby." He didn't look at her. "Are you all right?"

Abby, being helped to her feet by Peleg, dusted ice off her coat. "Yes, Nat," she said calmly.

"My apologies, gentlemen." Nat stepped back, smiling a little, though his gaze never left Jared. They might be separated, but the enmity between them was almost strong enough to feel. "It's been a rough week."

Some of the men nodded, as if in understanding; others

took Jared by the arm, pulling him away. The fight was over. It was not, however, done. Abby, feeling the tensile strength in Nat's arm, wondered if it ever would be.

"It's not over," Jared said, in an eerie echo of Abby's thoughts. "Remember what I promised in Hawaii."

Nat gave him a long, long look. "You'll fail at that, too." He turned aside, taking Abby with him. "Bastard," he added under his breath. "Did he hurt you?"

"No." She looked up at him as he settled beside her on the quilt, under the upturned boat. "What was he talking about?"

Nat shook his head. "Nothing. He can't hurt us now, Abby."

"I don't trust him anymore."

"It doesn't matter. He can't hurt us," Nat repeated and looked away. "We've already lost everything."

"Oh," Abby said. Though she was snuggled against him for warmth, she felt distant from him. The voyage and the marriage she had undertaken with such high hopes had turned out to be disastrous. She only hoped they could salvage something from the wreck of their lives.

After a cold, uncomfortable night, the group on the shore took to their boats again, pressing southward. The weather was miserable, with the wind blowing fresh from the southwest, spraying everyone with frigid water and threatening to upset the boats with each swell. Nat, taking a turn at the oars, had to fight to keep them heading into the seas, so they wouldn't be swamped. His shoulders ached and his arms burned, but he wasn't about to complain. He wasn't the only one suffering, and at least the exercise kept him warm.

He glanced quickly back at Abby. She hadn't said a word since they'd started out, but sat hunched into herself for warmth, her head down. How she must be regretting her decision of a year ago, he thought, pulling on the oars. If she'd chosen differently she would be safe at home now, with at least a little nest egg. Now she had lost everything, and it was his fault.

"Hey! Is that a flag?" one of the men called, and everyone in the boat perked up. The boat went into a trough, but as it rose again Nat could see it: a flutter of color on the horizon. Something inside him relaxed. Thank God! After the long, desperate journey south, help was at last in sight.

They set to with a will now, pulling on the oars with renewed strength. Slowly the flag ahead rose higher; slowly, the masts of first one ship came into view, and then another. There were seven ships awaiting them, so they had been told by the small expedition that had gone before, off Icy Cape. Seven ships, to rescue more than one thousand people. The ice was thick here, too, Nat noted grimly, forming a long peninsula that kept them from the ships. Nothing for it but to row around it and pray that safety was at hand.

Another man came forward to relieve Nat at the oars. Crouching, he moved back and settled beside Abby, gathering her close for warmth. As the sweat dried inside his clothes, he felt the first faint chill of fear. Odd. He hadn't been afraid off Point Belcher, even when the ice threatened to crush the *Aquinnah,* because he had trusted his own abilities. Nor had he been afraid getting into the boat and setting off on an uncertain eighty-mile voyage; he couldn't afford to be. Now, though, his nerves were singing. A rogue wave, a shift of the ice, and they could still meet with disaster. For that to happen with rescue in sight would be very hard.

For all Nat's fears, the passage along the peninsula of ice went fairly smoothly. Trouble came when the boats rounded the tip of the ice and met the southwest gale full on. The men at the oars had to fight against tremendous waves to keep from capsizing, while great sheets of water washed inboard. Everyone, including Abby, was frantically busy bailing, in spite of the fact that their clothes were soaked and stiff with brine and that their stores of bread and flour were ruined. Survival was all that mattered now.

Nat was so busy with bailing and with clutching Abby each time a wave struck that he wasn't aware they were nearing a ship until the wind lessened. Looking up, he saw a hull rising above him. They were in the lee of the *Europa,* on her starboard side. The removable bulwark, or railing had been taken away, to aid in getting everyone aboard quickly. Several boats were ahead of theirs, Nat noted, with men already scurrying up rope ladders to the ship's deck and railing, a perilous feat in seas that tossed vessels of all sizes about like so many twigs. As he watched, a familiar figure grabbed hold of a rope. It was Jared.

"Damnation," he muttered.

Abby peered up at him. "What?"

"Nothing." He shook his head. So, they'd be on the same ship as Swift. He thought he'd rather wait for rescue than to be so near to his adversary. For he had no doubt that Swift had meant what he'd said when he reminded Nat of his threat—and what better time to carry it out than now? Under such terrible conditions, any injury Nat suffered would probably be considered an accident. And Abby would be left alone. He would not, Nat thought grimly, allow that to happen.

"We're almost there."

"Aye. Abby, if anything should happen to me—"

She drew back. "Nat, what are you talking about?"

"Go home." He held her gaze with his. "Go back to your cousin Elizabeth or to one of your aunts. Go where people care about you."

"Well, of course, silly. But nothing's going to happen to you." She looked up at the rope ladder dangling over the ship's side, and for the first time he saw apprehension cross her face. "Go first, Nat?"

Nat glanced up at the ship, seeing only the seamen on deck, helping the survivors of the disaster aboard. Of Swift there was no sign. "Why?"

"I'm—to help me."

"I'll be right behind you, Abby," he said reassuringly, grabbing the ladder. "Good thing you wore your bloomers."

"Yes." She set her lips and then rose. "You promise you'll be behind me?"

"Yes."

"All right," she said grimly. Nat held the ladder steady and looked up. At the railing stood Jared.

It was only a fleeting look, but it was enough for Nat to see the look of triumph in Jared's eyes, a look that warned him immediately and yet not soon enough. Everything happened at once then, very fast and very slow. Someone yelled, "Look out below!" and there was a great rattling of chain as the heavy block used to hoist whales aboard for cutting plummeted downward, directly at Abby. "No!"

Nat yelled, and thought he heard an echo of his cry. He reacted without thinking, grabbing the ladder and yanking it aside. Abby cried out as she banged into the ship's hull, and at the same moment Jared dove overboard from the deck. The block caught him square in the back, and he fell, suddenly and limply, into the sea.

"God!" Nat exclaimed, scrambling onto the ladder, where Abby hung by one arm. "God! Abby!"

She turned a dazed, pained look at him. "Nat. What—"

"Stay calm, sweetheart. I'm going to get you to safety." Though the ladder swayed beneath him, he wrapped one arm around her waist. "Hold on to me."

"I—can't." Her voice was breathless. "Nat, my arm . . . "

He glanced at her left arm, hanging limp and useless. Dear God. "Your other arm, sweetheart."

"I'll fall."

"I won't let you. There. That's it. Hold on." Carefully he climbed the ladder, one slow rung at a time, until at last he reached the deck. Then hands were reaching out, pulling them aboard, and they were safe at last.

Nat swung his wife up into his arms. "Where—"

"Here." The ship's captain, a man Nat knew well, led them aft. "The cabin for now, and then we'll find someplace for you to sleep. How bad's she hurt?"

"I don't know. Her arm might be broken."

"That was a nasty knock. You can be sure I'll find out how that happened and who was responsible."

"I already know," Nat said, easing down the companionway and into the cabin. It was enough like the *Aquinnah*'s cabin that he felt momentarily disoriented, and then Abby stirred in his arms, distracting him. He nodded at the other man, already heading back out. "Thank you."

"Nat?" Abby's face still looked dazed as he set her carefully on the green tufted settee. "What happened to Jared?"

"I don't know." Nor did he care. It didn't matter that the man had tried to save Abby from his trap, not when he had put her in danger. It was unforgivable. Nat suspected, though, that Jared was far beyond his vengeance.

The ship's steward came in, carrying a basin and strips of cloth. Nausea briefly churned Nat's stomach. He'd set broken bones before; a captain learned how to do such things. The thought of doing so to Abby, though, terrified him. "Brave thing Captain Swift did, trying to save her," the steward commented, setting down the basin. "He'd deserve a hero's burial, if they could find him."

Abby looked up, her face ashen. "Burial? Nat—"

"You don't know?" The steward shook his head. "Poor man went down like a stone. Looks like he's dead."

Chapter 28

Much later that evening, Nat sat on the side of Abby's bunk, gently smoothing her hair away from her face. She had shed tears over Jared's fate and he had held her; whatever kind of villain Swift had become, in the beginning he had been her friend. In the end he had tried to save her life.

"All that distance traveled." Abby's voice was dreamlike; he'd given her a dose of laudanum a few minutes earlier, and it was taking effect. To his vast relief she had suffered no broken bones; she had massive bruises on her shoulder and upper arm and would be sore for a while, but her injuries would heal. Thank God. For one terrible moment he had thought he was going to lose her, and that made everything else seem trivial. "The bad weather, the high seas, almost being swamped—and we lose someone when we're safe."

"Let's just be thankful everyone else made it safely and that the ships were here." He glanced around the stateroom, made available to them because of Abby's injury, and because they were one of the few married couples. Otherwise, he didn't know where they would have slept. There were now well over two hundred men on a ship designed to support forty or so, and the situation was the same on the other vessels. Still, no one was complaining. Though they had lost their ships, though the rescuers were giving up any chance of profit by taking the refugees aboard, everyone was glad just to be safe. Tomorrow the fleet, much diminished, would set sail for Hawaii.

"He didn't have to jump the way he did."

"He was trying to save you," Nat said, the words sticking in his throat. Earlier the captain had spoken with him, furious that the line holding the block had apparently been cut. He would find out who'd done it, he'd promised, until Nat had quietly told him who the culprit was. The crewman who had attacked Nat had also confessed that Jared had paid him to do so. It galled Nat that Jared had died a hero's death, yet that was how things would remain. Abby's reputation would be hurt if the truth came out.

"He thought it would be you, didn't he?"

Nat went still. "I don't know what you mean, sweetheart."

"Jared. I saw his face, just as I got on the ladder. He thought you would be climbing it first, didn't he?"

Nat didn't answer right away. He would never forgive Swift. What good would it do Abby, though, if he told her the truth? "I don't know. I doubt it."

"He hated you," she said and yawned. "I never realized how much until today."

"It doesn't matter, Abby. It's over."

"No, it's not." She turned her head on the pillow, looking sleepily at him. "It can't be."

"He can't hurt you now, sweetheart."

"I don't mean that. Nat." She gripped his hand with her good one. "We almost lost each other. We can't let that happen."

He stared down at her hand. "I lost your ship, Abby."

"It doesn't matter."

"It was all you had. I'm sorry." He clutched her hand. "I tried to save her, Abby, for you. I did everything I could, tried to find a channel, prayed for the wind to change, and now— "

"Oh, Nat." With her last bit of strength she pulled his head down to rest on her bosom, feeling his shoulders heave in a way so unlike him. They had both suffered terrible losses: she, of a childhood friend, and a kind of innocence; he, the dream that had kept him going for so long. "Nat."

"I'd get her back for you if I could," he said, his voice broken. "I would, but I have nothing, Abby. Nothing."

"Shh." She feathered her fingers through his hair, coarse with salt. "You have me."

That made him look up. His eyes were red and he obviously was struggling for composure. "Do I, Abby?"

"Aye, Cap'n."

His eyes squeezed shut and then opened again. "Why?"

Because I love you, she thought, but somehow the words stuck in her throat. "We've lost everything else, Nat. Let's not lose each other too."

He nodded, his gaze on her hand, still in his. "Aye. You're right. But you're tired." He straightened, laying her hand gently on the quilt. "You need to sleep."

"I will. Nat, I have some ideas about what we could do—"

"In the morning, Abby," he interrupted, laying his finger on her lips. "We'll talk about it in the morning."

Abby nodded, letting her eyes close at last. She thought, though, as the darkness swept over her, that she heard a voice. She thought that it said, "I love you."

In the morning Abby awoke to a warm body pressed against her side. Momentarily disoriented, she gazed about the stateroom, gray with the early light of day, trying to figure out where she was. Her old stateroom on the *Aquinnah*? But no, she remembered, with a fresh wave of grief. The *Aquinnah* was gone, and so were her hopes of a new life. She had lost everything.

Everything except Nat. Turning her head carefully, to protect her arm, she looked at him, asleep beside her. He looked tired, she thought, older and vulnerable. Not a Viking god, after all, but a man. Only a man, but the one she wanted. Last night, as she'd gone off to sleep, he'd declared his love for her. At least, she thought he had. It might have been a dream.

For a long, long moment she studied him. Dream or not, the thought of it sent warmth through her, melting the last vestiges of ice. If he loved her, then there was hope. Somehow the past no longer mattered quite so much, not when compared to what they had gone through. Even losing the *Aquinnah* wasn't quite so important. When she had crashed against the ship's hull yesterday, it wasn't the first time she'd faced death. The threat of disaster had been ever present during the arduous trek in the whaleboats. Such an experience had a way of clarifying things. She loved Nat. They could face anything, so long as they were together.

Rising up on her good arm, she bent to kiss his forehead. "I love you," she whispered and was about to pull bac when his eyes opened. She was caught by an intense, and very aware, blue gaze. "Good morning."

Nat shook his head. "Did I hear you right?"

"Did I hear you right, last night?"

He hesitated, and then leaned over to kiss her, very gently. "How are you feeling?"

"Stiff," she said, disappointed that he hadn't answered her. "Sore. Scared."

He rose on his elbow, looking down at her. "Of what?"

"Life without you." she held his gaze. Now was the moment when all would be decided, if she only had the courage. If she could take the risk, as she had once before, leaving her comfortable home for unknown adventure. That the adventure had included loving this man was something she could never have anticipated. The thought, and what it meant for the future, made her almost giddy. "I love you, Nat," she said and, reaching up, kissed him full on the lips.

He responded instantly, molding his lips against hers, pressing her back against her pillow. She hooked her good arm around his neck, and it was only when she winced involuntarily that he pulled back. "I'm hurting you," he said in dismay.

"I'll likely be sore for a while. It can't be helped."

He shook his head and pulled back. "I don't have to make matters worse." He sat up, running a hand over his hair. "We have to talk, Abby."

"Do we?"

"Aye." He turned to look at her. "We both said some hurtful things to each other, a few days ago. And"—he paused—"I lost your ship."

She eyed him with compassion. "Nat, nothing I could say could make you feel worse about that than you already do. It wasn't your fault. Well, it wasn't," she insisted, as he shrugged. "If we'd left when I wanted to, I don't think we'd have been any better off. You saw what conditions were like all down the coast. Ice, everywhere. It wasn't because you were drunk, Nat, or careless, or used poor judgment. If that's the case, then thirty-one other skippers are guilty, too."

"I'll never forget it, Abby," he said in a low voice.

"No. I won't either. It was a terrible experience, but we don't have to let it rule our lives. Not any of it."

He settled on his side, facing her. "So what do you suggest we do?"

"This," she said and kissed him again. This time he didn't react, and so she pulled back, studying him. His eyes were grave, his face serious. "Well?"

"You're hurt. And it doesn't solve anything."

"It doesn't have to. I love you, you idiot."

That made him laugh, if briefly. "Never have such words been so lovingly said."

"They're true." She gazed at him for a few more moments and then pulled him to her with her good arm. "I don't want to lose you, Nat. You're the best thing that ever happened to me."

"Am I?"

She gripped him tighter in a mixture of compassion and exasperation. Just now, she suspected, his pride and his confidence had been shaken to their roots. It would take time for him to regain them, and she wanted to help him. Just as he had helped her shed the cold shell that had imprisoned her for so many years. "Do I have to prove it?"

He pulled back, and this time there was a glimmer of humor in his eyes. "How?"

"If you have to ask, you're not the man I think you are," she said, and kissed him again. He responded at last, but gently, his lips moving persuasively over hers, as if she were the one who was reluctant. But she wasn't, not anymore. She would never withhold herself from him again.

"Let me take care of you," he whispered, and turned her gently onto her side, so that they faced each other and her injured arm was protected. "Abby."

"Mm." She ignored the ache in her shoulder as she arched her head back to give his lips access to her neck. She shifted slightly, making it easier for him to pull free the buttons of the man's shirt she wore, borrowed from the captain. And when he slid his hand under the soft fabric, she lay still, knowing that, even though she might not feel anything, these caresses meant a great deal to him.

"Oh!" she exclaimed, as his thumb rubbed her nipple.

He pulled back. "Did I hurt you?"

"No. Nat!" She looked at him, stunned. "I felt something."

He smiled slowly. "Like what?"

"I don't know." She matched his smile. "I think we might have to try it again."

He sighed. "If you insist," he said and cupped her full breast in his palm. This time the sensation was unmistakable, a jolt of pure pleasure that arrowed down to her loins. She wanted to cry with the joy and the wonder of it. "Well?"

"Oh, Nat," she said, and pressed her face against his neck, unable to stop the tears that suddenly streamed down her cheek. She felt warm and whole and complete in a way she never had before, and it was because of him. "Nat."

"Hey." He eased back, alarmed. "Did I hurt you?"

She laughed, in spite of her emotion. "Idiot," she said and pressed his hand to her again. "Oh, my."

"Your what?"

"Heaven." She closed her eyes, savoring the sensations, new and yet somehow familiar and right. Though she couldn't return his caresses, still she could hold on to him, kiss him, murmur answers to his endearments. Then his hands were sliding down over her hips, pulling up the shirt, fondling her bottom and thighs. She opened for him, and he slid inside her, cupping her buttocks, moving slowly and smoothly and easily. The pleasure built inside her, and when at last they reached their completion together, it was sweet, almost gentle, and very, very fulfilling.

They lay in peaceful contentment, happy just to be together, to have found each other again. At length, though, Nat stretched and sat up. "I suppose I should go topside and see if I can do anything."

"I suspect there are enough men there trying to keep busy," she said.

"Aye, but we're a strain on this ship. We have to do what we can."

"Mm-hm." Her eyes drifted shut; she was more tired than she realized. "Where to now?"

"Hawaii, and then home."

"Home." Her eyes snapped open. "Why?"

"Because people there will want to know what happened."

"Oh." She frowned at the ceiling, displeased at the thought of returning to New Bedford. "The owners, you mean."

"Among others," he said, pulling on his pants.

"Nat." She turned back on her side. "I'm still the *Aquinnah*'s owner, even if she is in the ice. There's no need for us to go back."

He paused in the act of tucking in his shirt, as if startled by the thought. "We don't have to, do we?" he said slowly. "But what would we do, then? Stay in Honolulu?"

"I liked the Oregon territory," she said.

He looked at her in surprise. "The Oregon territory? Why?"

"It reminded me of home, in a way. But it's freer there, Nat. We could be what we want to be, not what people think we should be. Not Benjamin Palmer's daughter and not"—she leaned back, holding his gaze—"the skipper who lost the *Nantucket*."

He was quiet, mulling her words. "Start over, you mean."

"Yes. What is there for us back in New Bedford? The only relative I care about is Cousin Elizabeth. The rest made it clear how they felt about me when I decided to go to sea."

"I'd miss my sister," he mused. "Not that I ever saw her much anyway."

"And someday we can have a family of our own."

"Children." He smiled. "I like that idea."

"So do I. There is one problem."

"What?"

"The past."

"Abby—"

"No." She put her fingers to his lips. "I have to say this. Nat, what happened, happened."

He looked away. "I know."

"I don't know how to deal with it. Forgetting didn't work."

"It got you through."

"And nearly pulled us apart. Nat." She gripped his arm. "How do I deal with it?"

"Day by day, sweetheart." He bent down so that his cheek, raspy with stubble, was against hers. "Just the way I did with the drinking. And I'll help you."

"Will you?"

"You know I will. I love you, Abby." he sat up. "I think a fresh start might be a good idea, at that."

"I do, too. Shall we try it?"

"What would we do? I warn you, Abby, I don't want to go whaling. Not again."

"I think whaling's finished, Nat." She was suddenly serious. "We've seen the signs ourselves, this past year, and losing so many ships at once will be a terrible blow. It might take a while, but whaling will end."

"Hm." He turned on his back, cradling her carefully against him, and stared up at the overhead. "I could open a coastal line," he said finally. "Seattle to Sacramento, or San Francisco. Just us at first, Abby, and in time," he leaned up on his elbow, face alight with excitement, "maybe other ships, too."

"My heavens, Nat. Do you know what that would make you?"

"No. What?"

"An owner."

He gave a short bark of laughter. "So it would. With a partner." His face softened. "You'll be my partner, won't you, Abby?"

"Of course I will. No matter what?"

"Aye," he said, and somehow she knew he was thinking about all they had been through together, all they had been, all they had become. Just as she was. "Aye. Let's do it."

She pulled back, a little surprised that it had been so easy to convince him, and absurdly happy. A chance for a new life, together. "Really?"

"Really. I love you, Abby."

"I love you," she said, at last pledging herself to him completely, and hooked her arm around his neck. His mouth came down onto hers, and as she melted into his kiss, she knew that what they had lost was as nothing against what they now had. Far beyond the sea, they had each other, together, forever.

The End

Author's Note

This is the book I have always wanted to write. Because the sea is a part of my heritage, I often felt as if I were living events along with Nat and Abby. I hope that you, the reader, have enjoyed reading it as much as I enjoyed writing it.

As was stated earlier, this book is a work of fiction. While the disaster in the Arctic actually happened, and most of the ships mentioned in that section of the book were real, fiction demands that actual events must sometimes be altered for the sake of the story. (It is purely coincidental that one of the ships lost in the Arctic was the *Gay Head.* "Aquinnah" is the original Wampanoag Indian name for the town of Gay Head on Martha's Vineyard island.) It is also entirely possible that I have made mistakes in my research, though I was as careful as possible. If so, they will come back to haunt me.

Whaling was a rough, brutal business, the scope of which is beyond this book. It was also difficult to write about nineteenth-century whaling from a twentieth-century perspective, when whales are endangered and whaling is outlawed in most of the world. When Nat stated that whales had small brains, he was repeating the accepted wisdom of the time. An excellent book on whaling in general and on the 1871 disaster in particular is *Children of the Light,* by Everett S. Allen. It is available in maritime bookstores and in libraries.

The loss of the Arctic fleet dealt a devastating blow to whaling, an industry already in decline. Altogether, thirty-two ships were lost, with, remarkably, no loss of life. Though whale products were no longer in the demand they once had been, there was enough profit to be made to keep the industry going another half-century. In 1924 the bark

Wanderer left port with all flags flying. The next day a nor'-easter blew her up onto Cuttyhunk Island. Whaling in New Bedford had ended at last.

Whaling history, however, has been kept very much alive. Both the Old Dartmouth Historical Society and the Waterfront Historic Area League (WHALE) have done much to promote preservation of New Bedford's past. The historic whaling district has been designated as a national park, and many buildings and homes from the whaling era survive. One of the best is the Rotch-Jones-Duff House and Garden Museum, the only whaling mansion and garden in the city that survives intact. In this book it served as Abby's home.

I would like to thank my father, Bill Kruger, who saw the *Wanderer* sail; Jennifer Sawyer-Fisher, who helped shape this book; Joanna Cagan, for her support, understanding, and never-ending patience; and, as always, the terrific staff of the New Bedford Free Public Library.

I reserve my warmest wishes, however, for the people of New Bedford. I love this place.

I enjoy hearing from my readers and will answer all letters. Please write to me at:

New England Chapter/RWA
P.O. Box 1667
Framingham, MA 01701-9998